Head Count

A Romp

by

Adrian Truss

Copyright © 2009

Adrian Truss

ISBN 978-1-257-06037-5

Printed in the US by Lulu.com

CHAPTER ONE

BRAIN PAN

Albert Bader killed a dog. Stopped his bike in the middle of the road, took a big mother Wesson out of his denim jacket and shot the thing from about fifty feet away. Cage whistled low between what was left of his teeth.

"Nice one, Albert", he called back over his shoulder from where he sat on his bike. "Real clean..."

Albert smiled, sort of, squinted and blew coolly across the top of the barrel. Further up the road two other bikes (one a three-wheeled trike, built out of the backend of a Volkswagen) had pulled over and their riders were gazing idly back at the pair behind. Mystic Bob and The Crip watched the dog as it twitched its silent last and finally Mystic Bob hung his head. The Crip roared his hog around and sped back to Albert. Albert watched him come on, his smile fading.

The Crip hissed between closed teeth, "What the hell do you think you're doing Albert? What did I just fucking tell you not more than ten fucking minutes ago?"

"Calm down, man, it's just a dog; a stupid, fucking dog. What's your problem?"

"*He's* my fucking problem", said The Crip, pointing one half-fingered glove at the ramshackle house further up the drive from where the now completely dead Doberman lay. A man, small and dark and angry chomped his way down the gravel driveway carrying a baseball bat. "I just want to get to Newton, okay? Just a nice simple ride to pick up some goods and then a nice simple tool back and then you can kill all the fucking wildlife you want."

The Crip stepped off his bike and shut the engine down and began to walk toward the rapidly approaching man. As he walked toward him with his unsteady limp, his hand reached behind and clutched for the bone handle of the long Bowie knife cradled against the small of his back. "You're really starting to piss me off, Albert," he called back. "Now look what I'm gonna have to do."

Mystic Bob, meanwhile, had rolled the trike off to the side of the dirt road and now the only sound that broke the otherwise silent afternoon was the wind in the scrub and the cursing of the small, dark man. Then, suddenly, only the wind remained.

Mystic Bob took a small can of gas out of a side pack and started to walk slowly across the lawn and up to the decrepit wooden structure, lighting the stub of his cigar as he moved. He shook his head and chuckled to himself as he caught up to Cage dragging the body toward the house. Still on his bike, Albert watched as The Crip kicked the small man's head toward the door. It banged off the frame and gutter-balled inside; flecking the white frame with red wetness.

*   *   *

Karen Armitage woke up with the same familiar flutter in her stomach that had been there every morning for the past couple of weeks. She opened her eyes to the same strange surroundings that had been her home since early July when she had first taken the job at Newton Fairbanks High School, agreeing to make the move from San Francisco when the current English teacher suddenly "retired".

The rumours of what had actually led to Alan Delacrombie's quitting were rampant in the community and had more to do with the daughter of one of the town elders than with a desire for Freedom 55. However, there was no proof of any of this and no legal pursuit so it was just "retired". Not the sort of situation every new teacher would want to come into. But there you go.

Karen rolled over and gasped as Huxley, her large, grey tabby meowed loudly and leapt out from under her arm. "Sorry Hux, sorry, sorry. Are you okay? I didn't know you were there. Come here."

Huxley looked up with a slightly hurt glance, turned his substantial butt in the direction of Karen and strutted out of the room. "Damn..." Karen thought, "Can't afford to offend him." Huxley was the only part of her former life that she had brought with her from Telegraph Hill other than her clothes and some books. A fresh start...

This wasn't her first teaching assignment but it was the first outside of the state and the different rules would be one of the most difficult aspects to it all. Still, it excited her in some ways and the challenge of meeting the new students and staff and finding out what the specific needs of the community were took most of her attention. It also helped, in a way, to cover the uncomfortable hole in her heart where Steven had been.

She pulled on a house-coat, opened the bedroom blinds and looked out onto a view of the fields behind the apartment and then across the highway to the encroaching desert. Her tiny rooms were at the back of a large house owned by an expatriate Mexican family named Chavez. It was kind of cramped, truth be told, but the panorama of the mountains in the distance and the multi-coloured beauty of the sands between them and the town had convinced her... that and a very nominal rental fee.

She plodded into the kitchen where Huxley circled, waiting to be placated. She opened up a tin and filled the little bowl. "Here you go, baby... yay... cat food!" Huxley, with the bed-crushing incident now but a distant memory, started scrunching away.

Karen showered and dressed, ate something light and walked out into the street. She would walk the three blocks to the school; she would fix up her desk, lay out her course introduction and then proceed to wow her Grade Eleven class with a classic breakdown of 'On the Road'. Everyone would pass with 'A's and go on to become famous novelists or journalists, thanking her in book intros and retirement speeches across the country. Or maybe she would spend the first hour explaining who Jack Kerouac was. It could go either way.

*   *   *

The old Ford flatbed beat its way down the road like a drop of water hitting a skillet. Dust and pebbles spat up into the hot Arizona sun and fell back with a dry rattle into the smoky haze behind. A startled hare blinked once and darted into the scrub as the truck careened close to the side of the road overlooking a washed out rill, the wide tires almost dragging it into the sand.

Big Jim Ahiga gripped the wheel loosely, spun it to one side and laughed. Little Billy laughed back. It was the first time he had made a sound since leaving the Rez; sitting stern-faced, arms folded, gaze glued to the distant, shimmering horizon.

Big Jim looked over with a grin. "Well good, I thought maybe you was dead, Billy"

Little Billy just grunted and returned to his pout. He didn't like any of this. No sir, nothing at all. Bad enough to be going back to school, which he hated, but to have to truck into Newton every day to go to the public school there was too much. It stank. He wouldn't know anyone and fully expected to be confronted by a sea of pale faces; curious, probably hostile faces that would belong to people he really didn't want to get to know anyway.

"I don't see why I have to go to this fucking place."

Big Jim looked over at him, wanting to help his younger brother but not quite knowing how. So he just shrugged. "C'mon Billy, the Rez School is closed and gone. Nothing we can do. There just aren't enough kids out here anymore."

"So what? So I don't go to school…" He said the word 'school' like it hurt his mouth. "I could get a job at the centre or go work with you on the tours."

"You can't go with me. What am I gonna do, fire Joey? I only need one guy. There's hardly enough work for me… Besides, you can do better than trucking tourists around the mesa pointing at toads. You're smart."

"Yeah, smart. What about the Center then?"

"Gimme a break... What are you gonna do there, serve coke and fries? Work at the clothing store? You're crazy! Nope, you're gonna get some learning, kid."

Billy muttered into his jacket. "Who died and made you chief?"

"Nobody. It was a vote."

"Funny."

"So quit asking me then." He paused for a moment and then, "Look, Billy, just give it a try, okay? I know it's a drag and it probably won't be easy. But you'll make some friends and the teachers are supposed to be the best."

"I've got friends," said Little Billy

"Man can't have too many friends, Little Bill."

"Where'd you get that from, a fortune cookie?"

There was a brief silence and then they both started to laugh. Big Jim reached over and punched Little Billy in the arm. Billy smacked him back as hard as he could. Big Jim winced in pretend pain. "Man, you gotta stop with those steroids."

"I will if you will."

The truck bounced on.

*　　　　　*　　　　　*

In the staff room of Newton Fairbanks High, a tossed salad of instructional man-power paced about or slurped coffee or read the paper in the armchairs scattered about. Nobody was particularly talkative nor were they particularly happy it seemed. Morale was at an all-time low to kick off this semester. Alan Delacrombie had been somewhat of an institution at the school with his cocky attitude and ready wit and now the rare respite to the boredom of their various callings that he provided was suddenly and ominously gone. None of them really believed the innuendoes about the young female student and with that doubt came another, more shadowy, about what would happen if that same unshakeable, sinister spotlight ever fell upon them. Add to that the union's inability over the summer to force from the town council the funds needed to bring their pay up to state standards and you pretty much had taken the temperature of the room.

Into this stale air, on her first full day of employment at Newton Fairbanks High, stepped Karen Armitage. The smile that she had decided to plaster on her face, no matter what, really did light up the room as she came in, if for no other reason than by its singularity. Most looked up curiously, some didn't even do that. But Vice-Principal Morton Edwards made an attempt at least, rising out of his semi-recumbent slouch at the back of the room and tossing the sports pages into the waste paper basket.

Striding over to her he said, "Aha. You must be Ms. Armitage."

"I must be," said Karen and took his offered hand.

"Welcome, welcome. Let me introduce you around. We're so glad you could make it up here for first day. It would have been a big strain on everyone to have to cover off on the English this soon into the year. Here this is…."

And so it went, around the group, a blur of faces and names that Karen knew immediately she would forget by the time she left the room; except, perhaps, for that of Mr. Kilagrew, the gym teacher, who held her hand for just a little too long and twinkled his eyeballs at her just a little too much. She would remember his name.

But all in all not a bad bunch from the look of it and as she made her way with Morton Edwards to her home room she brightened considerably upon seeing some of the students who were getting themselves organized into small lockers and even smaller cliques.

Morton wished her luck and she shut the door behind him, stepped to the desk and put her bag and books down upon it. It was dark in the room and she realized the blinds on the windows were all lowered. She took off her sweater and moved through the gloom and started to pull open the blinds. A cough from behind her made her jump and she gasped as she turned around.

There in the back row was a dark, long-haired boy in denims and a hat. He sat still with his hands on the desk in front of him. He was native, she knew, and had suspected that there would be at least a few in her class seeing as Newton was so close to the huge Navajo reserve.

"Good morning", she said. "I didn't see you there. Who are you?"

"Billy Ahiga", said the boy. "Sorry. I didn't mean to scare you. I just didn't want to wait outside."

"Why not?" asked Karen. "I mean its okay that you're in here but it's still nice outside and early. Did you get your stuff settled into a locker?"

"Not gonna bother."

"How come?"

"Not gonna stay long."

"I don't understand," Karen said, vaguely.

"I don't belong here."

"Oh, I see," said Karen. She finished opening the blinds and looked once more at his nervous face. It was a young, nice face that offered up a good deal of bravado but not a lot of self-assurance. "Is this your first day at this school?"

"Yeah," said Little Billy.

"Mine, too," she said. "We have something in common there. I hope you're not as nervous as I am."

"I'm okay," he said, perking up slightly. She could sense instinctively that maybe now he felt he had an ally; a jumping off point for what must be a very scary day in this young man's life. Score one for the sensitive teacher, she thought.

The door opened and a few other students entered and Karen smiled to herself as their heads swiveled back and forth trying to determine which they were more curious about; the unfamiliar, pretty, new English teacher standing in the flash of sunlight or the much more interesting aboriginal boy sitting at his desk in the shadow of the flag.

*   *   *

A thunder head rose over Black Mesa and water splashed down on the hard, dusty rock. Monster-Slayer and Child-Born-Of-Water had gone to visit Ever Changing Woman and there was no one to look down upon the people. In this time of confusion, the spirits of evil monsters floated above the earth and searched across the mesa. They were angry as they looked upon the bodies of their ancestors, now turned to stone and existing only as outcrops and crags on the Black Mesa. But they didn't know what to do. If they tried to hurt the people in revenge, the sons of Ever Changing Woman would return and punish them, perhaps changing them into rock as well. As it was, they were imprisoned far below, shackled in stone. The more they thought about their impotence the more they wailed and tore at their hair. And the hair floated up from below on cold winds and was carried past the farms to the desert where Coyote was playing.

He heard their wail on the wind and ran as quickly as he could to Black Mesa to find out why the monster spirits wept. When he heard of their anguish, he said "Then you must find others to do your bidding. You must be asked to rejoin the world. Then the Changing Woman can find no fault." The monsters heard Coyote and thought that what he counseled was good and together they started to search about for the right way for them to enter the world. It would have to be sly and difficult to see so that Changing Woman would be fooled. They looked among the people and finally they saw Big Jim. And they saw his grandfather. They saw Big Jim's woman, Lucy, and Little Billy. Then they looked further and saw four white men riding roaring horses through the desert. And they knew then what to do. And the rain stopped.

*   *   *

Big Jim heaved the last of the supplies into the pick-up outside the co-op. He was sweating hard now and he hoped he'd be able to get home and shower before Lucy came in. It wouldn't do to greet your fiancé of less than twelve hours with a serious stink on. He paused and leaned against the fender of the truck and wiped his brow with his gloved hand. Just the thought of her name made him drift off for a moment and he gazed out over the desert toward the reservation and the small village where he and Little Billy and their grandfather made their home. A home that was soon to become one person more crowded when Lucy came and then perhaps not long after that... who knows?

He'd have to get some more clients. More tourists for the mesa tours. That much was for sure. The one or two tours he was doing every month wouldn't be enough; especially with the added cost of running Billy into school every day. Maybe he'd have to get him his own car soon. There was another worry.

Al McReary, the store owner, came out with the final bag of ammunition and plunked it into the back.

"I'll take that up front with me", said Jim. "It's too hot back here. We wouldn't want a nasty accident hitting me in the ass."

"Yeah, she's a hot one today and that's a fact", said Al. "Looked like rain for a while there," he said, peering at the sky. "Don't look like it now." Then he grinned at Jim, "So when's the big day, Jim?"

"Well, probably next month. Gonna come?"

"Wouldn't miss it. Where's it gonna be? On the Rez?"

"Yeah", said Jim. "Granddad wants it to be traditional. And that's okay with me and Lucy but it means guys like you will have to travel out. But we'll make it worth your while. Little Billy and granddad are planning quite the spread." Even as he said this he was doing the mental arithmetic and coming up with one more reason he'd have to get some more tourists out on the mesa. Marriage, it seemed, was going to be as expensive out there as it would be in town, what with one thing and another. Oh well, he thought, it only happens once... hopefully.

"Sounds great", said Al, smiling largely and pressing his big hand into Jim's equally impressive mitt. "Let me know and Sue and I will be there with bells on."

"You may have to be if Granddad has his way", laughed Jim, climbing into the cab. "See ya later"

"Later," called Al as he walked back into the store.

Jim hauled the Ford around and pulled out into the road, whistling to himself and looking at his watch. Almost three-thirty... time to go get Little Billy and head back out to the village.

Cutting through town, he pulled up across the road outside the school and sat and rolled a cigarette. He lit it and watched as students started to pour out of the school. Some had already exited and were loitering around on the lawn. Several minutes went by and the kids began moving off in dribs and drabs until the front of the school was completely empty. A few stragglers came out and walked off down the road. There was still no sign of Billy.

Jim finally got out of the truck and ground the cigarette out with his boot before heading up the walk and into the school. He entered the big doors and walked down the hallway. He'd never actually been in this school before and the sheer size of it surprised him. He began to appreciate just what Little Billy had been worried about and vowed to himself to be a little more patient with the kid.

He stuck his head into the first room he came to and spotted a young woman wiping off the blackboard in front of her.

"Excuse me, miss?" he almost whispered. The woman turned to look at him. A pretty good looking woman at that he thought and gave himself a kick, mentally. Can't be looking in quite that way anymore, he reminded himself.

"Oh, hello", said the woman.

"Hi. I'm looking for Litt... for Billy Ahiga. Would he be around here?"

The woman put down her brush and stepped over to him. "Are you related to him?" she asked.

"I'm his brother, Jim. I've come to pick him up."

"Oh, yes, he said you would be coming. I'm afraid there's been a bit of... an incident. He's down in the principal's office waiting for you."

"An incident", said Jim, his face darkening.

"Don't worry, it's nothing serious; just a scuffle with a couple of the other boys. Mr. Edwards thought it would be best if he waited for you in the office rather than outside. So there wouldn't be any more problems."

"Where's the office?"

"Just down the hall on the right." Then she added, "I wouldn't worry too much. He was doing fine all day really. I know he was nervous about coming here. He was great in class, answering questions and such. He just got a little defensive at lunch from what I understand. He's a proud boy."

"Yeah, he is that", said Jim.

"I know what it's like to be facing a strange group for the first time. Tell him if there's anything he needs to come and see me. I want to make things as smooth as possible for him."

"Thanks Miss…"

"Armitage… Karen."

Jim turned at the door before heading down the hall. "You're not just saying that because he's a 'Native American' are you, Karen?"

"No, it's my job", said Karen.

"Just asking", said Jim turning and leaving.

Jim walked down the hall and found Little Billy sitting on the floor outside the office. Billy saw him coming and got up, ready for the bust which never came. Jim put his arm around his brother's shoulder and silently they walked out of the building and got into the truck.

"You alright?" Jim asked eventually as they pulled away from the curb.

"It's cool", said Little Billy.

"How was school?"

"Loved every minute of it. Let's go."

*   *   *

Albert Bader clung to the throttle of his big Harley, his damaged fingers throbbing as he tried to keep up with the others. He had taken a bad beating from The Crip and the one blow he had managed to land of his own had resulted in another wound that now made it hard for him to focus. One eye was puffed shut and the knee of his left leg was

13

swollen and sitting at an angle that made it difficult to shift. He looked at his face in the mirror on the handlebar and scowled; cursing as he spat blood down onto the pavement; pavement that was getting to be of much better quality now that they were heading into town. He couldn't wait to get off the damn bike and get a drink.

Up ahead, Crip and Cage were riding side by side. Mystic Bob trailed slightly behind and pulled on a wine skin slung around his neck. Albert wished he had some of that right now, although what Bob drank and the rest of humanity drank were quite often at odds. Still, it would have helped with the pain that seemed to be attacking him from every side. He knew his days with these guys were numbered but he ached for some payback on Crip. Instinctively, his hand reached to his side to feel the Wesson that usually nestled there, only to remember that The Crip had it now. Albert smiled to himself though because he knew, as The Crip didn't, about the piece strapped to his leg. His time would come.

Crip said something to Cage and the three sped up to make the light at an approaching intersection. They crossed through as Albert twisted gingerly on his throttle, but the spring was too stiff for his numb fingers and the acceleration didn't happen. The light started to change and Crip was waving him through it as they tooled down the street. Albert couldn't see past a truck parked at the corner but he barreled on regardless. Then there was a deafening horn blast and a screech of tires as an ancient Ford F-10 with a couple of Indians in it ground to a halt half-way through the intersection. Albert swerved the bike to one side and just made it past the fender of the truck, hitting the curb lightly and bouncing off toward the others. Mystic Bob was howling and Cage grinned like a fool up ahead. Albert looked back at the truck and the face of the man in the driver's seat. He started to stop to go back but The Crip yelled and waved him on. Albert took one more look at the man in the truck and the kid beside him and caught up with the others.

Crip shouted over the brack of the engines, "Shit, Albert, you gotta be more careful. That's a hundred and eighty buck fine."

"It's not the fine, it's the points..." laughed Bob.

"There's The Jug", shouted Cage as they hit the outskirts on the other side of town. They pulled into the parking lot of the town's only strip club and got off their bikes, shaking the dust as they went. Albert was slower getting off his bike but much, much faster getting into the bar.

*   *   *

Karen let the warm fragrant water of the bath close over her like a blanket. She slipped back a little further and closed her eyes, opening one temporarily to spot Huxley on his hind legs, front paws hanging over the edge of the tub. She closed it again and said, "Hi buddy. So how was your day?" She reached out a hand and felt for the back of the cat's neck to grab the scruff the way he liked it. But he was already gone. Now he was at the bathroom door standing, in that disconcerting way that cats do, ears erect and staring at a spot in the living room.

"Hux, what do you see, baby?" Huxley stood still, staring fixedly. "Baby, don't do that okay? It freaks me out. Huxley?"

The cat bolted into the next room. There was silence for a moment and then a mad scrambling that sounded as if he was bouncing off every piece of the meager furniture in the apartment. There was a last furious scrabbling and then stillness.

Karen sighed and tried to relax again. But it was too late, the moment was ruined. She washed herself and sank one last time under the now-cooling water and then hoisted herself up and out of the bath, grabbing a towel from the rack as she did so. She dried off, wrapped herself in her housecoat and went to investigate.

"Hux...? What are you doing", she asked into the darkened living room.

"Kitty?" she called. "Where are you Hux?" There was a small mew from the corner behind the chair and she could see the cat's tail sticking out from under it, twitching madly. "What are you doing there?"

She got down on her hands and knees beside the chair and peered under but couldn't see past the cat. Reaching under she pulled Huxley back by his haunches. He resisted and Karen pulled harder. "What have you got there?" she asked and turned Huxley around to face her.

She screamed and let the cat drop, the dying mouse still wriggling in its mouth. Huxley's jaw dropped and came down hard on Karen's knee, snapping shut. The body of the mouse fell to the floor and the cat scrambled the other way meowing loudly. A ragged mouse head spat from his mouth and rolled under the TV leaving a thin trail of blood on the rug.

Karen watched this for a moment and then started to gag. She ran to the bathroom just in time.

*   *   *

Linda-Lou's head hit the table with a thump. She coughed a little and then rose up again and resumed her upright position against the back of the chair. Her boyfriend, Cooter, was still drunk as a boiled owl and was thumping with his fist on some buddy's back at the bar. She'd like to think this was another Saturday night but it wasn't. It was Tuesday. She rolled her head groggily to one side and spied Albert Bader again at the other end of the room with the same bunch of freaks he'd come in with. She'd noticed him earlier. He was a handsome guy even with the bruises around his eye and his limp. She thought she'd seen him get off a bike earlier. That was definitely cool.

Albert eyed the girl sitting alone and watching him from the other end of the room and saw that the guy that periodically came back to her table to get another glass of beer, was busy with some other dude at the bar. Albert was very aware of how she was looking at him and even though he felt like shit, he still wouldn't mind grabbing some ass back to his room and getting her to ease his pain. And he'd had just enough to drink to make her look passable.

The Crip and Mystic Bob were studying some map that Bob had come up with and Cage was already practically comatose. So Albert got up and limped over to the girl. Crip looked up momentarily and watched him go; Mystic Bob just chuckled and kept on peering at the map.

Albert reached the table and set his glass down on it as he sat. "Hey," he said. "Don't you know me from somewhere?"

After a second or so the girl started to laugh and then hiccupped and laughed some more. Albert smiled and started to say something but the girl just kept on going. She laughed and coughed and then Albert

16

thought, "oh god, she's gonna hurl." But she didn't. She suddenly became very calm and stretched one arm out and onto Albert's shoulder, not unlike a snake; a wet snake. The band was ripping out something outrageously loud and he could barely hear her. But he did hear her say "You're cute, you…"

He mumbled something back and cupped her breast with his hand and started to move his head toward hers when a hand landed on his other shoulder and pulled him around.

"What the fuck do you think you're doing?" said Cooter.

Albert stood up and on doing so was glad to find that he stood about a half a foot taller than Cooter and was about six beers more sober. He was about to deliver a head butt to Cooter when all of a sudden there were two more guys standing behind him. It seemed the bouncers that Albert had seen when they had first entered The Jug were joining ranks with the regulars. The white guy looked like ex-marine and the black guy seemed to have been recently carved out of a truck. Albert's sore leg started to throb with the anticipation of what was to come. The girl was standing now too and screaming at Cooter to fuck off.

Marine started to laugh as Cooter grabbed Linda-Lou's arm and then, suddenly, there was TheCrip standing beside the boyfriend. Crip took hold of one of Cooter's arms and steered him aside. The Truck started to move on Crip but Mystic Bob had a hand on his throat and a knife at his kidney before the man could get close. Marine stopped laughing and Truck waved him off as Crip took the boyfriend to the bar.

It looked, for all Albert could tell, like they were discussing a local fishing hole as Crip leaned in and whispered something into Cooter's ear. A concerned look appeared on Cooter's face and he got sort of pale. Then it became more like an expression of fear as The Crip continued to say whatever it was he was saying. Finally, Cooter left Crip and came over to the two bouncers, said something and they all three turned and left the bar. The girl was standing there like a statue and Albert was leering at her as Crip and Bob went back to their table. The band was crashing out now with music so loud that nobody outside of the immediate vicinity of the altercation even noticed that anything had been going on.

Albert grabbed Linda-Lou's hand and pulled her up the stairs leading to their rooms on the second floor. Linda-Lou was in big trouble and she knew it. But she didn't scream.

*   *   *

Changing Woman was visiting the home of Spider Woman and together they were weaving a pattern for the night sky. They laughed as they worked and watched as Monster Slayer and Child-Born-of-Water wrestled atop a nearby mesa. Spider Woman loved the two children of Changing Woman as if they were her own, for was it not she that had given them power when they were young. Was it not she who so loved the Dine (the Navajo people) that she had sent these two children to protect them?

The Sun-God was happy also and all about the land was bathed in a warm and even glow. Soon the tapestry would be ready and the night could proceed.

Suddenly there was a high-pitched yip and Coyote sprang from the bushes and lay down beside the loom of the two gods. "What do you want?" asked Spider Woman putting out a bowl of water for him to drink.

Coyote said nothing but took a long, cool drink from the bowl. Finally, he looked at the two children of Changing Woman, still cavorting on the mesa.

"Tell me," said Coyote "is that not Monster Slayer and Child-Born-of-Water playing there?"

"It is," replied Changing Woman.

"Interesting," said Coyote. "Who then is it that now protects the people near Black Mesa?"

"From what?" asked Spider Woman.

"Oh, you are right," replied Coyote. "All the monsters are dead." And he laughed and ran away calling back, "Thank you for the water!"

*   *   *

A lone Harris Hawk circled in the twilight of the Arizona sky, his endless search for prey his sole reason for cycling through the dusk. His eyes were clear and focused on the earth hundreds of feet below him, alert for any motion that would indicate even the smallest of his potential victims. He rose and fell slightly on the waves of heat that came up to meet him, dissipating and falling back to the sands to be heated again. Below, a Coral snake wound itself under a scrub cactus and watched the same prey, a small mouse, creep unwittingly towards its fate. The snake slowly coiled up, preparing to strike. But, from above, a brown flash descended like an arrow towards the rock protecting the snake. At the last moment, the hawk pulled up and landed with a flutter some five or six feet away from the snake and started to jump about and flap its wings. Its mewling craw broke the silence of the evening and the snake, startled by the action of the hawk, broke its cover and headed for a stand of cacti. Far too great a distance, that stand, however and within a second or two the hawk was skyward again, the writhing reptile grasped firmly in its razor talons.

From where he sat, alone on a blanket with his back to an outcrop of stone, Nascha Ahiga turned his old eyes to the sky and held a hand up to block the last rays of the dying sun so that he could watch the hawk. "Anaba," he whispered, naming the bird as he that returns from war, the war that all creatures waged to live and that, at least for today, the hawk had won.

Nascha Ahiga's leg was sore and he reached down to rub it gingerly. Later he would drink some Arnica tea. That would help even though it was a Catawba medicine and not Navajo. But it was soothing and worked and that was the main thing. Nascha was a Navajo medicine man but he was practical and equal opportunity when it came to cures, even if he had to go to the store at Wahspah Falls to get it. He felt along the rock and pulled his canvas bag towards him, and, feeling its contents, thought it had been a good day of gathering considering the heat and his age.

"Grandpa!" He heard the sound of his grandson Kai calling to him or, as he preferred to be known, Little Billy. Although Nascha didn't think that Billy enjoyed the "Little" part very much. That part just came with being Big Jim's brother. Even that wouldn't have come about if Big Jim had stuck to his aboriginal name, Mosi. "Grandpa!" the call came again; the thin voice just this side of reaching manhood. They wanted him for dinner probably. Nascha felt somewhat foolish being called like a child to his own table so he said nothing and waited, irascibly, to see how long it would take Kai to find him. He wasn't far from the house and from here could see the lights twinkling invitingly down below.

He waited, grew impatient, and was about to shout out to end the game because his leg was really throbbing now when a soft voice came down from just above his head, making him jump. "How was the search today, Granpa?"

"Good. Could have used some help, though Kai," said Nascha.

"Billy," said Little Bill.

"Help me up, Kai," said Nascha, obstinately, and put his arm out. Billy sighed and dropped silently down beside him.

"Is your leg hurting?" asked Billy.

"Like a son-of-a-bitch. Help me will you?" They started to make their way down the slope, slowly at first and then a bit quicker when the ground started to even out. At one point they stumbled but Billy bent over, almost at a ninety degree angle, and caught them up and they moved on. "See?" said Nascha. "Kai... willow tree. The name isn't for nothing."

"Anything," said Billy.

"What?" said Nascha.

"The name isn't for 'anything'."

"You're so smart," said Nascha. "You're so smart you smell funny."

Billy looked at his grandfather and wondered what the hell he was talking about. There was a lot he didn't understand. But he loved the old man to bits.

*   *   *

   The head...

Even through a casual examination of the human body one can see that the head is attached to the body by the neck. The head relies on the neck to communicate with the rest of the body. This

20

communication includes air and food passages, nerves, and major blood vessels and, of course, the all-important spinal cord. It is nothing less than incredible that within this extremely narrow area are housed these supremely necessary, vital structures and yet the whole thing is so built that it still allows for maximum mobility; fluidly permitting a great deal of different head positions relative to the rest of the body. And it's tough too... sort of.

The skeletal structure of the neck is basically that of the vertebral column. The aero-digestive space (the gullet and windpipe) is supported by the hyoid bone and laryngeal and tracheal cartilage. These hang, like fleshy monkeys, from the bottom of the jaw and the base of the skull by a series of ligaments and muscles.

Between all the tubes and the skin lie a group of strap muscles connecting the respiratory skeleton and the sternum (chest). There are also muscles attaching the hyoid bone to the tongue, the jaw and the 'styloid' bone. A muscle group called the sternocleidomastoid (but more easily referred to as the SCM) divides the neck into convenient muscular triangles. The posterior triangle is for support so that your head doesn't roll around like a bowling ball held up by a noodle, and the anterior triangle contains and protects the vital structures mentioned above.

The neck also contains major branches of cranial nerves as well as cervical roots. These nerves control and support facial expression and the tongue, amongst other things. Hence, the dazed, bedraggled, foolishly surprised look of the hanged man.

There are many glands hanging around here too, including the thyroid and para-thyroids that service the body and cause much consternation when they misbehave. And, of course, the lymph nodes, those little islands of energy that if you are unfortunate enough to get cancer in is, more or less, a death sentence; they too are snuggled in there.

Not to mention the jugular vein. Target of many a wolf, lion and lawyer.

*   *   *

Lucy soon-to-be Ahiga was coming in through the front door as Nascha and Billy were coming in the back. Big Jim was in the shower.

She dropped a bag of bread on the kitchen counter as Billy helped the old man lower himself into a chair.

"You okay, Grandpa?" asked Lucy as she took her jacket off and hung it in the closet. "You look a little red."

Nascha just waved her away and took a deep breath. "I'm all right. It's just my leg's sore. Kai, hand me my bag will you?"

Billy took the old leather bag, beaded and worn, from off its hook on the wall and handed it to Nascha and then turned and went to the kitchen to get some water. Nascha scrounged around in the old sack for a bit and then took something out and grinding it between his fingers and thumb, stuck it under his tongue and sat back. Billy came back and handed the water to his grandfather.

Lucy started making the meal and called in from the kitchen to Billy who was now sitting reading a book under the small lamp by the window. "How did it go today, Little Bill? Have fun?"

"It was fine," Billy answered.

Lucy came in wiping out a small clay bowl. "Just fine? What was it like? Pretty interesting I bet with so many people around and all. A big school like that."

"It's not so big," said Billy.

"Well, not by big city standards maybe, but bigger than anything you've ever been to. Weren't you nervous? I'd have been terrified. I was terrified my first day there."

"I wasn't scared, okay?" Billy said and got up and went out the front door letting the screen hammer behind him.

Lucy watched him go. "What's with him?" she asked.

Big Jim came into the room wiping his hair with a towel. "He got in a fight. Leave him alone."

"A fight? With who? Is he hurt?" said Lucy, worried now.

"He's alright. Some of the kids were giving him a rough ride, that's all. He'll handle it."

"Maybe we should talk to his principal. I could go in before work," said Lucy.

"He'll handle it, Lucy. Let it be," said Jim, putting a hand on her shoulder, turning her around and planting a kiss on her mouth. "Thanks though."

"'Course he will," said Nascha. "We gonna eat soon or what?" Lucy pushed Jim away and together they returned to the kitchen to finish making dinner. Nascha went to stand up but sank back down with a small groan. "Damn leg," he thought.

Later as they sat around the small table in the kitchen, Billy was quiet and Lucy and Jim talked about the day and about some people that Lucy wanted to have at the wedding that Big Jim didn't particularly know. Nascha was slowly poking a fork at his chicken.

"It doesn't have to be that big, does it?" said Jim, thinking in the back of his mind about the food costs and liquor expenses. As soon as he said it he saw the look on Lucy's face; not anger so much as a kind of quiet disappointment. "Of course," he said, repeating himself from the afternoon, "you only get married once. Sure, invite them."

Lucy smiled and put a hand onto Jim's. Jim kissed her on the back of the neck.

"Get a room, will you?" said Billy with a smirk. Jim took a fork full of potato and flung it towards his head. "Hey!" shouted Billy and took a carrot and was about to hurl it back when Nascha started to cough. "That's enough, Billy", said Lucy, "you're upsetting Grandpa."

"No, I'm not," said Billy. "Am I, Grandpa?"

But Nascha was still coughing only harder now and now his face was red and now he was clutching at his arm and now Big Jim was pushing his chair back and now Lucy screamed and then Billy jumped up too and now Nascha was falling backwards out of his chair and Jim was holding his head and Lucy was standing up, still, like she was frozen.

"Call 911!" Big Jim shouted over his shoulder.

*   *   *

Mystic Bob watched The Crip as he slept, turning and tossing in his sweaty bed. Bob was fascinated by The Crip and couldn't get enough of him. He'd been that way ever since the particularly vicious drug night that had laid waste to a lot of Bob's brain. He had been on the brink of the abyss that time for sure but in one, sudden burst of light (actually, just Crip returning from the bathroom and leaving the light on) Bob had been saved from the final drop. Since then Mystic Bob couldn't leave The Crip even if he wanted to, which he didn't.

Also, it was Bob that had been responsible for The Crip losing the lower half of his left leg. Bob's bike had broken down and Crip had to double him to the nearest town. Bob, for once not having to apply himself to keeping the bike up, rode behind The Crip, holding his arms up as he day-dreamed of flying along the highway. Dreamed until he actually fell asleep and started to fall to one side, upsetting the balance and causing them to veer into the soft shoulder that trapped the wheel. The bike came down hard and Bob was thrown clear but Crip was pinned and the manifold burnt right through the skin; almost to the bone. Crip didn't get it seen to properly and it festered and that was the end of the lower half of The Crip's left leg.

But The Crip didn't hold it against Bob. He held it against the world and as hard a man as he was before the accident, the fire from his bike's exhaust had tempered him into a steel-souled troll that felt no remorse for anything and no sympathy for anyone. Still Mystic Bob loved The Crip and was his ever-vigilant right-hand man. It wasn't really his fault that the only way that he could deal with the world at large was through a drug-fogged haze that helped tone down the monster that constantly saddled his back.

The crazy, blue light from The Jug's big sign flashed on his face as he rocked gently from side to side and slid into semi-sleep. In the room next door, the same blue light cut an angle across Cage's face.

Cage couldn't sleep tonight. In fact he couldn't sleep most nights. He was a nervous man. He was small and wiry and had no meat on him at all really. Probably as a result of the nervous condition that left him twitchy and skittish. They called him Cage because of the four vertical, black, tattooed stripes that traversed his face from top to bottom. Some years back Cage had been in a medium security facility near Mexico doing time for sexual assault. A facility that received very little state funding and was pretty much falling apart both inside and out. Surrounding the prison was a field with a ditch around that and on the other side of the ditch, an electric fence. Not a very good one, either. And on the night that Cage and another inmate decided to vacate the premises, it was particularly faulty owing to a rain storm earlier in the day. As they ran towards the freedom they thought lay on the other side of that fence, Cage tripped while jumping the ditch and hit the fence face first. He passed out and ended up with four, vicious, evenly-spaced, third-degree burns down his face which scarred into deep, ugly red welts. Eventually, not having any money for plastic surgery, Cage had the stripes tattooed black and now he peered out between his thick, dark bars; permanently incarcerated in his fleshy cell.

He got up and pissed into the open toilet. He filled a glass with some coke and drank it down to clear the bile in his throat. Then he flopped back down on the broken bed.

Down the hall, Linda-Lou waited until Albert fell asleep and when she was sure from his drunken snore that he was out for the night, she collected what pieces of her clothing weren't torn to shreds and dressed as best she could. It was difficult. She was pretty sure her right arm was broken and she whimpered as she pulled her sweater on over it. She bit down hard on her lip to stop the sound from waking Bader and when she finally got the sweater and skirt on she reached for the door handle and let herself out.

In the hallway the light was dim and the one, thin fluorescent bulb that still functioned in this section of the dirty ceiling hissed and spat and gave a weird strobe effect to the walls and carpeted floor. Linda-Lou crept along with one hand outstretched for she couldn't see very well through the one eye that wasn't swollen shut. She shook all over and could hardly stop herself from running. But she knew she couldn't see well enough to do that and so she inched herself slowly along towards the stairs. The stairs to the lobby were on the other side of a 'T' in the hallway and as she moved to cross and go down, a hand suddenly reached out and grabbed her wrist. Then another hand wrapped itself quickly around her mouth and her eyes glazed as Cage dragged her, kicking, through the open door into his room.

*   *   *

"You wanted to see me, Mr. Edwards?" Karen held onto the door and leaned in to speak to the vice-principal. Morton Edwards looked up from his work.

"Oh, hi Karen. Please, just make it Mort, okay? Come in." Mort stood up and indicated a chair near the desk. "How's everything going? Settling in okay?"

"Great, yes, fine…" Karen sat and was temporarily blinded by the swatch of sun beaming in from behind the desk. Edwards walked over and closed the slats.

"How's that? Better?" he asked.

"Great, yes, f…," Karen stopped herself short, realizing she was about to repeat herself. Not very creative for an English teacher. Mort caught the moment and laughed. He sat back down.

"Listen," he said, "I have a bit of an assignment for you if you're okay with it."

"Oh?" said Karen.

"Yes. This being your first year at Newton, it's become somewhat of a custom for a new teacher to go out on the first field trip of the year; you and a more experienced teacher of course."

"Well, that sounds okay, Mort," said Karen. "What sort of field trip is it?"

"Oh, it's a lot of fun. You and about twenty of the grade eleven students spend a couple of nights out on the desert. You do some geology and aboriginal history stuff and then everyone writes a paper on it when they get back. We usually let it come in at about ten percent of the semesters mark."

"A couple of nights?" Karen asked. She immediately thought of the requisite camping, which she hated. She hadn't camped since Steven had insisted on it the first summer they were together. She wasn't really the camping sort. They had ended up a Motel Six. But there wasn't likely to be a hotel involved this time.

"Now, I know what you're thinking", Mort said soothingly, "but you'll have Harry Babcock with you and he's done this sort of thing a thousand times. He'll have you in the lap of luxury, camping-wise. It's more of a chaperone sort of thing really. "

"Who is he?" asked Karen.

"Harry? Oh he does a lot of things for us. He's a retired cop actually, he usually volunteers for these trips; drives the bus and stuff. Great guy. You'll be plenty safe with him. Knows more about these lands than anyone else around except for the natives."

"Um, okay."

"And what he doesn't know Herman Kilagrew does so between the two of them…"

"Herman Kilagrew?" said Karen and she flashed back to her first day and the overly long handshake with the buff but somehow repulsive gym teacher. She was beginning to get an uneasy vision of the 'staff tent'.

"Yeah, he usually goes along. Puts the kids through a sort of wilderness training thing, you know? Lot's of fun. Although you don't have to get involved with that," he added quickly. "Unless you want to, of course."

"Well, I…" She was about to tell him about her more than average ability as a runner. An ability that had led to several strong finishes in the San Francisco Marathon. But she decided to let that sleeping dog snooze.

"Excellent. You'll find it's a great way to get to know the kids better and also to find out what this part of the state has going for it in the way of landscape and flora and fauna and such. I'll put you down for it then, all right?"

"Yes, yes. Of course." Karen was already resigned to it and if it was expected of the newbie well, she wasn't going to let a couple of nights in a tent ruin her integration with the rest of the staff. Could be fun, actually, she thought. She could handle Kilagrew.

"Great!" Morton came round the table and offered his hand. Karen shook it and headed for the door. As she was beginning to close it, he added, "Oh, and Karen. No need to worry about the snakes and coyotes and such. Harry carries his service revolver with him just in case."

*　　　　　*　　　　　*

Little Billy and Lucy sat and waited in the lobby outside of the ICU. They didn't speak but just sat, slouched, watching the endless parade of nurses, doctors and orderlies that scurried back and forth like ants.

Nobody had spoken to them for hours. Not since the emergency room intern told them that Nascha was being moved to ICU but that they shouldn't worry too much because it was just a precaution; that he was still unconscious and in a weak condition.

Big Jim came around the corner carrying some coffees and a box of sandwiches that he set down on the little side table covered with dated magazines and a phone that didn't work. Lucy had found that out when she tried to call work to tell them that she wouldn't be coming in the next day. Her eyes were red from crying and now that she had that under control she didn't say much for fear that she would start again. Nobody touched the sandwiches.

Billy was numb. It had never occurred to him that this could happen. Even though he knew that Nascha was an old man, he had seemed invincible. Like the bedrock and the desert that had surrounded him all his life. It didn't seem possible that Nascha might just disappear; that in one short moment he would be gone from his life and that all the things that they did together and that he loved him for would melt away and become just another set of dreams from the past. He kept wanting to cry but didn't, partly because of Jim and Lucy's presence. Partly because he still couldn't quite comprehend what had happened. A myocardial infarction the intern had said... heart attack.

Billy wondered if there was any connection with Nascha's leg problem. Or even the herbal remedy that Nascha had taken just before the attack. He considered this even as he wondered whether he would ever talk to his grandfather again.

"Do you think we should tell them about the medicine he took before dinner?" Billy asked.

"Nah," said Big Jim. "It was just herbal stuff. He's been taking that all his life. That wouldn't have hurt him."

"I'm not so sure, Jim," said Lucy, quietly. "Maybe he got something out in the desert today that he mistook for something else. Some mushrooms or something. His eyesight isn't like it used to be."

"If they wanted to know things like that they would have asked us," Jim replied.

Billy was about to bring up the sore leg business when a doctor appeared before them; almost rising like a ghost from the green-tiled floor. They hadn't even seen him coming. He had the slightly tired but compassionate composure common to many of his profession. Like an unspoken sigh.

The doctor looked at a clipboard and said, "Mr. Ahiga?" to Big Jim.

Billy's ears started to buzz then and he felt his face flush as he wondered if his head might explode. He could barely make out what the doctor was saying. The words drifted down to him like they were being spoken from the top of a well; dropping from a great height. He heard fragments and bits like "serious attack", "lack of oxygen" and then a phrase that confused him but sounded something like "potential brain damage."

Then the doctor was walking away saying something about them coming back tomorrow as there was nothing else they could do that night. Big Jim was talking to a nurse about tomorrow's visiting hours and Lucy was looking at him with an odd kind of expression on her face. He thought he must look sick or something. Billy was about to say that he would stay at the hospital anyway but suddenly he felt incredibly tired. He thought he was going to pass out. Then Big Jim was there putting his arm around him and Lucy put hers through his other arm and they all walked out to the parking lot. The night sky was brilliant with stars and as Billy looked up a meteor split a fiery path towards the horizon. Then another flashed after it, like twins chasing each other across a field of black grass. Then he started to cry.

*   *   *

Mystic Bob walked into Albert's room and laughed. It looked pretty desperate. Clothing strewn about, a broken bottle lying smashed against a dresser, what looked like blood on the edge of the mattress and Bader himself laying the wrong way round on the bed, one arm dangling, and his hand in a beery ash-tray.

"Bader," Bob called. "Get up. Crip wants to get going. We've got a meet in half an hour"

There was no response so Bob walked to the dresser, grabbed a bowl and filled it with water from the tap in the bathroom. He poured it slowly over Bader's head. Bader moved slightly and groaned. "Bader! Up and at 'em, man. Let's go!"

Bader rolled over and grabbed Bob's arm by its thick wrist. "What the fuck…" he mumbled. Mystic Bob yanked his hand away easily and picked up Albert's pants and threw them at his head. The buckle of the belt smacked down on Albert's cheek.

"In the lobby… ten minutes. Or we split without you," said Bob and walked out the room. Before he left he tossed his wine-skin at Bader. "Here, this'll get ya going. Bring it down with ya."

Bob walked along the hall and tried the door to Cage's room but it was locked. He slammed a big fist against Cage's door. "Cage!"

There was a pause and then a low voice, hardly recognizable as Cage, said, "Okay, I'll be right there."

"Let me in, Cage. Open up."

"I said I'll be right there, now piss off!" shouted Cage.

Bob hesitated. "Alright. Just hurry it up. The meet is on. Half an hour…"

"Okay," came the muffled reply and the sound of movement and a chair or something scraping away from the door. Bob turned and headed downstairs to get his bike going. It always took a few extra kicks first thing in the morning.

Inside his room, Cage sat on the edge of the bed and looked towards the bathroom. What was in there was bad and Cage knew it. He could split back to Frisco now but the others would rat him out in a second. He didn't have time to clean it up. Cage started to panic. Why was it he could never think straight when it counted? Others could. The Crip could. The Crip would rip his throat out if he thought he was going to get mixed up with cops just when they were getting close to the score.

Crip got up and looked out the window. In the parking lot, Mystic Bob was adjusting his carbs. He stood up and wiped his hand on his pants and walked back inside. Cage mopped his forehead with his shirt. Then he spotted Bob's spare gas tank behind his seat. Letting himself out of the room, he carefully locked the door behind him and then hurried down the back stairs to the side entrance. Watching for Bob, he quickly undid the bungee cord around the spare tank, grabbed it and pulled Bob's jacket down over the empty space. Then he moved back inside and disappeared down the stairwell into the basement.

The Crip and Bob emerged from the front of The Jug together and walked to their bikes. Crip was really juiced. This was going to be the biggest day in the small-minded career of a real punk. Do the meet, make the buy, head back to the city and it was easy street for a long time. He'd had to do a lot of bad things to make the scratch to pull this off. But it was nothing compared to what he had in mind once he had some leverage.

Bader struggled down the steps pulling on his dirty, denim vest. A vest stained now with all sorts of shit. He looked at The Crip and then tossed Bob his wine-skin. It had helped. But who knows what the effect would be an hour from now.

"Where the fuck is Cage?" The Crip growled as he started up his bike.

"I'll go back up," said Bob and started to move towards the door. But just then Cage came bouncing through the side door and up out of the stair well. Bob turned and saw him and headed back to his bike.

"Sorry, Crip," said Cage. "I couldn't…" Then he just stopped and stared moronically around him.

The Crip just shook his head. "Let's go," he said. "We gotta do about 20 miles."

"Where to?" asked Albert.

"Into the desert. Just shut up and ride."

They roared out of the parking lot and onto the main highway, passing nobody in the early morning hours of a town that hadn't woken up yet. As they rode under the "Thanks for Visiting Newton Fairbanks" sign, Cage looked back. He could just make out the smoke beginning to rise from the basement of The Jug. He smiled as he thought about just how fast that crap-house made of balsa was going to burn.

*   *   *

Karen stirred to the sound of sirens and the smell of smoke drifting in through her open bedroom window. She turned on to one side and pried an eye open to look at the time on the clock radio. It was six a.m. She groaned a little and felt with her foot to the edge of the bed where Huxley usually slept at this point. Sure enough the fur-ball was there and immediately started to purr at the human contact.

31

"What's the rumpus, Hux?" she murmured and pulled back the covers on the window side of the bed and got up, her pajamas slightly skewed around her waist. She heaved them up and lurched to the window and gasped when she pulled back the blind and saw what was happening.

"Oh, my god…" she whispered as she looked across the open field to the bar that was now engulfed in flames. People from up and down the street were walking across the grass towards the building to get a closer look. There were four fire-trucks that Karen could see and an ambulance and a police car with another just sliding into view and grinding to a halt. Officers jumped out and started positioning themselves to prevent curious onlookers from getting too close to the fire. Karen could see one or two of the students that lived nearby running up the road.

"Better go have a look," she said to Huxley as she quickly threw on some track pants and a sweater and ball cap and headed to the kitchen. She grabbed a bottle of water and exited out the back door and down the metal fire escape and out through the small gate at the bottom of the garden that led onto the field. The grass was still stiff and wet with cold morning dew and she wished now that she had put socks on as the chilly moisture clung to her ankles and calves like ice. Mr. Chavez stuck his head out the window of his downstairs bedroom.

"Look at that will you?" he said to someone inside and Maria Chavez' head appeared beside his. "Be careful, Miss Armitage!" he called out to Karen as she unlatched the old metal gate. "That place is on natural gas I think."

"Thanks, Mr. Chavez," Karen called back. "Are you coming over? I can wait for you."

"No, I've gotta get to work. Ain't that something, huh?"

"Incredible," said Karen and waved back at them as she started off across the field. As she walked she could see that the police were frantically trying to push people away from one side of the building. Karen supposed that it must be the side that housed the gas tanks. The fire crews were smashing windows on the second and third stories, trying to find out if any of the guests might still be in there. Karen shuddered at the thought of being in a fire-trap like that during something like this. She was starting to get scared now as the reality of the actual death potential sank in. But she kept going, a victim of the same hypnotic curiosity for disaster that was drawing the others.

She was about two hundred yards away now. The police were becoming more successful at corralling the bystanders towards a more-or-less protected area behind the fire-trucks which were spewing water onto the roof and upper stories. Suddenly there was a shout and a fireman with a yellow helmet that Karen guessed must be the one in charge, was screaming through a bull-horn at the men on the ladders to come down. He was pointing at the side of the building from which the police had been herding people away. The firemen started scrambling down; one of them even dropping from a height that Karen guessed must have been about 20 feet up. He hit the ground with a heavy thud and had obviously hurt his leg. Two other firefighters ran up and grabbed him under the arms and began to drag him away from the building towards the trucks. Karen started to run less directly towards the hotel and instead started to take a more circuitous route that would bring her up onto the road on the far side of The Jug.

But at that moment the door at the back burst open and a man, tall and thin, came stumbling out. Karen recognized him as the same man she had seen emptying the garbage two nights ago. He screamed as his burning clothes blazed around him. Karen came to a complete halt as the man's hair started to flame and he stumbled about, blindly, on the tarmac of the rear parking lot. She tried to shout to the firefighters to point them to the dying man, but she realized immediately that she couldn't be heard above the roar of the flames and the bedlam of the retreat of the bystanders. The man started to move again, clawing frantically at his burning clothes and as he did so he began to move, unknowingly, towards the side of the hotel that held the gas cylinders.

"No!" Karen shouted and started to run towards the man. A fireman near one of the trucks spotted her sprinting across the rear of the parking lot and began to shout at her and point. Others started screaming at her as well but it was too late, Karen could hear only the fading cries of the dying man and the heavy rumble of the fire.

Then she could hear nothing at all as a brilliant flash erupted from the building, obscuring everything. A shock wave hit her like a baseball bat, smashing into her and knocking her back ten feet into the field and the ditch of murky water that bisected it. She felt all the wind leave her lungs and the boom of the explosion that followed the flash left her ears ringing. She laid in the water, stunned, the sound of the explosion resonating and echoing around her and vaguely, too, the screams of the crowd.

Then there was a sharp splash and a spray of water as a heavy object about the size of a volleyball and smoking, hit the ditch a few feet from where she lay. She turned slowly to one side and watched as the steaming sphere bobbled up to the surface of the sludge and slowly rolled over to reveal the burnt face of a young woman. Cracked and scarred, its mouth opened and the tongue, split and cut in two, protruded from between the seared lips. Karen had had enough. Karen fainted into black relief.

*   *   *

Changing Woman and Spider Woman were deep in tense conversation as Child-Born-of-Water and Monster Slayer approached them. The children were hot and worn out from their furious play and wanted to eat the corn and mutton that were cooking on the fire. They wanted cool water even more. However, when they came close, Changing Woman beckoned them over before they could eat or drink and said "Children, you must return to Black Mesa and protect the people there."

"But Mother," said Monster Slayer, "We are hungry. There are no monsters there now. The people are safe. We know this."

Spider Woman told them of the visit of Coyote and the strange things that he had said before he left. It had made the women cautious and worried and now they felt that something must be done. But what Monster Slayer had said was true. There had been no trouble from monsters for many years nor had any been seen. Besides, Coyote was known for his trickery.

"Perhaps Monster Slayer is right," said Changing Woman.

"We could ask Father Sky to look from his height and warn us if such trouble is to come," said Child-Born-Of-Water.

"Good then," said Changing Woman. "Go to Father Sky and ask him for this favour and then we will not worry and can continue our visit here.

So Monster Slayer and Child-born-of-water rode a lightning bolt to the sky taking with them gifts of corn and bread. Father Sky welcomed them with open arms, his children sat and he listened to what they had to say. After hearing their story and looking down below, he finally spoke.

"I can see now that there are no monsters of the sky on or near the mesa. However, the people are not safe. There is evil in the land under which they dwell and we must be vigilant. Be ready at all times for men-who-are-not-people travel the desert and surely no good will come of this."

"Who are these men-who-are-not-people?" asked Monster Slayer. "We will hunt them down now and kill them."

"They are the lost ones. But now is not the time," said Father Sky. "Beware the rocks that live and move for in them are the spirits of the dead monsters from long ago. They wish only harm to all and there will soon come a time when they will walk again. I have seen this. And when they come among the people all will live in fear. It will be then that you must act."

"Can we not prevent this? Do we not have that power?" asked Child-born-of-water.

"That which I have seen must come to pass. It is not for us to change the way of the world. Go now and tell the women what I have said. Then return to Black Mesa and wait."

So the two children of Changing Woman flew back down from the sky on another bolt of lightning to tell the women what Father Sky had commanded.

Meanwhile, deep within the rocks of Black Mesa, there was movement. A vile, ancient evil stirred and the dark spirits that lived there smiled for they knew that their time was near and soon they would be freed from their prison of stone.

CHAPTER TWO

COMATOAST

Billy sat and chewed thoughtfully on a piece of stale chocolate. The only kind, apparently, that came out of the machine in the hospital lounge. The light from the window spilled in across the room and neatly dissected his grandfather's figure, separating it into two distinct forms; one radiant, the other a mordant echo. The lower half, from the shoulders down, was swathed in dark shadows, the IV and various other medically necessary devices which hung like spidery filaments from his arms and torso and controlled the row of monitors and feeders aligned along the bedside. Above all that, his grandfather's head, still and slightly moist, floated above the covers, suspended on his slim shoulders. His grandfather's smile had always seemed whimsical even when he was asleep at home and now was no exception.

Billy got up and went closer, bent over the sheets and with a small cloth, patted at the beads of sweat dotting Nascha's brow. He put the cloth in the basin and pulled his chair closer so that he could hear his grandfather's breathing. It came in short, even swallows and despite his warm temperature he seemed restful. It was two days since Nascha's admittance and it was now Sunday. Tomorrow Little Billy would be back at school; the school that he had not attended since his grandfather's attack. It seemed like it was the last place of any importance he could be but he knew Big Jim would insist on it. He wondered how it would be when he did return. Would the other students even remember the short-lived fight he had with the two jocks, Cam and Louie, or would they be sympathetic about his grandfather's situation (assuming they even knew about it or cared, for that matter)? The English teacher, Armitage, she would care in some way, Billy felt. She seemed to care about a lot of things. He sort of wished he could speak with her now. The notion of it annoyed him. Why should he care, one way or another, what she felt? She was just his teacher; his teacher for one day.

Nascha's hand twitched. Billy looked down at it and took it in his own. He knew now not to make too much of that. The first time it had happened he had run down the hall to the nurse's station, shouting at them and begging them to come with him. They had told him, after checking, that this was normal activity and didn't necessarily mean that he was even close to rising out of the coma. That might not happen for a while; if ever. Billy tried to drive that thought from his mind even though he knew the true potential of it.

A candy-striper by the name of Allison stuck her head in around four o'clock. Billy recognized her from his one day at school as the girl who sat near the front of his home room class. Pretty and red-headed with a soft voice that you could hardly hear. Ms. Armitage had to ask her several times to speak up. Billy wondered how many times she had actually announced her presence just now in the hospital room before he heard her.

"Excuse me, Billy?" she said, much louder than she would have normally. Yes, she must have arrived a little before he had become aware of her.

"Oh, hi, yes... um, what?" Billy said, now fully aware of her.

"We need to change some of your grandfather's things. Would it be okay for you to take a break for a few minutes?"

Billy looked at her blankly and then, when the question sunk in, replied, "Sure, yes, sure. I was going to leave in a minute anyway. Got to get home."

"I'm really sorry about your grandfather. I'm sure he's going to be fine."

"Oh, why is that?" said Billy and immediately regretted it. She was just trying to be nice and now she was blushing and starting to move back out into the hall. "Hey," he said, "Its okay." He got up and brushed past her into the hall, smelling as he did the sweet and gentle perfume that she had on; or maybe it was her hair. In any case, he found himself wishing he had been much cooler about the whole thing.

He watched as she went to Nascha's bedside and started to pull back the sheets. He couldn't begin to imagine doing what she did. Looking after all these people, most of them seniors, and not even getting paid anything for doing it. She looked back over her shoulder at him and smiled. He wouldn't forget that smile for a while.

Billy started out to the lobby and the main doors. He would catch the bus to the furthest stop and call Lucy who would pick him up on her way out to the house. He was just moving down the hall when Allison leant out of the door to Nascha's room.

"Billy, I don't know if you heard. Ms. Armitage is in room 311. She was in a fire or something."

*   *   *

The head of an animal is the anterior part of its body, in terms of anatomical position. It is comprised of the mouth, the brain, various sensory organs and the skull, the protector of the aforementioned, as well as the surface coverings of skin and hair.

But it is, of course, much more than the sum of its parts. It is the driver, the seat of knowledge, and as much as we would like to believe that love comes from the heart, it doesn't. It comes from the brain.

In most complex animals the head is joined to the body by the neck. In less complex animals the head is joined to the body directly. Sometimes this is true of football players.

Collectively, the bones of the head are called the skull. These are divided into the cranium (home of said brain), the mandible (or jaw or sometimes, colloquially, cake-hole) and, in the case of humans, three ear bones. All other animals have but one ear bone. And yet, for the most part, they hear much better than us. So much for intelligent design.

The cranium is actually a series of bones joined at various points by tissues called sutures. Most of these sutures are completely solid before birth, but there are three particularly vulnerable areas that don't solidify until puberty. These are called the fontanelles. You may know one of these as the soft spot on the top of a baby's head. Don't press here.

38

Other than the skull, the mandible or jaw-bone comprises most of the solid structure of the head. The jaw is connected to the skull at the temporomandibular joint. It is this that allows the mouth to move freely. Sometimes we might wish that it didn't function quite as well as it does.

When viewed from below we see that the skull contains several holes. These holes allow for the passage of various tubes, like veins and nerves, to extend down to the rest of the body through the neck (see above). Within the skull are several depressions upon which lay the sundry parts of the human brain. The brain without which, as mammals, we cannot function. Aristotle believed that although the heart was the centre of intelligence, it was the brain that separated us from the beasts because it was that which cooled the blood which fed the heart. Bigger brain equals better cooling equals greater intelligence. Of course, Aristotle wore a toga.

Despite the assertion by nervous people that butterflies live in our stomach, it is inside our head that the butterfly really finds a home. It is called the middle cranial fossa. The wings of this butterfly-shaped depression serve as a base for the temporal lobes. What is the difference between the brain and the mind? It is here that, perhaps, we may find the answer. In a purely metaphorical sense, if the brain is the hardware and the mind is the software then the temporal lobes are perhaps analogous to the RAM. As the system that is run by the brain, the body is at the brain's mercy. Remove the brain and the body is useless.

*   *   *

Karen was in a group ward with several other non-serious cases that were all in one stage or another of leaving the hospital. The woman in the next bed had broken her arm falling off a ladder; the man across the way was recovering from an asthma attack; and Karen herself was waiting to be released from her observational stay-over following Saturday's conflagration.

She felt stupid really, sitting here; she was fine. The blast had stunned her but not knocked her out. She had only fainted from the horror of the moment when that poor girl's... but no, she couldn't revisit that again right now. She felt the bile rise and her throat started to constrict with the memory of it; and the smell of the gas-fuelled fire and burnt hair... "It's only been two days," she told herself. The doctor who had treated her warned her that she would be getting flashbacks of the whole incident for some time, that it would probably even invade her dreams at some point but not to worry, it was normal. Normal. An interesting adjective to use to describe deep psychological trauma, she thought.

She would be home in a few hours and then she'd be back at the school on Monday. Karen wondered if she could even do that. Everyone must have heard about it by now. That was all she needed; to be the focus of attention and widen the scope of the magnifying glass that she knew was already firmly focused on her. She thought, for some odd reason but with relief, of Huxley and hoped that Mrs. Chavez had gone in more than once since her hospital stay. Hux would be so pissed off when she got home. Home... it was scarcely that; still just a holding area really.

She picked up her copy of Saramago's latest opus from the bedside table and started to thumb through the pages. She had planned to introduce the book into her course this year, but had decided to wait; best not to ruffle any feathers right away; just stick to the suggested curriculum and work the good stuff in later. Not that there was anything wrong with Moby Dick. She'd have to finish that book some day.

Then she was suddenly aware of somebody standing in the doorway and looked up. It was the native boy, Billy Ahiga, watching her from hallway. She motioned him in with a wave of her hand and, slowly, he ventured in and over to her bed.

"Hi there," she said. "What are you doing here?"

"I'm visiting my grandfather. Allison told me that you were in a fire or something."

"Well, sort of," Karen replied, "Actually I was near a fire. There was an explosion and it sort of knocked me over."

"A fire? Where?" Billy asked.

"That bar out on the highway. I think it's called The Jug or something like that. At least it was. It's just a pile of ash now."

Billy was amazed. "The Jug? You're kidding. That place has been there forever. I think it was there before the town was. But you're not hurt too bad?"

"No, it's nothing," said Karen. "I'll be back at school tomorrow. How's your granddad?"

Billy looked down. "He's had a heart attack. He's in a coma right now…"

"Oh, Billy, I'm sorry. What are they saying?"

"Not much, there are still tests and stuff to come back. I…," he went silent. "I don't know if he's coming home."

"You're pretty close, huh?" said Karen.

"Yeah, well since my dad died, it's just been Jim and I and grandpa out there. We spend a lot of time together. Now there's Lucy, too."

"Lucy?"

"Jim's girlfriend; they're getting married this summer. I don't think she's gonna want to live on the Rez and if grandpa's not around, that'll mean that I have to live with them in town."

"Would that be so bad?"

"Yes," said Billy. "Anyway, I just wanted to say hi and see how you were."

"Billy, I really appreciate you taking the time; especially under the circumstances. Will you be at school tomorrow?" asked Karen.

"I don't know… maybe. I may have to leave though."

"Of course. I'll see you tomorrow then, hopefully."

There was an awkward moment as Billy looked at the odd figure of his home-room teacher in her hospital bed with her flowery, flannel nightdress on. He felt he wanted to say something else but he couldn't think of what that might actually be. Then he heard a familiar voice from the hallway. It was Jim and someone else, the doctor he thought. He quickly turned and walked out of the ward.

The doctor was showing Jim a chart or something and Jim was looking on with a mixture of anger and frustration clouding his dark features.

Billy walked up and Big Jim hardly acknowledged him at first. Then he finally noticed him.

"Wait for me outside, okay Billy?" said Jim and turned back to the doctor.

"What's going on? Why are you here? I thought you weren't coming again until tomorrow," Billy said.

"They just called me in. Can you wait for me? I have to get this stuff straight. I'll be right out," said Jim.

Billy considered refusing for a second but then thought better of it. He wheeled around and walked quickly out of the building. The sun was starting to fall behind the town now, the heat making it seem to shudder in the sky and the fingers of light that stretched out over the mountains were as beautiful as ever. The temperature was as warm as ever; the sky as mauve and the clouds as billowy as ever. But everything was changing. Billy could feel it even though he couldn't put his finger on what exactly it was that was changing. He leaned against the hot metal of the truck bed and kicked at the gravel.

He watched as a long, black Chevy slowed momentarily at the stop sign near the junction with the highway. He recognized the driver as the creep that owned the pool hall and his slimy kid... Brixton he thought their name was. He'd seen them before. Some of the kids on the Rez bought drugs from the Brixton kid. He'd even seen the dad drop him off near the Center to do it. The Brixton "kid" was hardly that though. He must be at least twenty-five, if not older. He only looked like a kid because of his unnaturally young face; which, when he was with his father, appeared even younger because his dad's face looked like it had gone through a meat grinder. But he was just as notorious as his father. It looked like they were heading out of town; hopefully not to the Rez, Billy thought.

Billy looked up at the sound of a deep caw and a huge crow came flapping down and landed awkwardly on the stop sign, rattling it with his weight. It raised a wing and looked for all the world like it was signaling the Chevy on like some sort of avian traffic cop. The two in the car were pointing at it and laughing. Old man Brixton blasted the horn and the crow fluttered off, complaining, in a long, lazy loop towards the open desert. There was a break in the traffic and the car pulled out onto the highway and continued on its way. If Nascha had been there to see all that he would have said something about spirit messengers or something. Billy wished right now that he had paid more attention to that stuff. He would in the future, when they walked on the mesa again and the world stopped heaving.

"Billy..."

Billy jumped as he heard his name. He hadn't heard Big Jim come up behind him. He never did.

"Let's go," said Jim and they got into the truck.

"Well, so what's going on?" asked Billy. "What did they say to you?"

Big Jim looked straight ahead, silent for a moment and then said quietly, "There's been brain damage."

*　　　　　*　　　　　*

Moonrock. If it was up to Billy, that's what they would call the sort of yellowy quartz that cropped up here and there on Black Mesa. It was porous and shone kind of like the moon and at night, when earth's satellite was most ardent, it glowed.

Billy shivered and hunched up tighter under his rough blanket and gazed down at the house some half a mile away. On a night like this, cloudless and bright from the lunar bonfire, you could almost read. If you had a book... which he didn't.

Brain damage. What the hell did that mean? Was Nascha going to come out of this a vegetable? Were they going to have to clean him up twice a day as he drooled his way to the grave? It was so fucking wrong... Billy immediately felt guilty. Whichever way it turned out they would look after the old man, of course. But it just wasn't fair. Nascha was over seventy, closer to eighty probably. This isn't what he deserved. Of course his father hadn't deserved to drive his car into a tree at ninety miles an hour, drunk out of his skull a year after the death of his wife either. And Big Jim hadn't deserved to have to raise his infant brother and drop out of school to make enough money to feed them both. And he didn't deserve to be sitting here, freezing and wondering what the spirits could be thinking to bring this new tragedy on them.

Somewhere, close to where he sat, there was a scratching and scrabbling as some creature of the desert night hunted or built or fucked or something. Billy tossed a pebble towards the sound and it stopped immediately. He didn't know what small version of the Great Spirit's Will it was that was messing about there. Nascha would have known. Nascha would have said, "That's a Gila, Kai. Don't mess with them. They're poisonous and if they bite they just don't let go. And in the meantime, they're dripping their venom into your wounds and you're not going anywhere after that. But if you can get that venom, man you can do some serious healing with that."

Billy felt lost. He was going to school to please Jim and Lucy and really for no other reason. What was he going to do with a diploma, go to medical school? Become a lawyer? Not likely. So what was he doing it for? Why not live here like his grandfather had done? Like Jim was doing now. And get on with things. Maybe start his own business or something.

There was an idea that was starting to grow in the back of his mind that he would scarcely even acknowledge. Nascha was the only recognized medicine man in the vicinity. If he was out of commission, maybe Billy could...

But that was ridiculous, wasn't it? He knew nothing about it. Billy thought about this for a minute. It wasn't, strictly speaking, true. He had spent a lot of time out on the desert with his grandfather and knew a few things. But how could he learn the rest? Nascha, and in fact his whole tribe, had no written tradition. They passed stuff on by word of mouth, by story. Nascha had tried to do that, Billy realized now, on those many trips, but he had been too stupid or too young or both to get it.

Then he was struck by the thought that he was all set to believe that Nascha had one foot in the grave. Maybe his grandfather would not be so bad. Maybe Billy could start to absorb some of those herbal facts. Maybe, if he put his mind to it, he could pick up some of this stuff. Then the women of the nearby villages would come to him for help with their chickens-as-payment and the men would consult him before making any momentous decisions and pay him when they could. And in the meantime he could live in the house and...

He was distracted by yet another shooting star (there seemed to be a lot of them lately) as it disappeared behind the mesa, absorbed by it. Billy got up and walked further up the path that circumnavigated the huge geophysical structure. He wasn't really that high up but he began to feel light-headed anyway and thought about how it was some six or seven hours since he had eaten. He hadn't been able to eat the dinner as the three of them sat around the table, staring every couple of minutes at Nascha's empty place. So he had left the table and come up here. He slipped once as his footing gave way under the loose rocks of the trail.

He came to Face-in-the-rock. It was a small area some ten feet above the trail itself and it was here that Nascha always insisted on stopping and paying homage to the spirits of the rock. It was a strange looking thing. Somehow human in aspect, undoubtedly a play of the lines of the stone and the light angles, it was none-the-less, very much like a face. But a compressed face, as if a couple of thousand pounds of rock pressure from above was pushing down on it. And it was grinning. Billy looked up at it and wished he could remember the words that Nascha had chanted. He could remember little bits of it and he mouthed them, silently, before moving on. There was also another shape in the granite just above and to the right of Face-in-the-rock. Billy had always thought that it too resembled, in some ways, a sort of face, but terribly distorted with a large drawn hole in the centre that Billy always had thought resembled that famous scream mouth from the Edward Munch painting. Poised above the valley, these two figures guarded or threatened the landscape, depending on your point of view, for twenty miles in each direction.

Billy continued on up. He had only been on the roof of the mesa a couple of times because it was such a hard climb. He toyed with the idea of doing it tonight but then thought better of it and turned and started his descent.

With his back to the wall of the mesa he didn't really notice the slight variation in the diffused glow of the moonrocks; didn't really notice the fact that they were pulsing, ever so slightly, with the sound of each of his retreating footsteps.

*   *   *

45

In my dream I look up from the bed and see Nascha standing there. He doesn't say anything but smiles and I see that in his hand he is holding a book. It is bound in what looks like hide and the pages are worn and falling through and the whole thing is bound with a piece of tattered gut. He raises one hand and passes it across his mouth and I hear the words 'Tsa-Ond' but his lips don't move and the sound echoes through my head and I try to remember the meaning of the Navajo words. Rock... something. And I feel guilty that I don't know and that that part of me is slipping away from me and then I think, "But that isn't true. It's being taken away." I jump to my feet and then I am outside and looking towards the hills and Black Mesa and I run towards it but it just keeps getting further away and there looks as if there is a fire burning on the side of the cliff and it must be in a crevice or something. Then I am there at the base of the mesa and looking up and can see that it is a cave! Tsa-ond... rock cave. But there is no path up and then crow is there and he picks me up in his claws and lifts me to the ledge where the entrance is. The fire is inside and the walls are black and I can't see very well and so I take a step in and stop. There are rock shelves inside and there are things on the shelves. Strange things. I try to get closer but the fire is too hot. But I can now see the objects on the shelves and I'm scared. Fuck, they're...

A giggle begins at the back of the class and starts to grow into a wave that stops Billy in mid-sentence.

"Okay, that's enough, calm down," Karen says from behind her desk. "I'm sure we've all heard the 'f' word before. Go on, Billy."

"That's as far as I got," Billy said and sat back down at his desk.

"It was good; a really good flow of consciousness and some very evocative images. I think we can all see from the last few examples, what we can expect from this exercise. It's not to get you to write flawless prose, but to jump-start your imagination as you work. Attibi's story of his car breaking down was good but too pedantic. It didn't hold our interest because it relied too much on what he knows technically and didn't depart from that. Same with Cam's narrative on scoring a touchdown…"

"Like that ever happens," Louie quipped from the corner. The class laughed. Cam scowled at him and threw an eraser at his head.

The class bell rang at that point and the students immediately started closing books and shuffling about.

"I want you take these exercise results and do fifteen hundred words for next Monday, okay?" said Karen over the rising din of the exodus. A few groans. The kids started to file out as Karen pulled Billy aside.

"How's your grandfather doing, Billy? Do you mind me asking?"

"No, I don't mind. We're going there this afternoon and we should know exactly what's going to happen with him," Billy said, quietly. "How are you?"

"Oh, I'm okay. I was a bit shaky last night and didn't sleep very well, but it's nothing serious. I'll be fine."

"That's good."

"I think it's pretty brave of you to use your grandfather like that in your narrative; and to talk about your self-doubt. If you can use yourself like that without being too self-conscious, that's a great place to start as a writer."

"It was easy enough. I had that dream last night," said Billy. "See you later."

"Yes, okay. See you later."

Billy walked out into the hall and towards the change rooms for gym class. The first couple of days back at school had been okay and Cam Proctor and Louie Ostermann, the two kids he'd tussled with on his first day, had lain off although he knew they'd never accept him really. At least they had a respect for him because he hadn't backed down. Proctor was an idiot anyway so who cared if he liked him or not. Ostermann was a bit of an enigma, however.

He was a giant of a boy standing over six feet and weighing at least two hundred and fifty pounds. He was the center on the senior football team. That was no surprise. What was surprising was the fact that, against type, he was one of the smartest kids in the school with consistent A average and what looked like a certain scholarship to pretty much any school he wanted. What college wouldn't want a two hundred and fifty pound football player who was smart enough to become a doctor? And he had a great sense of humour, too. What he saw in Proctor to make them friends was beyond Billy. Maybe because Proctor had lots of girlfriends and was a party boy. Judging from the way they had behaved before the fight, Proctor was probably not above getting stoned at school either. Actually it had been Louie that had separated them and Mr. Kilagrew wouldn't have even noticed them if Proctor hadn't yelled at Louie to let him go.

Billy got changed with the others into their wussy yellow gym uniforms and marched with the others into the gym. Kilagrew waited, arms folded, near the stage.

"Okay, gentlemen, have a seat on the mats," he said and took a clipboard from under his sinewy arm. Kilagrew wasn't a big man but you could see that he was well-conditioned. Wiry was probably the word. "Okay, before we get into some serious calisthenics, I want to know what teams you want to try out for this year. Remember, everyone has to try out for at least one team. If you don't make any team you have to service one anyway."

The boys choked and laughed.

"Okay, shut-up! You know what I mean. You have to be a water-boy or something for the football team or assist with something else. Got it?" Kilagrew glared. "I can't hear you…"

The boys chirped back, "Yes, Mr. Kilagrew."

"Okay. Hands up for football…"

A bunch of hands went up, including, of course Cam and Louie's. Kilagrew took down the names. Billy just looked at the floor. "How about you, Ahiga? You look like you can run. Wanna try for wide receiver?" He looked from Billy to Cam at this point. Wide receiver was Cam's position. Cam flushed and glared at Billy.

Billy said, "No, I don't think so Mr. Kilagrew."

"Okay…"

They went through another few sports until there were only three boys left who hadn't signed for anything; Billy, a big Asian kid named Tommy Wong and the only disabled kid in the school, Virtual Jones.

"Okay," said Kilagrew, "that brings us to the rock climbing team. Tommy, I guess you'll be heading that up again, huh?"

"You bet, Mr. K." said Wong.

"Skip that, Wong, its Mr. Kilagrew to you, right?"

"Okay," said Tommy. Several boys chuckled until Kilagrew snarled at them. Billy looked over at Tommy Wong. Wong seemed to have no fear of Kilagrew. That was pretty cool. As he examined him, Billy could see why Tommy was into the rock climbing thing. His arms must have been almost as long as his body. Well, not quite, but pretty long. Slender, muscular arms with large hands and his legs were like that too. Not much body weight really. He wouldn't have to climb; he could just reach up and pull himself from ledge to ledge.

"Okay. You too, Mr. Jones?" said Kilagrew. Billy waited for the others to laugh at the thought of the wheel-chair bound boy climbing rock, but it didn't come. Billy couldn't even really understand why they would make the kid come out to gym. Didn't want to exclude him, he guessed.

"Yes, sir," answered Jones. Virtual wasn't his real name of course but he was known as that because of his keen ability with computers and graphics and such. "Wouldn't miss it..."

"Okay, that just leaves you Ahiga. What's it going to be?"

No-brainer, thought Billy. I climb more rock in a week than these guys probably have ever seen. "I guess I'll go with the climbing," said Billy and looked over at Tommy and Virtual. Virtual smiled, Tommy just stretched out on the mat and put his long arms behind his head.

"Okay, girls, up on your heels... You are going to hurt this afternoon!"

*   *   *

Karen sat in the lounge waiting for Herman Kilagrew to arrive for the pre-trip meeting. The Tylenol was beginning to wear off and the bruising along her back from the fall in the ditch was starting to ache. She shifted out of her chair and looked out of the window. Some kids hanging around; others were walking across the football field, the sun shining down. Everything was pretty calm; pretty relaxed.

She thought back on the last few days and what an odd situation she was in. Everyone wanted to know about the fire, of course. Mr. Chavez had made about a dozen trips up the stairs to "see how she was" but really just wanted more info about the... body part. I guess he couldn't be blamed for his curiosity but she had finally had to make it clear that she didn't want to talk about it. Chavez was okay with that and in fact had apologized awkwardly before Mrs. Chavez arrived with a peach pie and a tub of ice-cream. That hadn't lasted long.

The lounge door opened and Kilagrew entered, gave her a big smile and almost ran across the room to hug her. She thought he was going to tackle her at first and almost dove out of the way. But he caught her up in his bony but strong arms and held her close.

"Karen, how are you? I heard about everything. You poor thing, you must have been terrified!" Kilagrew gushed breathily.

Karen extricated herself from the human vise as quickly as possible, saying "oh, I'm fine. Thanks for the concern, Herman."

"Okay, that's good, that's good," said Herman, coming to his senses and backing off. Now he felt stupid and a man like Herman Kilagrew didn't like feeling stupid. Something time and repetition would have cured, one would think. But, like many overtly macho types, the moment he felt stupid he went into a defensive shell and would sulk for hours. He was confused now because he couldn't sulk, he had a trip to plan. So he threw a map on the table and waved Karen over.

"Okay, here, take a look," he said, pretending to stare intensely at the topographic spread. "Here's where we will set up base camp, okay?" Karen was becoming acutely aware of why the kids all called him 'Okay' Kilagrew.

"Base camp?" Karen replied, stifling an urge to laugh.

"Yes, we'll set up tents and um... facilities, here, okay? And then we'll foray out on mini-expeditions."

"I see."

"Okay, we'll go in teams, of course, you'll head one and I'll head the other. And then we'll get together for the longer trips."

"Well, I suppose. But you know, Herman, I don't really know anything about the area to show them," Karen said.

"Well, we've got two weeks; I'll give you some books. The kids are pretty much good on their own and I'll be giving them some briefings in geography class. Say, here's an idea! Why don't you come on over for dinner some night and I can show you some video that I have on the area? Fascinating stuff."

50

Aha, Karen thought, the trap. "Well, I'll see. I have a lot of work in the next week because of the time it took after the fire, but maybe."

"Okay, fine. Look here, I'll show you the camp setup. Here's where the fire-pit will be and the tents around it, of course. Here are the latrines and the cooking and storage tents. And over here, closer to the rock face is the, um... staff tent."

"Staff tent?" Karen asked, innocently.

"Yes, you and I and well, Harry Babcock of course, would share that; although Harry likes to sleep out under the stars most of the time." Herman Kilagrew coughed.

"That sounds nice," said Karen.

"Okay, but personally I find it too buggy. I suspect a woman certainly would."

"What should I bring with me?" Karen asked.

"Okay, you're going to need some good hiking boots; they're a must, and a change of clothes. Gets cool at night so bring a jacket and some bug spray, I guess. Other than that Harry does most of the outfitting. "

Karen was beginning to become aware that Herman had taught several gym classes in a row and his proximity as they hovered over the map was beginning to take its toll.

"Well, that's wonderful Herman, I guess I'll be off," said Karen.

"Okay, but we haven't gone over the student list and such. Don't worry, shouldn't take longer than an hour." Herman laughed, "I hope you haven't got a date!"

*   *   *

The long, black Chevy carrying Ashford and Lonny Brixton pulled up outside a pastel-coloured bungalow and sounded its horn. Someone inside pulled the curtains on the living room window open an inch and then let them go. A few seconds passed before the front door opened and Cooter Langford came out adjusting his sunglasses. He locked the front door, looked around carefully and then placed the key under a rock. From inside the Chevy a muffled outbreak of laughter could be heard. Cooter, resplendent in second hand military garb, strode down to the car. The trunk popped open for him and he threw the baseball bat bag he was carrying inside. It landed with a muffled thud on top of the ten tightly parceled bags of cocaine. Then he opened up the back door, jumped in and the long, black Chevy quietly pulled away.

"Well, hello my man Cooter," said Lonny, the younger of the Brixton's, turning around and looking at him, "All set for the big day?"

"Man, I am so ready," replied Cooter. "If you don't mind me saying, I can't believe you're dealing with these assholes, but hey, it's your business."

"That's right, I heard you had a little run-in with our boys," laughed Lonny.

"Yeah, a run-in… I would have done 'em there and then but the gimpy one told me who he was and I figured Mr. Brixton would want me to keep the peace for the time being."

"That's correct, Cooter. That was wise," said Ashford Brixton, peering back at Cooter through the rear-view mirror. "You see, Lonny? I told you we could trust Mr. Langford to do the right thing."

"Yes you did dad, and it looks like you were right. But Cooter, just because they took that skank away from you…"

"Linda-Lou Jorgenson."

"Whatever. We hope that isn't going to influence your judgment today. We need you calm and collected, got it? We're counting on you. We don't want any itchiness on that fine trigger finger of yours, comprende?"

"Don't worry," said Cooter. "Anything that is going to happen to them can wait until after the deal is done."

"Again, I say, a very wise young man this Cooter Langford," said Mr. Brixton. "What have you got for us in that big bag of yours, Cooter?"

"Just came in, sir. It's a beauty. It's a CheyTac .408 caliber intervention rifle. Armed forces issue."

"Fascinating, Cooter, tell me more…" said Ashford as Lonny tried his best to keep a straight face.

"Well, sir, the idea of this particular weapon is to provide effective long-range soft target interdiction. But to do so in an armament that is relatively compact and light. This it achieves, however it had to have a compatible cartridge to fire. Professor John Taylor of Baltimore designed such a cartridge and now it is available on the mainstream market."

"Like you," Lonny grinned.

"Like me, yes," said Cooter. He paused for a second wondering whether or not he was being made fun of. He decided to go on, the five grand made it tolerable. "It allows for target eradication at distances above two thousand yards but generates much less recoil than similar weapons and munitions."

"Accurate then, is it?"

"I could take the eyes out of a rattle-snake from a mile away, sir."

Lonny broke out into a long sustained laugh but finally managed to say, "A fucking mile away!"

"Yes sir; its computer driven."

Ashford Brixton allowed his first smile to break on the wrecked beach that was his face. "Cooter, you are too much."

"Too much," echoed Lonny.

"By the way, Cooter, we think it must have been them that burned down The Jug."

"I suspected as much, sir," said Cooter Langford, inspecting the back of Brixton's pock-marked neck and wondering what tensile strength of cord would be needed to cut it open.

"I owned a large piece of that establishment. And, actually, I did enjoy the occasional drink there... Understand?"

"Understood, sir."

*   *   *

Little Billy stood on one side of the bed, Big Jim and Lucy stood on the other. At the foot of the bed Dr. Resdon held onto the railing. In the bed Nascha was sitting with his head propped up with a couple of pillows and a small bib on a chain around his neck. The bib was wet with drool.

"You're looking at the drool," said Dr. Resdon, observationally. "I don't want you to get the wrong impression."

Big Jim looked at Dr. Resdon. "The wrong impression?" he asked.

"Well, Nascha here…"

"Mr. Ahiga," said Lucy.

"I'm sorry, of course, Mr. Ahiga," Resdon corrected himself. "Mr. Ahiga has suffered from blood loss to the brain, as we discussed. This doesn't mean that he will remain unaware of his surroundings forever. But you should know that the fastest recovery will be in the immediate and that further recovery slows with the passage of time. But it could be worse."

Billy laughed sardonically, "Worse? How could it be worse?"

"Well," Dr. Resdon replied, "for one thing, he could never have regained consciousness at all. Also, he could be in what we call a persistent vegetative state where he wakes up and sleeps but never really knows where he is. At least, as he is now, there is a chance that with care he can recover even more."

"That's ridiculous," said Billy, suddenly and violently. "If he's sitting up; if he can walk about; then he's getting better, isn't he? He can't stay like this!"

"Billy," said Jim, quietly, "Listen to what he's saying."

"Listen to what he's saying? Why? I'm telling you granddad isn't going to stay like this. I swear it!" Billy took hold of Nascha's arm and turned him to him. "Are you, granddad? Are you?" Nascha looked at Billy and his head tilted to one side almost as if he was listening. But all that came out was a soft murmur.

"Billy, for god's sake!" said Jim, sterner now. "Are you going to listen?"

Billy let go of Nascha's sleeve and slumped into the chair by the bed. Lucy came around to him and put an arm around him. Billy just looked at the floor.

Dr. Resdon continued, "Its okay," he said "it's okay to feel angry. It's not good to see someone you love like this. But I'm telling you, there is a chance things might improve. What we have to be careful with in the next while is that the brain swelling doesn't get any worse. I've already told you, Jim that we should really keep him here for further observation."

"I'm sorry," Jim interrupted, "but that's not an option. We can't afford to keep him here and if, like you say, we can manage for the time being, then we're going to take him home. There's a nurse on the reservation that can visit and make sure we're doing things right."

Just then Nascha started shaking, at least one side of his shoulder did, and the arm on that side. Lucy reached over and laid a hand on him and it gradually subsided.

"You can expect that from time to time," said Resdon. "It's called spasticity. Some muscles can receive abnormal toning due to the relaxation of other unused muscles so the newly toned muscles may quiver on their own. It's nothing to worry about."

"Nothing to worry about," echoed Billy.

"If, as we suspect, the brain cell damage was minimal, he might even regain enough memory to speak at some point. Then you must help him remember. But there's no telling exactly how much damage there was and dead brain cells don't re-grow. So don't put your expectations too high. I say this so you will stay patient with him. But don't be disappointed if he stays as he is now, mobile but dependant. If you have more questions or there is any new development, don't hesitate to call me whenever you want."

"Thank you," said Big Jim. "We can leave now?"

"Yes, I've done all the paper work. Sign this form and I'll take it down for you. You have transportation, I assume?"

"Yeah," said Big Jim searching Nascha's face for some sense of recognition and then looking at Lucy as he signed the form. Her eyes were full of just what he was feeling now. Doubt, shock, fear… they were all there. Billy just seemed to be dead. Dr. Resdon turned and left and Jim looked at Lucy again. "Better get his things."

As Jim went to get the orderly waiting outside, Lucy collected the few small items that had accumulated on Nascha's side table; an icon, a brand-new bible and some candy from someone. Jim took Nascha's arm and helped him move his legs around and off the bed. The orderly helped lower him into a wheelchair and together Jim, Lucy and Nascha moved off out of the room to the elevator. Billy watched them go. Then he remembered the medicine bag that he had put under Nascha's pillow on the first night. It had been forgotten but Billy picked it up now and shoved it into his pocket. He was no longer sad or mad or anything else. Now he was determined.

*   *   *

"There is no hunting like the hunting of man, and those who have hunted armed men long enough and liked it, never care for anything else."

Ernest Hemingway

It is very difficult to kill something from a long way away. That is why sniper squadrons in Iraq and Afghanistan drink a lot of champagne and sew patches on their hats when they actually hit something. In sport-hunting a vast majority of hunters find long-range hunting unethical. Of course, many others find the concept of ethical sport-hunting somewhat of an oxymoron.

Still, as with butchering small children and burning cats alive, there are a percentage of human beings who will do anything if they can convince themselves of its 'rightness'. So, the attendant industry has arisen and with it the 'science' of the long range kill.

"One of my favourite clothing patterns is camouflage. When you're in the woods it makes you blend in. But when you're not it does just the opposite. It's like 'hey, there's an asshole.'"

Demetri Martin

When attempting to end the existence of a living creature from anywhere over, oh say, a hundred feet away, there are factors that come into play that, although obvious to the experienced wraith, only a select few know about.

For instance: the notion of the ballistic coefficient. This is roughly the amount of drop a bullet will achieve at a certain range with a certain amount and quality of powder and the type of casing, rifle etc. Fortunately for the long-distance hunter or sniper or presidential assassin there are numerous computer programs on the market that will take into account these variables and tell you how to adjust your sights appropriately. The day of the sweating Jackal trying desperately to nail the president of France in the cross-hairs of his trembling scope is long gone. After entering the necessary info into the old portable Mac, you can adjust the sights and pretty much eliminate most of the guesswork.

For instance, if you know that when you slip a Sierra 338 Match King bullet into a 338-378 Weatherby, you will have a drop of seven inches at a thousand yards and up to thirty-three inches at fifteen hundred. But when those ranges start to get over the mile mark well, you need to be Einstein to calculate that stuff. And let's face it; there aren't a whole lot of those amongst the hunting set; hence the popularity of the computer read-out.

A list of the environmental conditions that can stop you from hitting that turban square in the middle includes: wind drift, altitude and humidity conditions (although the latter is scarcely worth mentioning).

For those hunting prey, either of a two or four-legged variety, in the mountains, you will find that the air density is offset by lower temperatures so you can shoot effectively without worrying too much about the effects of those things.

Uphill/downhill effect is another matter though and it is the good shootist indeed who can compensate for anything over a twenty degree drop in the landscape. As a rule of thumb, in terms of scope adjustment, one minute of angle at one hundred yards is equal to 1.047 inches in target drop. So, assuming you're using a decent rangefinder such as the upper end Barr & Strouds, do the math... if you can; twenty degrees at a mile?

Generally speaking, the heavier the rifle the more accurate it is. That is what is so special about the CheyTac .408 caliber intervention rifle. It maintains its heavy-type accuracy while only weighing in at three-quarters of the weight. It's great for slinging onto your back; along with your shooting bench, computer and Johnny Walker Red. And perfect for bagging that rabbit way off in the next county. Also, it comes with optional USB ports.

Of course, there are other things that come into play; intrinsic human qualities that no amount of technological finesse will eliminate. Things like stress, jealousy and self-doubt. Any or all of these can lend to the shoot an indeterminate variable that no amount of preparation can allay. And really, who's going to tromp a mile and a half over rough terrain to finish off a deer with one of its hind legs blown away when there's a case of Miller in the van?

(Footnote: Ernest Hemingway once shot himself in the calves while hunting sharks with a shotgun. He also shot himself in the face while hunting himself with the same weapon.)

*   *   *

From the soggy ground there rose a mist. And it obscured the moon that tried in vain to light the landscape. Through the mist there was a path and upon the path stood Nascha. He blinked and looked about him, trying to sense which way he should go. He could make out the moon through the clouds and the path for a short distance but all else was shrouded in the mist.

He was confused and he felt cold as the chill from the ground crept up around him, a cold which infused him with a fear that he could find no reasonable explanation for. Where were the others? Why had they left him?

He could make no sense of the land around him. This was certainly not the desert that he was used to and this cold wetness was like nothing he had ever felt. He tried to call out but although he could feel the air leave his lungs and although his lips moved, no sound emerged. No cry to break the dread stillness of the night.

He turned about and in doing so realized that there was no discernable difference to the tight, suffocating view no matter which direction he faced. And then he heard a rumbling; a low growl that seemed to come from all about him. And then, layered upon that a second growl, higher pitched that seemed to come from some place straight ahead of him. He felt a panic start to burrow through his gut and rise up to his heart; his heart, torn and weak. He chanted to himself. A warrior chant of courage but even this seemed to linger and waiver and die, the life sucked from it by the lightless vacuum surrounding him. The growls continued and seemed to be drawing closer and now he could sense shapes in the shadows. Just out of reach of the fingers of mist that swirled about the earth.

Nascha fell to his knees. He could not feel his own fingers or his feet and his breath came out in bursts, icy and ragged; forced downwards by the oppressive darkness. He wept. The tears flowed down his cheeks. Where were the others?

There was a sound now as if claws were being raked against the rock; a sound that sickened his soul. It was almost as if the sound was coming from within him and reverberating off the fog; bouncing back to him, infusing him with a fetid longing that he felt he could not endure for long. He could sense his mind begin to buckle and when the hot breath of the dark 'others' was upon his neck he moaned and gave up all hope. He knew now that he was dying.

But then he heard a noise that made him look to the sky and there, drifting slowly in front of the opaque moon, he saw the tip of a wing and as he watched, a single ebony shape descended from above and came to rest a few feet from his trembling hands. It was Crow.

Crow spoke. "Nascha," said Crow, in its dry, raspy voice. "You are afraid."

"Yes," Nascha admitted, "I am afraid."

"What is it that you fear?"

"I fear the mist. I fear the longing. I fear for my family and all that they must bear. I fear to be alone."

"All men are alone in this mist," replied Crow.

"Can you not free me so that I may go to my family?"

"It is true your people will need you soon enough. But not as you are. You are weak. Come, I will take you to a place where you may rest and regain your strength. Your time is not quite done."

Nascha got to his feet, heartened by this. And as he approached Crow he could see that Crow was now much larger than he had thought. He climbed up onto Crow's back and the great bird took to the air and carried Nascha to a place by a cool, green river where there was sun and water and food and Nascha sat by the bank of the river and watched the water of his life flow around him.

Black Mesa is, for a mesa, very large. In fact, it is three separate mesas caught at a stage where the sub-strata rock connecting them has not quite eroded to the point at which it could be defined as three distinct structures. There is a central rise that is larger than the two smaller ones that are at its flanks. The two smaller structures are known locally as Chindi Ridge (Devil's Ridge) and Tkele-Cho-G Ridge (Jackass Ridge). All together, including the series of other low-lying ridges and hills to the south-west, Black Mesa is roughly four miles long and runs back from its prime face to a depth of eight miles; huge by mesa standards. Some argue that it isn't even properly called a mesa.

Most of the area is part of the massive Navajo reserve although parts of it skirt the Arizona state highway. To the north, along Chindi Ridge, there is a small parcel of land that has been set aside as a National Park, even though there is little there to mark it as such other than some trails, a small camping area and a small sign out by the highway. There was never really enough archaeological interest in the area to warrant a station or any park personnel. The camping area is around to the north-west edge of the ridge and is some fifteen miles by dirt road from the main highway.

To the south, and snaking north-east between five small buttes, a rough road leads from the highway to the hidden face of the Tkele-Cho-G Ridge which contains the remnants of a small mining concern, long ago deserted when the expected silver ore failed to materialize in sufficient quantity to make it worthwhile. A single shaft, boarded and festooned with danger signs, descends through the rock to a depth of about two hundred feet, running downwards on a fairly steep angle. At the bottom is a larger cavern which had been carved out to allow for the drilling that never came to pass. The cavern itself is partially submerged now; filled to a depth of some twelve feet with black ground-water.

Nestled in front of the Black Mesa itself, at a point where it comes closest to the main highway, is the Navajo village of Tsas-Ka. All but deserted now with the slow exodus of the people to the larger towns on the reservation, it has a small store and about a dozen buildings including a school that has closed with the shrinking population. The town runs backwards into the mesa by way of a small canyon and, at the head of what really amounts to just a small indent in the main face of the mesa, is the beginning of a steep, winding path that leads upwards to the mesa's flat, barren top. But the wind and time have broken large pieces of the trail away and apart from a section that skirts the Ahiga property, there is little that is passable.

Unless you're a member of the Newton Fairbanks High School Rock Climbing team that is.

*   *   *

"I'm a what?"

"You're a gumby... that's what we call new guys in the world of rock climbing," Virtual Jones said to Billy, a large grin on his big face.

"Hey, I've climbed rocks before. We live on a rock," Billy answered, a little ticked.

"He means, new to the club; to the sport," said Tommy Wong, trying to help out.

Billy looked around at the strange equipment hanging on the spare-room walls. And then at the table at which he sat; then at all the other very empty chairs. Tommy sat across from him, Virtual sat in his wheel-chair at the head of the table. They were both looking at him.

"So where is everyone?" Billy asked.

"Um, this is it," said Tommy.

"This is it? There's just the three of us?" Billy almost laughed but didn't.

"Well, we had the Ridley brothers last year, but their family moved to Little Rock so they're not here... this year," Virtual said, trailing off as he realized he was stating the obvious.

Tommy spoke up, "And, of course, Okay is meant to be in charge. But he doesn't come around much except for the testing. And Mr. Craig, the French teacher, is our 'advisor'. I guess because he climbed a mountain in France or something. He comes now and then. In fact he should be here today. He's kind of weird."

"I know," said Billy, "I've had him for two classes. He reminds me of that guy in the Pink Panther movies."

"Except his accent's worse," said Tommy. They all laughed.

"And there's Mr. Babcock. When we go for a climb he usually drives us or lets us use his van," said Virtual.

"Babcock? Who's that?"

"He's this old, cop guy who helps out sometimes at the school. He'll be coming on the field trip."

"What field trip?"

"Every year the grade elevens get to go on an overnighter out to the mesas. You know, to hike and stuff. They do it every year," said Tommy. "Mostly it's just an excuse for making out."

"Assuming you have a girlfriend", a wistful Virtual Jones cut in.

"You have a girlfriend", objected Tommy.

"Cut it out will ya, I told you, Cookie isn't…"

"Where do they go?" Billy interjected.

"Different places. I think I heard this year it's going to be out at Black Mesa Park."

"You're kidding. That's where I live," said Billy. "Well, close. The park's on the other side of the mesa from the village."

"Your family lives in Sandy Hollow?" exclaimed Virtual, "That's pretty cool."

"It's called Tsas-Ka, actually," said Billy.

"Tsas-Ka, right, cool. Aren't there cliff dwellings there?" said Virtual.

"Sort of, they're more just holes in the rock now. Nobody goes there much and there's nothing inside."

"So how do you get to school? You got a car or does your dad drive you in?" asked Tommy.

Billy paused. Well, it was inevitable, he thought. All this pathetic junk would come out soon or later so it might as well be now, he figured. These guys seemed reasonable.

"My parents are dead. I live with my brother and my…"

And with that the few moments that he hadn't been thinking of Nascha came to a sudden, complete end. For a moment there, he'd almost forgotten the sadness that he'd been dragging around with him for the last couple of days. Nascha seemed like a ghost now; barely recognizable as the old, good-humoured man that a few days before had been poking around in the desert looking for herbs. Since coming home from the hospital he just sat, rocking slightly, in the chair out back of the house, looking into the distance. He said nothing and reacted only feebly when spoken to. Thankfully, he was aware enough to let them know when he was hungry or thirsty or needed tending to in other ways. But he wasn't really there. It was frustrating as hell because it was impossible to tell whether or not he was going to improve any or if he would be like this until he died. Although, it was true, as Lucy had pointed out that morning, he was looking a bit less pale and the shaking in his arm had stopped. For a second, Billy considered telling the others but what was the point of that really? So he just said…"And my grandfather."

There was a moment of silence and then Tommy said, "Well, I'm glad you decided to join up. If you didn't the club would have to fold. You have to have at least two…" Tommy stopped, glancing at Virtual. "Um…"

"Two guys who can support each other's weight," said Virtual. "School rule."

"Do you climb?" Billy asked, looking at Virtual.

"I have. If I can get up to the ropes on an aid climb, I can do some stuff. Obviously I'm limited though."

"What's an aid climb?" Billy asked.

"When you use slings and gear instead of just your hands and feet," Tommy answered. "But we have a little system we've developed for getting Virtual up on a free climb. You'll see. We'll be planning a climb for the field trip."

"Mostly I do the routing. You know, plan the ascent. I use topographical software and digital photographs to map out the best route," said Virtual.

"Doesn't that sort of take the fun out it?" Billy asked.

"Well, no not really. On the more difficult climbs it can just be a drag to keep feeling for the right route. Waste of time really. I only plan hypothetic ascents, you know? Input the beta? You have to find the jugs and buckets yourself."

"Sorry?" said Billy, this time laughing out loud.

"Hand-holds," said Tommy.

At that moment the door opened and Mr. Craig entered. "Pardonez moi," he said closing the door behind him while throwing his hat onto the table and knocking a can of coke into Virtual's lap. "Je suis en retard."

*   *   *

Nascha sat wiggling his toes in the cold mountain water. It was almost painful but he did it anyway, enjoying the effect that made the rest of his body feel even warmer in the summer sun. Crow hopped about from rock to rock poking his head down and trying for the small fish that played between the reeds. He came up once with a shining silver minnow in his beak and tossed it into the air high above him before swallowing it whole.

Nascha took his feet from the water and pulled down his pant legs. He stood and stretched and looked off up the river that ran for a couple of hundred feet before it turned a bend and disappeared between towering willows. He then turned and looked downstream and, similarly, the river bent off around some rocks, fading from sight in a misty spray.

The blue sky, the gentle breeze, the sweet chirping of birds in the trees...

"I love it here," said Nascha to Crow. "This is the nicest place I have ever known."

"Yes, it is lovely," replied Crow, flying up to a tree branch that hung over the water and starting to preen his ebony feathers.

Nascha picked up a smooth, flat rock and skipped it out across the slow-moving river. It bounced and skittered for some distance before sinking under the current. He sighed. He felt stronger now than he had for some time. And when he looked down at his hand it was no longer that of a seventy year old man, but the hand that had been his when he was young; the skin soft and not a flutter of motion as he held it out before him. He bent out over the water and looked down at his reflection. A handsome man with brown hair and deep, dark eyes gazed back at him nonchalantly.

"Why am I young?" he asked.

"You see your spirit, that's all Nascha. No great mystery, really," replied Crow. "Your spirit comes of age out of youth and remains that way forever. In the world, only the body grows older. You must feel that."

"It is true. Ever since I was thirty, I have felt more or less the same in my skin. Only the aches and pains change from year to year. The body grows weary."

"That is the way of things, all right," said Crow, flexing his wing.

Nascha looked up and noticed an eagle flying through the glade behind them and off into the clouds. "Crow," he said. "I am in this place of great beauty and my body is fit and young... Why am I restless?"

Crow regarded him in silence for some moments before responding. "I hear you, Nascha. You have asked this of your own will so I will explain. Here, in this garden, you may remain for as long as you wish. It is your right. But do you remember the day when I found you?

"Vaguely, it was so long ago. In the darkness, yes, I remember."
"And do you remember what I said then. What I told you of your people?"

"That they would have need of me; yes, I had forgotten. Well, not forgotten, but it is hard to understand. What it is that I can do?"

"You can return to them," said Crow, "Whenever you wish really. But you will be old once more and your mind will be weak still and it will take some time for you to be helpful. It will not be easy for you or for them."

A large fish jumped from the water and snatched a fly from the air. It hit back against the river with a large spray. Nascha knew then why he could not stay here. His love would not allow it. Then, suddenly, it seemed to him that he could hear music on the wind. A reed pipe and a skin drum, beating and whistling a high-pitched tune from his childhood.

"That is the sound of the world, Nascha. It says that you have made your decision in your heart."

"I have. Crow, will you help me?"

Darkness was beginning to descend on the glade from the north and Crow looked up at it. Nascha took a blanket from the ground and wrapped it around his shoulders. He climbed up on to the back of Crow, who once again had become mighty and together they rose from the ground on great undulations of Crow's glistening wings and headed towards the oncoming gloom. Nascha turned his head just once and looked back at the sunlit embankment, still glowing by the water, its soft grass billowing with the breeze. Looking down from the great height he could see the many twists and turns of the endless river and the many small fires that burnt beside it and the many small figures that stood or played or swam in the sun. Many faces turned to watch his ascent on the back of the huge bird. Then he turned and faced the darkness and pulled the blanket tighter about him.

*   *   *

Karen stood looking out over the piles of army surplus fatigues, camping gear, fleece liners and hiking boots spread across what seemed like an acre of Al McReary's store. She was frozen to the spot, mesmerized by the vast array of choice in a milieu of which she knew absolutely nothing. Around the store, a few other shoppers poked and prodded the goods on this particularly hot Saturday afternoon, occasionally picking something up and nodding to each other with approval and moving on to something else. Karen could not do this. Karen was a fish out of water.

Watching her from a counter on the other side of the store, Harry Babcock ran his hand gently over the bone handle of the new knife he was thinking of purchasing. Al McReary turned the page on the small pamphlet that came with the Idun Northern Lights hunting knife.

"Let's see, now… laminated steel, leather grip and a sweeping blade that means less meat damage while skinning… ," said Mr. McReary. "Sounds pretty good, huh?"

"Yeah, how much?" asked Harry keeping his eyes on Karen.

"Um, one hundred and sixty-five and that includes the leather sheath and a ninety day, no risk guarantee."

"Ninety days, huh? Not exactly a ringing endorsement of quality."

"Oh, I don't know. Pretty much all the knives come with ninety days, Harry. Some of the guys are pretty rough on them," said Al as he followed Babcock's gaze over to Karen who was still just staring at the racks.

"Know who she is Al?" asked Harry nodding towards her.

"Oh sure, that's the new teacher at the high school. Karen something... Armitage, I think."

"Not the one that was in the fire at the Jug?"

"Yep, that's her. That's something, eh? Can you imagine looking up and having that face staring right at you? All burnt up like that? Gives me the creeps just thinking about it."

"She looks okay now," said Harry. "In fact, I think she's coming out on the Mesa trip with us. Think I'll have a word..."

"Okay... You gonna take the knife, Harry?" asked Al, hopefully.

"Oh yeah, wrap it up for me will you Al? And stick it in with the supplies?" said Harry and started over towards Karen.

Karen was shaken out of her shopping reverie by the approach of what she suspected was a store clerk; a particularly beefy, tall store clerk with a big smile on his face. Karen considered running but decided to bite the bullet.

"You look a little..." started Harry.

"Stunned?" Karen finished. "I am. You have quite a bit of stuff here. A little overwhelming, you know?"

"Oh, I don't work here," said Harry. "I'm Harry Babcock. I understand you're coming out to the Mesa with us." Harry extended his hairy Harry hand to Karen who took it and shook it politely.

"Harry, right, yes. I've heard lots about you. How you do a lot for the school and such. It's very good of you."

"It's nothing really, um... Karen. Right?"

"Armitage... yes, sorry."

"Well, as I say, it's nothing. I love it really and the kids are always fun. Now that I'm retired it's time I can spare. Are you shopping for gear for the trip?"

"Sort of, yes, I don't have much in the way of camping clothes and such."

"Well, here, let me help you," said Harry, casting an eye up and down her frame. "Guess you'd be what, a medium?"

Forty-five minutes later, Karen was piling several bags and boxes into her car and waving goodbye to Al and Harry who stood on the store porch, smiling and nodding happily, one for purely mercenary reasons the other for reasons more obviously male. Karen didn't care about that. She wasn't above using a little feminine mystique to her advantage. Quite honestly, Harry had been a huge help although his taste in pants seemed to veer without exception towards the military end of the palette. But the boots were pretty cool and very light. She didn't really know what a Tilley hat was meant to do but it did look kind of cute in the mirror. And McReary had given her a hefty discount because of her affiliation with the school. So, all in all, the expedition had been good. Plus, she felt good about having an ally in place from the beginning of the trip; sort of a buffer against Okay Kilagrew.

As she drove home, she laughed to herself about these new-found attentions and realized that it had been some time since she had even thought about that kind of thing. Back in San Francisco, after the break-up, she had been able to melt into the generally indifferent metropolis and other than the occasional fresh cab driver or waiter she'd been left pretty much alone. But here in this small town she guessed that any fresh face would be given the once-over by the available men. She laughed again at that thought. So far, the field seemed to consist of an over-juiced, sweaty gym teacher and a retired cop.

These thoughts tumbled together as she headed to her house and the end result, of course, was the silent but looming image of Steven crowding in from the back of her mind. She hadn't thought of him every day but when she did it made her decidedly melancholy and just a little bit lonely. She wasn't even sure, since the fire, that she was doing the right thing here. Maybe she was just hiding out in this small town, maybe just avoiding things. But that was okay, wasn't it? For a little while?

She wondered as she pulled into the drive what he would be doing right now back in San Francisco. Eating lunch, out on a date maybe, camping... Well, it turned out to be none of these things. She realized that when she parked the car and found Steven sitting in the back yard drinking beer with Mr. Chavez.

*　　　　*　　　　*

In the razor-sharp confines of the inner surface of Face-In-The-Rock, a slight shift occurred as something hurried between the crags. As dark as the narrow shaft running perpendicular to the cliff face was, the small dribble of light that permeated the stone tube flared now and then in the eyes of the descending creature that now traversed it. Gila Monster paused and searched for a new foothold, the black pupils of his black eyes glistening and blinking slowly as he peered through the gloom. His big mouth opened and closed exposing his flat black tongue and rows of needle-like, backward slanting teeth. He hissed once and went on his way.

His heavy rear legs suspended him, completely inverted, as he dropped from small ledge to trough through barely passable openings. Still he continued on. He could hear his name being called on the stream of cold air that rose from below and he knew he must answer. And it brought him further and further down into the very bowels of the earth. Finally, with a push he shot through one last tight opening like a geothermal newborn and fell with a splash into a bowl of icy, green water. He climbed out and stood, blinking, in the dull light, looking about him for the source of the calls. Two foul shadows stared back at him from across the stone table on which he stood and there, held motionless in the living rock, were the two demons Tse-Nill Chindi and Naz-Tsaid Chindi. He could not see their faces properly, only the red gleam of the single eye of Tse-Nill and the even, steady blue-green glow of the mouth of Naz-Tsaid. This narrow vertical slit of oozing pestilence opened and closed as the morbid creature spoke through his prison of stone.

"Gila Monster... we have an errand for you."

*　　　　*　　　　*

About two miles in from the highway and half-way up the road to the adit of the abandoned Heminghurst Silver Mine, the long black Chevy came to a halt and its engine shut off. The dust settled around the car as three doors opened and the Brixtons, father and son, and Cooter Langford got out and stretched their legs. Ashford Brixton lit a cigarette and tossed the match into the ditch. He looked up at the small hills leading to the mesa proper.

"Tkele-Cho-G Ridge. Beautiful isn't it?" said Ashford, slowly blowing out a stream of smoke. "I used to come out here with my father years ago. You never did, did you Lonny?"

"What? No, granddad was gone before I ever made it out to the Rez." Lonny replied.

"You really should get up there, you know? It's really something to look down from the top."

"Too busy, pop... Product to deliver... Time is money."

Ashford turned and looked at his son. "You're a good boy, Lonny."

Cooter Langford had made his way round to the trunk of the car and removed his bag which he now slung over his shoulder. He adjusted the weight of it and began to check some of his equipment; water bottles and compass and the like. Lonny looked on.

"You look like you're going on an Iraqi patrol there, Cooter."

Cooter looked up through his aviator sunglasses. He had done two tours, actually. A fact he wasn't sure if Lonny knew. Again, he had the distinct feeling that these guys were yanking his chain. The five grand was beginning to seem like perhaps not enough now. He wondered, for a moment, what it would be like to send something hot and metallic into Lonny's big, soft gut.

He nodded to the small, secondary road leading up into the hills. "That's the path to the small mesa?"

"That's the one," Ashford said and pointed up to the west. "You track up there until you see a big spire of rock, okay? Get around behind that rock and up a little rise and you'll find yourself on a flat piece of ground in between two big Sorrels. From there, you'll be able to see the mine. Well, with the glasses anyway."

"Okay," said Cooter.

Ashford looked at his watch. We're meeting the boys at two so that will give you about half an hour to get into place. Should be plenty of time, right? Remember, the shorter one with the limp, he's the boss, so don't worry about him. Lonny will be watching him. It's the one with the bars on his face who's the trigger man so you cover him. And the younger one, you cover him too. I'll watch the freak."

"Okay," said Cooter and turned and started up the trail.

"Cooter!" called Lonny. Cooter turned and looked back. "Don't get lonely!"

Cooter thought to himself, "I don't know what the fuck you're talking about but someday you and I are going to have words, Lonny Brixton." He continued up as the Brixtons returned to the vehicle and drove off slowly towards the mine.

At the mine The Crip was arguing with Albert.

"I know they're fucking late! I can see they're fucking late, okay? Now shut the fuck up!"

Mystic Bob said, "Actually, they're not late. We said two, didn't we? It's only one thirty."

"What?" said The Crip, after a momentary pause as he stood facing Albert.

"It's only one-thirty."

"Holy fuck," said Albert and turned away in disgust. "We don't even know what time it is."

Cage was sitting on a rock running a gun cloth over his .32. "Hey, take it easy will you? They'll be here. Why wouldn't they be? They've got the merchandise, we've got the cash. They want the cash. They'll be here." He took out his water bottle and took a swig. "I'm going over there by the mine. It's a little higher. It'll give me a good position."

"Fine," said The Crip and threw a stone at a lizard climbing onto his bike peg. The stone neatly knocked the creature off and it fell, unconscious, about three feet away. Mystic Bob lit a joint. He took a long pull on it and handed it to Crip.

"It's cool. Don't worry, man," he said. "We'll be out of here in an hour and head back home and then we can all chill."

"Yeah, and not a moment too fucking soon," said Albert.

"Hey! I think they're coming," shouted Cage from up at the mine entrance. "I can see dust or something."

"Get the belts," Crip said and Mystic Bob went to his bike and opened up the saddle bag. He removed three large money belts and strung them around his neck. He felt for the sawed-off shotgun that was in its holster running down his back from his shoulder. It was loose in its sheath. Cage positioned himself beside a large, rusting ore car and waited. Albert took the Glock and put it down the front of his pants with his shirt pulled over it.

"Don't know what we're worried about," said Albert, "There're only two of them."

"That's what we told them. That doesn't mean that's what they're going to bring. Can you see the car? Is there just one?" Crip shouted up to Cage.

"Just the one!" Cage shouted back.

From the front seat of the Chevy, Lonny took a count as they drove slowly round the bend towards the mine. "Three by the bikes. The other one's up by the mine. Can Cooter see him from there?" he asked.

"Oh, yeah... Just fine," Ashford replied and pulled the car to within a dozen yards of the parked bikes. He switched off the engine and now all was silent in the canyon. They waited a moment for the dust to settle. The Crip raised his arm and waved. Lonny and Ashford smiled at each other.

"Shit, he can't be more than four feet tall," said Lonny.

"Come on, let's go talk to the fucking hobbit," said Ashford and they opened their doors and got out

On the rocky outcrop, some mile and a half away, Cooter peered through his field glasses and watched the men get out of the Chevy. He moved sideways and looked at the monitor on the laptop. The CheyTac's sighting system was engaged and the various bar graphs and needles were stable. He moved his finger to the left/right arrows on the keyboard and pushed the button to the left. The gun barrel sighting picture moved slightly to the left; the cross-hairs on the monitor lined up neatly with the base of Cage's skull. Cooter locked down the system and pushed himself up and across so he was level with the weapon. He gently put his head down and focused in through the eyepiece of the sight. Pushing the interlock button, he moved the barrel of the big gun until a steady beep from the positioning software signaled a sight match. His hand wrapped the trigger guard and his trigger finger tapped gently on the front of it.

He hummed to himself. A tune he hadn't thought of since he was a kid. Funny what goes through your mind at time like this, he thought. Camptown races run all day... doo dah, doo dah...

"Mr. DeSoto," said Ashford Brixton to The Crip.

"Mr. Brixton," The Crip replied. "Thanks for being on time." Albert laughed but stopped when Mystic Bob looked at him.

"Punctuality... The virtue of the bored, I'm afraid," said Ashford. "But I think I will be mightily entertained by the money you've brought us."

"Yeah, whatever," said The Crip, slightly confused. Mystic Bob shifted uneasily.

"This is my son, Lonny."

"Look, we're not here for tea. You have the stuff?" Crip shot back.

"Of course... No need to get antsy. Just trying to be friendly," Ashford said.

From where he was, Cage could only hear snatches of the conversation but he didn't like the tone of things. Something was off. If only he could hear a little better...

"Well, if you're in Frisco next month we can all go to the fair," said The Crip.

"Look..." said Lonny.

"Its okay, it's okay. Lonny, get the goods out of the car for Mr. DeSoto, will you?" Ashford tossed the keys to Lonny who, with a look back at The Crip, moved to the rear of the Chevy. The Crip motioned to Bob and Mystic Bob walked along a few paces back of Lonny. "Lonny's a bit agitated. We had a bad fire at our bar the other day."

"That's awful," said The Crip.

"Yeah, well, what are you going to do? Accidents happen…"

It was at that exact moment that Gila Monster sank his fangs into the exposed calf of Cooter Langford lying perched on his rock a mile away. Then Cooter did two things he shouldn't have. He pulled his leg the wrong way against the lizard's rigid, sloped teeth and he closed his finger on the trigger.

As it struggled to free itself, the lizard dumped a full load of venom into Cooter's leg. Cooter rolled over and off the ledge clutching madly at his wound while, a mile and a half away, Cage's head exploded.

Albert looked over at where Cage was when he heard the thud of the impact. "What the fuck…" was all he said. Nobody had heard the gun go off from that distance and for a second everybody just froze as they tried to decipher what had just happened. Cage's corpse with its bloody stub of a neck, meanwhile, tottered and fell to the ground.

Lonny wheeled and pulled his gun from his shoulder holster as Mystic Bob reached for the shot-gun. Lonny was just a little bit faster and managed to squeeze off a shot that destroyed a cactus about a foot to Bob's left and then the roar of Bob's shotgun and the upper right side of Lonny's body disappeared as his body flipped back over the bumper and into the trunk.

Ashford, who had looked back to see what was happening with Lonny, fired a shot into Mystic Bob's leg, then turned back to receive the full loads of Albert's and The Crip's clips into his mid-section and face.

This all took about eight seconds. And then there was no sound again except for the gun blasts echoing off down the canyon and the moans of Mystic Bob as he rolled on the ground.

"How the hell…" said Albert looking at The Crip.

Then, as they realized what had just happened, they both leapt for cover; The Crip crouching down behind the engine block of the Chevy and Albert behind the trike.

"I fucking knew it! Can you see anything up there?" Crip called back to Albert.

"No, nothing... He could be a mile away for all we know," Albert called back.

"Yeah, and he could be lining up another shot."

"What do we do?"

"We'll have to wait until dark."

"What if whoever was up there has gone for help?"

Mystic Bob had stopped moaning for the moment, having passed out from the pain. And now it was very quiet. The Crip sat back with his head against the fender. Albert crawled under the chassis of the trike. It was very hot. The Crip stared at his water bottle sitting uselessly on his bike a dozen feet away.

"Fuck..." said The Crip.

CHAPTER THREE

MIND SHAFT

Billy Ahiga, Tommy Chong and Virtual Jones stood (or in Jones' case, sat) and looked up at Face-In-The-Rock. The early morning chill was beginning to wear off with the sun breaking through the clouds and the mists from down below were clearing to reveal the highway in the distance and the Ahiga place just a speck beyond that further along the valley.

"That is pretty cool," said Tommy looking at the face.

"Yep," said Virtual. "Pretty cool... And look at that one there," he said pointing at the other ancient face peering from the rock.

"What's that opening way up there?" Tommy asked, perusing the side of the mesa wall about one hundred feet below the top, "Some kind of cave?"

Billy followed the line of Tommy's raised arm. "Oh, that's a cliff dwelling supposedly. At least that's the story, although I don't get how anyone could have ever lived in it. There's no way of getting to it that I can see."

"That sounds like a bet to me," Tommy said, winking at Virtual. "Nobody's ever been there, huh?"

"Some archaeologists ran a line down from the top of the Mesa about ten years ago and got in that way but they said there was nothing much there. No pottery or anything. Apparently the only unusual things were some shelves and a small opening at the back on the cave wall that they were going to dig into. But an accident happened and they abandoned the project."

"An accident?" asked Tommy.

"Yeah, they were lowering some gear down. Picks and stuff, you know? We were all watching from down there," he said pointing to a large area further down the trail.

He could remember that day pretty clearly even now; one of the last that he had spent with his father. His mother had been dead for six months and he thought, mistakenly, that maybe things were getting back to normal. Nascha and his father had piggy-backed him up to the clearing to watch the men climbing down from the top. It had been a pretty crazy day, the scientists sweating and cursing as they tried to access the cave. Nascha was killing himself laughing and it was the first time he had seen his father smile in a long while. But that hadn't lasted long.

"The line broke and the gear fell and then some guy got tangled in the rope and it yanked him off the edge and he got killed over there," he said, pointing to a spot on some painful looking rock fragments below the trail.

"Shit. And you saw that?" said Virtual.

"Yeah, I was just a kid at the time. It was pretty freaky."

"I'll bet... Bobby Ridley cratered last year on a climb."

"Cratered?" said Billy.

"Fell, decked... He was lucky, it was only from about ten feet but it broke his leg in four places," said Tommy.

"So nobody has been up there since the accident?" said Virtual.

"No. I heard that they wanted to go back but the reserve rules changed that year and they couldn't get the permits in place. By the time things came through I guess they were on to something else. They were pretty upset at the time, though; said they wanted to take a closer look at the window."

"The window...?" Virtual asked.

"That hole at the back. They called it a window; weird, huh? How can a hole at the back end of cave be called a window?"

"Well, I say..." said Tommy, looking at the others, "that we go up there and find out. How far up would you say it was, Virtual, eighty or ninety feet?"

"I'd have to use the gauge but it looks maybe more like a hundred," Virtual said, holding up a thumb for perspective.

"Pretty cruxy climb, side to side... but not too bad... And there's a bit of a tough undercling below the cave, see it?"

"Yeah, but in between there's lots of buckets and ledges. I don't think we'll need much stuff. I'll get a topographical together. It won't take long. Why don't you guys start bringing up some gear? I should have something in about half an hour." Virtual took his back pack from the side of his chair and took out what must have been the world's smallest laptop and an even smaller digital camera.

"We're gonna do it now?" said Billy, nervously.

"That's what we're here for isn't it?" said Tommy starting down towards the road.

"And don't forget my sling," Virtual called after him.

Tommy turned and looked at him. Virtual just stared back at him and then looked back down at the booting laptop. "Right on," said Tommy after a short pause.

"What did he mean by his 'sling'?" asked Billy as the two continued to walk down to the car.

"I guess he's coming up there with us," said Tommy. "This is gonna be fun."

*   *   *

A certain turkey vulture, with a particularly bad sense of smell, circled high above the Heminghurst Silver Mine and tried to understand what the other turkey vultures found so exciting. Even from this height, his long, v-shaped wingspan cast a shadow on the objects below; crossing the ground between the mine entrance and the bikes, flowing over the headless body of Cage Erlich, past the crouching, thirsty figures of Albert Bader and The Crip and taking a hard right at the Chevy which was alive with a coating of better-equipped turkey vultures. And not far from that, the prone, still shape of Mystic Bob.

The vulture, having sensed that maybe he was missing out on something good, descended, flapping his way to an ungainly halt on the sand about three feet away from Bob. He danced his way over, his little, bald, red head bobbing up and down. He paused and eyed Bob from that distance and seeing no movement and liking the general smells that were wafting his way, he advanced. In the trunk of the Chevy his feathered friends and colleagues ate like kings as they dined on Lonny. Why should he be left out? This was a road of sorts and this thing lying in it was surely road kill. He hopped on over, the anti-toxins that prevented him dying of botulism from fetid meat beginning to stream into his spittle, and jumped up on to Bob's chest.

Bob opened one eye. "Fuck off, you little fuck," he snarled, "I ain't dead yet." With a smooth, sweeping motion he brought the arm holding his knife up and the big bird's body landed on one side of him while its head flew in the opposite direction and bounced off the fender of the Chevy. This attracted the attention of one of the smaller birds who hadn't been able to shoulder its way into the mob chowing down on Lonny. The smaller bird, obviously not too worried about what the other birds thought about fresh kill, quickly jumped down and started pecking at the eyes of his dead cousin. Bob laughed, coughed and fainted again.

"He's alive," said Albert.

"I can see that," replied The Crip, his voice parched and dry. The temperature was at least a hundred even in the shade of the shaking Chevy.

"We've got to get out of here," Albert said, almost to himself.

"We have to wait until night."

"What for? We don't even know if he's still out there."

"So stand up and find out," The Crip challenged, hoping that Albert would take him up on it.

"Even if we wait for night, what does that do? Maybe he's got night-vision glasses or something. And maybe he's using a tripod. Maybe he can't adjust at that distance. We could just keep moving around." The Crip just laughed. "Fuck it. He's gone," said Albert and with that he crawled out from under the trike and stood up. "Hey, asshole!" he shouted to the silent hills, "Bring it on! Come on!"

Of course there was no shot, Cooter Langford was long since dead from the Gila bite and his body was already under deconstruction at the hands of an army of red ants. The desert doesn't wait around. The desert gets on with it.

"Told you," said Albert.

The Crip stood up, stretched and walked over to his bike, took the bottle of warm water from the seat and drained it. Albert did the same. Turning, The Crip grabbed another bottle and went to Mystic Bob and poured water into his face and mouth. Bob moaned slightly.

"Help me get him into the car," The Crip said to Albert. Together they hoisted him up into the back seat and closed the door. Albert walked around to the trunk and threw the empty water bottle at the birds that remained there; at those set against abandoning their buffet after most of the others had hopped off into the brush.

"Man," Albert said, peering into the car, "that's a real mess. He's all over the coke." He pulled at Lonny's shirt or what was left of it and it came away in his hands. "Fuck," he said. He closed the trunk lid.

"Drive the car up to the mine," said The Crip. "We'll take some of the boards off, drive it in and hole up there for a bit. How much food have we got left?"

"Well, plenty now that we're just eating for two," said Albert. "But why don't we just split? We've got the stuff and the money. Let's just get out of here."

"We can't. They might have people out by the highway. We have to wait it out for a bit."

"What about Bob? He won't last like that."

"We'll have to take that chance. I'm not going down now. Not when we're this close."

"I thought he was your friend."

"Jesus has friends," said The Crip. "Now help me get what's left of this other asshole into the car and then get up there and smash some of those boards off the entrance."

*   *   *

"You've got to be kidding me," Billy exclaimed, staring at Tommy and Virtual. Virtual was hanging from a leather sling that was secured by straps to Tommy's back. A bandolier Tommy called it. It sort of looked like a baby carrier only Virtual was higher up and sat over Tommy by the size of his head. From the front, it made Tommy look like he had an extra head growing from the back of his own. "You're going to climb up there like that?"

"Piece of cake," said Tommy. "It's actually easier in some ways. I now have four arms."

Virtual waved his arms around Tommy's shoulders while Tommy pranced and waved his own arms and together they did a kind of goddess-Kali thing. Billy laughed so hard he thought he was going to puke.

"I only weigh fifty-five pounds out of my underwear," Virtual laughed.

"Yeah, but you're wearing them now though, right?" said Tommy and they all started laughing again.

Virtual (born Virgil, but don't call him that) had lost his legs when he was eleven riding behind his older brother on a motorcycle. A tow-

80

truck, driven with usual tow-truck abandon, had side-swiped them coming out of an alley, pinning Virtual against the brick wall of a building. Small in stature to begin with, many people mistakenly thought it was disease that had left him in a wheel-chair and it was their own misfortune if they did. Virtual took great pride in the fact that he had lost his limbs being adventurous and told you so immediately if you let pity get the better of you.

Together they went over the route that Virtual had schemed out and Billy had to admit that it was pretty ingenious. He never would have thought of it just by eyeballing the slope. Up Face-In-The-Rock; using the facial elements and then onto the lesser face, then a small chimney and then pretty much just ledge-to-ledge up to the undercling. The tricky part would come then but Tommy figured with a Chicken Wing (the device they would use to scale the chimney) and a metal ring and rope known as a Carabiner, they could be up and over onto the ledge in forty-five minutes… with luck.

Tommy put on his best fake French accent,"Allez, mes amis. Let's Redpoint this baby!"

Billy watched as Tommy took the first few grips in easy stride. Virtual didn't even help. He just looked around smiling a lot. Then, after he had risen above Face-In-The-Rock, Tommy signaled Billy to start up. When they had made it to the chimney, Virtual took out the Chicken Wing and using it as a lever they made their way up the twenty feet or so that the chimney rose above Lesser Face. Billy's bridging technique in the tunnel was no match for Tommy's long arms and powerful legs, aided by Virtual clamping and releasing the Chicken Wing, and it took him nearly twice as long to complete it. Finally, the three of them were on a ledge about half way up to the cave. Billy's breath was coming in hard short gasps and his left leg was shaking violently.

"Disco Leg," commented Virtual to Tommy.

"Yep, he's doing the Wild Elvis alright. Don't worry Billy, it won't last long. It's just all the crap built up in your muscle from the bridging. Give it ten minutes."

"Weirdest thing," said Billy. "That's never happened to me before."

They fell silent as they sat there on the ledge in the midday sun, looking out at the magnificent view below and around them. In the distance, the sun pulled vapours from the desert floor and the shimmering mass of the mesa was reflected in it as if there was a second, ghostly mesa there in the wilderness.

"Beats football practice, wouldn't you say, Billy?" said Tommy.

Billy just nodded. "Guys," he said, pausing. "It's about the Billy thing."

"What, you prefer just Bill? That's cool," said Virtual.

"Actually my name is Kai. At least that's what my grandfather calls me. My Navajo name. I think I want to be called that from now on, you know? For his sake, kind of… and mine…"

"Kai is cool. What does it mean?" said Tommy.

"Um, well that's not important really…" said Billy-now-Kai.

"What do you mean it's not important? It's your name," said Tommy.

"Okay," said Billy, a little hesitantly. "It means willow."

There was a pause and then a sputter and then both Virtual and Tommy were chortling but trying very hard to suppress it.

"Yeah, okay, okay… see you at the cave you losers," said Billy and took to the wall once again. The jittery leg was gone and before Tommy could hoist Virtual back onto his sling Kai was ten feet from the undercling. But that was as far as he could go and he watched as down below Tommy and Virtual made their way up to him. When they were all assembled by the undercling, Virtual strapped the chicken wing to a length of rope and while Tommy leant out from underneath, he tried to toss the wing up and in between two rocks that jutted out from the cave mouth. He finally managed to hook it in after several unsuccessful attempts and now they had a length of rope hanging down from the five feet that stood between them and the cave buttress.

As they had planned, Kai took to the rope and hand over hand he made his way up, his feet dangling below. He slipped once but in not too long a time he was pulling himself up over the edge. He got to his feet and peered into the yawning black mouth of the cave but could see nothing. Down below, Tommy took off the sling and attached the clips to the rope. Giving a call and a tug, he signaled Kai who pulled Virtual and the sling up and over onto the ledge. You could have launched a ship on Virtual's smile as he screamed a loud yahoo across the mesa.

Lastly, Tommy came up with almost scary ease and the three of them were perched there, a hundred feet above the trail.

"And that, my friends, is what you call a first rate Avue!" cried Tommy. "Straight up... No probs, no falls, no flappers."

"I've got one," said Virtual displaying the piece of flesh on his finger that had been torn up and was now bleeding slightly as a displaced section of skin 'flapped' over his knuckle.

From his backpack, Kai produced the flashlight they had had the foresight to bring along and he switched it on and probed into the darkness. Near the entrance there was a box marked Sandford University and in it was a pair of gloves and an old, kerosene lantern. This sudden reminder of what had happened ten years ago sobered them all and they looked at each other, sharing it.

"Let's be careful," said Kai.

"You got it," Tommy replied and Virtual nodded.

Inside, the cave was a little disappointing really. It only ran about twelve feet from side to side and the back wall was about forty feet from the entrance. There wasn't anything particularly special about the cave at all really, except for a series of what looked like shelves carved into the rock and the window. The square hole in the rear wall was about three feet by three in width and height and, upon further inspection, it was revealed that a tunnel of the same dimensions went in for about four feet and then seemed to disappear into blackness.

Shining the light down the tube, Kai said, "That's weird, the light doesn't pick up the wall at the end of the tunnel."

"Maybe it opens into another, larger cave," said Tommy.

"Full of gold probably," said Virtual, mysteriously. "But I guess we'll never know." Tommy looked at Kai and they both looked at Virtual. After a moment Virtual said, "Okay, tie me up."

Securing a rope around Virtual's middle, Tommy and Kai lifted him up and pushed him head first into the tunnel. There was quite a bit of room around him and no chance of his getting wedged in so he began to squirm further in, pushing the flashlight in front of him.

"Hold on for a minute, Virtual," said Tommy. "We can't see back here. I'll get that lantern." Pulling the lantern out of the university gear pack, he struck a match from the box and lighted it. The glow filled the cavern and all of a sudden the whole event took on a feeling of intense purpose. Tommy returned to the tunnel. "Okay, keep going."

"What can you see?" said Kai, unable to contain himself.

Virtual's voice echoed back to them. "Well, there's a wall but it's covered in something and doesn't reflect the light very well. Then the floor of the tunnel ends and there's a shaft that goes down for... just a minute, I can't see. I have to shine the light down there." There was a momentary pause and they could see Virtual's butt and the stubs of his pant legs as he squirmed to get a better position. "It looks like it goes down about eight feet and then veers off horizontally again. How much rope have we got?"

"About twenty feet left," Tommy called back.

"Okay, I'm going to lower myself down to the next level and take a look."

"I don't know about this," Kai said to Tommy. "If he gets stuck, what are we gonna do? Neither of us can fit in there."

"Maybe you'd better get out of there, Virtual," Tommy called in. "We can come back with better stuff."

"Nah, it's okay. Don't worry. There's plenty of room in the shaft. I won't get stuck."

"What if the rope breaks?" Kai called.

"It's braided Dyneema. It ain't going to break. Here I go..."

They felt the rope go tense as Virtual lowered himself over into the shaft and started to pull it through their hands in small lengths. Then suddenly the rope went slack. Tommy looked at Kai.

"Virtual," Tommy called. "You okay?"

There was no reply. Kai started to get a sick feeling in his stomach. He leant forward into the tunnel and listened. There was no sound. "Virtual!" he shouted.

"Yeah, I'm okay!" Virtual shouted back to the relief of the others. "There's something down here. Hold on, I've got to get the light around. I can't quite get... holy shit!!"

Tommy shouted, "What? What is it? Virtual...?"

"Pull me out! Pull me out!" Virtual screamed. Tommy and Kai yanked hard on the rope and it started to retrieve with Virtual wriggling on the end like a bass caught on a fishing line. He was thrashing about and almost crying. "Hurry up!"

When the rope got to the inside edge of the tunnel it jammed on a piece of rock and Virtual's panicked movement just made it worse.

"Virtual, relax will you? You're jamming the line!" Tommy shouted and the rope, correspondingly, relaxed somewhat. They could hear Virtual whimpering and swatting at something with his gloved hands.

"Pull!" shouted Kai and together they gave a heavy heave that pulled the smaller boy over the ledge and propelled him down the slight grade of the tunnel towards them. Virtual popped out of the tunnel mouth knocking them all down onto the cave floor. Tommy and Kai just sat for a second and stared at Virtual, not sure of what it was they were looking at.

"Get them off!!" screamed Virtual. He was frantically rolling around, covered from head to foot in massive black spiders. The other two started swatting at them knocking them from his hair and face and picking them from the folds of his clothing and then swatting at the ones that were trying to make their way up their arms. Finally they were all off and those that hadn't been killed in the removal were quickly stomped on. The three fell back, Tommy and Kai exhausted but laughing. Virtual just lay there breathing hard.

Tommy stopped laughing long enough to say, "So... no gold then?"

The renewed laughter caught itself against the quartz and feldspar and bent its way into the tunnel and down the shaft, bouncing from one side to another, resonance being shaved on its downward journey, until what was left was thin and high-pitched like the laughter of young girls. It went deeper and deeper, winding its way until it fell against the shifting sub-strata that held tight the hard, rancid casings of the two demons Tse-Nill and Naz-Tsaid. They strained and struggled against the bindings that held them, put in place so long ago by a force more powerful than they and that, even now, was resisting their mindless desire to rise to the surface, to find the interlopers and to make their flesh sing. But the confines that restrained them held fast and they screamed in the agony of their frustration and they bit their own tongues and ached for the day when they would be free. For, they did have their plan and they did have their agents. But this was of little comfort now and they screamed again in their rage to be free.

"Did you hear that?" said Kai, listening at the mouth of the tunnel.

"What *was* that?" Virtual asked, calming now from his spidery encounter.

"I think we should go down, now," said Tommy and without another word, they did.

*   *   *

The boards masking the entrance to the Heminghurst Silver Mine came away easily in Albert's hand, the rotten wood flaking as it pulled against the rusty spikes holding it on. In a couple of minutes he'd cleared enough away to pull the big car through into the larger space immediately inside. He turned off the engine and stepped out, immediately slipping on the wet slime that surrounded the vehicle and falling against the door, jamming his shoulder. He cursed and rubbed his arm as he looked around in the gloom. He reached into the dashboard and turned the lights onto high beam. The beams cut through into the tunnel, eventually hitting the ceiling as the floor of the shaft sloped away into blackness.

It was dank and wet and somehow there was a cold breeze coming up out of the yawning black hole in front of him that, after the searing heat of the desert, quickly chilled him to the bone. The Crip was outside trying to cover up the blood and mess on the road. Then he would bring the bikes up to the mine. Albert walked around the car and opened the front passenger door. He reached in and grabbed Ashford Brixton by the feet, his body having been shoved upside down into the foot well. He pulled the corpse out and dragged it off to one side and into a small room cut into the wall of the mine. Now he had to figure out what to do with the mess in the trunk. He didn't feel like shoving his bare hands into the bones and viscera of what was left of Lonny after his dinner date with the vulture sisters. He spotted a shovel and an old, rusting wheel-barrow in the smaller room and pulled them over to the rear of the car and popping the trunk, looked down onto Lonny. What lay there was hardly even recognizable as human. What the shotgun blast hadn't already made a mess of, the vultures had chomped and chewed away into stringy, bloody sausage. The only thing that kept him interested in this task at all was the ten kilos of coke under the brown sludge. So he grabbed the shovel and started transferring bits of Lonny into the wheelbarrow.

Outside, The Crip finished brushing over the blood-stained sand with a piece of scrub until it looked more or less normal. You could see that the dirt had been moved around but not significantly. Then he took the first of the bikes up to the mine. He pulled in and saw Albert at his task near the car and then walked back for another machine. When they were all stored, side by side, in the cave, he took a beer out of the trike's case and sucked on it, drinking the whole thing down in a matter of seconds. It didn't take the acidy taste out of his mouth though.

Albert came over and took one himself, cracking it open and drinking slowly. He walked over to where the shaft started to wind its way down into the depths of the mine. He couldn't see far down the line by the light of the car headlights so he walked a ways along the mine-car tracks that ran off into the darkness. He stopped when he heard a strange sound emanating up from below. It was something like a moan and also a little like rotten timber creaking in the distance; a strange noise that continued for a minute and then suddenly ceased.

The Crip came up behind him. "Did you say something?" he asked.

Albert put his hand up for silence and listened again for the sound but there was nothing now. "No. There was some noise down there. Could have been an animal or something..." He put his hand on the butt of his gun to feel its reassuring presence.

"Look, I've been thinking," said The Crip. "You could be right about getting out of here. But we have to be sure that these two clowns haven't tipped off the cops or something, because we could move out of here and run right into something. One of us will have to go into town and try to get an idea if anything's going on. We could get some stuff for Bob, too."

"You gonna go?" Albert asked.

"No. I'm not leaving this stuff for a second. Nothing personal you understand."

Albert considered this. "Yeah, what if I go and you take off in the other direction."

"I'm not gonna do that."

"Oh, okay then… I guess I won't worry."

The Crip thought for a second that maybe he should slap Albert around a little but decided against it. He needed him as the only other physically fit tool he had.

"All right… You go into town. I'll give you the keys to all the other vehicles and you can take them with you. That way you know I'm not going anywhere. Okay?"

Albert could see no problem with this. "Okay. Where should I go?"

"You can start at the grocery store. Get enough food for a couple of days. Then go to the pharmacy and get some bandages and stuff and some surgical sutures if you can. And get some blankets and junk for us to sleep on."

"How am I going to find out if anyone else knows about us?"

"The Brixtons own a pool hall on Fleming Street. Go down there and hang around for a while. See what you can find out."

"What are you going to do?"

"I'll get Bob out of the car and see what I can do for him. Tie off the wound maybe. Oh, and get some booze will ya?"

"Anything else, honey?"

"Just get going."

"Okay."

"And Albert…"

"Yeah?"

"Put the coke you got shoved in your armpit back into the car before I blow your fucking head off."

*   *   *

88

"What are you doing here, Steven?"

"Well, hello to you too."

Steven had risen out of the lawn chair and now the two ex-lovers stood face to face in the hot Arizona sun; two gunslingers with hearts and words instead of, well, guns. Mr.Chavez got up too and made an awkward excuse as he moved off into the house. Like townspeople scurrying off into doorways to avoid the hail of bullets about to be unleashed at the OK Corral. But it wasn't going to be like that. Karen brushed past Steven and went up the stairs and was trying to get her keys out of her bag with an armful of groceries and getting panicky when Steven came up behind her.

"Here, let me help you," he said softly.

"I can manage, thank you," said Karen, curtly and balanced one bag on the railing as she grabbed her keys from her purse and slid them into the lock. But as things go sometimes, she couldn't, in fact, manage that and the bag of boots and mosquito repellant fell to the ground and scattered on the driveway.

"Damn it!" she muttered and went into the apartment to put the rest of the bags down.

"I'll get your stuff," Steven offered and went down the steps and started collecting the things together. Karen quickly came down as well and started grabbing things away from him.

"Your taste is changing," he said, holding up the hiking boots and a khaki shirt.

"I'm going camping, if you must know," she said snatching the clothing and then their eyes met and it was ridiculous and she knew it and they both started to laugh. "Come inside," she said getting up and walking upstairs.

"Would you like a drink or something?" she asked once they were in the apartment. "I've only got lemonade."

"That would be nice, thanks," said Steven looking around the living room. "This is pretty nice. Where's Huxley?"

"Probably asleep in the closet," Karen replied, joining him and offering the glass of lemonade. And then, after a pause, "Why are you here, Steve?"

"I was worried about you, that's all. I read about the fire here last week in the paper and saw your name and the... thing that happened to you. I tried phoning but I couldn't get your number from directory assistance."

Karen knew this could be true. She had had this problem ever since she got her new phone. Her mother had encountered it as well in the twenty seconds or so between her moving in and Dorothy trying to contact her. In a way it had been a blessing but still, as it was proving now, inconvenient.

"I'm having trouble with my phone. I keep calling them about it. You mean all that stuff was in the paper? In San Francisco? I don't believe it."

"Well, it was kind of freaky, you must admit and I guess it was newsworthy. Seriously though, are you okay? I'm sorry I couldn't have come sooner."

"You didn't have to come at all. I'm fine," she said and went back into the kitchen to get herself a drink and buy some time for her face to return to its normal colour. "You could have tried the school," she called back.

"I did but they wouldn't give out your number, which I figured would be the case. I left a message though."

"That's odd. I didn't get it."

"Right..."

"Honestly, Steven," Karen said, coming back from the kitchen. "I didn't. I would have called you if I had. I wouldn't want you to worry about a thing like that."

"Okay," he said, sitting down, "Everything going okay here? Are you really going camping?"

"School trip," she answered, folding onto the couch. "No option there."

"I see."

There was a pause and they both just sat there sipping lemonade. Steven smiled. She liked that smile. She always had. Why was she here, living alone again? Oh yes, the other woman...

For a couple universally declared to be ideal, it was somewhat of a surprise to find out that he was doing some co-worker behind her back. But when the co-worker turned out to be the female cop that he had been riding beside for the last two years, Karen supposed it wasn't really that shocking. At least that's what she thought now. But back then... Was it five years ago? No, eight months... Well, back then it was the end of the world. Steven had ended it with Leanne and Leanne had transferred and they had tried to recover from it all but it was no good and Karen had decided to move out and away. Not running. She just knew she couldn't get started again in Frisco. Her whole world there had been about being a cop's wife and teaching was a thing she did well and it had taken her mind off the constant worry she had when he was on the job. When that was gone, well, it was time for a fresh start.

As it turned out (as it frequently does when times are bad) things happen... things that would be considered great under better circumstances. About two weeks after she had moved out, Steven got his chance for a detective's shield and now he was on the drug squad. Better pay, slightly more dangerous at times but less on-the-street playing about. It would have been a good move up for both of them. And might have been the opportunity that would have allowed Karen to pursue her writing, which is what she really wanted.

But, there you go...

"It was a long drive just to find that out," Karen said. "But I appreciate it."

"Well, as it happens, I'm sort of killing two birds... sorry, bad phrase. There's an ongoing investigation into a ring of small-time thugs that's been developing."

"In Newton? I find that hard to believe."

"It's everywhere, Karen, you know that. But it isn't locals. It's a Frisco gang that intelligence says is heading here to score with some locals. There have been some incidents in this area lately and we think Newton could be their destination. They might already be here as a matter of fact. Anyway, I asked to be assigned to the follow-up and here I am."

"How long are you staying here, Steven, I... No, you know what? I can't deal with this," she said, getting up. "It's really unfair, you know? It's nice of you to be concerned but I'm just getting settled here and it's hard enough and then with the fire and..." She stopped suddenly. Oh god, she thought, I'm going to cry.

But Steven spoke and her tears didn't come after all. "Look, its okay. I knew it would be awkward." He got up, too, and put an arm around her shoulder. She just looked at him. "I just wanted to check in on you. I'm not going to interfere with your life. I'm staying at a hotel on Oak Street for a few days, that's all. You won't even know I'm here. I'll be with the local department most of the time."

"Of course, I'll know you're here, you idiot, you just told me where you were going to stay and for how long."

Steven laughed, "I guess I did, didn't I? I am an idiot. Sorry." Karen laughed, too. She had to. Besides, she wasn't a child right? She could be grown up about this. "Look," he said, "I'm going. If you would like to have dinner or something while I'm here, that would be great. You can call me at the hotel. If not, then, well, not. I really did just want to find out if you were okay and I guess to see you as well. I worry about you, Karen."

"I know," she said quietly. "I worry about you too. But that's not the point, is it?"

"No, I guess not," Steven said. "I'll see you later."

"Goodbye."

After Steven had gone, Karen sat back down on the couch. Huxley poked his head around the corner of the cupboard door. She patted her hand against her lap and Huxley padded over and leapt up onto her with a small meow. As he settled down, Karen sighed and rubbed Huxley's neck and ears. "Well, you were a big help," she said as she watched Steven's car drive off down the street.

*   *   *

Albert wheeled his Harley-Davidson Street Bob into the parking lot of the MX Pharmacy just as Cam and Louie were exiting, their arms full

92

of chips and pop and other party fixings for Cam's 'Pre Field-trip Choose-yer-partner Soiree'. The black denim paint job on the gas tank shone warmly in the hot sun and the deep throated thrum of the 1450 CC engine cut through the blare of ordinary traffic like a knife through custard. Louie stopped dead in his tracks.

"Oh, man… will you look at that," he stammered. That's the new FXDB1. Man…"

Albert shut off the motor and put the bike on its stand a few feet away from the door to the drugstore-slash-supermarket. He eyed the two boys staring at his bike and wandered over to them. Cam looked at Louie as the dusty, bedraggled Albert approached them.

"How's it going?" he asked them.

"Um, good…" Louie managed. "That's a sweet bike, man. I've been reading up on it. The Street Bob, right? It looks great."

"Yeah, it's pretty good, a little soft in the mid-range," said Albert looking Louie up and down. "Big man like you should be riding a Glide or something though shouldn't you?"

Louie just laughed. "No, man, the Bob would do just fine."

"Listen," said Albert, "I'm looking for a pool hall in town run by a guy named Brixton. You know it?"

Cam answered Albert as Louie went over to get a closer look at the bike. "Oh yeah, that's The Delta. It's over on Oak. Couple of blocks that way…" he said pointing southwards into the downtown area. "It's right beside the Hayward Hotel. You can't miss it, there's a big pirate sign over it."

"Good, thanks kid. See ya," Albert said and walked off into the store.

Louie came back over to Cam. "I haven't seen him around before. He looks like he just got run over," Cam said, laughing.

"Yeah, right, you should go tell him that, Cam."

"He's going over to Brixton's," said Cam. "Guess I know what he wants there. Think I might take a little trip over there myself before tonight."

"Yeah right... Well, let's get going," said Louie, shaking his head and imagining the sight of Cam Preppy scoring drugs at The Delta. They walked over to Louie's Rambler Classic, got in and drove off to prepare for party night.

Inside the store, Albert walked aimlessly around the first-aid section wondering what the hell he was supposed to be buying. He grabbed some bandages and a couple of tubes of Ozonol. Not finding the sutures he went up to the pharmacist.

"Can I help you?" she said, looking him over and wondering what kind of pain-killers or downers this trash was going to try to get out of her.

"Yeah, I'm looking for some, um, surgical sutures," he said, throwing one of his winning smiles her way.

"You want surgical sutures?" she replied ironically, noticing the smarmy grin coming out of the scratched face; and the really, really odd smell that accompanied it, "What for?"

"My, uh, dog. He had a bit of an accident. A car..."

"Why don't you take it to the vet?"

"Can't afford it, ma'am... Gotta take care of it myself... He's in an awful lot of pain."

She considered this and thought about refusing but was it really worth the potential hassle. What did she care what he wanted them for?

"Here," she said handing him a box. "Thirty-two bucks. I hope your dog gets better."

"Me too, ma'am... Me too... Thanks."

"No problem."

Albert paid and left the store, throwing the supplies into the knapsack he'd brought with him. He started the bike and rode out of the lot, turned south and headed for The Delta. He found it without much trouble, as Cam had said, right beside the hotel and under a grinning, skull-faced pirate sign, the neon in which fizzled and popped every time it lit up. As he parked the bike he didn't notice the serious-looking man watching him from a car that had just pulled into the hotel parking lot. Albert walked into the dimness of The Delta as Steven Walker got out of his car carrying his small bag of clothes and his police issue service revolver and the massive chip on his shoulder that had re-appeared after his visit with Karen. He watched as the door closed behind Albert. He would have to have a look at this place later after he had spoken to the local cops. But, having a nose for such things, he suspected that this seedy place would be a good spot to start looking for visiting desperadoes.

Inside, Albert strolled over to the bar and ordered a beer. Half a dozen people sat around the place, smoking or playing pool. The room was cool and dark. Albert had always liked pool halls. He felt at home in them which wasn't surprising as he had practically been raised in one. The bartender was a hard looking dude with a broken nose and what looked like half his hair missing on one side; like he'd been burnt or something, although there was no scarring on the flesh. Classic, thought Albert. The waitress that served the tables was a different story though and Albert felt that old familiar tug as he checked out the fluid motion of her ass in its pair of tight blue jeans. She noticed him looking and smiled. Yes, siree, thought Albert, I surely do like pool halls.

*   *   *

Not too much later, the kids were arriving at Cam's house. Conveniently, Mom and Dad Proctor were at a business weekend in Winslow and baby brother Sammy was in the care of the grandparents and the stereo was cranked and the place was starting to rock. Cam was juiced and had been since about five o'clock and Louie was rolling a doob ensconced in his favourite la-z-boy in the rec room. Every kid in the class that was going on the trip was invited, which was a rarity at Cam's affairs because he tended to mostly invite his version of the cool kids and, of course, the girls. But tonight was a mega-blind and all were welcome.

Tommy Wong came into the living room with two beers and tossed one to Virtual who was out of his chair and on the couch. Virtual cracked it open and they cheered and drank and waited for the chicks to show up. It didn't really matter which chicks, although they had their favourites, because they wouldn't know what to do with them anyway.

Allison Donkers, the candy-striper from the hospital and the subject of Kai's attentions was already there and was talking to Micki Valence, the tiny, exuberant girlfriend of Louie. She could have fit into Louie's pocket actually. They were the 'cute' couple. But Micki was no slouch athletically either and was an all-state high-school gymnast.

The Remo twins, Attibi and Enye, showed up a few minutes later carrying a lot of CD's and a bottle of expensive wine. The Remo twins were black, tall and, sexually speaking, evenly divided by gender although, in their long, lanky not-quite-developed bodies, they were fairly androgynous and could be mistaken for each other and very often, were.

Somewhere, screaming in the back yard out by the pool, Ricky Ray, class clown and all around goof-ball was pretending he was going to dive in with all his clothes on; holding his nose, bouncing up and down on the diving board until, of course, he did fall in and had to go home to get changed. Fortunately, that was right next door.

Alice Bird and Linwood Desmond arrived. She was a shy, quiet kid and he was a smart-ass from England that had just joined the school last year when his parents immigrated. Despite her waif-like appearance she was probably the prettiest girl in the school actually and Cam had been mightily disappointed when she had fallen for Linwood's semi-sophisticated charm. Cam had actually had a fight with Linwood until it turned out that Linwood was a trained boxer and could handle himself pretty well. In the microcosm that was high-school, this translated into status and Cam and Linwood had become fairly good friends. Linwood also had a lot of money. That helped. Anyway, Linwood had quickly tired of Alice's soft demeanour.

Finn Esterhaus was in the bathroom being sick. He was a nervous kid who hardly said a word; ever. He was ridiculously ham-handed and couldn't relate to anyone very well. The fact that he was even at this party was a miracle and a large part of his presence there, and subsequently in the bathroom, was due to the insistence of his mother who was determined to get Finn out of the house for reasons other than school for at least ten minutes a week.

The cheerleading squad, senior girls variety, who for some reason always traveled in a clutch (if that's the right collective pronoun for a group of almost revoltingly perky girls who laughed and pointed a lot) arrived like an explosion. They were Angela McReary (head cheerleader and current flame of Cam), Melissa Heels, CJ Hayford and Hattie Conway; all pretty and, contrary to type, generally pretty bright too.

Cookie Johanson, the girl that Virtual would love to sit next to for at least part of this evening, was a strong, capable girl, with huge blue eyes and a pleasing temperament who worked part-time at the humane society. She was an animal lover to be sure and lived just outside of town on a farm with her aunt and uncle, her parents both having passed away some time ago. She liked Virtual; Virtual liked her. And that's where it sat.

David Smith, a bookish, conservative boy who somehow managed to look Dickensian in ordinary clothes, arrived shortly after that with his cousin, Anton Remy, a Cajun kid who always had holes in his clothes. They kind of looked like the city mouse and the country mouse when they were together.

And walking up the street, really only going because Tommy and Virtual had made him go, strode Kai Ahiga. He didn't really know why he had come tonight. He was torn between the teenage angst about fitting in and worry about his grandfather and resentment about even being forced to make a decision like this. But he felt like getting drunk and this was surely a good excuse. And then there was Allison...

So there they were; twenty young people, the pride of Newton Fairbanks; twenty kids that would party the night away (at least part of it); twenty kids who would soon be camping together in the shadow of the Black Mesa; ten of whom would be dead within a week.

    *   *   *

"6 Baker to dispatch..."

"6 Baker to dispatch, come on..."

"Dispatch, 6 Baker. That you Rick? You're breaking up..."

"6 Baker..."

"Come again, 6 Baker..."

"Fucking thing... 6 Baker position report and..."

"6 Baker?"

"Hell... Never mind, I'll check in on the other side of the mesa."

"6 Baker?"

"Fuck off."

Officer Richard Jennings slammed the mike down onto the seat beside him and cursed again. He had a bad headache. In fact he was hungover and this patrol was hot and the god-dammed air conditioning in his unit was dribbling out with an ineffective whine and a mere puff of semi-cooled air. He switched it off and opened all the windows and then looked at his watch; half an hour to go. He floored the car a bit and sped past the northern edge of Black Mesa and then past the boarded up gas station, almost painted over solid with really rude graffiti, some of it in Navajo. Then he slowed as he passed the village of Sandy Hollow and its fifty mph zone.

About a mile on the other side of the village and just past the Ahiga place, Rick pulled the car over to the side as a man, a Navajo by the look of it, waved him over with a blanket. Rick sat for a moment in the car and looked around as the man walked towards him. He was an older man, maybe in his fifties. He was carrying a bag and was wearing a broad-brimmed straw hat. Rick rolled down the window as the man approached.

"Can I help you, sir?"

"Yes, I heard shots…"

"Gunshots you mean?"

"Yes, sir, lots of them."

"Whereabouts?"

"I was in the field looking for rabbits."

"No, I mean where did the gunshots come from?"

"Hard to say… They was all around, coming from the rocks like. If I had to guess, I would say it was coming from out near the mine."

"You mean the old silver mine? Maybe it was someone out there hunting."

"I don't think so. This was a lot of shots and different sounds, you know?"

"Different guns, you mean?"

"Ya-hey…"

"All right, I'll run out there and take a look," he sighed. "Thanks. Can I get your name there please?"

"Lenny."

Rick waited. "Lenny what?"

"Just Lenny…"

"Where do you live, just Lenny?"

"Tsas-ka… anyone can tell you that."

"Okay, good enough. See ya later, Lenny."

"Bye now," said the man taking off his hat and wiping his brow with a handkerchief as Rick pulled out onto the highway.

"6 Baker, RMP, to Dispatch. Out at Heminghurst Mine, report of gunshots…."

Only static responded. Rick looked at his watch again and wondered about the old man. Seemed a bit simple and even if he had heard anything it was probably just hunters or something. Only twenty minutes to go until end of shift and Newton was still thirty minutes away. And his head hurt. And it wasn't his jurisdiction. And it was hot…

He slowed the car at the turnoff to the mine road and peered up between the rocks. He listened and heard nothing. He was about to roll up the window and call it a day when he spotted the last of the turkey vultures; little black dots circling high in the sky a mile or so up the road. He put the car into reverse, backed up a little and then headed along the dirt road towards the mine. He tried the radio one more time with no luck.

As he drove the road he could see that the vultures were flying over an outcrop of rock up on the side of one of the hills where a smaller road, not much more than a path really, veered off. He started to pull the car up the track road but the big Ford couldn't make it over the first of the little rock piles that were scattered here and there along the way. He shut off the engine and started walking up the trail, checking his revolver as he went. He knew this was kind of stupid, that he shouldn't be doing this without checking in, but his head and his hang-over got the better of his usually good judgment. Finally he was standing on the outcrop looking down on the mine some mile away. He couldn't make out what the birds were interested in. He couldn't see anything down where they were concentrated and flying about; not more than a hundred feet from where he stood. Then he spotted the laptop sitting on the rock; a USB line stretching from one of its ports and disappearing over the edge of the ledge.

He walked over and picked up the computer. It was still on, in standby mode, and as he moved it the computer kicked back on and showed a weird picture of a bunch of scrub but the picture was panning back and forth over top of it. And what looked like a hand was stuck out of the scrub and coming into frame every time the camera waved by. He followed the wire over the edge and saw, hanging down from it and secured by a snag on a dead tree-root some four feet below, a long, black rifle. The USB lead was wrapped around the butt and the gun was dangling from the branch. The picture he was looking at on the laptop was apparently coming from the sight and as the gun swayed in the breeze the picture of the ground, some fifty feet below it, was moving. A close up of a bad accident it looked like.

A hunter who fell, was Rick's first thought and he put the laptop down and ran back to the car to drive around further and see if he could get to the man below. He slammed the door shut and the gravel flew up as he drove around the hill. He realized quickly that he wouldn't be able to circumvent the hill before getting to the mine. This meant that the only way down there was up and over the hill and for that he would need ropes and more men. So he turned the car around and was about to head into town for help when he noticed the boards on the mine entrance had been ripped away and tire tracks led from a few feet in front of it into the black entrance. Probably just kids, he thought, but he stopped the car anyway, got out and headed up to the entrance…

Inside the mine, it had not been a good afternoon. Bob had started moaning as soon as Albert had left and The Crip had gone to him to see what he could do. Lifting up the cloth around the wound, he could see that the bullet had not hit anything serious and although he was bleeding slowly it didn't look too bad. He had poured some water over it and tied it off with a bungee cord and the bleeding seemed to have more or less stopped a few minutes later. Of course there was the chance of infection if they didn't do something about it soon but The Crip couldn't help that. The Crip had a mission.

Bob slipped in and out of consciousness but at one point sat straight up and in an almost normal voice said, "Get me my bag."

The Crip knew which bag he meant and searched the box on the back of the trike until he found Mystic Bob's 'medicinals'. Bob went through it and finally pulled out something wrapped in tin foil and about the size of a marble. He couldn't get the foil off though so he handed it to Crip who, carefully unwrapping it, revealed a lump of something black and dotted with bright green spots that were almost fluorescent. Bob took it and slipped it under his tongue and then fell back and passed out again. He didn't moan much after that and then The Crip was on his own with the two dead bodies.

The Crip was pretty much dead emotionally, but even he began to see the weirdness in the situation. He walked over to the car and turned on the radio but couldn't tune anything in so he switched it off. He walked around a bit and then tried lying down on the back seat of the car. But the smell starting to drift up from the trunk began to make him sick so he got up and shut the doors. In the side room where Ashford was stored he found an old wooden chair so he propped it up outside in the shade against the stone wall, tilted it back and tried to sleep. He had been that way for about an hour when he heard Rick Jennings patrol car approaching...

Rick made his way slowly up to the mine entrance and paused, looking into it, his eyes adjusting slowly to the gloom. Then he caught sight of the tail end of the black Chevy; then the line of bikes. And then, out of the corner of his eye he saw, for a brief instant, the flash of The Crip's big knife. Then Rick Jennings headache was gone.

*   *   *

"Kai..."

That was all he had said, but for that one brief instant Nascha had been there. Not just staring quietly around him, or mesmerized by bird sounds outside or sitting still at the table while somebody fed him. And for that the Ahiga house was in rapturous turmoil.

Big Jim rushed to the phone and called the doctor at the hospital. Lucy headed to the truck to go to town and buy some celebratory beer and Kai just sat with his hand on his grandfather's arm and waited for more. It was what they had all been waiting for; the first real sign.

But that was all old Nascha had to say, at least for the time being. "He probably won't do much more right away," the doctor said, "but that's fantastic news, Jim. And it's just what we would hope for in this short a time period. Rapidly regaining motor response and cognitive awareness; recognition of family members... Fantastic!"

"So what do we do next?" Big Jim asked.

"Do?"

"Yeah, what can we do to speed this thing up now that he's talking?"

"Well, look Jim, it was just one word after all and who knows what was going through his mind when he said it. It may just be a temporary thing, so just keep doing whatever you were doing. You can't rush it. There's no set pattern to recovery in these cases. Just make sure he's eating well and engage him as much as possible. Who is Kai?"

"Oh, that's Little Billy. You met him at the hospital. He's using his native name now for some reason. I guess to honour his grandfather. Nascha always calls him that. He was just coming in from school; walked in through the front door, Nascha looked up and said his name; real loud, too."

"Excellent, well call me if there are any further developments."

"Yeah…. alright then… Thanks Doc, I guess we just got a little excited here."

"With good reason… Bye Jim."

Big Jim hung up the phone and went into the living room and watched Kai and his grandfather. He was having trouble remembering to use Kai's Navajo name. Kai was playing softly on a reed pipe that Nascha had made for him many years ago and Nascha was swaying slightly in his chair, his eyes closed and what appeared to be a smile on his face. Kai was actually pretty good on that thing.

Jim was so proud of Kai he could burst. The moaning about school had stopped and Kai had friends, the two funny kids with the climbing club thing, and he had spent every spare hour he could with his grandfather. It sounded like there was even a girl in the works. Jim hoped that it would last. He had had to go out twice on short day trips and those had gone extremely well. The clients were real happy and had promised to bring him some more business soon and tipped him a hundred bucks as well. So some of the bills were paid and the wedding (which they had all agreed should proceed) was not so daunting a financial load.

The phone rang and Jim answered it.

"This Jim Ahiga?" sounded the voice over the wire. A strong, aggressive voice... A no-nonsense voice...

"Yeah, speaking..."

"Gordon Stemrow gave me your number. He said you were the best man in the area to see about a trip out into the badlands."

"Yep, I can probably help you out there. When did you want to go and for how long?"

"Well, we want to get out maybe the week after next, for three or four days. Five of us. It's a corporate kind of thing. You know... a motivational trip? We won't want any molly coddling. Roughing it, you know? See what we're all made of."

Jim smiled to himself. Well, if tough is what you want then that's what you'll get, mister, he thought. Less supplies, less overhead, more profit. "Sounds good," he said.

"Any fishing to be done out there or is that a stupid question? Is it all desert?"

"Oh no, there's a little bit of everything in the Sonora. Some pretty good fishing in the Gila. Although, to be honest, I've never been at this time of year. But hey, that's part of the adventure, huh?"

"Damn straight, it is. I like your style, Ahiga. I think this will be fun. I'll have my secretary call you in the next couple of days and set things up."

"Don't you want to know what it's going to cost, Mister...?"

"Henson is my name. Bill. Nope. I trust you, sir. I'm sure you won't hose us because if this trip works out well, you can expect a lot more work of this kind. We have a big company and a lot of wusses in need of some backbone, if you catch my drift. Besides, you come highly recommended."

"Okay, well... great. I'll wait to hear from you."

Big Jim hung up. Was this a great day or what? What was that, happiness he was feeling? Lucy came back just then with a couple of big bags of goodies and Jim quickly helped himself to a beer still ice-cold from the beer store. Perfect.

"Who was that?" she asked as she started to unload the groceries.

"I'll tell you over dinner. You go sit with Kai and grandpa; I'll put the steaks on."

He watched her hang up her jacket, her pretty calves straightening as she reached up for the hook. Man, he felt good.

"Lucy?"

"Yes?"

"I really love you, you know."

"Yeah, I know."

She went into the living room and sat quietly until Billy finished playing and Nascha was fast asleep and snoring.

*   *   *

"It's just a perfect day; I want to spend it with you…"

Lou Reed

Albert moved his arm in the dark and felt around for the motionless form of Rachael Malone. In his semi-conscious state he felt wetness. Don't tell me the bitch has puked, he thought. Fuck. But I don't smell anything horrible, so…

Albert rolled over and felt something hard against his eye. He tried to open the lid and as the last vestiges of the vision of water that had been his dream dried up and drifted, along with him, on the river of a slow awakening, he managed to pry it past the hard thing. And then he was looking down a tunnel; a long, black tunnel with a spiral cut into the wall and what looked like a subway train sitting still, at the end.

The Crip cocked the .32. "Wake up, you bastard."

Albert lifted his head away from the barrel of the big Smith and Wesson. "Crip…"

"I should fuck you up right now…"

"What's the matter, Crip?" said Albert, awake now and struggling to rise to one elbow.

"What's the matter? It's fucking two o'clock in the morning!"

"I was on my way back, Crip. I got everything you wanted. It's on the bike. And I found out what the Brixtons were doing, just like you wanted. I was just taking a little, you know, time for myself..."

The crack of the gun barrel against Albert's head sent him spinning away towards the wall and with a soundless impact he was face up against Rachael. Rachael's eyes were open and for some strange reason, as Albert followed her line of vision upwards, she was staring over his shoulder at the ceiling fan. And she didn't blink. And she was dead as a doornail.

Albert wiped at the blood that was beginning to stream down into his eye from the cut above his brow. And he noticed his hand and the blood already on it from Rachael. He twisted back towards Crip. "Take it easy," he managed to get out, lamely.

"I'll take it easy. Get dressed you moron."

Albert rose up and grabbed at his jeans hanging on the back of a chair. He pulled them on as Crip watched him, cloaked in shadow, from the corner of the room. Moonlight was streaming in through the one cracked, dirty window and Albert could see down onto the street and a cop car parked beside some garbage bins.

"Oh Christ, Crip, there's a cop down there. They must have heard something."

"He didn't hear anything, believe me. Get going."

Crip opened the door to the room in the low-rent boarding house where Rachael, the waitress from The Delta, roomed and now had died. They left down the back stairs and out into the street. Crip walked behind Albert with the gun leveled at his hips. They walked towards the patrol car.

"Get in the driver's side," said the Crip.

"What are you talking about," said Albert, looking down at the pile of something in the back seat.

"Get in."

Albert opened the driver door and slid behind the wheel. The Crip moved behind the car and got in the passenger side. Albert looked back over the seat and caught the arm and shoulder patch of the dead officer.

"Oh, man, you didn't…"

"Drive," said The Crip.

"Where to?", Albert asked, feeling now as though he had perhaps not, in fact, woken up. That he was now mired in phase-two of a ridiculous nightmare.

"Where's your bike?" asked Crip.

"Back at the pool hall... We came here in her car."

"Go to the pool hall."

"Man, somebody is going to spot us in this fucking car! Are you nuts?"

The Crip scratched at his ear. "I would have thought that was readily apparent, Albert. I've killed five people in seventy-two hours. Now drive."

Albert pulled away slowly and following the theory of 'hide in plain sight' they made it, miraculously, to the pool hall undetected. He pulled into the lane behind the Delta and parked a short distance from the bike.

"Wipe the steering wheel and get out," the Crip ordered. Albert did so and they went to the bike and started it up. "Now drive us back to the mine."

"Back to the…"

"We'll have a talk when we get there."

The next forty minutes were numbing as the cold desert air whipped Albert who had not worn his jacket for the hot ride into town earlier in the day. He could feel The Crip's legs, strange and unbalanced, pressing against his outer thighs. He could hear The Crip's breath in his ear. He could feel his own heart beating wildly against his ribs. The town gave way to the desert, shining below a moonlit, cloudless night. Albert wondered if this would be the last thing he would ever see, this winding drive on the smooth blacktop out to the reserve. He was calmer now and considered that he was still needed; that The Crip couldn't just finish him. He'd be mad, sure, maybe even beat him with the gun a little more. But he couldn't kill him. And that would mean time, and that would mean a chance, eventually, to waste this malignant little weasel and move on.

Yes, that was his plan and when they were within a quarter mile of the turnoff to the mine he opened the Harley up a bit. And he heard the roar of the big engine and felt its strength and he got lost, for the moment, in the bizarre strangeness of it all.

And then he hit the coyote.

*　　　　　*　　　　　*

"Why are you limping?" Spider Woman asked Coyote as she washed her hair in the stream of night. Stars splashed about here and there as she did so, sparkling and shining in the blackness of the void.

"I always feel pain when one of my brothers passes between worlds," Coyote answered and sat down by a rock and licked at his hind quarters. The pain throbbed in his hip and he was worried that it might interfere with his plans. The time was drawing near for the big event and he didn't want to miss out on any of it. Not a single moment.

"You seem anxious, coyote," said Spider Woman and drew her hair back behind her and tied it with a peyote root. She stepped from the water, her smooth skin glistening with the moisture and she picked up her dark, red cloak and put it around her shoulders. "You aren't planning some of your trickery are you? Some game to pass the time at our expense?"

"Crow has brought Nascha back to the real world," said Coyote suddenly, hoping to change the subject. Damn this Spider Woman and her meddling. She would ruin everything if she knew, as he did, what was soon to occur. Did she know?

"Yes, I know. I am surprised he did not remain by the waters. He is old and has served his time among men. He should rest now and enjoy that which follows. It is well earned."

"I think he feels he has a duty of some sort to perform," Coyote said, his voice barking with sarcasm. "He feels he has to remain among men until it is fulfilled."

"Well, it is good that the people have their allies, is it not, Coyote? To help when mischief has its way and evil comes to bear?"

"I suppose that is true, Spider Woman. But what mischief do you speak of?"

"Coyote… make sure you know who it is that controls the way of things; for it certainly is not you."

"That is not why I am here, to be sure. It is for me to make sure that the world is not taken for granted," said Coyote and under the stern gaze of the Spider Woman he trotted back to his lair to ponder what had been said.

A realm away and slightly to the left, Kai sat and looked at his grandfather. He was happy and amazed.

"What did you just say, grandfather?" he asked, hardly able to contain his excitement as Nascha had just uttered his second sound since the heart attack.

"That is not why I am here…" said Nascha looking at the sky.

"Grandfather…"

"Kai…"

Kai went to Nascha and pulled the blanket up closer around him. "How do you feel, granddad?"

"Like I have walked a very long way."

"Here, sit down," Kai said, and led Nascha to a stool in the shade of the porch. The old man slumped onto the chair and sighed long and deeply. "Can I get you something? Some water?"

"Yes, some water, Kai."

Kai ran to the kitchen and poured a cup of water. Big Jim and Lucy were in town and he ached to be able to tell them about this new session of speaking. What if Nascha was silent again when they returned? They'd never believe him.

He went outside and found the chair empty; then he saw that Nascha was standing up again, propped against the fence post at the back of the yard. He was looking out at the Black Mesa and had an apprehensive, questioning look on his face. Kai noticed for the first time that Nascha's hair was even whiter than it was before the attack. It almost glowed.

"What is it, granddad?"

"I don't know Kai."

"Do you remember anything about what happened?"

"I remember you and Jim and Lucy looking at me. I remember thinking that the chicken smelled really good and then not much until yesterday. Everything is a little hazy, you know?"

"We thought…" and Kai stopped. He felt his throat tighten and he started to cry into his grandfather's shoulder. Nascha put his arm around his grandson.

"I can imagine what you thought. It's hard but you know, Kai, death is always there, waiting. I will die one day, soon probably. I am old. You too will pass from this world; long after me, hopefully. But it is not something to fear. It is something to embrace; a part of the order of things. You know, the best thing about death is that it makes you realize how good you've got it now. I'm tired, boy. Help me to bed, will you?"

"Sure, granddad."

Nascha paused and looked up. "Kai, see that crow there?"

Kai looked up towards the mesa and could see a large crow circling. As it flew it seemed to cock its head towards them.

"Yes, I see it."

"He's a nice guy."

Kai looked into his grandfather's faltering eyes and saw the mist that had accumulated there. He knew that the old man wasn't raving. He was special now. He knew the old man was truth in a nutshell.

*　　　　　*　　　　　*

Lygophobia *(ly-goh-foh-bia) n.* fear of the dark

Interesting, isn't it, that when on our own, even in familiar surroundings like an apartment or house, and given the right mood, the right time of night, the right set of pre-event circumstances, our blood can still run cold when we have only risen from our bed for a quick glass of water. Perhaps we neglected to turn on the light, either from sleepiness or a sense of reckless abandon, and found ourselves listening for a noise from the black, back room to repeat itself; or the notion that, out of the corner of our eye, we just saw something move across the hallway.

The usual first reaction is to think, hey, this is my apartment, nothing has ever happened to me here, nor is it likely to. Then, another part of the brain, some might say the more cynical part, adds its two cents regarding the recent rise in home intrusions. But is that which spooked us really just the notion that a couple of misinformed burglars are here to steal our CD collection? Or is it (as some behavioural specialists might argue) that at some point in our past somebody or something caused us a fright as we lay in awake in our crib and now it is re-playing itself?

Probably not... In all likelihood it is, indeed, from our past. Not our immediate past, mind you, but from the grey days of our evolution when we dwelt in dark caves and twice a night "they" would come and snatch those furthest from the fire when they weren't looking and drag them off a short, dark distance to munch and crunch on femurs and skulls. What if, in the brief instant that the abduction took place, the adrenalin gushed in such super-charged quantities into the various areas of our ancestor's autonomic response systems that permanent and indelible changes were wrought in the collective consciousness and remain lodged deep in the very marrow of the tribe even today?

So here we stand, some one hundred thousand years later, trembling in the dark and for one brief second entertain the possibility that something very large with hair on it is about to rip us into bloody pieces. But, of course, it doesn't and we stumble back to bed, pull the blankets up and comfort ourselves with the thought that things like that hardly ever happen nowadays.

*   *   *

Albert wheeled the damaged bike into the Heminghurst silver mine, the front end still wet with animal viscera. The front forks were badly damaged. There's a couple of grand of repairs, he thought, angrily. The Crip came in behind him, sore and tired not only from the spill after hitting the coyote but also from the hour-long walk up the mine road, swearing and pushing the injured motorcycle in front of them. The only thing that had kept him going was planning and imagining how he would take it all out on Albert's skull soon enough. But they had to bring the bike in for the same reason that Crip couldn't just dump Albert's body in the brush. If he was going to get out of this at all it would have to be by covering up every possible trail to them. Albert could be reckoned with a little now and a lot later; just enough to punish him for his stupidity but not enough to lose his physical help.

Albert pulled the bike up onto its kickstand and knelt down to inspect the front end. "Shit," he said, "I don't believe this. This is fucked. This whole fucking trip is fucked. Look at the forks, man." He looked over the seat towards The Crip who was just leaning against the wet stone wall staring at him. He thought what he might do is just rush him and hope that The Crip wouldn't be able to aim and fire quickly enough to do any damage.

Just as he was thinking that, The Crip said, "Albert, you know what? I feel like killing you. And I think you probably wouldn't mind doing me either. But look, there's a few million dollars of coke sitting in the trunk of that car. I'm not going back inside and if we stay cool we might just get out of here in one piece. So, I'm not going to kill you. You are going to help me get Bob better. Then we are going to wait one or two days and then we are going to get the fuck out of here, sell the coke and live like fucking kings for the rest of our days. Okay?"

Albert quickly weighed this up. The Crip might be on the level or he might just be stalling for more time to rest up and then take Albert out with refreshed enthusiasm. On the other hand what about the dead cop? That was a major piece of work and the whole area was going to be crawling with feds and such when the word got out.

"What about the cop?" he said.

"What about him?" The Crip replied as he went to the water and took a drink.

"You killed a cop. They're not just going to let that go."

"By the time they figure out that he wasn't killed in the parking lot of The Delta and figure out where he was killed, we'll be long gone."

"And the Brixtons…?"

"Well, you see, when the Brixtons turn up missing, the cops are going to figure that they did it and split. There'll be an 'all points' out for a crater-faced old man and his fat son driving a black Chevy, right?"

Albert had to admit that this was so. As diversions go, they couldn't have planned it better. As long as no-one came to the mine. And as long as no-one had seen them dump the cruiser behind the pool hall they'd probably have the time they needed.

"Alright, but what about Bob? He's not going to be able to ride with a hole in his leg."

"We'll do what we can for him. I owe him that much. If he can ride when we leave, okay, if not then... I'll take care of it."

"Where is he?"

"In the side room... stoned out of his mind. Did you get the bandages and stuff?"

"In the bags..."

The Crip came over to the bike and opened the leather saddle bag and took out the medicine and walked over to the small room. Albert was beginning to feel a little shady what with the spill from the coyote and the disgusting stench that was beginning to build up from the now-spoiling carcasses of the Brixtons. He took some water and ran it over his head, feeling the coolness slide down his neck and through his shirt. He pulled a piece of chocolate from his coat pocket and sat against the bike and ate it.

Then the Crip came back.

"He's gone!"

"What do you mean?"

"I mean, he's gone. He was in the room over there."

"Maybe he went outside when he realized you weren't here."

They went out into the night once more. The moon was beginning to drift down as the dawn approached and the wind and the crickets were all they could hear. The Crip motioned Albert off to the right and he went left. They walked along the Mesa wall and then turned off after a while, circling about, peering under brush and rock until they met up again a hundred yards or so out from the mine entrance.

"Nothing," said the Crip. "You…?"

"No. Maybe he went to the highway."

"He couldn't get that far on that leg."

"Let's search the cave again."

They walked back to the cave and turned the lights of the Chevy on, lights that were beginning to dim as the battery gradually wore down. They looked throughout the area. Mystic Bob was nowhere to be found.

"Well, if he wandered out into the desert, he's probably dead by now. Or will be soon," said Albert.

"We can't leave him out there. Someone might find him."

"Well, we won't find him tonight. We don't even have a flashlight."

"You didn't get a flashlight?"

"You didn't ask me to get a fucking flashlight!"

"It didn't occur to you that, spending a couple of days in a cave, we might need one?"

Albert was about to call the Crip something unsavoury but was stopped by a laugh. A distant, insane cackle that started off low and built and echoed from the walls until it was a deafening cacophony of confused hilarity that bounced and careened from the cave sides.

"He's down in the fucking tunnel," said the Crip.

"Fuck me," said Albert.

"Let's go," The Crip said and started for the tunnel.

"There's no light down there," said Albert.

"Pull the Chevy as close as you can to the tunnel and shine the lights down."

"Look, the angles too steep and I told you before I thought I heard an animal. It could be a fucking bear. I'm not going down there."

The Crip pulled out his gun. "Stop your fucking whining will you? Get the shotgun. If there's a bear down there we'll have it for fucking dinner, won't we?"

Albert went to the car and drove it as close as he could to the descending mouth of the tunnel. Even from here he could see that the light only intruded to a depth of thirty or forty feet. He hated the dark; always had. He took the sawed-off twelve-gauge from the back seat and checked the magazine. Full but for the one shell that Bob had used to turn Lonny inside out.

As he came back to the Crip there was another burst of maniacal laughter but it was suddenly cut off and there was only a repeating echo of it fading away into the darkness.

"Let's go," said the Crip and began to walk down into the wet gloom of the tunnel. Albert followed behind about ten feet. Inside of a minute they were in relative blackness and what light still permeated from the car was rapidly growing dimmer. Albert could just make out the shape of the Crip ahead of him, limping down into the nothingness.

"We can't go much further," he said to the Crip in a tense whisper. There could be a shaft in the floor or anything down here."

"If Bob can make it down here, we can,"

"Fuck this," said Albert. "I'm going back."

Then there was another shriek of laughter that made his heart skip a beat. But it was much closer now and somehow, from up above. He looked up. Then the Crip tripped over something as another, larger something seemed to be moving up the tunnel ahead of them. Was it Bob? Then the car battery died and the lights sputtered out. There was a short, silent pause before the boom of the shotgun exploded with a ferocious flash into the dark. Then everything was quiet again.

CHAPTER FOUR

TETE A' TETE

The sunlight bouncing off the dresser mirror caught Steven flush in the face. It had for the last few minutes as a matter of fact and the smell of the smoke-infused hotel room was an instant reminder of where he was. But it wasn't that which had woken him, it was the sound of police radio chatter and cars and men talking in somber voices below his window. He recognized it immediately as the matter-of-fact, let's-get-this-job-done, seriousness of a crime scene investigation.

He pushed back the covers and went over to the windows where he pulled at the blinds cord, opening it enough to be able to glance down into the parking lot beside The Delta pool hall. There were three cruisers and half a dozen police down there... and an ambulance. They seemed to be concentrated around another cruiser parked towards the back entrance of the hall. The area had been taped off and one or two passers-by were watching two paramedics struggle to get something out of the back seat of the cruiser. Steven watched as the body of Officer Rick Jennings, his open shirt covered in blood, was extricated and laid on the ground beside the vehicle.

"Man, I don't believe this," Steven said to himself and hurried to dress, not worrying about cleaning up. He hastily pulled a sweater over his head and scrambled to put on some jeans and his trainers. Then he grabbed the key to the room and his wallet and headed out of the door and down the back stairs that he figured would come out onto the lot. They did.

He walked out into the crisp morning air and made his way over to the tape line and the uniformed cop that was guarding it, keeping the gathering crowd at bay. He could see two plain-clothes guys talking to the paramedic who was shaking his head. Not good, he thought. That doesn't look good.

He spoke to the uniform. "Hey there," he said. The uniform said nothing, his attention focused on two guys who were pushing to get through the tape.

"Back off there, Mitch," he growled. One of the two men turned.

"Come on, Bill, what's going on? That cop dead?" the man said.

"Looks pretty bad to me..." said the other. "Oh Christ, is that Rick Jennings?" Then he whispered something to his colleague and headed off up the street.

"Just lay off the tape will ya? You guys will find out when we all know, okay?"

The two guys were obviously press. Steve leant into the thin cop. "Officer, I'm Steve Walker. San Francisco PD," he said and flashed his detective's badge at the uniform. The officer glanced down at it and then back up at Steve, a confused look on his face.

"What do you mean? You're here from Frisco?" he said, trying to put the two things together and remain professional with his dead friend lying but twenty yards away.

"Look, sorry, it's on something unrelated. Is that your captain over there?" he said pointing at the older of the two plain-clothes. The other reporter was starting to take an interest in their conversation and Steven felt kind of trapped now.

"Captain McKinney, yeah," said the cop.

"You think I could have a quick word?" he asked.

"Listen Sergeant, he's pretty busy right now, I don't think..."

"I know, I know. I don't want to chat. I stayed at that hotel last night," Steven said, pointing up at his window. "I checked out that pool hall a bit before I turned in, might have something useful about all this. I'm not trying to intrude."

The cop looked him up and down for a second. "Wait here," he said and walked over to the growing group of plain-clothes staring at the body and the cruiser. He touched the shoulder of the big man in the middle and received a quick glare before pointing over to Steven and saying a few words. The expression on the other policeman's face changed to something like interest and together the two walked back to where Steven waited. The reporter, definitely aroused now, hovered closer although not too close to get shoved off.

"You're from Frisco?" said McKinney as he got closer. "You the guy they sent up about the other killing south of here?"

"Yeah, Steve Walker..." He held out his hand that, after a moment of hesitation, McKinney took a hold of briefly. "Sorry to see all this."

McKinney looked him in the eye for a second. "Yeah... Look, we're pretty busy right now..."

"I know. I just wanted to let you know that I was hanging around here a bit last night. I saw one or two people... of interest, going in and out. I was gonna go in there today to start trying to get a feel for your town... at least that particular element of it."

"Did you see the cruiser come in?"

"No, I was out front as late as nine and then I went up to my room. Right up there," he said pointing out his window. "I looked out before I went to bed, around eleven, and it wasn't there then; just a couple of cars and a bike."

"Okay, well that's helpful Steve. Look it's going to be nuts for the next while. I know you were planning to come into today, but it might be better to make it tomorrow. You're seeing Lewison, right?"

"Yeah, your drug squad leader..."

McKinney laughed, humourlessly. "That's rich. Lewison *is* the drug squad. This is a small town Walker. You'll find that out quick enough."

"Okay, I'll check in tomorrow. If there's anything I can do, please call me here at the hotel. I'd be happy to help out any way I can."

"Good. Maybe write down anything you can think of that you saw. Describe the cars and the bike and so forth, and you could bring that in with you tomorrow," McKinney said and started to walk away.

"Good luck," said Steve.

"I don't think we'll need it," said McKinney over his shoulder. "It looks like the scumbags that ran this dump are in the frame. They

117

haven't been seen since yesterday." He stopped for a moment and glared at the reporter who just put up his hand, guessing what the big man was about to say.

"Its okay, Captain, I get it."

McKinney turned and walked away. The reporter came over to Steven. "Did I hear that right, you're here to investigate that murder down on the highway?"

"Something like that… See you around," said Steven as he walked off to get some eggs.

*   *   *

Kai watched Nascha from the back porch of the house as his grandfather made his way slowly up the trail to the Mesa top. Kai was a little nervous about this. His grandfather had made a lot of improvement in the last couple of days and was talking more, eating fairly regularly (at least as much as he'd ever done) and seemed pretty mobile as evidenced by his fairly rapid advance up the rocky slope. Kai had wanted to go with him but Nascha had insisted on going out for a bit by himself. To think, he had said. It was four o'clock in the afternoon and Kai had been home from school for about twenty minutes before Jim had gone with Joey Wencha, his part-time helper, to scout out some areas for the upcoming corporate walkabout. Kai had been anxious to spend time with Nascha only to now see him go off by himself. As he watched Nascha climbing up higher and higher on the narrow trail, he thought to himself, "this is crazy, I should be with him." So he went inside to get a jacket and go up after the old man.

He entered the kitchen and grabbed his leather jacket from the back of the chair and took a couple of oranges from the bowl on the table before stepping out again onto the porch. He glanced up at the trail but could see nothing of Nascha at all now. Maybe he was sitting down to rest Kai thought but further inspection of the cliff face revealed no sign of him.

Kai started running, passed through the gate at the back of the property and sped up the first slopes towards the trail and the side of the mesa that was just under Face-in-the-rock. He slowed down a bit as he hit the part of the trail with the greatest angle of rise so as not to exhaust himself. He knew better than to try to run up a mountain. The two visages stared down at him as he passed onto the portion of the path where he had last seen Nascha. Still there was no sign of him and he was quickly approaching the area where the trail was eroded and getting to the next solid part of the path was problematic at best.

When he got to the eroded cliff face he looked down with some hesitation into the ravine that separated the two sides, half expecting to see Nascha's broken body lying down below. But there was nothing. Then he heard his name being called and looking up he spotted Nascha standing on the first rocky ledges of the Mesa top. Kai hadn't been up there for weeks because of the severity of the climb and yet there was Nascha, smiling and waving down at him and beckoning him up. Kai stood there, stunned, looking up. Then he started picking his way over the broken boulders to the other side of the path. When he had accomplished this, over the course of about ten minutes, he continued up to where Nascha was sitting on a pile of stones.

Out of breath and panting fiercely, Kai made the last few steps and fell on his butt beside the old man. Nascha was not only breathing easily but almost seemed sleepy.

"How the hell..." said Kai in between gasps, "did you manage that?"

Nascha opened an eye and pointed to the sky. Kai looked up, shading his eyes against the sun but could see nothing.

"What?" he asked with something like frustration in his voice. "I don't see anything."

"Look again," said Nascha. "High in the clouds..."

Kai peered upwards and finally spotted a small black dot drifting between the white cirrus.

"What's that? A hawk?" he speculated.

"Crow," Nascha replied and stood up and continued walking along the rim of the mesa.

Kai shook his head and rose and followed his grandfather. "What, you're saying the crow brought you up here?"

"Well, I can't fly, Kai."

"But..."

Nascha held up a hand indicating he wanted Kai to shut-up. He did. "Listen."

They stood silently on the barren roof of Black Mesa and the wind whined and moaned around the rocks and stumpy cactus heads. Kai loved the sound of the wind up here. It was alive and breathing like an animal. It moved and changed its mind on occasion and sometimes hid altogether. Then would pounce on you as you rounded a boulder, pushing you this way and that and then letting you go. There was hardly a day when it wasn't this way, except before a storm when all would go still and the silence would, as they say, become deafening.

"There's something different. Do you hear it?"

Kai strained to hear what his grandfather was talking about and, for one moment, thought he heard something; a soft murmur underneath the ever-present voice of the wind. But then it was gone.

"I don't know, granddad."

Nascha looked at Kai and studied his face for a moment before putting out his hand and touching the top of his head, running his fingers through his hair. "Tell me about your school, Kai," he said, softly.

"My school...?" Kai replied. "There's not much to tell really. We study, go to class. It's stupid. I don't enjoy it."

"How come?"

"Because it doesn't mean anything to me. You mean something to me. This place, Jim and Lucy and the other people on the Rez, they mean something. They're important. What happened in Europe in the seventeen hundreds...? I don't care about that."

"They're just stories, Kai, people's stories. Like ours I suspect."

"No... not like ours. It's mostly about who owns what and when."

"Possession is nine-tenths of the law." Nascha said slowly.

Kai looked at his grandfather. "Are you feeling okay, granddad," he asked.

Nascha took a friendly swipe at his grandson. "I heard that on TV once. It's what they believe, you know. It's not their fault." He could see that Kai wasn't following him. "It doesn't hurt to understand other people, Kai. People are people. Have you got friends now?"

"I guess you'd say the two guys I climb with are my friends."

"And you like them?"

"Sure, they're okay. They're pretty funny actually."

"Are they both Europeans?"

"No, one is Asian and the other is African-American."

"What about a girl?" Nascha asked.

Now Kai was getting a little awkward. "No... well, yeah. Kind of, I guess."

"What's her name?"

"Allison."

"White?"

"Yeah..."

"Well, there you go."

"What do you mean, 'there you go'?"

"If you want to know about her you have to know about her people, don't you?"

Kai could see where this was going and was getting annoyed. It wasn't that simple. The Europeans were all over the place. Their stories were all over the place. You couldn't pick up a book or turn on a TV or walk down a street in town without hearing their stories. He was fed up to death with their stories.

"If I never heard another white story or saw another white movie, I'd still have more than enough to go on," Kai said.

Nascha laughed. "Yes, I suppose that's true. Just try to keep an open mind, will you?" He paused. "Is she pretty?"

"Oh yeah," said Kai. Then he laughed. What was he getting upset for? He was sitting on a mountain top with his rapidly recovering grandfather shooting the shit. He relaxed physically with a sigh as the two of them stopped and looked down. After a moment of stillness, Nascha spoke again.

"Kai, things are changing; have changed. I think that something big is coming our way and we have to be ready for it."

"Like what?"

"Not sure exactly, but look... You can help me, huh? My strength isn't good and I may need you. We may need each other."

"I've always needed you, granddad," said Kai.

Nascha put his arm around Kai's shoulder and they stood for a moment like that. Then Nascha laughed. At nothing, really, and Crow cawed up aloft, his own, belligerent, crow laugh drifting down and mixing with that of the grandfather and his grandson as they made their way back down the trail.

*　　　　　*　　　　　*

"Karen! Come on in!"

Okay Kilagrew held back the screen door to the small red-brick bungalow that sat at the very end of the very last street in town. Karen looked in and the wild idea of running away came to her but she didn't. She smiled instead but her feet still weren't moving forward. She started to feel panicky. Suddenly, a moth the size of a small bird winged in past Kilagrew's head and headed for the bright lights of broadloom.

"Damn!" said Kilagrew. "We're being invaded!" and he let the door go bang in her face and chased into the house after the dusty intruder. Karen laughed and pressed her nose against the screen and watched the mayhem unfold inside. Kilagrew, having disappeared into a cupboard, re-emerged with a rolled up magazine.

"Should I open the door?" Karen called in. "Maybe it will fly out."

"Yes, yes... come in, okay?! And no, close the door behind you," he called back and Karen made her way into the foyer as the sound of furious pursuit and paper bashing against walls ensued. There was a final smash accompanied by the sound of something small and made of glass hitting the floor. Karen peered around into the living room to find Kilagrew looking down at a broken figurine. The flattened moth fell from the wall where it had been temporarily pasted and landed on the floor with a diminutive thud. Kilagrew covered it with the crumpled men's health magazine. He looked devastated.

"That's a damn shame, okay?" he said. "That was a real beauty of a Kachina doll."

"That's too bad Herman. Did it completely shatter?"

"No, no, the doll's made of wood. The case it was in shattered, okay? But the glass cut the head off."

Karen looked closer and saw that this was true. The main body lay on the lamp table, the head, appropriately enough, on a cushion. Karen's eyes focused in on those of the Kachina head. Something inside her fluttered.

"Can it be glued back together?" she murmured, after a moment.

"I guess," said Kilagrew.

Great start, thought Karen. She had been worried about this evening since the first time Kilagrew had mentioned it. She had hoped that if she got through it all right then maybe the trip could be a normal outing for two colleagues. At first she had thought that it might be better to have him over to her place, on her own turf sort of thing. Then she thought no, it's easier to leave somewhere than to get rid of someone. She had toyed with the idea of dressing like a slob but then realized how ridiculous she was being. It's not like Kilagrew had groped her in the school lobby or something. And now, as he stood there looking at the head of the broken doll, she almost felt sorry for him.

"You collect those, do you?" she asked.

"Oh yeah, I'm a big fan of all things native. Can I get you a drink or something? Some wine, maybe?"

"Oh, no thanks, bit of a headache; maybe tea?" she asked.
"Hmm, no tea… just coffee, okay?" Kilagrew said with just a hint of disappointment in his voice.

"That would be great, thanks." Herman went off to get the java. "So, you have some slides from last year's trip, you said?"

"Yes, ma'am," he called back from the kitchen. "Video actually, we can watch it down in the den, okay? Just got a big-screen TV. You'll love it."

"Okay," said Karen, immediately aware that she was falling into the Kilagrew 'okay' vocal pattern. She wondered what it would be like to be married to Okay Kilagrew for some time, pick up the mannerism and show up at functions on a sea of 'okays' that would echo and re-echo as she matched and parried his okays with her own. Or perhaps she would develop her own verbal peculiarity as a counter-point. Perhaps something that rhymed with his... like "say" for instance. "Say, would you like some lemonade?" she would call from the screen door as moths by the thousands flew by. "Okay," the hearty reply would be heard from the garden as Kilagrew paused from mowing the lawn. Karen stopped and wondered for a moment if she was going mad.

"Here you go, Karen," said Herman handing her a mug. "Come down to my... lair." Kilagrew laughed after saying that; the kind of laugh that usually accompanies a joke that one has used many times.

With that laugh Karen knew she had nothing to fear from this man. She felt quite bad now that she had ever even considered it. Twenty years living in the big city she guessed. Not everyone was as conniving as the world would have you think.

She gasped when she walked down the stairs and entered the den. From floor to wall to ceiling the entire thirty by thirty foot space was covered with Native American paraphernalia. The walls were covered in tapestries and blankets, photos and paintings and masks; the floor awash with hand-woven carpets and baked, hand-made tile; from the roof hung dream-catchers and staffs. It looked like someone had opened a store for native art in his basement. She felt like asking how much for the coyote mask that stood out prominently above the brand new 53" Sony television monitor, isolated in the middle of one wall, lonely and self-absorbed in its twenty-first century casing.

"This is really something, Herman," she said.

"I got it at Best Buy" he replied.

"No, I mean the crafts and carpets and things."

"Right, yes. Sorry. Do you like them?" he replied. "I've been collecting for years now."

"You really have a lot of... items."

"Just over three thousand, okay? Worth about a hundred grand now I think."

"I hope you have it insured." There was a pause as Herman considered this. A look of panic started to come into his eyes. "You mean you don't?" Karen said.

Then there was a sound of bells tinkling. Not unlike that bells that native dancers wear around their ankles during ceremonies; only electric.

"Well… the doorbell. I wonder who that could be?" Kilagrew said and bounded up the stairs, grateful for the opportunity to escape the insurance issue. A moment later she could hear two male voices talking. Karen wandered over and took the coyote mask from its holder. The face was almost hypnotic. She noticed a mirror near a bar made out of cactus barrels and went over to see what it would look like on. She placed it gingerly over her face and attached the string to one ear. She leant her head to one side and then the other, pleased with the match of the colour of the mask and her hair. It looked like the hair was actually growing out of the mask. Then she heard the sound of two pairs of feet tromping down the basement stairs. She quickly tried to take the mask off but the string was caught in her earring. She struggled for a second and then turned to face the door, half-woman and half-coyote. Kilagrew entered with Harry Babcock on his heels.

"I'm sorry," she said sheepishly, her voice reverberating from behind the papier-mâché. "I was trying on the mask and…"

"Mask…? What mask?" said Harry with a laugh. Kilagrew went over and helped Karen untangle herself.

"I'm so sorry, Herman. I hope I haven't damaged it," she said.

"No, no, it's fine. You look great in it," Okay replied.

"Say, what were you two getting up to down here, anyway?" Harry leered.

"Harry was just passing by," Herman explained. "He lives the next block over and thought he'd drop in."

"Didn't mean to intrude," said Harry.

"Not at all Harry; it's good timing actually. We were just going to watch some video."

"Oh yes?"

"From last year's trip, okay? Then discuss some planning," Herman said.

"Why don't you join us?" said Karen as she sat down with as much dignity as she could muster.

"Don't mind if I do," Harry said, "as long as I don't have to wear the bull mask over there."

Harry and Karen both laughed. Herman didn't.

*   *   *

A mineral laden drop of water flashed down from some unseen height, free-falling like an aquatic sky-diver down between gaps and crannies and landing, flat-faced, with a plunk into a pool of rank cave water not far from the ear of Albert Bader. Small specks of the brown water thrown up from the pool gathered near his brow and dripped slowly down his cheek, winding their way between his nose and its clotted blood and running over and through his slightly parted lips. He gagged slightly and rolled to one side, coughing. His arm hurt, his leg hurt and more or less every other part of him. And for some reason he couldn't hear out of one ear. He pushed his way up into a sitting position with his back against the sharp rock of the cave wall. There was a dim light coming from above and now that he had both eyes open his pupils were doing their best to widen to the right aperture that would allow him to look about. He was in a smaller cave now, a cave that somehow had been dressed up as a disco. The walls were lined with what looked like sunken strips of faded tin foil. They were all around, up each wall and across the floor, reaching up towards the light coming in from above.

"It's silver," said a voice from across the space... The Crip's voice.

Albert forced his sore neck to pivot slightly to the left and could see The Crip, sitting in much the same position as he was, about fifteen feet away.

"I can't believe it. I come nine hundred miles to score drugs and I strike silver," he said and laughed a dry laugh that ended up as a cough.

"Where are we?" Albert asked as he tried to stand up. He could do it but it hurt so he slumped back down.

"In a side cave off the main shaft... When you fired off that shotgun a hole opened up in the wall and the ground gave way and we slid down here. There's the hole up there." He pointed to an opening about twenty feet up the wall at the top of a ramp formed by the crumbled line wall.

"Well, let's get out of here," Albert said and once again raised himself up to his feet.

"We can't," said The Crip.

"What do you mean we can't? We can climb that rubble easy enough," Albert said looking up again at the hole in the wall.

"He won't let us," said The Crip.

"He...? Who? Who won't let us?" Albert asked.

"Bob. He's sitting up there at the opening. He's got a gun. He says we can't come up. He says we're evil."

"What are you talking about," said Albert. "I'm getting out of here. You stay if you want." He started to scramble up the side, his feet slipping and sliding away but making progress as he clawed his way upwards. Suddenly there was the easily identifiable click of the hammer of a .45 being slapped back.

"Go back," came the tense whisper of Mystic Bob's dry voice.

"Bob?" said Albert.

"Don't try that Bob stuff on me, you evil bastard. I know what you are. I've seen you. I know what you look like. I know..." Then there was laughter; the crazy laugh that one usually associates with somebody that has lost a major chunk of reason.

"Bob, you let me out of here man."

"Bob. Bob. Bobby bob bob," was the lunatic response. "Bob bob bibbidy bob bob," ...blam came the explosion of the .45, one step ahead of the bullet that whizzed past Albert's ear and ricocheted at least ten times off rocks and stones before spending itself in the dirt. Albert raised his face from the rubble where he had hit down hard as the gun went off.

"Bob, fuck off!" Another click but this time, no roar... The gun had jammed. "Ha!" called Albert. "You are dead now you asshole," he yelled and started to crawl furiously up to the hole. The Crip was up now too and starting to climb.

"Get him, Albert," he yelled as he fought his way up on his withered leg.

Albert finally got to the opening and pushed himself into the main shaft. There was light now in the shaft, too, coming from the entrance. The Crip appeared moments later, breathing heavily.

"Where is he?" he said.

"I don't know. He must have gone down the shaft again or he's pushed the boards off the entrance and gone outside.

"Forget him. Let's get the bikes."

They went up into the main cave and got the bikes over towards the entrance. "Help me get the stuff and we'll get out of here," The Crip said and they went to the long, black Chevy to start hauling the bags of coke into the trike. But when they pried the lid up the only things they were confronted with were little bits of Lonny and nothing else.

"What the hell..." mumbled Albert.

"He took it!"

"Who...?" Albert asked, dazed.

"Who do you think? Bob! The bastard took the whole stash."

"How... when? We were only in the hole for half an hour."

"He must have taken it out when I went to town to get you... Fuck! The money..." The Crip ran to the trike and opened up the hatch. "He took it! The bastard took everything!"

"Where could he have put it?"

"I don't know. He couldn't carry all of it around at once so he must have stashed it. Either deeper in the cave or outside somewhere."

Albert stared down the mine tunnel. About the last thing in the world he wanted to do was go back down there. "Maybe we should just blow this thing off, Crip," he said. "This fucking thing is cursed six ways from Sunday. We should just get out."

The Crip just stared at him for a second and then said, quietly, "Listen, Albert. I am not going back to Frisco with no money and no stash. And the only way you're getting out of here without helping me is in a box. So pull that trike over to the tunnel. We'll wheel it in as far as we can for the light. If the stuff is down there Bob would have had to do the same thing."

"What if he's not down there?"

"Then we start looking outside. He couldn't have gone far."

"How the hell is he getting around like that with a fucking bullet hole in his calf?"

"Something's happened to him. He's nuts. He always was nuts. Maybe the shit he was taking for his leg pushed him over the edge. Let's go."

Together they started up the trike and slowly began to make their way into the shaft. As they disappeared into the hole, the roar of their engine reverberated around the hills and died gradually, like so many other things, on the parched floor of the Arizona desert.

$$*\qquad\qquad *\qquad\qquad *$$

"Who is this?"

"Rosemary Clooney."

"Oh yeah, I forgot, the jazz thing."

Karen put down her knife and fork. "What do you mean 'oh yeah, the jazz thing'?"

Steven looked up at her. "Now don't get hot. I didn't mean anything by it. I was just remembering your musical preferences."

"You asked me to put something on the juke box."

"Yeah, but… look, skip it, okay?"

They sat in silence for a few minutes; Steven trying to induce appetite for his rapidly cooling spaghetti and Karen chewing on a piece of 'Italian' bread. The Matsoh Gazumba was really the only decent restaurant in town other than an over-priced Thai place near the city hall, so this was really the only place to come to for their dinner; Jewish-Italian cuisine… only in Newton. There was a pretty nice place in Steven's hotel too, but there was no way Karen was going there. She looked over at him and felt nothing but confusion. Compared to this her strange night at Kilagrew's, trading quips and stories with Okay and Harry Babcock had been a piece of cake.

"Maybe this was a mistake, huh?" she said, tipping a glass of merlot and watching the legs splice down the side.

Steven looked up. He felt sad. Sad that it had come to this; sad that a friendship and love affair had dribbled out to nothing; sad that something with such potential had become a burden to them both. And sad, also, that he had not been man enough to deal with it all before getting tangled up with Leanne. Still, as he looked into her eyes, he felt something; a reasonable facsimile of the tenderness that they had held for each other for so many years.

"Don't say that, Karen. We're just a little tense that's all. It's normal."
"I'm not tense," she lied.

"Okay, well, I am. It would have been hard even without this killing... Maybe it was stupid of me to think that we could have any kind of normal time with all this going on in the background. But, dammit, I couldn't come here and not spend time with you could I? You're important to me. It was the only reason I asked for the assignment out here, like I said."

"What's happening with the case?" Karen said, hoping to change the subject for a bit, "Any developments?"

"Well, everyone they have is working on the murder so the drug thing is on hold for a few days. They want to get it sewed up before the feds get involved. I told them I'd help out with any leg work they need done and San Francisco said okay. I can't really discuss the details but between you and me, I don't think they're on the right track. The funeral's next Saturday."

"I heard they think it's the Brixton people."

"You heard that? But it's just a day old," he said, amazed.

"It's a small town, Steve… no secrets here. I'm sure they already know about you and me if Mrs. Chavez has anything to do with it. Why couldn't it be the Brixton people?"

"Why would they kill a local cop? He wasn't investigating them. And why leave his car in their parking lot? I don't know. It's too easy. Doesn't smell right..."

"You sound like Sam Spade when you say things like that. Well, it's not like they're the mafia or something. They're just local thugs aren't they? Maybe they were just stupid local thugs."

"There's something else going on, too; something about this cop, Jennings. People are pretty tight-lipped about what's in the coroners report."

"Coroner, okay... can we change the subject now, Steve?"

"Yeah, of course, I'm sorry. How's the school life going?" He poured the rest of their litre of house red into his glass. He wished he had about four more litres going.

"Fine, we're gearing up for the big overnight out at Black Mesa. I can't believe that I'm actually looking forward to going camping. The kids are busting to get there."

"I can believe that. The mesa's out on the reserve, right?"

"That's right."

"I'm going out there tomorrow, actually. I said I'd ask around the reserve town about the Brixtons and such. Apparently the reserve police and the Newton police don't have a great relationship, so they thought it might be good for me to take a trip out there as an 'independent' kind of investigator. They don't have any jurisdiction anyway."

"How's your hotel?"

"Well it's great if you don't count a view of the murder scene."

Karen laughed.

"It's nice to hear you laugh, Karen," he said quietly. "I miss your laugh."

"Don't, okay Steve?" she said and put down her wine glass and then, after a moment... "Can you take me home do you think? I've kind of had enough for right now."

"Are you sure?"

131

"Yes. It's not you. I guess I just wasn't ready for this. Maybe we can see each other in a few days. Would that be okay?"

He was going to protest but thought better of it. "Sure. I'll get the check," he said and took out his wallet.

He paid and, together, they walked out into the cool evening air. The sound of music from a nightclub up the way drifted on the breeze and there was a smell of flowers that came down from somewhere to the north. The night sky was ablaze with stars even with the diffusing effect of the city light; in any other situation, romantic...

As they walked to the car Steven took her arm in his. She let it stay there.

"Steven..." she started to say.

"I know," he replied and opened the door to the car to let her step in.

*　　　　　*　　　　　*

The concept of genetic determinism ("I can't help it, I was born bad.") is not a new one. However, with advances in brain scan technology and DNA decoding, the future looks pretty bright for those who embrace the 'born bad' theory. PET scans can now be used to show, in some detail, the broken brain. Of course, it's used mostly for physical illness prognostications. More recently, however, mental illnesses such as depression have been shown to the world in full, 3D, Technicolor glory. An alcoholic who would rather reason his problem away than actually abandon the habit can now point to genetic sub-markers and bright blue blips on the old resonance scan to elude the hoary finger of personal responsibility. And in some cases, like alcoholism, the reasoning fueled by the need is obvious. "If I can justify it to myself then, by god, I can keep doing it."

But what about the career criminal? The one whom, studies tell us, doesn't give a tinkers cuss as to whether the sentence for armed robbery is five years or ten, they're damn well going to do it anyway. The psychos; the Natural Born Killers that people seem to be able to stomach on screen, in films and on television ad nauseum, because, let's face it, aren't they just a little bit sexy, those wild, we'll do anything and then fuck in a hidey-hole kind of folks.

132

Some might say, "sure, those psychopaths are sick, but you know what? If I didn't have to go to work at the bank everyday, I too would like to become a desperado. Not that I would want to kill anyone, mind you, because that would require extremely heavy penalties (and let's face it, it's the penalties that stop a lot of people from doing a lot of bad things) but I'd at least like to rob a bank or lead a gang or run a multi-national corporation... something despicable."

A few years ago, the American government, always on the lookout for clever ways of repressing its people, commissioned a study to look into the possibility of drugging urban youth before they became aggressive in later years; to remove the gang mentality by intervening intravenously in the lives of likely young street combatants. The plan only floundered when the man running the commission likened the subjects of his study to young primates in the jungle. Bad analogy... But, hey, the thought was in the right place. It is not hard to imagine this as a tip-of-the-iceberg scenario. Perhaps the results of this study have already born fruit in a mutually beneficial co-production with McDonalds, ensuring that the very grease in which all those charbroiled cow bits stuffed into all those sugary buns are sautéed, contains the neural inhibitors necessary to suppress all those delinquent hi-jinx.

Of course, for a large percentage of miscreants, the more obvious street crime is committed because the perpetrators don't have the brain power to reconcile their need for worldly goods with their intellectual lot in life. And, on the higher and more seamy levels, the corporate crimes (with their far larger victim manifests) well, here we are basically talking about morally bankrupt rich people. And morals, or a lack thereof, come with age and experience. So they can't use the born bad defense.

Some studies show, as in the case with alcoholism for instance, that certain genes can be "turned on" by certain experiences. So here we have a sort of fifty-fifty scenario in which a person pre-disposed towards evil because of genetic markers but never having displayed said evil, is suddenly called upon to, say, go to war for his country. He arrives on the sandy shores of 'Fill-in-the-blank-istan', watches his buddy's insides erupt all over the side of his Humvee and click, the little switch is turned on and Mr. Hyde leaps onto the scene... and then takes a plane home. Sometimes the choices that we make turn out

133

okay. And sometimes they make us into evil monster killing machines. Who can say what would have happened if Hitler hadn't dropped out of art school?

*   *   *

The Brixtons were one ugly family. Steven couldn't get that thought out of his mind as he headed into the murky confines of The Delta Pool Hall and Bar. He had been given pictures of Lonny and Ashford; Ashford with his caved-in face and Lonny with his obese, distended gut that almost looked like it had something growing inside it. Now, as he stood to one side of the bar and sized up Windover Brixton, standing behind the bar dispensing beer and eight-balls, he realized that the worst had been yet to come.

Windover had been burnt or something on one side of his head. So the hair that was left there hung in ratty snatches down the back of his neck starting at what would normally be the hairline. That was on one side. On the other, the greasy orange hair was receding from the right side of his scalp to the ear. It looked like something that had eaten an orangu-tan had crapped on his head. Then there was the burn mark on his left cheek running over his eye. Closer examination though, revealed that it wasn't in fact a burn but rather some sort of congenital aberration. Questioning this freak wasn't going to be as difficult as being forced to look at him.

Steven was here with another officer. One of Newton's finest. He had been allowed to accompany him as this was more or less connected with his mission in town, to locate and identify the source of the drug trade in the area and any possible connection to San Francisco's gangs. Detective Sergeant Morris Lewison was heading over to the bar to speak with the Brixton boy so Steven went with him.

"What do you guys want? I already talked to McKinney. I don't know where my dad is."

"What about Lonny?"

"Same. I have no idea."

"When was the last time you talked to them?"

"Day before yesterday. In here."

"And they didn't say they were going to be gone for a while?"

"No."

"Was Officer Jennings in here that night?" This came from Steven, the first time he had spoken. Windover looked him up and down.

"Who are you? You're not local. You fed?"

Lewison got a little closer to Brixton. "Never mind who he is, Winnie. You gonna give me something or are we gonna close this place down for a bit?"

"You can't do that."

"Try me. We've got a dead cop, Brixton, and his car was in your parking lot and you say you never saw him at all. And you don't know where your family is even though you never blow your fucking nose without telling them. Things are going to get mighty hard for you if you don't come up with something." Lewison had a strange look on his face; sort of somewhere between amusement and hunger. Steven had already started to like this diminutive copper the moment he had met him; big city attitude fighting a small town demeanour. Sort of like Andy of Mayberry on steroids.

"You guys don't want to hear anything about Jennings," Windover said, barely audible.

Lewison shot a glance at Steven. "What do you mean by that, Winnie?"

"You guys look after your own."

Lewison's arm shot out and he grabbed Brixton by the shirt and jammed him down hard against the counter top.

"If you're even beginning to suggest that Rick was on the take, you scumbag, you'd better think real hard about that, Winnie," Lewison snarled in his ear. Steven stepped back and took a look around at the one or two other customers in the joint. One of them had noticed the conflict but looked quickly back down at his cue stick as he sized up a shot.

"I'm not," moaned Winnie.

"Then what are you talking about?"

"He was a party guy. You know that. There's more than one guy with a good looking wife who wouldn't mind seeing him go away... out of town, too."

"What do you mean 'out of town'?" Steven asked.

"You know, out on the Rez. He had a piece going out there too."

"How do you know that?"

"We have… um, friends out there. He was out there every weekend." Lewison released Windover who straightened up, rubbing his chin which had just been dragged across the counter.

"Okay, I want a list of everywhere you think your father and brother might have gone. Phone numbers, everything, got it?"

"Yeah, alright… It'll take me a few minutes."

"Do it."

Windover went over to the back of the bar and took a piece of paper from a pad and started scribbling some stuff down on it.

"What do you think?" Steven asked Lewison when Brixton had gone.

"Bullshit mostly… Its true Rick got around. It's possible if he was screwing around with some lowlife's broad that maybe he got careless. But get this Walker, Jennings wife and kid are going to be burying him on Saturday and we don't want any of this spilling into that."

"I hear you. But listen, if there's anything to this we're going to have to go there sometime. If we don't the feds will. Somebody might have even been blackmailing him."

Lewison considered this. "Yeah, I know. But we can't be going too deep into that right now. We, the department, I mean…" Lewison looked at him. Steven knew what was coming.

"I could look into a couple of things," he offered. "Maybe start out on the reservation. Keep whatever I find to myself for a bit until after things cool down." Steven hoped he was giving Lewison what he wanted to hear. He was.

"Yeah, good… You know we want to find out who did this, don't you?"

"Of course… But there are other considerations. Anyway it will help me to get to know what's been going on out there drug-wise"

"Right. I appreciate it, Steve. Everyone will."

Windover came back at that moment and handed over the list. "That's all I could think of. And I wrote down the name of the chick out on the Rez that he's been seeing. She actually lives in town most of the time. A Summer I guess."

"A Summer?" Steven asked.

"A white chick that gets off on the Native American thing," Lewison informed him.

"I see," said Steven. "This is her here?" he said pointing at the list.

"Yeah, that's her. Lucy something..."

*   *   *

The softness of her lips still clung to his in Kai's fevered mind and as he pulled the big pickup into the driveway of his home he almost hit the old wheelbarrow laying there. It's not like he had never kissed a girl before, but man... this was definitely different. He couldn't have had a clearer impression of something in his head if it had been whacked there with a shovel.

He got out of the cab quietly and stood for a moment with his back up against the hood and felt the heat rising off the engine block. Then he walked up onto the front porch and stuck his head around to look inside the picture window. Nascha was there, sitting in the big easy chair with a tray in front of him. He was slowly going through some of his herbs, sifting some and cleaning the detris from amongst the roots. Big Jim was at the table reading some sort of pamphlet. It looked like it was probably a manual for some of the new equipment he had bought for his big trip next week. Lucy was nowhere to be seen. Maybe she was staying in town tonight.

Kai jumped off the porch and ran around to the back and sprinted up the path to the meadow and towards the mesa. The moon was bright and the wind was warm and as he ran he startled a deer in the brush that sprinted away in the same direction, its white tail bobbing up and down for a moment in front of him until it veered off to one side and disappeared into the night. He felt pretty much like that deer as he bounded through the scrub on his way to the cliff face.

His big date with Allison (that he had decided on after his talk that night with Nascha) had come off better than he could have hoped.

They had a great time, they laughed a lot, genuinely, and the dinner out was pretty sophisticated for a kid who had only eaten in two or three restaurants in his life. He hadn't made a fool of himself with the ordering anyway. And he had received what might possibly be the best kiss that anyone had experienced, ever. So soft that... Kai laughed again at the thought of it.

It was all good. There had been a bit of a tense moment when he had shown up at the Donkers house. What a last name. Allison had told him that she hated it and Kai had to admit it did have its problems. There had been a visible look of relief on her father's face when he came in. Kai had never had his hair very long anyway but from Mr. Donker's reaction, it looked like he had been expecting Crazy Horse to show up. But Kai was no fool. He knew the kind of thoughts that even well-meaning people like Mr. Donkers had, no matter how liberal they thought they were. He knew that even if he was the president of the Young Republicans and arrived in a tuxedo it could never be enough for a girl's father. So after a moment or two of small talk that had become increasingly friendly in tone, they had left and Allison had smiled and assured him that her father seemed to like him. She said she could tell this because he hadn't given her a curfew.

Then they had gone for dinner at a fancy Thai place that Allison knew. He had never had Thai food before and immediately found that he loved the peppery soups and dishes. There is something so magical about sharing the discovery of certain foods or places with someone you're crazy about. It seems like everything couldn't be more perfect and you think about nothing but the other person, the sensations of what you're eating or the air in the place you're standing. There is no threat in the future and your past seems to have led, unerringly, to this single event.

They had talked about school, of course, and the upcoming field trip; gossiped about this couple and that and even touched on the subject of the murder of the cop, but not for long. She talked about her job at the hospital and how sorry she had felt for Kai when he was going through the stuff with Nascha. And she talked about his taking up the name Kai and how she wished she could do that with her last name. He had made a lame joke about how Kai wouldn't make a very good last name but she had laughed just the same and told him how she thought the name Kai suited him much better than Billy. Then he had paid (he liked that sensation, too, for some reason even though it had completely drained his resources) and they had gone for a walk by the river and sat on a bench by an old, yellow tree. The water had rippled along and every now and then a fish would jump in the shallows.

In the end, he had worked up the courage to put an arm around her; her small shoulders feeling slim and delicate beneath his hand. Despite the hormonal urgings that all this had elicited (and that he had no choice but to recognize), he really didn't want any more than this and when, upon parting from the riverbank, she had raised her face to his and they had kissed, it was with the sweetest and most innocent of intentions. And yet, wow, how it had knocked him over! He had spent the last half hour, driving her home and saying goodnight and driving again back to the Rez in a complete fog. He thought at one point, they should add love to the influences under which you really shouldn't be driving; D.W.I.L. He laughed to himself when he realized he couldn't remember the last twenty minutes of the drive because he had been singing at the top of his lungs.

He thought about that moment in the park over and over again. Then he began to realize that now he couldn't wait to get back to school tomorrow. Because she would be there; and they would smile at each other and maybe she would even be willing to let others know about their night out. And then they would be a couple; boyfriend and girlfriend; Kai and Allison. Man!

*   *   *

"Cheap bastards!"

That's what was going through Steven's mind as he headed out of town towards the reservation in his rented Ford Focus. Grey and shapeless and no power... that was sort of how he was feeling in general so maybe the car was just a grim, particularly appropriate extension of himself. The office in San Francisco, already unhappy that his stay was going to be longer than he had anticipated and in a man-power shortage themselves, had reluctantly given him permission to rent the car, but at a minimum cost. Even this piece of crap had been an upgrade.

And the sun had been replaced by rain clouds and his relationship with Karen was going nowhere fast, although he had had little hope that it would really. He knew in his heart that he had dealt her a blow back in Frisco that would take an awful long time to make up for, if ever. He wasn't sure whether perhaps he should have just left her alone and let her get on with things. Of course he should have but then again he did still love her and he was, in fact, concerned when he had heard about the fire and in some way, a little guilty. If she hadn't come here, she wouldn't have been in the fire, etc. The convoluted logic of a man who was obviously trying to find a way of taking responsibility for things he should have accepted two years ago. Oh well, mistakes… what are you going to do?

He thought about the events of the last few days. The last thing he'd have thought he would be doing right now was playing private detective on a cop's murder. But in a way he liked the challenge and as long as he didn't offend anyone either out here or back at the department, he should be alright.

He pulled into the bypass leading into Sandy Hollow (or Tsas-Ka as he had to keep reminding himself.) As he rounded the bend leading past the main highway he spotted two native cops parked in a white SUV with Navajo Nation Police written on the side. He pulled over and got out. The two cops watched him as he walked over to their truck. They looked pretty severe.

"Hey there," he said as one of them rolled down the truck window and a blast of heavily conditioned air and cigarette smoke hit him in the face.

"Good day, sir, can we help you?" said the older of the two cops.

Steven pulled out his badge and flipped it over to show them. "I'm Detective Sergeant Steven Walker." The officer took the I.D. from him and gave it the once over.

"San Francisco PD... You're a long way from home aren't you?" he said handing it back to him.

"I talked to your commander this morning, Captain Dale? I'm on my way to see him about the cop murder in Newton. You must have heard about it."

"Yeah, we heard. Some of us are going to the funeral on Saturday."

"Oh yeah? That's great. They'll be glad."

"I doubt it," said the younger cop. "But we'll go anyway. He was a brother."

"Never mind that, Jack," the older cop said, then to Steven, "The main office is in Tuba City but I guess you know the Captain came out here for the day."

"That's what he said, yeah," said Steven. "Is it right in the village?"

"No, keep going into the valley a bit, about a quarter mile. You'll see the station on the left as you go."

"Thanks guys."

"No problem."

Steven returned to his car and headed into the town; if you could call it that. A few buildings in various states of collapse; what looked like an abandoned school on its own road between the main highway and the cutoff and in the distance he could see what looked like a Quonset hut. He headed for that and found that it was, indeed, the local office of the Navajo Nation Police.

But there was nobody home. This wasn't going to be easy, he realized, and headed back to the cutoff to speak to the two cops. But when he got there they too were gone.

"That figures," he said to himself and drove back to the village. They must have known there was no one there; the bastards. There was a small convenience store with a couple of gas pumps outside and he pulled in and shut off the engine. There was no movement from inside, in fact there didn't seem to be any movement in the village at all. As he got out of the car he felt like he was standing in the middle of a film-set from a western (other than the modern props provided by the gas station and the scattered phone and electric poles, some leaning crazily to one side.)

He walked to the screen door of the store and went inside. There was a man standing behind the counter looking at him and two other women sitting beside a barrel and talking. They looked up for a moment as he came in and then returned to their conversation. The man behind the counter spoke:

"Can I help you?" he asked.

"Hi, I'm a police officer attached to the Newton police. I was supposed to meet a Captain Dale here in town? But he isn't at the office. Do you know him?"

"Sure. Fayette Dale? He's my cousin."

"Really. Did he stop in today?"

"Yep. 'Bout an hour ago. On his way out of town."

"Don't suppose he left a message for me?"

"Nope."

"Do you have a land phone I could use? My cell doesn't seem to work out here."

"No, there's been a problem with that lately. It's the hills I figure. Full of iron, you know?"

"Really? Well, thanks, if I could use your phone I could call and see if he left a message for me at our office."

"Right there by the door."

"Uh-huh. Thanks."

Steven dialed up the desk at the Newton office and there had in fact been a message. Dale had to get back to Tuba City as there had been an armed robbery and he couldn't hang around. He suggested talking to an officer named DougWencha who was local. He might be able to help.

Yeah, fine… That was undoubtedly Wencha in the white SUV that was now nowhere to be seen. It looked like he was going to have to start from scratch. He returned to the counter and the old Indian behind it.

"Listen, I'm looking for a woman; but I only have a first name. Maybe you know her. Lucy?"

"Lucy, huh? No, can't say I do."

"How about Big Jim's Lucy?" said the larger of the two women by the barrel.

"She's white," said the old man.

"Well, that could be her," said Steven. "We don't know for sure if she's native. Just that Rick Jennings, the Newton officer that was killed the other day, may have met her out here."

"Yeah, bad business that killing. But this Lucy wouldn't have had anything to do with that. She spends a lot of time out here with Jim Ahiga. They're engaged. And why would she have met a Newton policeman out here?"

"Well, maybe I can find that out. Where can I find the Ahiga place?"

"Back down the highway a bit towards Newton. Close to the mesa."

"Okay, well, thanks. You've been a lot of help."

"Okay then," said the old man as Steven left the store.

The old man was right, of course. Why would Jennings come out here to talk to some woman he could talk to back in town? And surely he wasn't having an affair with the woman right under the nose of her fiancé; a fiancé with the imposing name of Big Jim. Of course, that might explain his present condition of non-living.

Five minutes later he was banging on another screen door. This one belonging, he hoped, to the Ahiga family. There was a sound of movement from within and then there was an old, smiling face looking at him through the mesh.

"Jim Ahiga?" Steven asked.

"Nope. He's out back." Nascha replied.

"Okay." Steven walked around the side of the house and found Big Jim Ahiga cutting up some fire wood. Jim stopped when he spotted him.

"Yes?" said Jim, picking up his shirt and wiping the sweat from his forehead.

"Steven Walker. I'm a detective helping out in Newton with the police killing."

"What can I do for you?" said Jim as he walked over to the porch and took a long drink out of a pitcher of water. He offered it to Steven.

"No thanks. I'm actually looking for a woman named Lucy."

"Lucy Fleming? What for?" Jim asked, confused.

"Routine questioning, that's all. Her name came up in connection to Jennings, the dead officer, and we wanted a word with her. She actually lives in town, I understand."

"Yeah, but if you know that what are you doing here?"

"Well, I just found that out. We only knew her first name and that Jennings may have met her out here."

Jim frowned and sat down on the deck. He didn't say anything for a minute and then got up and went inside. Steven was beginning to wonder what was happening but a moment later Jim returned with a photo.

"Listen, I'm going to tell you this so maybe it will save some trouble for Lucy, okay?"

"Well, okay…"

"This is a picture of Lucy and her sister Mary."

Steven looked at the photo of two pretty girls sitting together on a beach near an ocean somewhere. They both had matching red sweaters on and had the same long auburn hair. They were virtually identical.

"They're twins?" asked Steven.

"No but they might as well be. You can see how much they look like each other. They're actually a year apart. People are always getting them confused. Anyway, Mary, the one on the left, was seeing Jennings. I told Lucy that Mary must be crazy. Jennings was married and all. Anyway they'd been carrying on for about a month before Lucy told me about it. Mary and Rick used to meet at the old Motel 8 up the road on the other side of the Rez. They'd shack up on the weekends."

"Did they do that last weekend?" asked Steven.

"I don't know. You'd have to ask Mary."

"Can you tell me her address?"

"Yeah, I'll write it down. Listen, you'd have found out sooner or later anyway but don't tell them this came from me, alright. I knew she wouldn't be able to keep the affair a secret after the murder. But wherever this is going, I can tell you one thing. Mary is as gentle as Lucy and there's no way she'd kill anyone."

"I appreciate your help."

"Yeah, well…"

At that moment Nascha came out onto the porch with a cat in his arms. He put the cat down on the step. It immediately dashed off into the tall grass.

"Phone call, Jim; it's Lucy. She can't find Mary."

*   *   *

Meat jump… me lasting a night-sky… creepy crawly desert thing… shivery skin inserts that bite…

These and other thinky fragments toured the various synapse locations of Mystic Bob's brain, stopping here and there for a visit to the museum of Bob's memories or riding on the roller coaster at the fun-land that was Bob's imagination. His sensory inputs were overwhelmed. The cornucopia of pharmaceutical agents that had found their way into his blood stream in the last forty-eight hours was having its way with Bob.

He crept, Gollum-like, through the scrub of the Black Mesa, hands and feet scrabbling over rocks and pausing every now and then to observe some light phenomenon playing out through the ends of his fingers.

He had been in relative control immediately after the shooting, having assuaged his throbbing calf with some highly opiated hash that had left him feeling, well, not a lot actually. He had laid in the back room of the cave with the body of the deceased Ashford Brixton until the smell had permeated even his wrecked nasal membranes and he had crawled out into the main room to watch The Crip kill the cop and drag his body out to the cruiser. Then The Crip had come back and, seeing that Bob had wormed his way out into the cave, tried to pull him back into the smaller room. But Bob had resisted and managed to mumble out something about wanting to stay away from Brixton. The Crip had told Bob that he had to go into town but the warped sound of the words flowing from his mouth in a sort of mixed soup of verbiage, coloured and high-lighted here and there by the effect of the drug, meant little to Mystic Bob. Bob just stared up at the melted, twisting shape of The Crip's face until it went away.

This wouldn't do. He had had a lot of experience with being completely wasted and he knew, not unlike a sort of anti-medicine man, what the various combined effects of his drugs would do. What he needed now was some natural amphetamine; which he had if he could just find his fucking bag. Then he realized that it was where it usually was, hanging from his neck, but it had twisted around and was hanging over the shotgun holster still attached to his back. He took some of the water that The Crip had left him and poured it over his head and with this temporary, relative return to consciousness managed to roll over on to one side and unclip the holster. It fell away and the rawhide bag containing his stash swung back around to his chest. He opened the bag and took out a vial of bluish liquid and loosening the top poured three or four drops onto his tongue. The effect was immediate and he felt energy return to his limbs. The cold increased and the pain in his calf came back but not prohibitively. His mind 'cleared' if you could really use that word with such a one as Bob.

Then he heard his name.

It came into him and was warm and seductive. He almost felt turned on. It wasn't so much a whisper as a soft pulse and, if he had been in tune with it, he would have realized that it probably matched the tempo of his rapidly beating heart. Somewhere in his head he knew that everyone that he had come here with or met in the last while was either dead or outside the cave. But logic was running like a bunny in the wind. All he could really think was that he had to get to the source of that voice and that it was coming from down the tunnel.

Taking a broken shovel handle from against the wall he pushed himself up into a standing position using the tool as a crutch. He hobbled to the mouth of the tunnel and looked down into its mouth. The walls waved and pulsed and in his head he could hear the name being repeated over and over, slowly, softly... he took his first few steps into the dark.

For some reason he could see in this pitch black womb. He could see for a distance of about twenty feet even though there was no apparent source of light. He made his way along the abandoned mine car track and eventually came to a fork. One side seemed to end in a rock face about ten yards away, the other continued into the murk. He took that route and soon found himself against the end of that tunnel, too. But there was a crack, larger than a crack really, to one side and he found if he put his ear up against it he could hear the soft pulse of the voice calling him emanating from within. He squeezed one shoulder in and then the other and finally pushed his chest, which seemed to give way like rubber and allow him access to the larger space on the other side.

Then he was not alone. There was some sort of snake… no, lizard, on the ground in front of him that looked up at him with nonchalant friendliness. That was freaky. But not nearly as freaky as when it opened its mouth and said his name.

This was new to Mystic Bob. In his past, in the heady days of his big acid experiences, he had spoken to things before and even had a conversation with a tree once, but there was no acid now. He was, however, prepared to learn. He was an astronaut in the unexplored regions of outer consciousness and he had a lot of confidence in his ability to return in one piece. He had made a career out of it actually. Despite the fact that he rode a bike now with The Crip and his loser friends, Mystic Bob was more than the sum of his parts. This was but one phase in the juicy if somewhat self-indulgent life that had been the journey of Mystic Bob. He had been a soldier, an actor, a long distance truck driver, and played in a high-profile rock band. Not in that order, of course. Now he was into the most extreme set of circumstances he could come up with, riding shotgun on The Crip's stage coach. He'd never had a moment in his life that he could look back on and say, "Well, that was normal." But there was more to Bob than his drugged out wastrel image. Bob had a mission of sorts and that was to push himself, in a sort of hyper-Castenadian fashion, until he met with some ultimate conclusion that would explain and soothe his constant sorrow. It looked like it might be just up ahead. At least that's what the lizard was telling him.

But even the hallucinogenic meanderings of his most visual drug experiences couldn't have prepared him for the confrontation in the cavern ahead. And when he found himself standing face to face with two ancient demon entities, trapped and struggling in the crystalline rocks and felt their presence and heard their words, it was game over. The safety line that he had always used to drag his ragged mental space-suit back to the mother-ship snapped and he floated away, into an abyss from which he would never return. But it was alright. The sorrow was gone. He knew now why he was never able to quite 'get it'.

There was nothing to get. Or rather, there was so much to get, that in his little brain pan, or that of Sartre for that matter, there just wasn't enough storage space. You couldn't run the software of the real universe on the primitive operating system that was the human brain.

And so he gave himself over to the first of the demons and knew that, temporarily at least, he was safe, because he was needed. True, it was on the same level as the lizard that was now scurrying away, his own mission accomplished, but nonetheless he would continue to exist. There was no panic in Mystic Bob, just a kind of warm complacency and the knowledge that he was serving a greater power whose plans were older and more convincing than his own.

His instructions were simple. Force his other two companions to follow him out into the desert. That's all the demons wanted him to do. Mystic Bob laughed when he was asked if he could do this simple thing. A laugh that now somehow strangely resembled the tone of the monsters inhabiting the back of his skull. Of course he could do what they wanted. He had everything he needed stashed in the back of the trike.

And so he had returned to the surface, taken the trike out into the sand and buried the stash and the money. Then he had returned to the cave and run, now that his leg was returned to decent use under the benevolent care of his new masters, back down to his new friends. They had instructed him on how to behave with his former cohorts and how best to confuse them and make them think they were creating their own plan and not following his. The Crip and Albert had returned then and Mystic Bob had played the part of the freaked-out druggie. Now he was outside and leaving a not terribly difficult to follow path for The Crip leading out into the badlands. Then, well, and not to overstate the obvious, all hell was going to break loose.

*　　　　　*　　　　　*

For Steven, coming from San Francisco where the weather changed regularly, being at a funeral in Arizona almost seemed a contradiction in terms. But perhaps that wasn't an entirely bad thing. The sun sparkled off the grass and quartz driveways of the cemetery and the uniformed policemen, many from other jurisdictions, marching into the grounds made it almost seem like a May Day parade. Even the piper who played the men and women to the gravesite made his sorrowful dirge seem almost gay.

Now they were gathered around the big hole in the ground that would soon swallow up the earthly remains of Police Officer Richard Jennings, Award of Merit (Posthumous), and with him the secret, still under investigation, of who put him there. The pious words had been said and Stephanie Jennings had stepped forward and their young son had received the folded flag. Steven wondered, as he watched the pretty young woman and the two children, whether she had any idea of Rick's true nature. He was pretty sure she must. And then he glanced at Karen who was standing beside him. She had actually offered to come with him. She had received a lot of sympathy from the Newton police regarding her 'incident' and was there out of respect for them even though she didn't know Jennings personally. Steven wondered at the irony of the situation; him investigating a cop who was cheating on his wife while on the job. Karen looked great; her slim figure set in a suit of dark, conservative clothes the likes of which he couldn't remember ever seeing on her. She looked inviting and mysterious with her dark glasses and broad-brimmed hat. Like something out of a Hitchcock film. She noticed his stare and looked over. Steven looked away.

He saw the small contingent of native officers from the reservation, there as they said they would be and largely on their own as they had also said. The big officer from the SUV that Steven had come to know was Wencha looked over at him and their eyes met. Wencha smiled slightly and looked back to the ceremony.

With the service over and the rifle reports from the salute echoing off across the lawns, the crowd started to break up and move off. Some lingered to speak with Mrs. Jennings as an older woman, probably a grandmother, took the kids off to a waiting car. A couple of reporters followed them, one of them Steven recognized as being the reporter that had approached him at the murder scene. The other man tried to take a picture of the kids and the old lady but was blocked off and turned away by a trio of large policemen.

Captain McKinney motioned to Steven that he wanted to speak to him so he turned to Karen and excused himself for a moment. He had made a sort of report, briefly, to McKinney at the station, telling him about the situation with the girl Mary and her sister and mentioning that Mary was temporarily missing. Nobody had reported that situation to the police so Steven had guessed they were trying to handle it themselves for the moment. He had agreed to leave it with McKinney and had received a curt thank you but it was plain that he still didn't want to think that anyone but the Brixtons were responsible for Jennings.

"Hello, Walker," McKinney said as Steven approached him. "Thanks for coming out today."

"Glad to," Steven replied. "A good turnout from outside…"

"Yeah, a good turnout…" They walked past the trees where the Native Police were hanging out looking unsure about what to do next.

"Is there a reception of some sort?" Steven asked.

"At Stephanie's… Mrs. Jennings house over on the north side in about an hour. You coming?"

"Oh, sure. Okay if I bring Karen?"

"Don't see why not," said McKinney. "Look, Steven, I've been thinking about things. Maybe it would be a good idea for you to keep pursuing this girlfriend thing. We don't seem to be getting anywhere with the Brixton angle. And that's just between you and me, okay?" he said, looking at the Newton Nugget reporters regrouping after their run in with the honour guard.

"Of course," Steven said. "You want me to see if they found the sister yet."

"Yeah, exactly. A couple of the fellas are going to take the other Brixton kid for a bit of a ride and see if they can't get him to remember something he may have forgotten to tell us."

"A ride?" said Steven. "Does that still happen?"

"Around here it does."

"Bit of a stretch isn't it?"

"What's the matter, Walker? Things in Frisco must have gotten a lot easier. Or do you guys just file it under 'Who gives a shit'?"

"I'll see what I can find out from the girl's family."

"Good."

They walked past the group of Native Police and Steven again caught Wencha's eye. "I have to have a word with this guy," he said to McKinney.

"Okay, I'll see you at the reception."

"Yep, good." Steven paused, "Do these guys know about the reception?"

McKinney stopped for a moment and with no expression in his voice at all said, "No, and let's keep it that way, alright?"

Steven didn't say anything and McKinney turned on his heel and headed to his car. He felt somebody at his back and found Wencha standing behind him.

"Howdy," said Wencha. "Nice ceremony."

"Yeah, it was quick. That was merciful anyway."

Wencha laughed. "That your wife over there?" he asked, looking at Karen.

"At one time, yeah," said Steven.

Wencha looked him in the eye and then after a moment said, "Look, sorry about the other day."

"That's okay. You guys must get tired of white cops showing up on the reservation every time there's a problem that can't be solved in Newton."

"That's very perceptive of you, Detective Walker."

"Uh-huh."

"By the way, Dale really did have to go back to Tuba City. He wasn't messing with you."

"Okay."

"I just thought you might like to know that they found Mary Fleming."

"Who did? Where?"

"Her family. She was getting on a bus. Jim Ahiga talked her out of it."

"Good thing."

"Yeah, anyway, she's out at the Ahiga place now. You know where it is?"

"Yeah, thanks."

"No problem, see you around. Have a nice time at the reception." Wencha smiled and turned and walked away. Steven watched as the group of Indian cops piled into the big white SUV and drove away and then he returned to where Karen waited.

"Who was that?" she asked as Steven approached.

"Native cop from the reservation. He had some information for me."

"There's a reception," Karen said. "Do you want to go?"

Steven thought about this for about a half a second as they walked to the car. "Nah," he said finally. "I've had it for today. Let's go get a drink."

*   *   *

"I'm sorry Jim…"

Jim Ahiga turned away and looked out the window at the rain coming down in sheets over the highway and battering the aluminum sides of the little bungalow with a steady rhythm. Like thousands of fingers tapping to get in, he thought. In the gloom of the living room (nobody had made a move to turn on the lights) the family sat in silence. Kai and Nascha sat at the table looking, sort of, at a magazine on climbing; Lucy in the arm chair and her sister, Mary, like a slightly smaller, carbon copy of her, in the rocker. Mary had a blanket around her and looked very unhappy. So did Lucy for that matter.

"Well, I guess I'll have to try Joey again… Maybe he can get out of his other job for a day anyway." Big Jim turned and looked at his family. Mary stood up slowly and walked out of the room and they heard the screen door close as she went out onto the back porch.

"You can see the way she is, Jim," said Lucy. "She's on the verge of a breakdown or something. I just can't go."

"I guess not," Jim replied, with a sigh. "This is a big job, Lucy. It could mean a lot of money for quite a while if it all goes well, you know that."

"I know."

152

"I don't see why I can't go," Kai added, looking up from the pictures. Nascha looked at him and smiled.

"No," said Jim. "You've got school and your field trip. Besides, there's grandpa to see to. I'll figure something out. If Joey can't come, I'll do it alone. Just more work, that's all... and not as much fun," he added, looking at Lucy.

Lucy smiled. "I'll make it up to you, Jim," she said softly.

"Hey, nobody asked me if I need taking care of," Nascha chipped in. "What am I, a ghost?"

"He didn't mean anything, granddad. But there's stuff around here you can't do by yourself yet," said Kai.

"Didn't mean anything..." Nascha muttered and got up and went into the kitchen. They heard the top of a beer bottle being snapped off.

"Should he be drinking that?" Lucy asked.

"Ah, leave him be," said Jim. He went out the front door and over to the recently packed truck and checked again to see the bungee cords were firmly in place over the tarp. He'd checked them three times already. He peered under one corner at the equipment and gear and tents and food and wondered if he had forgotten anything. He had a list of course, but what with running into town to nab Mary at the bus station before she could take off and make things really bad for herself, and the rain and trying to track down Joey Wencha, things that had at one time seemed to be going very smoothly now looked a little problematic.

The cool rain ran down the back of his neck and he shivered. He looked up at the mesa which was living up to its name at the moment and appeared as a series of black towers fading into a grey background of clouds and mist. He shook his head and tied the corner of the tarp back down.

Bill Hennings from the Movatron Corporation had called and said that he had read the forecast and he hoped that that wouldn't slow things down. Jim had been glad to hear that. Many others would have cancelled altogether.

"Nope, son..." said Hennings, "that's what this trip is all about. Making do with what you have. Am I right?"

Jim liked Hennings although they had never met. Their conversations had been firm and to the point and no back-tracking. It made things a lot easier. He still didn't quite understand what it was that Movatron actually did but that didn't matter. He had a mental picture of Hennings and looked forward to seeing if it actually matched the man.

He opened the cab door and looked again at the gas gauge. Full, of course. As he adjusted the map case on the back of the seat, he heard a car pull into the driveway and he backed out of the truck to see Steven Walker's little grey car come to a stop. Okay, here was another complication.

Steven got out and walked up to Jim Ahiga and offered his hand. Jim shook it, saying, "You'd better come inside out of the rain."

"Going on a trip?" Steven said indicating the truck and its full load.

"Outfitting some business guys into the desert," Jim said as he led the way into the house.

When they got into the house, Lucy had gone to join Mary on the back porch. Kai and Nascha looked up as Steven entered.

"This is my brother, Kai and my grandfather, Nascha," Jim said. "Have a seat."

"Thanks," said Steven, "pleased to meet you both."

"Are you a cop?" Kai asked.

"That I am, son."

"I guess you'll be wanting to speak to Mary," Jim said.

"Yes," Steven replied. "I thought it might be better for me than some buddy of Rick Jennings."

"Yeah, you're probably right there. I'll go and get her."

Jim went out onto the porch. He glanced at Lucy who returned his look nervously.

"Was that a car I heard?" she asked.

"Yeah, it's a cop to talk to Mary about Rick."

"Oh god…" Mary started to say and she backed against the wall of the house and looked like she was about to collapse.

"It'll be okay, Mary," Lucy said soothingly. "You haven't done anything to worry about. You had nothing to do with any of this."

"Yes, I did. He was with me. If it hadn't been for me he'd still be alive."

"That's ridiculous, Mary," Jim said. "Rick was his own man, he did what he wanted. Whatever happened to him that night, it wasn't your doing."

Inside, Steven sat quietly and watched Nascha and his grandson. They watched him. Nobody said anything. A lizard ran up the wall. Steven started to move, but the other two didn't flinch so Steven relaxed again. Then the others came back in. Just as Jim was about to introduce the two women to Steven, the telephone rang and Kai answered it.

"It's some guy for you, Jim," he said offering the phone to Jim. Jim took it and suddenly everything seemed absurd; the six of them all standing in the small living room looking at Jim who didn't want to have a conversation in front of them all. Lucy saved the moment.

"I'll make some coffee," she said. "Why don't you come in with Mary and me, officer...?"

"Walker."

"Walker. We can talk in the kitchen."

"That'll be fine," Steven said and followed them in, Mary staring nervously at the floor in front of her.

On the phone it was Bill Hennings. He and the others were in their SUV downtown in Newton.

"I'll be there in about thirty minutes," said Jim. "Why don't you go to Dooley's on the main street and grab a beer and I'll come and collect you."

"Excellent suggestion," the big voice on the other end of the line boomed, "Thirty minutes then?"

Jim hung up. "Okay, I have to go," he said loudly to everyone in general.

"Have a good trip, Jim," Nascha said getting up. Kai just watched as Lucy came into the room and took his arm. They walked out to the front yard.

"How's it going in there?" Jim asked.

"It'll be alright, don't worry," said Lucy. "Mary's pretty nervous, but this Walker guy seems okay. He's from San Francisco."

"I know," Jim said and drew her close to him. He wished he hadn't said that, realizing what it implied. But Lucy didn't pick up on it. Or if she did, she said nothing. "Just tell her to be honest about all this and it'll go away. Everyone knows about the affair by now anyway."

"Okay. Don't you worry either. If Joey calls I'll send him out after you. Have a good trip and I'll see you in a few days."

"I love you Lucy."

Jim gave her a short kiss and got into the cab. As he drove off down the highway he looked in the mirror and saw that she was standing there, in the drizzle, watching him as he headed for the town. The further he got from the house the more the rain and mist obscured his vision as he looked back and forth from the road to the bungalow, but still she stayed there, an image from a book of the past, in her grey dress, a black and white picture gradually fading away until only her face was visible and then that, too, was gone.

The truck sped down the road passing the fences and fields separating the reservation from the rest of the world and on one post set a little further back than the others, a large black crow hopped from one foot to the other and put its head to one side as it eyed the driver. Then it took off from the post and with a cry disappeared into the blackness of the thunderhead.

*   *   *

Carol Wencha dished out the meat and potatoes onto Doug Wencha's plate. He looked down at the steaming pile of protein and carbohydrates and sighed to himself. A sigh of contentment, mind you, not one of resignation. This was easily his favourite time of the day; the evening meal with his family. And bedtime, of course, he enjoyed that too. And he was kind of partial to stepping out into the early morning sun as well. In fact, Doug Wencha was the kind of man who liked a lot about his life.

His eldest son, Joey, sat beside him already half way through a pork chop. The only thing missing was Mo, the youngest.

"Where's Mo at, Carol?" Doug asked, pushing a pat of melting butter deep into the hot spuds.

"I don't know. In his room?" she guessed.

"He's out in the garage with Squirrel," Joey said, his mouth full of chop.

Carol sat down and, catching Doug's eye, said hesitantly, "They've been out in the hills all day." Squirrel was Mo's best friend but on a miserable day like this Doug couldn't easily understand why they would blow off school to head out into the wet countryside. Still it was a rare occasion that Mo would dare to do it. Doug decided he was going to let it go this time. Kids need to feel their oats sometimes. Besides, he was looking forward to his chops and didn't want anything to spoil them.

"Joey, Jim Ahiga has been calling all day for you," Carol said.

"I know. He wants me to go out on a trip with him, but I can't. I have to work at the Center all this weekend. I told him that a week ago."

"Doesn't sound as much fun as going out with Jim," said Doug munching a mouthful of beans.

"I can't give up my job at the Center for a once a month trip with Jim," said Joey. "He doesn't pay me enough."

"You saying he's not fair with you?"

"No, he's fair. He just doesn't charge them enough. He's got no business sense," said Joey.

"Not practical like you, huh?" Doug said, looking over at him. And then before Joey could argue the point, "Go get Mo will you? And tell Squirrel to go home, it'll be getting dark soon."

Joey made a noise of protest but Doug shot him a look and Joey got up reluctantly and headed for the kitchen door. But he stopped dead in his tracks when the gunshot went off.

"What...?" he managed to get out and turned against the counter as Doug pushed him aside in his rush to the door. Carol gasped and stood up.

"Both of you stay inside," he shouted as he grabbed his service revolver from its belt by the door and ran outside where he was met

157

with a soft wave of the rain that was now nothing but a light mist. He looked around the yard and ran to the corner of the house where it became part of the garage. There was a door slam and when he rounded the garage into the driveway, he saw Mo and Squirrel speeding away on their bikes down the gravel road.

"Mo! Get the hell back here!" he bellowed and the two bikes slowed down and then stopped about fifty yards away. They said something to each other and then Squirrel started peddling off slowly in the direction of her house looking back over her shoulder occasionally. Mo turned and, head down, started reluctantly back towards his home.

Doug went in through the partially opened door of the garage. Inside the windowless box, there was the smell of smoke where, other than from the door, there were only two sources of light. One was a ragged six inch hole in the rear wall through which a shaft of late afternoon light was punching though the haze. The other was the soft glow of a laptop computer screen that gave a muted metallic shine to the barrel of the CheyTac .408 caliber intervention rifle resting on its slightly bent tripod, the smoke from the barrel still oozing out slowly from the business end.

"What the hell?" Officer Doug Wencha said to himself.

"We didn't know it was loaded," answered the half-spoken, half-whimpered voice of Mo Wencha from outside. "We was gonna tell you."

*   *   *

"Steven, its Captain McKinney…"

"Yeah, good morning. Listen, I want to come in and give you a report on this Mary Fleming thing." Steven wiped the sleep from his eyes with his free hand and then reached for the water beside his bed, almost dropping the phone.

"That's gonna have to wait. There's been some action out on the reservation. You up yet?"

"Oh, yeah, for a while…" Steven lied.

"We'll be there to pick you up in five minutes. You may as well come on this, it kind of involves you."

"What do you mean?"

"I think we found the Brixtons."

In what felt like much less than the promised five minutes, Steven was in the back seat of the Captain's car with Lewison and trying to sip at a cup of impossibly hot, hotel-lobby coffee. He didn't know the driver; Jennings' partner apparently. They sped through the city and headed to the reservation; no sirens, no lights, just speed.

"Couple of native kids playing in the hills found a weapon. Kind of a break actually, it was Doug Wencha's kid."

Steven looked in the rear-view mirror at McKinney as he spoke, "Wencha the tribal cop?"

"Yeah... Otherwise the gun would be in the hock shop by now," McKinney said. The cop driving the car grunted his agreement.

"Wencha seems okay," Steven said, his liberal hackles rising slightly.

"Yeah, well, nothing against him, I guess he's okay but some of his people are pretty fucked up." Steven was about to point out that some of theirs were pretty fucked up too but left it. "Anyway, he took some guys out there and they found a body at the foot of a cliff; local hump name of Cooter Langford. He works for the Brixtons occasionally. Crack shot with high-powered armaments, ex-marine. The gun they found was a CheyTac? Know it?"

"Nope."

"Long distance sniper rifle. Wencha had the good sense to call us after they investigated a mile or so from the ledge he fell off."

"What did they find?"

"More bodies... in a mine. Tell me about this Mary Fleming," McKinney said.

"She was with Jennings that night alright. While he was on his shift actually," said Steven, trying to gauge what McKinney's reaction would be.

"Stupid bastard," McKinney said. The driver looked at Steven in the mirror and scowled.

"Anyway, he left in the morning from the Motel 8 out here and without Mary. The manager can confirm that. And there was no boyfriend…"

"Okay, so she's out of the picture for the moment," McKinney said. Steven sat back and tried to relax a bit. When they neared the reservation highway, they could see a Tribal Police truck up ahead.

"That's the road to the mine," said Lewison. A huge native cop waved them through the turn and they could see further up the road another truck parked by a turn-off.

"That it?" said, Marksly, the driver cop.

"No," said McKinney, "Keep going, it's about a mile on."

Steven shut the window on his side against the dust that still hung in the air from what must have been a busy vehicular morning. As they pulled around the last big boulders before the mine, he could see a car and a meat-wagon up ahead near the opening of what had to be the mine. When they got close, Wencha strode up to their car as they got out.

"Captain McKinney…" said Wencha as he approached.

"Officer Wencha… thanks for the call. We appreciate it," said McKinney as he looked at the mine and the ambulance.

"No problem, sir. But Captain Dale wanted me to remind you that this is a tribal crime scene. You're free to look around but this is our jurisdiction."

McKinney's face got that darkness that Steven had seen more than once now. "Is that so?" he said.

"Just passing along the message, Captain… Dale will be here in a while if you want to chat about it. You want to go in? I'm warning you right now, it's pretty unpleasant in there. The bodies have been rotting for a few days now."

"How many?" Steven asked.

"Three. The two Brixtons that I think you're looking for. And some other guy…"

"No I.D.?" McKinney said.

160

"Nope, no face either. In fact, not much left of a head. We figure the guy with the rifle got him, judging from the wound."

"But he's inside," Lewison said.

"Yeah, tough one to figure..."

The four white officers moved up to the mine entrance and McKinney led the way into the dark cave. Wencha had set up a couple of lights inside and as they entered further into the cave it became more illuminated. The stench of spoiling flesh was instantly overwhelming. Lewison got green in a flash and had to leave quickly. Steven put a hand over his mouth and went up to the back of the long, black Chevy. What was in there was not even worth trying to dig out. McKinney was bent over the remains of Ashford Brixton.

"That's Brixton, alright," McKinney said. "And if I had to guess I'd say that must be what's left of his kid. What the hell happened here?" Then they went over to the body of Cage, freed at last from his facial tattoo prison in a break-out of the most radical kind. "No I.D. on this one, huh?" McKinney called over to Wencha who waited by the entrance, having had enough of this hole for one day.

"No, nothing," he replied. "Nothing on the bikes yet, either. We're running a check on the plates, but they're probably stolen."

"Well, that accounts for seventy percent of the Newton drug trade," said McKinney, nodding at the Chevy. "I guess that winds up your job here pretty neatly."

Steven looked around at what he saw. "Maybe... There's at least one other person unaccounted for though," he said. McKinney looked over at him.

"What do you mean?" said McKinney.

"The other biker..."

"How do you know the Brixton kid didn't ride out here on a bike?"

"The plates on both the bikes are California. So where's the other Californian?" he said.

Wencha cursed himself for not having thought of that and called out to one of his men for some flashlights. "He may still be down the tunnel," he said. "We'll take a look."

McKinney grabbed one of the flashlights from Wencha who just shrugged at Steven and they started down the tunnel. Steven trailed behind a little as Marksly went out to check on Lewison. They had only moved a few yards down the shaft when Steven got a feeling in his stomach. He hadn't felt that particular feeling in quite a while. But it was unmistakable; at least for someone from San Francisco. The others had felt it too but, being from Arizona, didn't have the required sense memory.

"What the hell was that?" McKinney said.

"Captain, we have to get out of here now," Steven called out. McKinney and Wencha stopped up ahead and shone their lights back at him. McKinney was starting to ask him something when the rumbling started and a few bits of rock descended from the ceiling. Then they were running back towards the entrance; then they weren't so much running as being thrown, with that sensation that the world has suddenly gone wrong that only an earthquake can give you. Not like the shaky camera from a cheesy Hollywood movie, but the distinct impression that parts of your body are moving away from others, like you somehow took the first step onto a rapidly moving airport walkway without being at the airport.

McKinney pitched headfirst into the dirt and Wencha grabbed him by the collar and hauled him to his feet. Steven stopped and made a step back towards them but Wencha waved him on.

"Go!" shouted Wencha as the dirt and rock began to cascade down in a dirty, jagged curtain.

The three cops flung themselves out of the mine entrance as the entire roof of the Heminghurst Silver mine crashed down onto the metal and flesh of the dead criminals, sealing it forever. Creating an impenetrable tomb that Lonny, Ashford and Cage could never have imagined they would be sharing together for the rest of eternity; and sharing it not just with each other but with two that had been sealed there for a very long time and would greatly enjoy the pleasure of their company.

CHAPTER FIVE

SKULLDUGGERY

Coyote lay at the back of his lair, staring out of the opening at the endless plains and forests of the spirit world. Here and there animals and men walked together talking of their days in the world and discussing the events of those days. The breeze was warm and even and penetrated the lair, rustling up bits of leaf and grass that Coyote used for his bed. Coyote coughed, he was in a bad mood. He contemplated going out amongst the spirits and causing a little havoc, but couldn't bring himself to rise from his mat and do it. He was restless and impatient waiting for the conditions down below to favour his latest oeuvre. He wished things would happen faster, that people would stop messing around and get on with it.

He managed to prop himself up on his front paws and with a little push on his hind legs he padded quietly to the entrance of the lair and laid back down, his tail smacking at the dirt like a cat's. There was a bit of a noise and from around a rock Gila appeared.

"You shouldn't come to my cave," said Coyote, annoyed, "Spider Woman might see you."

"My tooth hurts," said Gila, sucking at the fang that had almost broken loose when he had sunk it into Cooter Langford's leg.

"Well, unless you want me to chew if off for you, there's not much I can do," said Coyote, wincing at the thought of putting his head anywhere near the ugly creature's scaly body. "Why are you here?"

"The monsters sent me to tell you that things are almost ready, that you should do what you must to distract Child-Born-Of-Water and Monster-Slayer so that they will not interfere."

"I have been thinking on that and this is my plan. When the time comes I will trick Spider Woman herself into calling them to do her bidding. Then I will create a false threat that they will pursue and that is when our friends will be unleashed upon the Fourth World." Coyote listened to his own words with great admiration. This would plainly be one of his best and most elaborate of plots. There would be songs made of this one that was for sure.

"When will the monsters be free?" asked Gila.

"Four days from now," said Coyote, "Nothing can prevent it."

"And it will be a man that frees them?"

"Nothing can prevent it. Three days hence I will do my part. Then when Spider Woman and the Sun-God's children are gone from Spider Rock, we two will have the best seats of all to watch what happens below."

"I will tell all of this to Tse-Nill and Naz-Tsaid. They will be happy."

"Can a demon be happy?" asked Coyote, more to himself than to Gila and not really caring, one way or the other, how such monsters felt.

Gila looked at Coyote with some confusion and then turned and scurried away to return to his masters. Far away, Changing Woman felt the breeze against her face grow cold and she stopped her work on the loom for a moment to listen. She tilted her head from side to side, as did Crow who sat atop the loom. Together they tried to understand. But there was nothing else.

Changing Woman looked back down at her tapestry and sighed. A stitch had come loose and had broken away. The sky that formed the cross poles of the loom had grown darker and the cords of earth that held the loom aloft had grown dry. She knew that this meant hard work in the coming days. She took the white shell, weaving comb in her hand and drew it back and forth across the pattern, trying to ease the tension in the thread, but it was of no use, the unraveling continued and finally she had to cut the strand with a knife to prevent further damage. She would have to work very fast to save the tapestry, the tapestry that had always unfolded as it should since the days of the creation of the Fourth World; after the Dine, the Navajo, had arrived.

Coyote drank from the pool of water beside his lair and chewed some corn to get ready for his long journey to Spider Rock. When his belly was full and the night was approaching he set out, trotting quietly along the spirit trail. His gait was lively and he almost leapt into the air at times because now he was in motion and he no longer felt impatient. Now he almost wanted things to slow down so that he could savour the moments. He breathed in the cold air and his breath returned out with short bursts of mist that filled the canyon. The moon hung in the clouds and, for a short time, stood alone against the black firmament. Coyote stopped and looked and, raising his head, let out a long coyote yowl which of course, to them, is a laugh of joy.

*   *   *

From where he stood, atop his converted school bus, Harry Babcock felt like Moses overseeing the flight from Egypt. The entire school parking lot seemed to be covered with students and their camping gear. Even though there were only twenty of them, they seemed to him to be a great mass of badly dressed humanity, seething about, their voices pumped by the giddy adrenalin rush provided by the prospect of a couple of nights together with little supervision. In fact the din was almost overpowering. Then Okay Kilagrew's whistle blasted and the noise subsided somewhat to low murmurs and giggling. Harry turned and checked the bolts on the luggage racks he had attached to the top of the bus. Then he climbed down to check the hitch for the small trailer attached to the back. Everything seemed okay, although he found it hard to imagine all this gear packed away in any short amount of time.

"I see the notion of one small bag and some food seems to have escaped some of you, okay?!" Kilagrew shouted through his small megaphone. "Anything we can't get up on top stays here, you know. I hope you understand that, okay?" he added. "Okay, its time for a headcount! I will call out your name and you will respond as follows: Here, Mr. Kilagrew."

A few giggles burst forth as a few of the boys shouted out in girl-like voices, "Yes, Mr. Kilagrew."

"Okay, stow that right now!" Kilagrew shouted through the megaphone, a device which only served to make his voice sound even thinner than it already was; albeit at a much higher volume. In her mind Karen rolled her eyes. She felt a little foolish standing there in her camping store outfit, mostly khaki, and her Tilley hat that seemed largely like overkill. The kids were dressed in all manner of cool outfits, the girls mostly looking sexy and the boys loose. She also wished her outfit didn't quite so closely resemble that of Harry's but when you get fashion help from a fifty-five year old ex-cop that's the risk you take, she supposed.

"After your name is called you may carry your things to the bus and Mr. Babcock will help you stow it, okay? Here we go... Kai Ahiga!" shouted Kilagrew. There was no response.

"We're picking him up en route, remember?" Karen said. "He's on the way to the site."

"Okay, that's right," said Kilagrew. "Alice Bird?"

"Yes, Mr. Kilagrew!" called Alice, her voice, like her name, a shrill call from the back of the group. Everyone laughed.

"Linwood Desmond?"

"Affirmative...!" Linwood pulled down his jaunty cap and placed a foot on his duffel bag revealing a muscled calf much to the delight of the girls in his near vicinity. Cam gagged.

"Yes, Mr. Kilagrew!" shouted Mr. Kilagrew.

"Yes, Mr. Kilagrew!" Linwood shouted back in exactly the same tone.

And so it went on, each student in some way frustrating Okay Kilagrew who rapidly grew more and more annoyed. Karen sat down on the step of the bus. The trip would be over before they got aboard at this rate. Harry did the same on the trailer hitch. Everything chugged along though until they got to Virtual Jones.

"He's not here yet, sir," Tommy Chong shouted.

"Is he not coming?" asked Kilagrew.

"No, no... he's coming. I have most of his stuff here. He was up late working on... something."

"Well, if he's not here by end of count, we'll be leaving without him," Kilagrew said.

166

"Hey, there he is!" shouted Louie, pointing across the road. "What the hell is he riding on, a lawnmower?"

Virtual Jones wheeled noiselessly along the sidewalk in a chair that looked like a cross between a lunar rover and a miniature jet pilot's seat. He approached the relatively steep curb and the whole group watched him silently and held their collective breath as he broached the height. But when it looked like it would surely tip over, the contraption seemed to fold under him as each huge, balloon-like wheel moved independently and he rolled smoothly down onto the main street, across the grass and climbed over the cement parking lot slabs that separated him from the group. As the last tire bounced down over the seemingly insurmountable concrete barriers a cheer went up amongst the students and with a grin Virtual Jones rolled to a silent stop.

Harry Babcock, closest to the boy, went over and looked down at the machine. It put Virtual at about half the height of his regular chair. "That's a remarkable piece of thing you have there, Jones," he said as others gathered round.

"Thank you, sir," said Jones, "I call it the Jones Device. It's based on the Mars rover that they used to collect samples and such. Independent four wheel drive, battery operated and better climb than an ATV."

"Remarkable..." Babcock repeated. "Let's get it into the trailer. Is it heavy?"

"Light gauge, hi-tensile aluminum, sir" said Virtual, "donated by Versagrip industries, my uncle owns it. I weigh more than the machine, except for the battery."

"How long will the battery last?" Babcock said.

Virtual grinned. "Back of the chair has a solar panel to recharge it every day."

"Remarkable..."

"Ahem..." A megaphone-assisted cough was heard from the direction of the bus. "Do you think we could continue with the headcount? Cam Proctor?"

"Here, Mr. Kilagrew!"

When Anton Remy, the Cajun kid, heard his name called he responded, picked up a large bag and carried it nervously towards the trailer. He stumbled slightly as he approached the bus and dropped the bag against the side of the trailer. The bag emitted a low whine and started to wiggle. Babcock looked down over the edge of the trailer. "What the hell?" he said.

Kilagrew came over and nudged the bag with his toe; another short yelp. "Open that bag Remy!" he said, scowling down at it. Anton did so and a small, black, scruffy looking dog tumbled out caught up in a pair of jeans and some underwear and began to amble about excitedly to the 'aws' and 'oohs' of the cheerleader squad.

Anton looked up at Kilagrew and then, not liking what he saw, down again at his feet. "My mom went away for the weekend. I had to bring him; there was nobody else to look after him. He won't be any trouble. I can't go if we can't take him."

"No way, Remy, no way," muttered Kilagrew, "Anything could happen to him and we can't have a dog barking all night."

"He won't bark, Mr. Kilagrew," Remy said. "He's pretty old and he's only got about four teeth."

Harry leant down from trailer. "It'll be okay, Herman," he said. "There's room and he's pretty small. I'll keep an eye on them." Kilagrew looked around at the group. Everyone had stopped talking now and there was silence as they waited to see what he would do next. The last face he came to was Karen's and she, too, wondered what he would say. A quite a few things went through his mind as he weighed his options. In the end he figured he would amass quite a few brownie points if he looked the other way on this one.

"Alright, but if he doesn't behave out there he gets tied up."

Another collective cheer and Anton Remy's face lit up and he and the dog, whose name it turned out was Éclair (to more 'aws' from the girls), climbed aboard the bus.

"Can I go and get my dog?" said Ricky Ray. "He's cute, too."

"No!" shouted Kilagrew through his megaphone about four inches from Ray's head. He turned and marched to the bus door where he continued the headcount until all were stowed and aboard the bus. The bus door hissed shut and with a jolt, the kids and bags and dog and trailers and Karen and Harry hauled out of the parking lot. "Okay," said Kilagrew, now speaking over the bus p.a. system, "Here are some bus safety tips…" There was a collective groan and a single bark as they started down the street.

Meanwhile, in his bed in his house on the reservation, Kai Ahiga slept the sleep of the innocent. There was a dream happening and it had something to do with a bird and some fire and then there was a girl there, of course, and what sounded like thunder. And the thunder grew and eventually it became Lucy Fleming calling through the door, "Kai, wake up, the bus is here!"

The surge of panic that drove through his body like a knife pulled him from his somnambulistic bliss into a state of high anxiety. If he was sixty he would probably have had a heart attack right on the spot. How could he have overslept on this day of all days? The bus horn greeted him as he ran from the bedroom to the bathroom, quickly urinated and grabbing a piece of bread and a banana from the kitchen table he seized his bag and hurtled out the door, almost bowling Nascha over as he came in from the living room.

"Have a good time," Nascha said to the already empty doorframe. He went over to the door and yelled through the screen, "See if you can find some Box-Thorn. I have a toothache!"

Kai scrambled up the steps and onto the bus and ran into Kilagrew who was standing and reciting camping safety info to the students. The group laughed, not just at the collision but the state of Kai's hair that was wound up on the top of his head like an ice-cream swirl. Kai glared at them and they stopped and he walked down the aisle until he found the only remaining empty seat. And it was being saved for him by a smiling Allison Donkers. And he relaxed as the chatter returned and they pulled out onto the highway and headed for the park on the far side of the mesa.

*   *   *

"Mr. Rose, Mr. Ellis, Mr. Tinker… meet Big Jim Ahiga."

From their barstools, Emerson Rose, Gary Ellis and Graham Tinker got up as one and waited in a row to shake Jim's hand. Bill Hennings stood to one side beaming at his protégés and watching as Jim made the rounds. Jim was amazed at how three men could look so out of place in something as simple as blue jeans and sweat shirts. Their stuff looked like it was fresh off the store shelf but had been dragged through the dirt or something. Oh well, Jim thought, at least they're not wearing fatigues and carrying guns.

"How about one for the road Jim, before we hit the wilderness, huh?" said Hennings and Jim took a seat at the bar even though he really just wanted to get going. You gotta be a team player, he thought, and ordered a draft.

"I've told Jim that we don't want any babying out there. We'll be on our own, making our own decisions and what-have-you. Each of you boys will get a turn to lead the group on a hike or something and we'll see what you make of it. Are we all set for gear then, Jim?"

"Yep, all set," said Jim, swigging down his beer in a couple of gulps. "I brought some extra fishing tackle in case you need any. You said you might want to fish…"

"I must admit, next to corporate takeovers, fishing is the next best thing, my man. Actually, it's kinda the same thing, come to think of it. Choose the bait, set the hook and reel 'em in!" Hennings laughed, loudly. The chorus line joined in with that loud, not-quite-sincere kind of laugh that businessmen do to stroke each other. Jim was beginning to think maybe he hadn't charged enough. Oh well, big-city guys, you can't expect too much, he figured.

"I think we should get on the road, Mr. Hennings…" he said.

"Bill! We're all on a first-name basis out here, isn't that right Emerson?"

"Sure is Mr.… Bill," Emerson said, catching himself but wishing he hadn't just called his boss Mr. Bill. Rose leered at Tinker as they got up from their stools again and headed out of the saloon. The gold Humvee parked outside had attracted a lot of attention as it, of course, was meant to do. Jim looked askance at his old Ford nestled behind the glittering mass of motorized affluence. Hennings caught his look.

"Tell you what, Jim, why don't I ride with you and we can chat about what we're going to get up to as we drive out, huh? No sense you riding by yourself." Bill said.

"Well, okay, but I gotta warn you, the seat on the passenger side ain't too soft."

"Doesn't matter, Jim, I got lots of personal padding," Bill said with a laugh, patting his ample buttocks." Emerson laughed loudly and then stopped, realizing he was the only one. Strike two, he thought miserably, and we haven't even left the town yet. Bill Hennings climbed into the Ford beside Jim and the others got into the Humvee and Jim led the way out of town.

"You can see we've got our work cut out for us with this crew, you and me," Hennings said after they had hit the highway. "Just between us, Rose is on the bubble. I brought him along so that maybe he could show me why I shouldn't can his ass."

"He does seem a little nervous, I guess," said Jim.

"You can say that again, Jim. And if there's one thing you don't need in the farm fertilizer business, its nervousness."

Jim tried to figure out what that meant exactly but quickly gave up. He had picked a spot for the group that was off of his usual grounds. It was an extremely beautiful spot; about five miles past the mesa, a short drive to the river and there were a couple of old abandoned shanties that could be used to store things while they forayed out into the desert. And clean water, too.

"I thought I should mention that we've been having a bit of trouble with cell-phones anywhere north of the mesa lately. I hope that won't inconvenience you, Bill."

"Nope, as a matter of fact I made the boys leave all their toys back at the office. Notwithstanding that I don't want to eat toads for four days, we're looking at doing this on the rough," said Hennings.

Jim wondered how anybody driving a luxury Humvee into the desert could consider themselves 'roughing' it. Maybe they were planning on turning off the A/C.

Following along in said 'luxury vehicle', the others were having a serious discussion about what was expected of them on this trip. Emerson kind of knew that this was his last chance but nobody was talking about that exactly, although he was certain that Gary and

Graham saw this as a golden opportunity to bypass him and head up the new department.

"Why do you think he took our cells away?" Emerson said nervously from the back seat. "Do you think we're supposed to come up with some way of connecting with the office anyway?"

"Like what," said Gary, "smoke signals?"

"I don't know maybe we're supposed to get back to town or tap into a telephone line or something."

Graham turned and looked at Emerson. "Em… you are really starting to lose it. Just relax okay? It's only a couple of days of camping. Soon as he gets a bit of sunburn the old man will want to head back, you watch."

"I don't know about that, Gray…" said Gary. "You've only seen him around the office; I've seen him playing flag football. He's nuts when he gets into something. I'll bet he has us doing twenty mile hikes and living off lizards. Last man standing gets to keep his job." He winked at Graham, surreptitiously.

"You really think so?" said Emerson as he shifted from one side of the truck to the other to avoid the sun. "God, I don't think I could eat a lizard."

"Don't worry, Em… I've heard its not too bad, sort of tastes like snake."

Gary and Graham laughed. Emerson just put his chin on his hand and gazed out the window and watched the arid land slide by as he sipped his double espresso, low-fat latte, still warm from the Humvee's heated cup-holder.

*   *   *

Nascha and Lucy sat on the back porch, Nascha rocking slightly and gazing up at the Mesa, Lucy reading a book. Nascha shaded his eyes with his hand and searched the cliff tops for any sign of Crow. It had been two days since he had last seen him and he wondered what it meant. It had only been a few hours since Kai had rushed out the door but he had spent so much time with him in the last while that his absence, too, felt strange.

"What are you looking for up there?" Lucy asked, putting her book on her lap.

"A bird… Can you see any up there?"

"What kind of bird?"

"Crow…"

Lucy scanned the mesa and the field in between. She had pretty good eyesight but couldn't see anything moving at all. "No… as a matter of fact I can't see any birds at all. Isn't that odd?" she said. "For this time of year, I mean."

"It'd be odd at any time of year. There're always birds," said Nascha. There was a stirring behind them and the screen door squeaked open and Mary Fleming came out. She sat down on the steps.

"How are you feeling, Mary?" Lucy asked.

"Oh, I'm fine, really," said Mary, quietly, and then said, "Lucy, I feel real bad about you not going out on the trip with Jim. He obviously needs you."

"He'll be okay. It's only for a few days. And he's with a group of guys so they aren't completely helpless. I hope. Besides, it would be weird being out there with all men."

"You're just saying that. Listen, here's what I think. You should go out today in the car. Nascha and I can stay here and look after things. I don't want to go back into town just yet anyway."

"I don't think that's a good idea, Mary," Lucy said.

"No, I mean it. If you're worried about me, well, it's bothering me more that I'm making you stay than if you went. Besides, I'd like some time by myself…" she looked at Nascha, "I mean without being fussed over."

"Yeah, fussing can be a real pain in the ass," said Nascha.

Lucy laughed. "Come on, granddad, you love it."

"Kinda…" said Nascha as he got up and walked out into the garden.

"Do you really think you'd be okay," she said to Mary.

"Absolutely… It would be good for you guys to work together out there. It sounds as if this trip is pretty important for you both. So go, okay?"

Lucy looked into Mary's face which was a lot like looking into a mirror for her. She saw the darkness there that the death of Jennings had caused; the sadness in the eyes. She knew Mary had wanted to get out of the affair for a long time but hadn't had the strength. And now there was just grief and guilt left for her. Maybe it would be some help to her for Lucy to trust her now and let her feel like she had her life back to some degree. And Nascha could help with that, too; giving her someone to be responsible for besides herself. She watched Nascha amble about the garden, bending over now and then to pick some weed out of the vegetables or to peer once more into the sky, like he was expecting rain or something. He was almost his old self again, just a little frailer, but his mind was fine.

"Are you sure?" she said hesitantly.

"Yes," said Mary, brightening considerably as she sensed that Lucy was being swayed.

"Is it okay with you, granddad?" she called down the yard.

"Go…" Nascha called back with a wave of his hand.

It was with some concern that Lucy stood, about half an hour later, beside the car and looked back at Mary and Nascha standing on the steps, arm in arm. She was worried but it was being balanced out quite well by excitement at the prospect of being with Jim and how happy he would be when she showed up. She held the map of the trip site in her one hand and the bag of things that she had packed a week ago.

"I'll be back in two days. I won't stay for the whole trip, just to help Jim get started."

"That's fine," said Mary, "have a good time. Don't let him make you do the cooking."

Lucy laughed. "Bye, Granddad," she called as she got into the car.

Nascha didn't answer. He was looking at Crow who had reappeared and was sitting on the mailbox staring back at him. He held something in his beak which he dropped into the grass as Lucy drove out onto the road. Then he cawed loudly and flew after the car, easily keeping up with it as it rounded the first bend. The car turned right, the bird flew right. Crow was following Lucy.

Nascha didn't quite know what to make of that and as Mary went back into the house, he walked over to see what the big bird had dropped. He stooped down and picked up what looked like a piece of a different kind of bird. It was a claw, ripped from its haunch and Nascha shuddered as he turned it over in his hand. The feathers were brown and mottled with white and grey and a few small specks of blood were splashed here and there. He had seen its kind before; but not for a long time. It was the claw of an owl. Nascha grew cold and tossed the thing down into the ditch where it sank in a trough of leftover rainwater. He turned and hurried back into the house to get his cleansing herbs. He wanted to flush the filth from his hands for this was omen and it was bad. For his people, from time before memory, the souls of the dead that had escaped back to the world had assumed the form of these owls; flying through the night, searching for the life that had left them. When he got up onto the porch he stopped, turned and looked down the road, but Lucy was long gone.

*   *   *

Ricky Ray lay on the ground, a tent pole through his heart. Finn Esterhaus and Kai stood over him; Finn beating his shallow chest and Tarzan-yelling and Kai shouting "At last! At last!"

"You boys get that tent up! I'm not going to ask you again! Do you want to spend the night sleeping on the rocks?"

Ricky rose up, Lazarus-like, at that threat from Kilagrew and removed the pole from under his armpit. He grinned at Kai and Finn and they started, once more, to put up the impossibly clumsy bivouac tent. The tent was a left-over from the basement of Harry Babcock. Some of the kids had brought their own and those that didn't have one at home had rented. The only rule was 'at least three in a tent'. That was Okay's way of ensuring (at least in his mind) that there would be no hanky and/or panky going on. Kai turned and watched Allison, Micki Valence and Enye Remo struggling with their smaller, but equally difficult Babcock tent. Kai caught Allison's eye and smiled. Allison blushed. Micki got her hair caught in a lanyard.

Anton, David Smith, Cam and Louie had been handed the job of digging a latrine hole and were sweating it out some distance from the tent ground.

"Well, better to be digging it than filling it in," David had said to the general agreement of the others. Filling it in before they left would be the task given out as punishment to any malefactors over the weekend. For some it was reason enough to be good, for others it was the price they might just have to pay. David was a skinny kid related vaguely to the mayor so he was tolerated but under any other circumstances he would have been regarded as a classic nerd. But he had a great car and that helped his stature. Somehow the coach had even found a position for him on the football team. Éclair barked and jumped around and rolled around in the dirt and chased things and was clearly having more fun than anybody else.

CJ Hayward, Melissa Heels and Hattie Conway, having put their tent up very quickly (because it was brand new and simple and courtesy of Melissa's very rich father) were now in shorts and tank tops and sunning themselves on a large, flat rock that formed the natural wall that Okay had thought was a good place to set up camp. Harry had tried to point out that it was a long way from the small stream that would be their washing and cooling off area (they brought their own drinking water) but Okay was more interested in not being woken up at six in the morning by kids going for a swim.

The walk in from the road where they had left the bus had been a long, hot one. The only one who didn't seem to mind that much was Virtual who buzzed along on his Jones Device, which, it had been revealed, even had a sun canopy. Cookie Johanson had tripped over it at one point and skinned a knee (for which a mortified Virtual had happily agreed to carry her stuff) but that had been the only mishap as they tromped the two miles up the canyon to the spot that Okay had selected.

Tommy Wong was helping Alice Bird build a fire pit. Alice Bird, her thin, white arms flailing away with a small hatchet at the ground and Tommy digging in with a collapsible (otherwise known as 'useless') shovel. The pit was meant to be four feet wide but Tommy was already on the verge of protesting the dimensions to Harry Babcock who was overseeing the operation from the shade of the awning on the Staff

Tent. Karen came out of the tent with a tray with four plastic glasses of iced-tea on it and handed one to Harry.

"Having fun yet, Karen?" said Harry after thanking her for the drink.

"Well, so far I've killed two spiders in the tent," she replied as she placed her drink beside a camp chair.

"What colour?" said Harry.

"Brown and white, why?" said Karen as she walked towards the fledgling fire pit to bring some relief to the two exhausted diggers.

"Oh, brown and white, well that's okay. If you see any black and red... well, better call me," Harry called after her.

Karen laughed, but when Harry didn't laugh back, her laugh trailed off. "Here you go guys? Need a hand?" she said to Alice and Tommy as she handed out the drinks.

"Oh no, that's okay Miss Armitage, we can manage," Tommy said. "But I think the hole will have to be a little smaller than Mr. Babcock was saying. This ground is too hard."

"Well, I'm sure it won't matter too much. I'll look around and get someone to help you."

Karen took a stroll around the site that, under Kilagrew's design and supervision, was beginning to look something like a small, canvas and nylon city. The tents were laid out in two rows that intersected to form a cross. He had built a little wooden sign for the centre of tent town with mildly funny directions like 'Tokyo – 2000 Miles' on it. The staff tent, located there in the crossroads, loomed over the other sundry dwellings like a great, green city hall made of cloth. Karen didn't realize they even made tents that big and when she went inside and realized that there were actually separate 'rooms' in it, she felt like laughing; until she spotted the first brown and white octoped crawling towards her cot.

She stopped at the tent containing Linwood Desmond and Attibi Remo and called through the mesh, "Anyone home?"

The two boys emerged, sweating from the heat that was already turning the tents into canvas ovens. They were in their bathing suits.

"Hi, Miss Armitage, we were just going for a swim. Want to go?"

"Sounds like a great idea but we're having a staff meeting in a few minutes to plan the first walkabout. I was going to ask you to help Tommy and Alice with the fire pit. But as you're already in your suits, it's okay."

"I can get changed again," Linwood offered, reluctantly.

"No, that's okay, you two go along. I'll find someone else."

The boys looked at each other and then back at Karen. "Okay" they said, almost in unison and were gone before she could change her mind. Oh well, Karen thought as she headed back to the pit, I guess it won't hurt to do a bit of digging. But she found Harry, shirt off and big chest heaving, in the middle of it all, attacking the ground with a metal pole.

"This'll break it up," he was saying to Tommy while Alice slumped in the shade of her tent, sipping on an ice tea. Karen was starting to like Harry a lot.

Looking down at the whole sprawling mass of kids and teachers was like peering into an ant's nest from up atop the height of the mesa; which was where Coyote sat, watching the proceedings with great interest. He saw the leaders and the followers, the shy and the bold, the budding lovers and the friends and all the rest, including those whose time among the living was growing shorter by the second. He barked a short laugh and trotted away over the rocky path that led towards the second mesa peak. Before long, because he was very quick, he was on a spot some fifteen miles or more by road and overlooking another group of nature lovers. This one significantly smaller and better organized but every bit as doomed. Coyote lay down under a shady spot and trained his especially good hearing upon the ground below.

In a testimony to the shared and inherent goofiness of the human male at any age, Gary Ellis lay on the ground, a tent pole through his heart exactly as Ricky Ray had done some time back and some distance away. Graham Tinker and Emerson Rose stood over him; Graham laughing and holding his stomach and Emerson looking worriedly about and saying "Come on, you guys. Bill almost has his tent up by himself!" Coyote shook his head.

"Look, relax will you Emerson, it isn't a 'see-who-can-get-it-up' contest," said Gary and got up and dusted off his pants.

"If it was, my money'd be on Big Jim there," said Mike, watching Jim haul the last of the food hampers towards the larger of the wooden lean-tos. Jim's tent, which he'd pitched a thousand times, was up and he already had a fire going and was getting ready to roast some chickens for lunch.

Bill walked over, having shored up the supplies in his small pup-tent with a bottle of Jack Daniels and a box of cigars. That was all Bill would need in the way of supplies really. He lived hard, something he'd learned how to do while he was carving a niche for his company in an over-crowded and cut-throat market. He had no time for slackers or even for `get-by-ers`. He wanted drive and he didn't care how you fueled yourself as long as you came up with the goods.

"Come on, boys, we've still got some hunting to do before sundown so get a move on." He brandished a cross-bow. "What do you think of this?" He displayed the shiny, aluminum weapon to the others.

Graham whistled. "Wow, that's a beauty Bill. What'd that set you back?"

"Enough," said Bill, "but it ain't about the money, Graham, get my drift?" Graham didn't actually but still nodded in agreement.

"What are you going to hunt, Bill?" said Emerson.

"Jim tells me there are some pheasants around here somewhere and we could be eating pretty if I bagged a couple, huh?" said Bill.

"Well, I said there might be," said Jim Ahiga, walking up to them. "They're kind of rare these days. And you should have a permit for them really."

"Well, I have my Arizona Hunter and Angler permit," said Bill.

"Not much good on the reservation though," said Jim and let it go at that. The chances of these guys getting close enough to kill anything would be pretty slim and there weren't any patrols out here this time of year anyway.

"Well, you let me worry about the legal aspects," said Bill and walked back towards his tent. Graham, Gary and Emerson just stood and stared at Jim. Nobody had ever contradicted Bill Hennings, at least not in their collective memory. Gary was just about to say something to that effect when the sound of a car interrupted them and Mary's old grey heap came bouncing along the grassy road and to a stop beside the trucks. Lucy got out and Jim ran over to her.

"Lucy, what's up? Is everything alright? Is Granddad...?"

"No, it's okay. I just decided to come out and lend a hand. Mary's staying with Nascha. She's feeling much better."

"Well... good, that's great!" he said and gave her a squeeze. "But I don't know how much fun it'll be for you. These guys are a little... well, stiff might be the word."

"That doesn't matter. I'll just stay until you head out for the fishing and then I'll drive back."

"You're the best, girl. You really are. Come on, I'll introduce you around."

Coyote watched as Jim took Lucy over to the others. Well, he thought, this was a bonus. He heard a flapping of wings and Crow landed on the stone above his head.

"Why, hello Crow," Coyote barked up at him. "Come to watch the fun?"

"Fun?" said Crow, looking down on the scruffy trickster.

"Down below... fishes-out-of-water..." Coyote said innocently. "Always good for a laugh, don't you think?"

Crow didn't respond. His eye had already been distracted by another motion. With his keen sight he had spotted two other sources of activity; one close to the young people, the other to the elders. The one, a single human, dirty, disheveled and clearly mad, crawled on his hands and knees and knelt to take a drink from the stream a short distance from the student's tent city. The other, two men, paused from their pursuit of the first and sat beneath the shade of a dead tree and ate some stale bread.

"I haven't seen this much activity in the desert since the monsters walked the earth," Coyote mused. "It's almost as if life has returned here."

Crow looked at Coyote and remembered back to the days when there *were* more people here, until Coyote had turned the world against them and the yellow sand turned crimson in the sun.

Four silent figures sat hunched over coffees at the Motel 8 restaurant. Officer Wencha gazed out the window as cars zipped by on the highway. Beside him, Steven stirred his coffee slowly while Lewiston watched. Captain McKinney inspected Wencha.

Steven eventually broke the impasse. "So... what now?"

McKinney looked at him, "I don't really know, Steve," he said and looked out the window as well. "I'm still getting over my near-death experience." Wencha chuckled and looked at McKinney.

"More coffee, gents?" A passing waitress, flask in hand, stood above them and without waiting for a reply proceeded to ruin Steven's recently prepared cup. Steven looked up and stared at her until she shrugged and walked away.

"Half the mesa came down on that cave," said Lewiston. "It would take weeks to clear it out and then what? Any evidence is ruined and the trash that's in there ain't worth burying anyway."

"Well, we're still missing a man," Steven remarked.

"Yeah, according to you... We searched all over and found nothing."

"That doesn't mean he doesn't exist," said Steve, starting to get a little exasperated. "And there're still the drugs..."

"They may be down in the cave," said Wencha, joining the conversation for the first time. "For that matter, the missing guy may be in there too; down the tunnel."

"Yeah, and he may have gotten out and into the desert when he heard us coming."

"Well, he wouldn't get far on foot."

"Maybe he had a car. Maybe the shooter on the plateau had a car somewhere," said Lewiston.

"I don't think so, we found no tracks to the ledge," said Wencha.

"Well, fuck then," said Lewiston, helpfully.

"How do we even know there were any drugs," Wencha asked. "Maybe it wasn't about that."

"No, there were drugs for sure," said McKinney. "The brother spilled that once the boys told him his folks were part of the mesa now. Look, Jennings is still dead and we don't have anyone to hook this on. Anyone alive, that is, so we keep looking for this other guy. I've put out an APB for him, although that won't get far because we don't know what the hell he looks like."

"In the meantime, I think we should assume he's still on the reserve and search there," said Steven.

"I agree," Wencha added. "I'll have an extra patrol circle the Mesa a couple of times and see if we can spot him. You've got a helicopter, don't you?" he said to McKinney.

"Grounded... no budget," said McKinney.

"Also, I think we should pull in that High School field trip that's out there," said Steve. "If our guy's out there he'll be pretty desperate."

"I'm not starting some sort of panic, Steve," said McKinney. "I don't want people thinking there's some maniac on the loose."

"Isn't that what they said in Jaws just before everyone got eaten," said Steven.

McKinney eyed Steven and was about to say something when Wencha interrupted. "Look, I can send a car out to check on them. If there is someone out there I don't see how he could get all the way around the Mesa on foot. It's like fifty miles. I'm more concerned about a tourist party that's out there somewhere. They're closer to the mine. Trouble is there's no communication out there right now. Even the two-ways aren't working."

"Okay," said McKinney. He turned to Steven. "I've got a dead cop, dead drug dealers, dead bikers; not to mention that guy over in Mohave County that got his head cut off and his house burnt down after they shot his dog. I gotta start tying some of this up, you know?"

"Don't forget the Jug burned down too," said Lewiston. "And that woman..."

"Yeah, thanks...," McKinney said, cutting him off. "I can't wait to see what the papers are going to say on Monday." He looked at Steve. "You gonna stick around?"

"Yeah, I'll stay. I want to question Brixton again if that's alright with you. But I'm sure looking forward to getting back to San Francisco," said Steve. "It's so much calmer there."

There was a long pause and they fell silent once more. Wencha was staring out the window again.

"What do you keep looking at out there, man?" Lewiston asked.

"There's no birds…" Wencha said quietly.

*　　　　　*　　　　　*

They say that when the spirit (or in his case, spirits) moves you, you can do amazing things. This is what Mystic Bob was thinking as he whisked across the landscape. He'd had this dream before, this flying dream. Only he was awake now, sort of, and mused that even in his dreams he had kind of known where he was going and could, to some degree, control the direction of his flight. And he was much higher in his dreams, altitude-wise. Here he saw the sands and cactus and stone glide by as if he was walking, but quickly and tirelessly. He must have covered thirty miles this way. He thought back on the books of Carlos Castaneda. He'd read them all by the time he was twenty and he wondered what would become of himself if he dared to turn and look at the face of that which conveyed him. Would it be the end of what remained of his self? Would the line finally snap on this journey into the abyss?

Well, as it turned out, these were questions he wouldn't have time to answer as he dropped to his knees with a yell. He was on a ledge of stone that jutted out above a small cliff which sloped down to a peaceful looking stream. He looked down at his skinned and bleeding knees and at the gun wound that looked much worse but that he could scarcely feel. As a matter of fact, he couldn't feel very much of anything right now, but he was thirsty.

He scrambled down the embankment and threw himself into the cool water and drank it and submerged his head in it. Then he realized, after a moment, that he had no desire to remove his head from the water; that he wasn't struggling for air, so he held it under for longer; one minute, then two, then five. He didn't particularly need to breathe. That's a new one he thought and, sitting up on the rocks once more, he reached into his bag for an upper of some sort. Just as he was about to ingest the tubular purple pill he hesitated, his gaze held by a cactus. But not just any cactus... Again he smiled and was reminded of just how Castanedian these circumstances actually were as he reached down and pulled at the flower of the peyote plant at his feet. It had budded.

In for a penny, in for a pound, thought Mystic Bob and tossed the button down with a swig from the stream. He had a feeling that his sponsors on this trip might not like him fooling around with this right now but, dammit, they could tell him what to do but not what not to do.

He spoke a prayer that he had been taught as a child. He couldn't remember all of it, just the first few lines. He didn't even really know why he was saying it. He said it out loud so that anyone could hear it. But if anyone had been thereabouts all they would have seen was a frightening looking beggar with wild, frayed hair and even wilder eyes, sitting on a rock, more or less naked, and babbling incoherently.

Bob looked down at his right hand. Something about it was bothering him, like a painful itch, but what? Then he focused on the middle finger of his right hand and the ring that he had worn since his more conservative days when, as a ranch hand, he had married the sweet young thing on the next farm and been thrown over for a banker on a dude ranch. But he had loved the sweet young thing quite a lot, so he had been unable to throw away the ring. Now it looked very ugly and almost alive in the way it seemed to stare up at him with its little jade eye. So he took the Crip's Bowie knife that he had lifted from the car and sliced his finger off at the upper knuckle. He held up the separated digit and laughed and threw it in the water. He looked at the wound. It wasn't bleeding and it didn't hurt.

There was a slight ringing in his head, like someone was trying to get him on an internal line. But there was nothing to answer; he was just to move on, to get on with it, to do something that he wasn't quite sure about. He guessed it would become apparent when the time came. He looked at the afternoon sun, getting ready to dip behind the peaks, and the rosy fingers that extended from it sickened him. He looked at a small blue flower growing amongst a sea of red ones on a bush and it sickened him, too. He looked at a small bird winging its way away from the mesa, its tiny red head surrounded by a slew of yellow feathers, and again the nausea rose in him to the point that if he had wings himself he would have caught that bird and torn it to bits.

Everything that had once held beauty (for someone such as him) was now revolting to him and the more beautiful the thing was the greater his desire to destroy it. He was beginning to understand what it was he was meant to do. He was to do that which the mountain kings tucked away in their rocky prison beneath the mesa could not do. He would find the joy and extinguish it, he would find the beauty and defile it; he would erase life where once it had breathed and replace it with despair. And this would set him free. If only he had known this when he was younger! He could have saved so much wasted time. He would be free at last; free to die.

*   *   *

Five crows for silver,

Six crows for gold,

Seven crows for a secret never to be told.

(Part of an ancient rhyme)

"Oh, amazing bird, you crow. You with your jet black feathers and your fine black eyes. Perfectly adapted for seeing each other by day (which might account for your loving social life) and easily disguised at night (which certainly accounts for your enduring survival). You have flourished in lands inhospitable to others and have carved for all time a place in the mythologies and legends of the world. To some a harbinger of doom, to others a sign of great import, you hop about in your 'murders' and 'mobs' and bring your wise eyes to bear on the foibles of men.

Oh, amazing bird, Corvus. You fly by and fluff your feathers and find yourself a mate and, once you do, that's it for life. No feathery infidelities for you, noble crow. You build your nests and have your chicks and do the parenty thing, but should one of your kind be in danger or distress, you will come to its aid even if you are unrelated to it. Not many birds would do that. Not many men would do that.

And you don't fly the nest, you young crows. You take from the parents, learn to fly and then for the next year or two, while waiting to mature, you hang about and help with the next years nest-building. Nobody tells you to do this; nobody bribes you by letting you use the car for a date.

Oh, most intelligent of birds. You who have, alone amongst non-primates, developed the use of tools. Freud once wrote that tool use was among mankind's first acts of civilization. Are you becoming civilized? Or were you always civilized and it is we who are losing our civility and can no longer judge? You cut sticks with your beaks and shape them so that they are serrated and then use these to cut other sticks and give them barbed ends which strips back the thorny bark on tender branches. Creative crow!

You can count! Why, it has been observed that if three hunters go into a blind, the crows will wait, out of range. If three hunters then emerge and leave, the crows will go about their business. If only two emerge, the crows will maintain their place until the third also leaves. Amazing!"

"Yes, yes," said Crow to Coyote with a sigh. "Is there a reason for all this? Do you think that if you flatter me enough I will drop my guard and no longer watch out for what you do? I am not like the crow of fable that drops the fat to look at his image in the stream because he has been told how handsome he is. I am Crow, of dream and visions. I am Crow who watches and protects. I am the messenger and guide of the spirit world."

"There is no motive in these things I say," said Coyote, and rolled onto his back on the grass, his tongue lolling out disgustingly. "I like you, that's all."

Crow cawed a laugh at this and, shaking his head, hopped into the stream. He stuck his beak into the water and drank but spat the liquid out. It was foul and bitter. He gazed about this way and that and smelled at the air but sense of smell was not his strength so he took to the air and realized now, as he peered to the north, why Coyote had been talking on and on. While he, Crow, had sat and listened to this drivel, the man-monster slave of the imprisoned rock gods was creeping ever-closer to his purpose.

"You have tricked me!" shouted Crow to the Coyote below who was now sitting on his haunches watching him.

"Yep... that's what I do," Coyote yipped and sprang away in the direction of Big Jim's campout. "Let us see you warn the children of the spirits now! Ya-hey!"

*   *   *

"Maybe he doubled back..."

Albert sat in the relative shade of the dead tree and watched The Crip move back and forth on the dune, poking at it with a stick as though he expected the stash to reveal itself in the loose sand; green leafy bundles of cash, springing, weed-like from the dead, dry earth; bags of coke floating up through the grey rubble like crispy bubbles in a pot of desiccated stew.

The Crip stopped and looked back at him. Albert couldn't understand how he could stay out there in this sun. His brain must be cooking like soup in that pointy skull of his. He laughed at this.

"What's so funny, Albert?" Crip asked, menacingly. "So what if he doubled back? It's the stash we want; we can deal with him later."

"But he's the only one who knows what he did with it."

"It's long buried by now. He couldn't keep it on him; too much weight. We just have to find out where he went."

"This is the fucking desert man! What are we going to do, dig it all up looking for it? It's fucking nuts! You're fucking nuts!"

"You keep saying that, Albert... Look, I don't care how drugged up he was, he couldn't have gone more than a couple of miles carrying those bags on that leg. We'll either find his burnt out carcass or some place he would throw the stuff. Look around.... That tree you're lying under was the first thing that wasn't rock or sand we've seen in the last four hours. He'd have to leave it somewhere he could find it again; by a tree like that or a weird looking boulder or something. We just have to go in a circle checking out things like that and we'll find it. And if you call me nuts again, I'll cut your ears off."

"There's not much water left," Albert said, checking the bottle in his back pack. We'll have to go back tomorrow if we can't find any. I'm tired of eating this fucking jerky too."

"Albert, you have to be cheapest fucking crook I've ever hung with, you know that? Man!" He threw the stick at Albert and it clattered off the dead branch above his head. "Let's go…"

Albert struggled to his feet and put his hat back on. Nothing for it, he thought, this guy is going to be the death of me.

They made their way up a ridge of broken rock and dirt and stood facing the southeast. The sun was starting to get a little lower now and the heat was a little less crazy. They walked in what was now a parallel direction to that which they had been following. Crip was right about one thing, there was precious little in the way of natural markers to hide things by.

"There's a bunch of boulders over there. We'll make for that," said The Crip. Albert swatted at the bugs on his neck. How did things like this live out here? What did they eat when he wasn't here for them to feed on?

It took about a half an hour to reach the rocks that The Crip had spotted and when they did, he immediately started to poke around in the thousands of nooks and crevices. Madness, Albert thought. There wasn't a single sign to point towards anyone ever having been here at all let alone in the last twenty-four hours. Albert thought again about jumping Crip and bashing his brains out with a rock, but Crip was still pretty energetic and wary so Albert figured to wait a little longer until he wore himself out with his constant prodding and digging.

Suddenly, Crip stopped his searching and stood peering off into the distance between two rocks. "Got you now, Bobby…" he said in a low growl.

"What are you looking at?" said Albert coming up behind him.

"Smoke, about a half mile down there." The Crip said, pointing down the slope and taking out his gun and checking the load. A thin wisp of smoke curled up from behind a small rise, spreading out across the desert in the weak head-breeze that blew hot wind against their faces.

"What if it's not him?" Albert said. "Could he start a fire out here? He couldn't start a fire…"

"Who gives a shit? If it's not him, they've got water and food whoever they are. And maybe they've seen him. Either way, we'll go check it out." He crawled between the rocks, popping out the other side like a snake from its hole. Albert felt a lot better thinking about someone cooking something edible. And maybe beer... Together, they strode, side by side, down the slope. Each, in his own way, hungry; each thinking that whoever it was on the other end of their walk was in deep trouble.

*   *   *

Karen crossed over the campgrounds and wandered down by the river. It was too hot, way too hot. She could hear the kids splashing and laughing in the larger swimming hole located upstream but she took a fork in the footpath and walked south a little, enjoying the cooling effect of the few stubby, desert willows that grew near the water. Even the bedrock and sand felt a little cooler down here and she stopped and sat and removed her boots and socks. She left them under a stone and continued on to the waters edge.

The water moved sluggishly at this point but from where she stood, ankle deep in the surprisingly cool water, she could see that the water sped up a little further down, near a bend and a rocky outcrop about ten feet higher than the water level. She strode through the stream, kicking the water up a bit, loving the feel of the sandy silt between her toes. She paused for a moment when she caught sight of a couple of small fish skittering about in a rocky bowl submerged by a bank. If she'd known that they were pupfish and that they shouldn't have been there and that the only way they could be there was if something had ruptured underground, many miles away, she might have wondered about it. But she didn't. She just watched them play for a couple of minutes. Then she realized that she was also watching something else, something floating on the surface above the diminutive fish. That something was a face; a reflection... She jerked her head up and looked to the outcrop a few feet away but there was nothing there to be seen so, after a minute, she continued on downstream.

The water gurgled and spun about her feet as she stood looking back towards where she had come from, wondering again at the face in the water. She thought she heard a noise to her left and turned as a rock skittered down from above and splashed into the water. It was suddenly very quiet and she couldn't hear the kids anymore. Even the sound of the water seemed muted and a chill ran down her spine.

Again a rustle from above and she thought now that it was probably just a couple of kids making out in the bushes on the far bank. As much as she didn't want to be the matron on this trip she was, in fact, just that so she put on her 'stern' face and pushed through the stream towards the bushes. Any kid could get carried away in this setting and make the wrong decision. She coughed warningly as she moved, hoping to alert the lovers, but before she could make the other bank a dark shadow flashed across the stream towards her. The cry of a bird from above and then Karen was running back towards the other side as a huge crow flew above her, lunged at her and almost landed on her head.

Karen let out a short scream... then there was silence again. She collapsed on the bank and looked over at the ridiculously large crow now perched on the ground across the stream from her. The wind ruffled its feathers as it stared at her.

"Stupid bird... What the hell are you doing?" she panted out. "You scared the shit out of me!"

The bird just sat there, its blank, black eyes motionless in its head. Then it started to hop up and about the ledge upon which it sat and began to caw loudly at her. Karen had had enough of this. She got up, brushed the dust off her knees from when she had scrambled up out of the water and started to walk back towards the camp along the river, just once glancing over her shoulder at the bird.

Crow watched her go. Then he looked back into the bush where Mystic Bob, flat on his stomach, his hands drawn into little straining claws, watched Karen go as well, confused about the conflict between the desire to destroy that was urging him to run after her and the unreasonable fear he felt for the black bird that stood between them. He eased himself back down into the bush and tried to control the shaking that paralyzed his guts. Crow watched him for a moment and then took to the air.

Meanwhile, Emerson Rose, account executive, was having his own wildlife encounter some miles away. It was his job, he had been told, to get further up the ravine, make a lot of noise at an appointed time and supposedly flush many pheasants up into the air and to the east, where Bill and the others waited. Then Bill, supposedly, would kill one with his crossbow and they'd all eat it later.

This, to Emerson, sounded patently ridiculous but Bill called the shots and this was his first 'challenge' so he had to make good. He knew that one more mistake would be the end for him and he might as well just leave and start looking for another job. Of course, he couldn't just leave because he had no way of getting out of this stinking hole of a desert. He felt like crying and sat down on a log to do just that.

As the first tears of frustration were pumping up from his tear ducts to the surface of his eyes, he felt something move inside the log... something alive. Could it possibly be a pheasant? Could he trap it and kill it and parade it, he, Emerson, the successful hunter, down to the camp and throw the bird, its neck wrung forcefully and finally, at Bill's feet and proclaim loudly... "How's that Mr. Bill! I didn't even need a bow!" The fantasy had already played itself out in his head successfully as he knelt down and peered into the open end of the long-dead tree.

He couldn't see anything at first but then, as his eyes grew accustomed to the interior of the stump, he spied two shining dots. He couldn't remember anything about pheasant eyes or indeed anything about any part of any bird but he fancied that this would be the obvious hiding place for a ground bird. Nesting, he thought, that's what it's doing. He pulled back and thought about what to do. Smoke it out? No that would be stupid and would probably result in about four hectares of burnt scrub and possibly the deaths of the very people he wanted to impress. The opening in the log was about two feet across. He was a small man. Emerson took out the camping knife that he had bought at the Sears down by the coffee shop in the nameless suburb in which he lived and eyed it with anticipation. After all, it was just a bird. How hard could it be to kill? Simply crawl into the log, knife the bird and return to the world a hero. He knelt down again and, hands forward, wriggled his soft shoulders into the log.

Gila Monster, however, saw it this way... A huge animal with a single shining tooth was cramming itself into his lair to kill him. Venom sacs went stiff with anger and began to feed a stream of toxic death into the twin hypodermics that were his fangs. He had killed one of these things that smelled like meat before, recently in fact, and he could do it again. Another four inches should do it...

*   *   *

Mystic Bob peered through the dirty rear window of the converted school bus. Standing on the trailer hitch of the baggage carrier he whistled a little tune between his yellow teeth, many of which were now either missing or reduced to craggy little fragments wedged into his gums. When he jumped down to the ground he left two soggy handprints to mark his having been up there. He looked at them and laughed, sort of, and waved to them. He then picked up a largish rock and smashed it through the bus door. Reaching in and springing the hinge he jumped up the stairs and gazed solemnly at the driver's seat. He sat in it. There was a ball cap sitting on the dashboard. He put it on his head. He started to sing... "The old gray mare, she ain't what she used to be... everybody now!" Then he stopped suddenly as he spotted the two-way radio in its sling under the dash. It had been left on and was hissing slightly. Bob kicked it to pieces.

Releasing a catch that he found beside the steering column, he leapt down from the bus and raised the yellow hood, looked down at the big engine and with one motion severed the leads from the distributor with his knife. He laughed again. He had killed a bus. He started to cry. He ran to the bush and turned around and made an exaggerated sign of the cross with his greasy hand and then he disappeared quickly down the embankment.

Two miles upstream, Kai Ahiga and Allison Donkers held hands and walked beside the glistening water. He was relaxed and happy and loved being in this element with her; his element. The heat made their hands clammy but neither minded. She looked so lovely in her shorts and blouse and Kai's heart was pounding in his chest. She looked up at him.

"What is it?"

"Sorry, what?" he asked, missing some breath.

"What are you staring at? There isn't a bug on me is there?" she said trying to see her shoulder.

Kai laughed. "No, no bug." Then he stopped. He didn't know what to say next. They had stopped near the outcrop that Karen had been under during her encounter with Crow. Kai was struggling to think of what to say next but Allison prevented anything stupid from coming out when she kissed him lightly on the lips. Then she pulled away.

"Hey," she said. "Look at that. Is that a cave or something?"

Kai looked to where she was pointing and could see that there was, in fact, an opening about three quarters of the way up the bank. They climbed up and looked in and could see that it was quite sizable inside.

"Let's go in," Allison said and, pulling him by the arm, they entered the cave. Inside it was remarkably cool and moist and behind the small wall of the entrance there was a layer of thick Spanish moss stretching, like a yellow carpet, to the rear wall. Up above, light entered thinly from a crack and the moisture of the wall reflected it around the room. Within a few minutes they could see well. "This is amazing," Allison said. "Let's not tell anyone about it." She turned to Kai and for the moment, when their eyes met, she had nothing more to say. Kai took her hand and they knelt down on the moss and their mouths came together passionately. His hand folded through her hair and down the nape of her neck, softly finding her shoulder beneath the lapel of her shirt. They lay down as she sighed and they clenched together tightly as the desire that had been building between them these last few days took control of their young bodies.

So taken into each other were they that they didn't notice that the room had gone slightly darker because the natural skylight was being blocked; blocked by the slightly trembling shape of Mystic Bob as he watched them, a schism of anxiety opening between two equally strong forces in his ravaged mind. He clenched his knife to his chest and the blade bit between his ribs, drawing a small trickle of blood.

Just before the incident at the bus, Bob had reached for the last time into his bag of tricks. It was pretty much empty now except for a small plastic box containing two tabs of purple micro-dot acid that he had had in there since the early 80's, a memento of happier times. He had looked down at them and thought about the days when he had actually believed that he could adjust himself for the better psycho-actively. Unfortunately, if there is any truth at all to the concept of permanent positive personality change through the use of such drugs, Bob was not in a position to figure it out. He had just added further fuel to the fire that was his maladjustment. However, it has to be said, that LSD is a powerful thing and that, depending on the person, it can bring about some beautiful things for the mind; at least most of the time.

As Bob looked down at the young couple, beautiful in so many ways, on their golden bower below, his eyes began to water. The Lysergic acid coursing through his brain linked all that was left of the godhead in Bob to the essential life below and effectively, if temporarily, screened out the psychic intrusion of the two demons some miles away. Still trapped in the rock, they screamed their frustration and anger.

For the second time that day Mystic Bob failed to kill and as he rolled off the rock he started to run to the south. In the brief time that the last of his drugs had bought him Bob wanted to be back with the only love he knew, the only family that he had really ever had. Bob wanted to be back with The Crip.

*　　　　　　*　　　　　　*

"Emerson... what the hell do you think you are doing!"

Bill Henson, Gary Ellis and Graham Tinker stood atop the rise overlooking the shallow valley in which the log with Emerson's semi-articulated body laid, its legs protruding out into the rapidly darkening sands.

It was at that second, strangely enough (and as strangely as things usually happen), that Gila lunged out at the approaching hand of Emerson Rose. The shout from above caused Emerson to ram his head into the top of the inside of the log and his hand jerked uncontrollably towards his chest. Gila's fangs, like an arrow shot at a ghost, missed their target completely but took root in one of the white plastic bags that lay all around him. He struggled madly to free himself, ripping it open. The venom from his bite shot downwards into the ninety percent pure cocaine that was contained therein and as he drew the fangs out he sucked a mouthful of the virtually pure nose-candy into his stomach. Gila died numb, but died nonetheless.

Emerson scrambled out of the log and jumped up, grabbing at his glasses that had fallen off and lay on the ground in front of him. "Bill?" he called out as he scrubbed at his glasses with his shirt tail and peered into the growing darkness around him.

"Yes, god damn it, who do you think? What are you playing around at down there?"

"Pheasants, sir... I think they're in this log!"

Gary and Graham guffawed and Bill whirled on the two of them, saying, "Will you two shut the hell up!" They did shut the hell up. Bill Henson looked down at Emerson with his dirty shirt and soiled glasses and even he, Bill Henson, head of a mighty corporation dedicated to the sustenance of a nation (or at least the shit it grew in) had to take pity. He lowered the cross-bow to his side and walked slowly down into the gulley.

"You found some pheasants, did you Em?" he said, softly.

He looked into Emerson's eyes and at the tear stains crawling like little, tell-tale worms down his cheeks. The man was obviously close to a breakdown. Bill didn't want to destroy Emerson; he just wanted to find out what he was made of. And now he knew. He thought, maybe, that he could find something else for him to do at work.

He put his arm out around Emerson's shoulders and tried to stop the sobs that were even now beginning to wrack the top of his frame. Gary and Graham looked away awkwardly.

"Really, Bill, I think..." choked Emerson.

"Let's take a look shall we?" said Bill and leaned over to investigate the log. "Well, there certainly is something down in there. Give me your flashlight, Gary." Gary handed it over and Bill flicked it on. "What the hell...?" he said and knelt down. "Grab the end of this thing, you two, and tip it down towards me."

Gary and Graham did as they were told and lifted the end up. Gila and ten kilos of coke and three plastic money belts containing about five hundred thousand dollars in hundred dollar bills slid and spilled out of the dead deciduous and landed in a pile at Bill's feet.

They all stood, silently, looking down at the stash. Gary's eyes went immediately to the clear plastic money belts and the cash therein. Graham's went to the bags of coke and his mouth watered and in a flash he was back at the hotel in Santa Monica with the hookers that he had hired, fruitlessly.

"Well, it's not pheasant but I think we should take this back and show Jim." Bill said.

Gary looked at Graham, Graham looked at Gary and then they both looked at Bill. Interesting things were going through their rapidly spinning minds at this point. Emerson was just thanking whatever gods existed that, whatever the outcome, he was probably off the hook for now. Gary and Graham were thinking exactly the same thing as each other... How can we suggest to Bill that we keep this stuff? Would Bill go along?

Bill stood up and coughed. No, he wouldn't go along. There was no way these drugs and this money were going to get into their respective hands. Not without a lot of killing and covering up and who-knows-what. For some reason Gary was reminded of the old film, Treasure of The Sierra Madre. A lot of needless hardship in a vista of shifting sands only to end with death for all.

"You're right, Bill, Jim will know what to do," Gary said.

"Unless it's his, of course," said Graham.

"Don't be stupid," said Bill. "He wouldn't bring us camping half a mile from his drug stash. Let's get this stuff back to camp."

"What about this thing?" Emerson said, poking with his foot at the lifeless Gila Monster.

"Bring it along," said Bill. "I'll have it stuffed. We can give it out as a trophy at the next awards dinner. We'll call it the Em Award. Presented to people who look into things other people wouldn't think of." Bill looked meaningfully at Graham and Gary. Emerson felt like kissing Bill at that moment, but held off.

*   *   *

When the four got back to the campsite, they could see Jim sitting at the fire. Across from him sat a figure with their back to them. At first they thought it was Lucy but as they drew near it became apparent that it was a man; a short man with a rifle lying across his knees. They all stopped. After a second Bill walked up to the fire. The flames played across his face.

"Company, huh, Jim?" said Bill, "Friend of yours?"

"No," Jim said quietly, not taking his eyes off The Crip.

"Why don't you all come over to the fire?" The Crip said standing up, the rifle barrel slowly starting to angle up.

196

"Stay where you are, guys," Bill commanded, backing off slightly, his hand tightening on the stock of the armed cross-bow.

"Do what he says, Bill," Jim said. "They've got Lucy."

"What do you mean 'they'" Bill said, his voice wavering now. There was a noise behind the Humvee and Albert came forward, his arm around Lucy's neck; a gun in his hand.

"Come over by the fire," Crip said again. "I won't ask again. And drop the cross-bow, okay?"

Bill looked at Jim and Jim was giving him a look that was more or less a plea. Graham and Gary inched forward. "Better do what he says, Bill."

"The hell I will," Bill said. "I've dealt with his kind before. They've..."

And that was the last thing Bill Henson ever said as The Crip fired a bullet into his throat. Bill's body crumpled to the ground as Jim leapt to his feet and with one motion knocked the rifle from The Crip's hand and in a second had him on the ground, his elbow at his windpipe.

Albert screamed at him, "I'll kill her!" Jim looked down at the Crip smiling up at him despite the fact that he was slowly beginning to lose consciousness and then at Lucy, her eyes wide with terror. Emerson was on his knees, crying and still holding onto the dead lizard. The Crip forced his way out from under Jim's weight and picked up the rifle. He tapped the barrel of it slowly and lightly against Jim's forehead. Then he went over to where Graham and Gary stood gripping the drug bags and money belts.

"Well, what have we got here?" said The Crip taking one of the money belts. "This is certainly a turning point in our vacation, Albert. Yes, sir, things are definitely starting to look up. You weren't planning on running off with our property now, were you fella?" he said to Graham.

Gary spoke up. "We found it out there. We didn't know it was yours."

Crip laughed. "Well of course you didn't know it was mine, fella. You only just met me didn't you? Tell you what, why don't you take these bags and put them in that car over there for me, huh?"

"Okay," said Gary.

"Okay," said The Crip. Gary looked at Graham and they walked to the car, skirting the still body of Bill Henson. They deposited the bags in through the open window and returned to the fire. Jim was still standing, watching Albert and Lucy. Albert was staring at Jim.

"I know you, don't I?" Albert asked Jim. Jim said nothing. Lucy, calmer now, waited. "Yeah, I do. You're the fucker that almost knocked me off my bike the other day; in town, right?"

"Look," Jim said, turning to the Crip. "You've got what I guess you wanted out here. Why don't you just take the truck there, take the keys to the cars and get going. It'll take us a day to walk out of here. You'd be long gone."

"Well, you see, the problem with that Jim... It is Jim, right? The problem with that is I just killed that old guy there and you all saw me do it."

"Oh, fuck," Emerson wailed, "they're going to kill us all!" And he fell on his stomach and started to puke.

"You see, Albert?" The Crip said loudly, pointing at Emerson. "That's what's wrong with America today. Yes sir, that is it in a nutshell. You, girlie," he said to Lucy and aiming his rifle at her, "you get over with boyfriend there." Lucy ran to Jim and he put his arm around her and felt her tremble. "Albert, get these three into the Hummer."

Albert rounded up Graham and Gary who helped lift the paralyzed Emerson from the ground and prodded them into the truck.

"Tie the door handles together with that tent rope there," Crip said and Albert began to fasten the doors so they couldn't be opened from the inside.

Jim turned Lucy's face towards his own and looked into her eyes. All their life passed between them in that look, all the love that he felt for her or would ever feel; all their hopes for the future; the children that they wanted to have; everything. Lucy knew now what Jim was thinking. These men were going to kill them if they didn't do something, anything. She smiled and nodded at him. Jim smiled back, touching her cheek. Then he pushed her, stumbling, towards the bushes and threw himself towards Bill's body and the cross-bow at his side. The Crip fired at him as he moved but missed, the bullet smacking the sand a foot from Jim's head. Albert ran towards his gun, left on the hood of the truck.

Jim rolled over the body, grabbed the cross-bow and fired in one motion. The bolt whined by The Crip's face, missing it by half an inch and disappeared into the Humvee near its gas tank. A slow stream of gas began to ooze from the hole.

The Crip dabbed at the trickle of blood that the feather on the shaft had grazed into his cheek "That, you see, Jim is why you don't bring a cross-bow to a gunfight," said The Crip. "One shot and then... well, what you gonna do then? Go get the girl, Albert."

Albert grabbed a flashlight and ran after Lucy. Jim stood up. The Crip walked over to him and stopped about five feet away. "Get down on your knees, fucker," he said. Jim didn't move. Instead, Jim threw all his weight at The Crip. The Crip fired and the bullet ripped through Jim's left eye. Big Jim Ahiga landed in a clump at The Crip's feet, dead.

Albert re-appeared moments later dragging an unconscious Lucy. "Put her in the car, we'll take her with us. She might be useful." Albert looked down at the pretty woman and silently concurred. He pushed her into the back seat and jumped into the driver's side. He started the car with a roar and Crip came over and threw his rifle into the passenger-side foot-well.

"What about them?" Albert asked. Gary and Graham's faces were pressed, frozen in horror, against the tinted windows of the Humvee.

The Crip looked at them, studying their faces for a moment. Emerson was nowhere to be seen. "Seems a shame, doesn't it," he said, admiring now the lines of the shining gold SUV, its chrome and colours highlighted by the red and orange flames of the campfire. It looked like an ad in a magazine. "Still, we wouldn't get far in that..."

The Crip walked over to the fire and pulled a piece of glowing wood from it. He tossed it near the gathering pool of gasoline pouring from the hole in the truck. As he walked back to the car the fire ignited the pool and then the Humvee was engulfed in flame. The Crip got into the car and they drove away into the night. The muffled screams from inside the Humvee eventually died away also.

CHAPTER SIX

CEREBELLUM

Lucy's grey sedan rolled to a stop on the gravel shoulder not fifty yards from her house.

"What the hell's the matter?" The Crip asked, his hand clenched on the door handle.

"I don't know. It just stopped," Albert replied, both hands gripping the wheel and searching the dash board for some mechanical answer. There was a soft moan from the back seat where Lucy lay, crumpled in a heap against the door. She was starting to regain consciousness to some degree but still struggled to find herself after the sharp blow to the back of her head that Albert had administered as he grappled with her in the desert scrub.

"What do you mean, 'it just stopped'? Is it the battery?"

"No. I mean, I don't think so. The lights are still on. It just died."

"For fuck's sake..." Crip looked around in the dark and back to the house that they had just passed. "Well, get out and fix it before those people get nosey."

Albert popped the hood and got out and stood, staring down at the motor. He jiggled the battery connections. He tapped on the distributor. He pulled at the spark plug leads. That brought to an end the full gamut of his mechanical knowledge. He just rode engines, he didn't fix them. He went back to the driver's seat and tried to start the car. Nothing happened. No sound. No steadily declining battery whine, no unresponsive starter motor; nothing. He looked at The Crip.

"Well?" said the Crip.

"Well, what?" replied Albert.

The Crip sighed. "Alright… go and see if they have a car at that house."

"There's nothing in the driveway."

"Yeah, I can see that. Maybe there's something out back; a truck or something."

Albert got out and walked towards the house. Through the window he could see a figure walking into one of the front rooms, their shadow cast across the window drapes. He skipped across the drive and into the side yard. Sticking his head around the side of the building he checked out the back area. There was nothing, obviously. All the Ahiga vehicles were in use.

Then as he turned and started back towards the car a light broke across his path and when he looked up he was confronted by somebody's shadow, standing silhouetted against the front door frame, the screen held open by a thin, pale arm.

"Who's there?" The voice of a young woman…"Is anybody there?"

"Um, yeah," Albert called up to the porch. "Sorry, we've had some car trouble; down on the road there. I was looking to see if anybody was about." He started to inch towards the porch.

"Well, you should have just knocked on the door. Do you want to use the phone?" the woman said. Her voice, brave enough, still had a tinge of nervousness to it that was unmistakable.

Albert stepped up on to the porch but then stopped dead when he caught sight of her face. He was standing three feet away from the woman he had just left in the car unconscious.

"Who is it, Mary?" came a voice from inside and then suddenly an old man was standing behind her, staring over her shoulder at Albert.

"I don't know," Mary Sanford said. "He says his car broke down."

"That one there?" said Nascha, looking over at the grey car. "That looks like Lucy's car."

Mary looked over at the grey car, recognizing it instantly; then back at Albert and then there was a brief moment of silence. Albert started to reach for the gun in his belt, but Nascha acted faster, hauling Mary by the scruff of her sweater back into the house and slamming the door. As Albert leapt to it he could hear the bolt on the safety lock ramming home.

"Open the fucking door!" he shouted, pointlessly.

"Get around to the back" another voice bawled loudly behind him. Crip grabbed Albert's elbow and shoved him in the direction of the back yard. Albert ran, hoping to get to the rear entrance before they thought of locking it, but before he could even reach the back door there was a shout and the sound of glass smashing. Albert put a foot into the flimsy wooden door and it gave way immediately, splintering at the latch. He ran into the small hall and kitchen and then into the living room where Crip stood, shotgun in hand, and the two occupants of the house were pressed against the back wall. Crip was staring at Mary.

"What is this?" he said, with an odd, even tone in his voice. The gun barrel shook slightly.

"I know," said Albert. "Fucking freaky, huh?"

"Where's Lucy?" Nascha said in a low tone, his arm around Mary.

"Well, this is just a guess, but I'd say she's outside in the back seat of the car," said The Crip and sat down in the armchair.

"Is she hurt?" said Nascha.

"A little bump on the head... You got a car here?"

"No."

"Well, now that's a situation, ain't it," said The Crip. He looked up at Albert and Albert just looked back and shrugged. "Take the old man and bring the other girl in here. We'll figure out what to do in a minute." Albert motioned to the old man and together they walked to the car leaving Mary and Crip inside.

"Why are you doing this?" Nascha asked. "If you want the car, just take it. Just leave the girl."

"Shut up," Albert replied. He opened the door with his left hand and nodded to Nascha. "Get her out."

"Get who out?" said Nascha.

Albert looked into the car. Lucy was gone. He ran out on to the highway and stopped on the tarmac. He looked back at Nascha. Nascha was smiling at him. He looked into the ditch on the far side of the road and up and down the highway. Then back at Nascha. Nascha just shrugged.

"Now, that's a situation, ain't it," Nascha said and started to walk back to the house. Albert caught up behind him and shoved him to the ground, viciously, with a blow between the shoulders.

"Pretty fucking smart, aren't you old man," he cursed down at him.

"No, not too smart really," Nascha said, looking up at him, his breath coming in short gasps. "But I know when things are going badly."

There was a pause and Albert kicked him in the back with his boot. "Get into the house."

In a moment they were standing in front of The Crip. "What do you mean, she's gone?" he said getting up slowly.

"She must have come to and got out when we were getting into the house."

"Yeah, no shit, professor. Thank you," said The Crip and walked over to Mary, turning on the front porch light as he went. He stepped behind her quickly and grabbed a handful of her hair. She yelped in pain. He pushed her over to the door and out into the front yard and tossed her, like a rag, to the ground. "Don't move," he shouted at her.

"Listen… Lucy… Is that it…? Lucy?" Crip shouted into the night. "Well, you have about five seconds to get your ass back here or I am going to water your lawn with this girl's brains." Mary started to cry.

From across the road and down a bit, a figure rose from the ditch and walked the ten yards or so to the driveway. Lucy held her head and staggered slightly as she crossed the lawn to Mary. Mary jumped up and ran to her. They held each other in the orange glow of the house light. Lucy tried to comfort Mary as best she could. She could see that Mary was in trouble and was barely hanging on. Crip stepped down from the porch and walked over to them. He stood and stared at the two.

"Well, now that is really something. Sisters, huh? What are the chances? Get inside," he ordered.

"No!" Mary screamed back at him. Her voice echoed out across the desert and then died on the uncaring sand.

"Its okay, Mary," said Lucy. "It'll be alright, don't worry. Besides, there's Nascha."

Mary looked into Lucy's eyes. Lucy knew that if she was there with these men that probably Jim was dead. But she tried to look as confidently as she could back at her sister. Somehow they had to figure this out. She helped Mary inside and when they stepped into the living room Nascha came over to them and helped Mary into a chair. Lucy saw the grazes on Nascha's face and hands from his fall.

"You alright, granddad?" she asked softly.

"Don't worry about me," Nascha replied.

"Get us some food," The Crip said, closing the front door and locking it.

*   *   *

Mystic Bob was only propelling along at half-speed now that the connection with his buried masters was diminished, so covering the distance spanning the width of the mesa took a bit of time and more than a few stumbles and cuts. But he knew instinctively where the Crip would be, or at least had been, and almost by smell found the conflagration that was Big Jim Ahiga's expedition station.

The Hummer was still on fire, although it was mostly the tires that fueled that. The frame was blackened and most of the glass cracked but not shattered; except for one. What looked like a burnt boot on the end of a charred leg hung, uselessly, from one of the rear windows. Someone had made some kind of effort to get out; for a second or two, before being overwhelmed. The campfire was just a pile of smouldering embers now and Bob almost tripped over the prone body of Bill Henson as he headed towards Jim's pickup truck, still parked by the sheds.

He gawped down at he remains of Bill and Jim and tried to remember where he was and what he was doing. His face, blank and disinterested, registered nothing as he perused the carnage. He knew who had done this, which was all that mattered really. Like a blood-hound, he sniffed at the air and tilted his head to one side, listening. The night was silent, although he thought he could hear, in the distance to the north, something that sounded like a train approaching from a long way off. He knelt down by Jim's body and rolled him over. He held Jim's heavy head up on an angle and studied the face. The eye not shot out was still opened, gazing at nothing, staring up through him, lifeless and cold. Then that one lid closed, an automatic response, leaving the face winking at him, noiselessly; the bloody hole looking now like one remaining, red-rimmed eye. Bob grinned and let the head drop back into the sand.

"I know," Bob whispered. "It's all a big joke, isn't it?"

He looked at the stain on his hands from where the bullet had exited Jim's skull and wiped them on his pants. He stood and picked up a banana from the open cooler by the fire, peeled it and stood munching it in the glow of the Hummer for a moment feeling the pulpy fruit slide down his dry throat. Then he tossed the skin down and walked over to the old pick-up. The keys were still in the dash, so he climbed in, took one more look at the mayhem around him and then started the engine and began to drive away. The sound from the distance was getting louder now and a few grains of sand whiffed against the windshield, thrown by the child of a softly groaning wind. He drove out onto the stony road.

A couple of minutes later, as he headed towards the highway, he spotted a pair of headlights, bouncing across the landscape, coming his way. So he turned off his own lights and pulled into a small break in the rocks and waited for the other vehicle to pass. The police SUV of Doug Wencha drove slowly by and Bob could see the officer's tired face reflected in the dashboard light. When the truck had rounded the bend, out of sight, Bob drove back onto the road and continued on his way. He left his lights off. Bob didn't need them on. Bob was on auto-pilot.

*　　　　*　　　　*

There was a grayness starting to edge up over the horizon and infuse the sand with its own colour. The featureless landscape of night was giving way to the slightly less featureless landscape of early morning and things were changing over slowly but surely. The night guard gave way to the day shift as certain insects and lizards disappeared down holes and into trees and were replaced by different Mojave folk, flying here and there and scurrying or creeping to begin the day's activities.

Doug Wencha sat in his truck and looked straight ahead. He was still trying to breathe. He kind of didn't want to blink, so his eyes were getting watery. He had headed out to the desert to talk to Jim and his party, hoping to catch them before they ventured out on a fishing excursion or an early morning hike. Now, at the site, he shook all over and sweat was forming on his cheeks and, in opposition, his mouth was as dry as the dust that was sweeping up and over the boiling hood of the SUV. His hand went down to the radio mike that he knew wouldn't work.

"Wencha to base. RMP 15... come back." Static and nothing else; a dry, useless haze of sound crackled from the speaker. He hung up the mike. Sometimes you're all alone, he thought.

He opened up the door and stepped out onto the sand. There was a whine that he could hear and the fine, granular desert floor was being whipped up and it pecked at his cheeks like small bugs. The occasional grain hit his eye and he wiped at his face with the back of his hand. Despite the lack of light he pulled his sunglasses from his jacket pocket and put them on. Now there was a steady flick of sound added as the sand hit the black glass.

He took his revolver from his belt and studying the surrounding cover as he went, advanced towards the horror that lay in front of him. He knew before he was anywhere near the bodies that one of them was Jim Ahiga. Arriving at that body first, he knelt down and felt the neck arteries for pulse. There was none. He reached over and did the same for Bill Henson and the result was the same. The bodies were cold now and were becoming part of the landscape; cold and gray.

The smoking hulk of the Hummer was next and he winced when he spotted the leg. He moved over to the car and reacted back as the heat from the still-steaming metal caught him in the face. He moved upwind and around to the cooler side and peered into the broken window. He counted two bodies until he pushed on the front window of the driver's side with a stick, and the shattering glass revealed a third, fire-eaten corpse. There was no sound but the sand buffeting the side of the big luxury vehicle and Wencha gagged and bent to one side and threw up into the scrub. He started to cry, not very different really from the tears that Emerson Rose had shed a few hours before; tears that ran because of the sheer repulsiveness of the situation; tears of frustration in a world that seemed to just turn its back.

What the hell was happening here? There was so much death and so little to explain it. He was frightened. Doug Wencha moved in a world that kept one foot firmly planted in his native life and the other, as a professional lawman, in a society that seemed to want to pull him apart from it. He knew that men, men who were close at hand, had done this. But his heart told him that there was more to all this. That there were elements involved that had more to do with corn and fur than metal and machines. There was a sound behind him and he turned to view the empty desert. What should have been an off-white-coloured surface was being draped by a dark curtain that was advancing rapidly towards him. He hadn't seen one for many years but he knew this for what it was; a sandstorm.

He looked back to the crime scene and knew that, within a very short time, this area would be scoured clean of any forensic evidence. He ran back to his truck and popped the rear hatch. He reached in and took out small camera and started taking pictures of the Hummer as quickly as he could. Even as he did so the wind was rising and the whipped sand was becoming painful. He started to cough.

After having taken as many pictures of the truck as he could, he turned to do the same with the bodies by the fire pit. He stopped though, thoroughly confused by what he saw. A large, reddish coyote stood looking down at the body of Jim Ahiga. It bent its head down and nosed at the corpse. It licked Jim's forehead. Wencha yelled at the dog and moved towards it. The big coyote slowly looked up at him for a moment and then turned its attention to the body of Bill Henson.

"Yah! Get!" Wencha shouted. But the animal just stood its ground. The wind was growing louder now and the sand on the back of his neck was becoming more painful. Wencha stooped and picked up a rock and tossed it towards the shaggy beast. It just stood its ground. It opened its mouth and yelped. Not once, but several times. Wencha's heart skipped a beat. He drew his revolver again and fired into the air. Then the big coyote rose up on its hind legs and yowled in response, walking five steps towards him on its hind legs alone. Wencha moaned and dropped to his knees. He knew now what he was facing and all the fear and doubt that this forty-one year Navajo had ever felt about his place in the ruptured society in which he lived flooded to the surface and his body erupted in waves of cold terror. The coyote was laughing at him, he was sure of it. He raised the gun in his hand, took as careful aim as he could with the crazy epilepsy that was wracking his arms and fired. There was no way he could have missed and yet the coyote didn't flinch. Their eyes became fixed on each other and then Coyote spoke, speaking his name in a long, drawn-out growl...

"Wencha..." And it turned and, dropping back onto all fours, moved to the edge of the hollow. "Yoo'į" it said to him. "Best leave..."

And with that Coyote laughed into the wind and jumped from sight. Wencha stood up slowly, his head spinning, and looked at the spot where the dog had disappeared. Then there was a tremendous loud groan and he turned, saw what was almost upon him and ran to his car just as the leading edge of the sandstorm smashed into the back of the big SUV.

*   *   *

Rolling along at sixty miles per hour, a sandstorm of any magnitude can create a leading wall as tough as an abrasive scouring pad and as high as five thousand feet. By meteorological standards, sixty mph may not be that fast, but when you're running from one, a sandstorm can be pretty imposing. When the wall hits, the sand turns day into night and the lungs rapidly start to lose their capacity to ingest oxygen as the bronchial tubes become clotted with grit.

The usual first problem for a man caught in a sandstorm is that he almost immediately loses his sense of direction, partly because of the lack of light but more so because of the effect of the swirling sands, caught up and cannonading around the head and ears and eyes. Machinery of most kinds, except those built for this type of thing, are fairly useless and the systems generally break down quickly.

What has happened is that the floor of the desert has become super-heated, usually because of the sun but sometimes, although pretty rarely, from what lies below the surface of the earth, breathing and yearning and trying their best to manipulate the lives of the people above. The sand itself becomes airborne at a low altitude, not more than fifty centimetres off the ground, but then the particles begin to collide with such force that now, added to the heat and wind and sand is their main rival for attention, electricity. As the heat inside the storm increases the air rises and vast differences in temperature and air pressure are formed. Massive and numerous vortexes appear, whipping the dust and sand into a wild frenzy. The storm, now electrified, seeks a way out of itself and begins to move and, like a beast tormented by its own cries, it progresses along the path of least resistance; mindless and uncaring of any insignificant life-forms that may be in its way.

As the cooler winds rush in from above the storm reaches its maximum pressure and the power becomes immense. Big enough, in fact to move or erase entire sand dunes and obliterate roads. In 1991 a 120 mph sandstorm in California caused such mayhem that a 164 car collision occurred, killing 17 people and injuring 151.

The roar of the wind in the distance is the first sign, then the first few stinging particles, then the black wall, then…

*   *   *

"I said get back in the tent, Tommy! Now…!"

The wind was hitting the back of Okay Kilagrew's head like a swarm of angry bees and he was scared. Tommy's head disappeared back inside the pup tent, one side of which was already almost fully coated with sand. Nervous voices inside were asking Tommy about what was going on. Nobody had even seen the storm coming. One moment most of them had been swimming in the cool liquor of the Gila River; the next they were running for their lives as an immense wall of driven sand descended on them from around the mesa like a biblical plague. He had twenty kids under his control and Okay couldn't even begin to imagine the nightmare that would accompany any loss of life on this trip.

"Karen! Karen!" he shouted, his voice already beginning to harden and choke off with the silt starting to pile up on his larynx. He hawked and spat to the ground.

"Herman!" Karen shouted back over the apocalyptic din of the rising wind. She could make out his shape, standing at the corner of the intersection of tent city. He was gesticulating wildly towards the southeast quadrant; a grim, gray shadow in the dust.

"Check the kids down Tokyo Street, okay?" he bellowed. "Where's Harry?"

"Right here!" Babcock's voice rose over the roar and his formidable silhouette joined the other two at the rapidly disappearing intersection. They tried to shield their faces with their hands as they spoke.

"Take the Northeast quadrant, okay?" Kilagrew tried to shout, a hoarse croak all that was escaping from his vocal chords.

Harry looked around, not knowing what he was talking about. "I'll go down here!" he called back and, turning, tripped over a tent cord, spilling his frame into the dune that was accumulating in the fire pit. He cursed and pulled his hand back as it singed on one of the few remaining coals from the breakfast fire. He pushed the dangling tent peg back into the ground with the palm of his other hand and struggled up to his feet and continued on. He hoped with all his soul that all the kids had made it back to the tents.

Karen's eyes were watering now from the constant abrasion and she had to feel her way forward with her hands to the entrance to the furthest tent. "Who's in there?" she shouted. A thin voice answered back all but drowned out by the ferocious flapping of the nylon walls. "It's Hattie, miss. What's happening?" The voice was on the verge of tears.

"It's all right, Hattie. Don't worry. Is everyone in your tent that's supposed to be there?"

"Yes. CJ and Melissa are here too."

"Well, stay put in there okay? Don't try to move about or you'll get lost!"

"Okay, Miss Armitage," Melissa's voice responded. She was sounding very controlled, obviously for the sake of the others.

"Good girls," Karen called back and moved on.

Harry was beginning to think he'd twisted his ankle. He hobbled down the row of tents and with each visit had to make up some reason for the strain in his voice. The kids were terrified. He was terrified, too, but relieved when he had visited each tent and made sure of his charges there. He turned and fought his way back to the staff tent pushing inside and quickly zippering up to fight the dust that was trying to squeeze in through any available opening. Karen was there already and in a few moments Kilagrew floundered in and flopped with a sigh onto his cot.

"For fuck's sake, okay?" he managed to get out. "What the hell is this about?"

"Sand storm," Babcock replied.

"Yeah, no fucking kidding," Okay gasped. There was a pause. "Sorry, Harry," He added. Harry considered this.

"Never mind, Norman," he said, looking over at Karen. Karen was trying to wipe the grit from her nostrils and ears with a handkerchief.

"What should we do?" she asked.

"Is everyone alright?" Kilagrew said.

"Everyone I checked," Babcock answered, "How about you?"

"Oh, I'm okay," said Kilagrew.

"I think he means the kids," said Karen.

"Yeah, yeah, okay. They're all accounted for, thank God."

"Well, mine too," said Karen. "What should we do now?"

"Nothing to do," said Harry. "We'll just have to ride it out and make for the bus when it stops. Hopefully it'll still start with all this shit in the air. It was pretty touchy to begin with."

"Maybe the tribal police will come out to check on us," Kilagrew said hopefully and took a drink from the water container. He spat it out almost immediately. His spit hit the tent side in a splotch of black ooze. "Shit, sorry," he said looking at the others and then took some more water.

"Maybe," said Harry," but they'll have their hands full with this. The highway will be a mess, that's for sure."

"I think we should just stay here, even when it clears," Karen said, slowly.

"How's that?" Okay asked. "Why?"

"Well, the sand might make the trail hard to see. We could get lost. Maybe we should wait for the parents from town to get something organized to come out. They must be worried already."

"Yeah, she could be right Norman." Harry looked over at Norman. Norman was looking out the little flap window. The sand that hit his face caused him to immediately zip it back up. "At least we're kind of sheltered here by the mesa."

"No. I don't think so. Who knows? This might be just wave one. If another storm hits it could blow the tents right away."

"It hasn't so far..." Karen was about to say when the peg holding one corner of the "front room" of the staff tent pulled away and caused a huge sag in the center of the tent. Kilagrew yelled and jumped up and held the middle support pole while Harry hauled the big food cooler over and secured the corner with its weight. The sag disappeared.

"Okay, when the wind drops we make a move. Keep to the same quadrants you just checked out and organize the kids. Tell them to leave their tents and stuff; we can come back for them. We'll meet up downtown." Kilagrew splashed some water on his face.

"Downtown?" Harry asked.

"At the corner of Tokyo and London streets," Kilagrew replied, his voice edged with exasperation.

"Oh, okay," said Harry grinning at Karen. Karen laughed a little and choked it back when Kilagrew glared at her.

"Should we set our watches?" Harry asked.

    *   *   *

It was slow-going for Doug Wencha as he tried to regain the highway, the visibility reduced to a few yards ahead. It took him the better part of an hour and a half to negotiate the dirt road past the silver mine. As he passed it he couldn't help but glance in its direction and was amazed that, for a split second, he could see what was left of the boarded up entrance and the yellow police crime-scene tape. He had almost died in there. Now he was fighting his way through another life and death experience and people were dropping like flies around him.

The truck was bucking and the engine sounded like a whooping cough patient as it struggled to feed gas and air to the carburetors, only to have walls of sand and dirt pushing back the other way. It was a wonder it ran at all in this. He might as well have tried to drive under the ocean. Finally the highway came into sight, what wasn't coated with sand and growing dunes, and he began to pick his way back towards the town. His first concern at the moment was for the people in the village who would be starting to wonder what they were supposed to do. There might have been injuries and certainly there would have been a car accident or two. What was already a problematic radio situation would be doubly so with this storm so he knew that he was on his own, other than the two deputies assigned to this area that would probably be holed up in the hut waiting for instructions. Hopefully they would have started some sort of highway sweep.

He could see the lights of the Ahiga place up ahead. At least the power lines were still functioning. He thought for a moment about Jim. He knew Lucy would be there and maybe he should stop there first, she would be worried. To say… what? Could he just tell her that her fiancé was dead and then move on? And the sick old man, Nascha, and Kai… then his heart stopped. He had completely forgotten about the school trip out to the river. Well, that would have to wait. His town came first and then he'd send a truck out to check on the kids. Probably they would be alright if they just stayed put for the time being. This kind of storm couldn't last for too long. But what if it did? He'd better send a truck out right away. There'd be hell to pay if something happened and he hadn't done enough for the town kids.

He was closer to the Ahiga house now and was beginning to form the thought in his mind that he would leave them for now. It wouldn't help to have the stress of the news on top of coping with the storm. Seeing Lucy's face when he told her was something that he could well put off for a little longer. However, this plan, as pragmatic as it seemed, was not to be.

He noticed that about a hundred yards up ahead there was a car on the side of the road with the lights on. There didn't seem to be anyone in it and Wencha figured the driver must have gone into the house for shelter. The engine in the SUV seemed to be firing on one cylinder now and as he came to the front yard of the house it quit altogether and the big tribal police truck rolled to a silent stop right behind the small gray car.

Well, it looked like his decision was made for him. He could either walk the two miles through the storm right now or see if the land line in the house was still working and call one of the deputies to come get him. Of course, going inside meant other unpleasantness but he really should check to see that every one was alright anyway.

As he left the car and started up the drive he thought he caught, for a moment, a movement from behind one of the curtains. They must have heard him coming he thought. He mounted the porch steps and knocked on the heavy screen door. In a moment Lucy appeared. She smiled at him but didn't move to let him in.

"Oh, hi Doug," she said. He thought he detected an edge to her voice; due to the storm no doubt.

"Hi Lucy; quite a storm, huh? Everyone okay here?"

"Yes, we're fine. Thanks for stopping. You must be pretty busy in all of this."

"Actually I'm trying to get to the village. The truck just conked out. Is your phone working?" In his head he was struggling badly. When should he talk about what had happened? There was so much to try to think about. Keep it all in order, part of him was saying, prioritize. Still, here she was; sweet, good Lucy, with a sword hanging over her head that she knew nothing about; a sword that he would soon have to bring down.

"Um... no, actually. We just tried to call out."

"Damn, I hope that isn't the case all over. Look, Lucy, can I come in? We have to talk about something." It must have been the look that was in his eyes or the tone in his voice but Lucy new instinctively what was to come. In fact, she had already resigned herself to the fact that Jim was probably dead. She would allow that world of grief to enter later, once the family was safe.

"Well, Granddad is really sick right now, so if it can wait, then maybe we could talk tomorrow."

This was pretty strange. Here he was talking to Lucy and she was treating him like it was a normal day. They could hardly see each other what with the sand streaming around them. Why wasn't she letting him in? There was something else…

"Lucy, can I come in for a minute? Get some water? Then I'll run into town."

A look of panic started to edge its way across Lucy's face. Now, Wencha new something was up.

"Doug, I…"

"Lucy, never mind," he said slowly. "I should get right into town anyway. I'll send someone out later to see if Nascha is okay, alright?" He started to back away off the porch.

"Okay," Lucy said. "Thanks for stopping."

Lucy closed the door and the porch light went off. Wencha walked down the driveway about ten yards and when he was sure that the dust was obscuring any sight of him from the house, he ran around the back and slowly worked his way to one of the kitchen windows. He got in close and with his back to the wall, craned his neck around to look inside. He could see Nascha sitting with his back to the window and a girl, he guessed to be Lucy's sister, Mary, was standing against the corner peering into the living room with a very frightened expression on her face. Wencha, tapped lightly on the glass, trying to get the older man's attention. Nascha's head spun around and his mouth opened slightly. Wencha put a finger to his lips and the old man stifled his words. Wencha signaled to him to indicate whether the kitchen door was locked or not. Nascha raised a hand to signal 'no' but before he could his eyes opened wide. Wencha got a puzzled look on his own face and then wondered why he couldn't feel his left leg anymore. He looked down at the knife sticking out of it and started to scream in pain as he fell to the ground. The Crip looked down at him with a smile.

"Welcome, to the party," he said as he smashed a board over Wencha's skull.

*   *   *

Steven stood at the foot of the cheap bed in the cheap walk-up apartment belonging to a girl, all but forgotten now in the mayhem of the past few hours, that had walked willingly and with a smile into the last minutes of her own life, beckoning Albert Bader through the door and into her room.

Steven wasn't new to crime scenes. He had seen a dead body or two in his time, usually with a syringe lying nearby, however; all the details of an ugly drug death repeated with sickeningly blasé repetition across downtown San Francisco. Here was something he hadn't seen though; a young girl with her throat slashed but no signs of a struggle, like she had been asleep at the time, which she probably was. Asleep; post-coital with whomever it was that had left his jacket hanging on the back of the rickety frame chair by the window.

The girl had been dead for a while now and if hadn't been for the neighbours below, alerted to her demise by the beginnings of the cloying, sweet smell of death that was forcing Steven to keep his hand on his mouth even now, she would be lying there still.

Ericsson, the county forensics officer, was putting the last of his swabs away.

"What do you think?" Steven asked.

"Well, it's probably about three days old. Died quickly, no struggle, as you can see. Quick, clean cut. It was asleep alright. Some signs of sexual activity."

'It'... He stared at the technician who blinked back at him and then turned away. Three days would put it around the same time as the murder of the policeman Steven thought. The jacket hanging on the chair revealed little, nothing in the pockets. Still, Steven thought that maybe he had seen this before. The red, devil-head insignia on the breast pocket he knew from a cadre of cheap bike thugs in Frisco. And had he seen it here? His mind worked back through some of the events of the last couple of days. He had arrived, seen Karen, checked in to the hotel.... That was it, the man entering the pool hall as he had parked his car.

He left the apartment and returned to the police station where a constant stream of citizens concerned about the sand storm that was encircling their town flowed around the front desk, seeking information about this or that. As Steven walked past to talk to the captain he heard one pair of parents who wanted to know why nobody had been sent out to check on the high school trip. The desk sergeant was in the process of telling them that there was a local tribal police detachment and that they would be looking in on them.

"How do we know they are?" the father was saying.

"Because they're in charge out there and they're very efficient," came the reply

"Well, these are Newton kids and I think Newton police should be doing something," the wife was saying.

"Look, lady, there are about two dozen accidents that are being seen to right now. The kids will be okay."

The frustrated parents turned away and Steven watched as the man put his arm around his wife to comfort her. He walked up to them.

"You have a child out on that trip?" he asked.

"Yes," the man said. "Our son; Tommy is his name. Tommy Wong."

"Okay, well look, I'm an officer, from San Francisco. I have to talk to the Captain here about something right now but when I'm done I'll try to get out there."

"Oh, thank you," said the woman. "Thank you very much."

"That's alright. I have a friend out there too; a teacher. And if it makes you feel any better, she is very smart and extremely competent and I'm sure they have everything under control. But I'll go out. Leave me a number where you can be reached and I'll call you when I know everything's okay, alright?"

The man reached into his wallet and took out a business card. "That has my home number on it. You can call me there. I'll call some of the other parents and tell them what's happening."

"Good idea." Steven looked down at the card. "I'll call as soon as I can... Mr. Wong."

Steven turned and walked down the hallway and into the office of Captain McKinney. The big cop was on the phone, trying to get some idea from the meteorological service about whether the storm was going to hit Newton or not. He was just in the process of hanging up.

"Okay, keep me informed... Hi Steve, this is a bitch huh?"

"Yeah, I was over at the apartment. Forensics says the girl has been dead about three days. Around the same time Jennings died."

"What? Oh, right the pool hall girl… I was talking about this fucking storm that is going crazy everywhere in the county except here."

"I think the girl is connected to the other killings. I want to talk to that Brixton kid again. I think I may have seen the guy the girl was sleeping with at the time."

"Well, that'll have to wait until tomorrow anyway," McKinney said. "We have our hands full right now."

"I want to take a run out to the reserve and check on that high school group, too, okay? Some of the parents are getting pretty worried about it.

"I don't know about that Steve, it's pretty bad out there. The storm seems to be centred right over the mesa. You probably won't be able to get through."

"Well, I can try anyway. Can I take one of the department trucks?"

McKinney walked over to his window and stared out at the distant storm that had all but obscured the mesa, usually visible from here. Dawn was beginning to rise and the land on all sides was blowing dust and the northwest, towards the reserve, was the worst.

"Yeah, okay, take an SUV. Take one of the boosters for the radio; too, it might keep you in contact here. Check in every so often. If you can't reach us then come back. The storm can't last too long and if it does it might be a job for the National Guard."

"Okay, I'll talk to you when I see the kids are alright."

"Thanks Steve," McKinney was saying as the phone rang again. He picked it up as Steven let himself out of the office and made his way to the garage. Twenty minutes later he had gassed up and was headed on his way into the dark wall that was now retreating from the town. Alone now he let himself admit that he was worried about his wife.

*   *   *

The Crip was stuffing his face with chicken and potato chips. Nascha, expressionless, watched him eat. His head and back were sore from the kicking and he phased in and out of semi-consciousness, struggling to

218

stay awake. His eyes would close entirely now and then and he'd jerk back to the room with a sudden twitch.

Lucy watched him nervously. She wondered how much more the old man could take; how much any of them could take for that matter. She gasped lightly as an image of Jim crowded in. She fought it off. She looked at The Crip with a kind of hatred that she had never felt before. He caught her glare and grinned; a big piece of chicken fat hanging from between his teeth. He sucked it out and swigged it down with beer, leaned back satisfied and thoughtful.

"That was good chicken, Lucy; very tasty. Did you make that?"

"Can you let Nascha lie down somewhere? He's not well," she replied.

"I'm alright," Nascha said, not taking his eyes off of Albert.

"Crusty old bird, ain't he? He can lie on the floor if he wants but nobody leaves the room."

Albert was sitting backwards on one of the old wooden chairs in the kitchen doorway and in front of the prone figure of the still unconscious Doug Wencha. He hadn't taken his eyes off of Mary for the last twenty minutes. Mary sat in the yellow rocker, swaying slightly, glassy-eyed. She stood up suddenly and Albert's hand flashed down to the hilt of his knife.

"I... I want...," she stammered, then just stood there.

The Crip laughed and sat back down from where he had also jumped to his feet. "Don't be startling me like that okay?" he said. "We're all a little tense here."

Lucy went over to Mary. "What is it?" she asked, gently putting an arm up and stroking her hair.

"I want to go to the bathroom."

The Crip laughed again, loudly this time. Albert did too.

"Can I take her?" Lucy asked.

"No," The Crip shot at her. You stay here. Albert, take her and watch the door."

Mary stared at Lucy with a wildness that made Lucy grip her arm tightly. "It'll be alright, you go," she said.

219

Albert followed Mary down the hall and stopped her before the bathroom. His hand lingered on the back of her neck. "Wait a minute," he said and when she had fully stopped he let his hand slide down her back and over her buttocks. She shivered and backed towards the hall wall. Albert stepped around her and entered the bathroom. He checked the small window by the toilet to make sure it was locked down. Then he moved back to the door and held it open for Mary. She walked in slowly, sideways past his raised arm. He made a sudden movement and she jumped back. Albert laughed and stood aside. Once inside, Mary tried to shut the door but Alert stuck his boot in the way.

"Uh-uh," he grunted and Mary left it as it was.

Mary lifted her skirt and sat down on the toilet. She could see Albert's shadow from the hallway where he pressed against the door. Mary began to cry. Crying and urinating at the same time, her body shook. Her hand went up to the sink and she felt for the taps but instead her hand hit the hilt of Big Jim's straight-razor sitting in its cradle. She looked up and grabbed it from the holder and clutched it to her stomach. Then she rose and pulled up her panties and put the razor into the waist band. She flushed the toilet and turned to the sink smoothing her skirt. She let the water get warm and soaped her hands as her thoughts tumbled frantically around her head. After she had rinsed off she turned to take a towel but found Albert there, his hand grasped her at the hip.

He pushed her back hard to the wall between the sink and the toilet and crushed his mouth onto hers, his hand pressing down on her breast. Mary tried to scream out but couldn't find enough air to do it. Instead, she reached down to her skirt and fumbled for the razor there. Albert whirled her around, face to the wall, and was ripping at her underwear. Mary, her hands now in front of her, snapped the razor open and then let herself go limp. Albert stopped pressing her down.

"That's better, baby," he whispered, his mouth against her ear. "You just be good, okay?"

He turned her back towards him and as he did, Mary's hand came up with the blade gleaming in the fluorescent bathroom light and swiped at Albert's face. He caught her hand as it went by, a thin, red line slowly appearing on his left cheek, just under his eye. He dabbed at the

220

cut with the back of his free hand and looked at the blood in the mirror.

"Big mistake," he croaked.

He slammed her hand down hard against the sink, breaking it near the wrist; forcing her to release the blade which clattered to the floor. He raised a fist above her head. But the blow never came down. There was shattering of glass as the window next to Albert's face smashed into pieces and a dirty, scarred arm flung inwards and grabbed him by the hair.

Albert spun and gripped the hand holding his hair at the wrist and cut it with the razor. There was a yowl outside and the hand was yanked back. As Mary ran from the bathroom Albert moved up onto the side of the tub so he could see out. He slowly put his hands to the window and unlocked the glassless frame and slowly raised it up. Then, even more carefully, he put his face to the edge of the sill, examining the ground below.

A hand came streaking through again and dug five dirty nails into Albert's neck. He yelled and pulled away grabbing at the flesh of his throat, coughing as another hand, the one with the cut, pushed through and attached itself to the window frame. There was a grunt and faster than Albert would have thought possible Mystic Bob was through the small opening and standing before him.

Albert didn't move. He couldn't quite grasp this. Bob was there, red-eyed, ripped and torn, but there, crouching before him. Bob straightened up slowly until his six foot four frame towered over Albert.

"Hello, Albert," he said, his voice a dirty whisper. "Miss me?"

Then he sprang at Albert. They crashed together and tumbled through the doorway, across the hall and into the living room. Crip had his gun pointed at Lucy and Mary who were huddled together in the corner. Nascha was standing still and watching the melee spreading across the carpet towards them. The two figures rolled to a stop at The Crip's feet; Bob on top and reaching for Albert's face.

"Get him off me for Christ's sake!" Albert screamed, struggling to free himself.

With one solid, sideways blow, The Crip smashed the butt of the shotgun against the side of Bob's head. Bob groaned once and fell to the side. As Albert scrambled away from the twitching figure, Crip rolled Bob over with his foot.

"Get some rope from the car and tie him up, Albert," The Crip said. Albert moved to obey as The Crip gazed down at Bob. He brushed the hair out of Bob's face with the barrel of the shotgun. The Crip smiled. "Truly amazing... welcome back, Bobby," he said.

*　　　　　　*　　　　　　*

Steven was inching along at a couple of miles an hour, the black curtain in front of him drawing back ever so slowly to reveal short stretches of highway, lingering for a moment then gone. The truck was holding up okay but he had, of course, lost radio contact shortly after entering the storm. The truck had GPS and the finder still worked, keeping a blinking eye on him as he headed out past the village towards the turn-off for the camp road. He hadn't gone this far before and if it wasn't for his electronic guidance system, he would have turned back. He had thought about it when he passed the Ahiga place, especially when he saw Wencha's truck there. But the need to see Karen and make sure she was okay was a formidable force within him and he drove on. Wencha was probably checking up on all the families along the line.

The GPS kept him informed to a twelve-foot variance and he soon found the turn-off and bumped along slowly for about forty minutes before he spotted the school bus in the lot attached to the park. He was glad to see that the engine hood was clear even though the back half of the bus was almost obscured. The door glass was broken though, that surprised him. He jumped out of the truck and climbed into the bus, looking around with a scarf tied around his face to keep the sand and dust out. The bus was bare, all the luggage racks empty. So the kids were still out on the campground. Then he noticed the busted radio and then the side of the hood that had been left open. He got out and stared down at the ruined distributor system. What the hell had been going on here?

Beside the bus on a large wooden sign, yellow and fading with age, he came across a map of the paths leading out to the camping area by the river. Around two or three miles he gauged. He toyed with the idea of the taking the SUV overland but decided not. He just didn't know the nature of the place or what it could do. He took a pack with a hand-radio (for what good it would do him); a flashlight, some water and a first-aid kit and headed down what seemed to be the shortest path to the site.

As he hobbled along, the sand driving against his side, he paused every now and then and listened. Ever since he had left the truck he had felt like he was being followed. But not followed, really, accompanied. Off to one side, to the mesa side. But whenever he paused the sensation ceased and he moved on. At one point, just clearing a jutting, ragged boulder, the itch that he felt came from above and when he raised his head he could swear that something moved up there, on the rock, pulling back quickly out of sight.

Stupid, really, he thought. As if anything would be out in this. Then again, he was. He struggled along, missing the path occasionally and having to backtrack, for about two hours. Soon he was dazed by the constantly buzzing sand around his face and he began to wonder if maybe he had made a mistake in this. Fortunately, the trail markers came up fairly regularly, assuring him that he was going in the right direction.

He almost tripped over the first of the tents in the line as he came to the campsite. He could see that the flap was slightly unzipped, so he put a hand in to it and called out.

"Hey, anyone there?" he shouted and realized immediately that if there were kids inside he would be scaring the life out of them. He lowered his voice. "Inside... anyone there?"

"Who is it?" came a soft reply, a girl.

"Detective Sergeant Walker, police. It's okay. I'm coming in, alright?

"Yes, come in," This time another, younger voice. He pulled back the flap to find three kids huddled in the center of the small tent. "Have you come to rescue us?" the biggest of the three girls said.

"Sort of," Steven said. "Where are the teachers?"

"They're in the middle of the town; in the big tent. They told us to stay here."

"Yeah, that's good. Stay here. I'm going to go and find out how everyone's doing, okay?"

"No, don't leave!" cried the smallest of the girls, tears welling up in her eyes.

"Quiet, Hattie. He'll come back," the older girl said.

"That's right, I will. Just stay inside your tent and everything will be okay. Do you have enough water?"

"Yes," the girl said. "But we're really hungry."

"I'll try to bring back something for you right away," Steven said.

"Yes," said the little one. "Something for the doggie, too."

As Steven pushed his way through the tent opening he looked back. "Doggie?" he said.

The wind rose and screamed in his ear as the older girl said something he couldn't quite catch and as he folded the canvas down and did the zipper up he thought he caught a flash of reddish brown fur move behind the girl's backs. The older girl pinched the younger one's arm as Steven finished doing up the flap.

He half-walked, half-crawled down the line of tents, slowly, so as not to trip over the many ill-placed guy-wires left by the inexperienced campers. From time to time he could hear the voices inside, some afraid, some enjoying the whole thing immensely and calling out to the tents beside them, fearsome voices trying to induce terror in their neighbours; sometimes with great success. Kids, Steve thought as he moved on, they can be pretty unforgiving.

Finally he came across the largest of the tents and started to work his way in. From inside he heard a shrill teacher's voice call out... "I thought I told you to stay in your tents!"

"It's alright," Steven called out before sticking his head in. "SFPD." He immediately felt really stupid saying that. He usually said that at the doors of frightened robbery victims. On second thought, he mused, this isn't much different.

"Steven?" Karen shouted, entirely confused.

Steven piled in through the opening that was smaller than it should have been because the zipper had become stuck half way up and as he pushed through he tripped on the lip of the tent, rolled and landed on his back in the middle of the floor.

"Hi," he said, looking up with a grin at the three adults standing there. "I've come to rescue you."

*   *   *

Changing Woman looked at the stain where the dust and dirt of the sandstorm was settling on the tapestry. Ragged holes were appearing and, try as she might, Changing Woman couldn't keep up with the swiftly unraveling threads. The shell loom-comb flashed this way and that as she worked away furiously, her hands a blur over the colourful cloth.

Spider Woman sat some distance off watching the frantic work. She knew that Changing Woman was the better weaver and at this pace Spider Woman would only get in the way. Child-Born-of-Water was there too, disgusted at the sight of the land below, blown this way and that and the loss of precious life of the animals and birds that lived there. Monster Slayer had left in anger and frustration and even now tried his best to walk through the storm the monsters had coughed up and try to find them.

But somehow he knew it was in vain, that they were still below the earth and that as long as they remained there he could do nothing. There were other forces at play as well. Even the Sun God had difficulty seeing Black Mesa through the carpet of sand that swirled about it. But Sun God was wise and knew this for what it was; an event of his children's doing. So instead of interfering directly the Father of the Earth allowed huge clouds to form over the landscape to the east, waiting for the moment when there would be enough strength there to let loose a deluge that would cleanse the desert and stop the storm.

Spider Woman sighed and took the Child to her breast and comforted him. She could feel his pounding heart and the hot blood coursing through his veins. "This is the Coyote's work," she murmured. "You can be sure of it."

"We should destroy Coyote," Child Born of Water snarled. "Remove him for all time. Be rid of him!"

"He is a god, he cannot be destroyed," Spider Woman answered, soothingly. "He is part of the order of things. Sometimes the balance has been pushed so far off that in order to right it again, harsh events must occur. But take heart…"

"It is useless!" cried Changing Woman and backed away from the loom with tears in her eyes. "Even I cannot keep up with it."

"Do not try," said Spider Woman, "do not try."

And they stood, shoulder to shoulder and watched the slow, inevitable undoing of the lives of the women and men below…

*   *   *

Albert Bader held the curtain back and looked out from the bedroom window down the highway towards the town. The fact that he could now make out the bend in the highway told him that the storm was letting up. Maybe they could finally get out of this place. He turned to look at Mystic Bob stretched out and hog-tied to the bed post. Bob was awake now and staring at him. He didn't say anything, however, the gag in his mouth prevented that. Albert grinned at him. Mystic Bob grinned back. He looked a little demonic with the blood that had infused the whites of his eyes glowing crimson in the light from the hallway; demonic, but kind of like he used to.

Bob motioned with his gaze down to the binds on his legs. He obviously wanted to be released.

"No, I don't think so, Bob," Albert said. He lit a cigarette and leant back against the dresser and let the smoke drift idly from the corner of his mouth. He looked now to the cop; Wencha was still out but was making signs of life as his left leg twitched a little and a soft moan escaped from his chest. This house was getting pretty crowded, Albert thought. He didn't know what The Crip had in mind now, whether he would waste the cop and Bob or just the cop and let Bob go, or what. Albert realized that he never really knew what was going on in Crip's mind and didn't know if he'd want to even if he could. Albert was tired. Tired and sore and just wanted to get out of this place. He imagined himself back in Frisco, a Frisco that seemed like an eternity away, lying on his bed with his regular; Denise. Yes, a long way away.

Wencha's eyes were open now and he struggled to sit up. His leg wound made him cry out in pain but it had stopped bleeding. He pushed himself up on to one tied elbow and righted himself against the cupboard door. He wasn't gagged.

"Can I have some water?" he said, spotting Albert in the corner.

"No," Albert said and left the room, pulling the door closed behind him. Wencha pushed himself up a little further and then realized that he wasn't alone. He leaned himself a little to his right and saw Bob staring back at him. Who the hell was this? Some friend of Lucy's? He could see that the man was badly cut around the face and neck and had a nasty wound on his arm that was seeping slowly but steadily onto the woven rug. And the eyes, what the hell had he done to his eyes?

Doug Wencha thought about his wife and kids. They'd be pretty scared right now, what with the storm and him not calling in. He cursed his stupidity in not hearing the approach of whoever had knocked him out. He'd made every mistake he possibly could this night and he swore to himself he wouldn't make another.

He tested the rope holding his hands behind him and felt that they were well-tied. Same for the cloth tied around his ankles. Then he realized that the other man was trying to get his attention. He followed Bob's disturbing gaze to where he was trying to show Wencha the broken bottle near the door. The broken glass...

Outside in the living room, Albert was telling The Crip about the cop. Mary and Lucy were back on the couch with their arms around each other. Nascha, ghostly pale now, was staring at the ceiling from his place in the old rocking chair by the fire. He rocked back and forth and, very quietly, chanted a song. He gripped his medicine bag tightly in one hand and the arm of the rocker with the other.

The Crip and Albert were close together now, speaking in hushed tones. Albert looked up every now and then and said something about the women. The Crip was shaking his head slowly. Nascha knew what was going on. The men were getting ready to leave and Albert was trying to get The Crip to let him take Mary. But Nascha knew that there was no way the crippled man was going to let any of them go. Not now...

The Crip said something vehemently and then Albert got angry and left out the front door. The Crip looked over at the others and smiled. Then Nascha could hear the engine of the little grey car turn over and after a few tries the engine came to life. Nascha knew their time was almost up. His chant raised in volume.

227

"Will you shut the fuck up!?" The Crip rasped, suddenly furious. Nascha ignored him and continued. The Crip stood up and started to walk over to Nascha. Lucy leapt to her feet.

"You leave him alone!" she screamed at him. Mary got up too and stood behind her sister, shaking. Nascha's voice rose, the song filling the living room. The Crip swore and then turned and went to the window where the shotgun was resting and picked it up, pumping the action at the same time.

Albert came back in. "The pick-up won't start but the sedan is running. The keys are missing from the cop truck." Albert stopped talking when he realized what was about to happen. But instead, The Crip turned to Albert and tossed him a sack that he had been sitting on.

"Go and fill this with any food you can find," he said. Nascha had stopped singing now that Lucy had gone over to him but continued to rock, mouthing the words to some forgotten chant, his brow soaked with sweat. Mary had sat back down. The Crip went closer to Albert. "I'm going to finish this in the bedroom," he said. "Don't come in there until I'm done." He turned back to the others. "Get up and into the bedroom," he said as Albert left for the kitchen. He didn't need to watch this and was glad for the task.

Lucy and Mary got up, Mary crying now and walked slowly towards the hallway. The Crip prodded Nascha with the end of the shotgun and Nascha got up slowly and followed the women. When they got to the door, The Crip pushed Nascha in the back. Mary sank to one knee and Lucy tried to help her up but Mary had become dead weight.

"Help her," The Crip commanded and Nascha bent to lift Mary as Lucy pushed open the bedroom door. Then, suddenly, there was a blur of motion from inside the room and Wencha was flying through it and straight into the mid-section of The Crip. Lucy tripped backwards and fell over Mary and they both hit the floor by the front door. Nascha staggered back and was bowled over by Albert who was running back in from the kitchen to see what had happened. Nascha crawled off towards the kitchen as Albert tried to pull Wencha off of The Crip. Wencha had a handful of The Crip's hair and was punching him in the throat with his other as they fell against the couch. Albert caught Wencha's fist before it could hit again and wrenched it back. There was sickening crunch as Wencha's femur broke and the big Indian moaned as he fell to the floor. But before Albert or The Crip could take advantage of that there was another addition to the melee. Mystic Bob...

Bob had a chair in his hand and brought it down against Albert's back and Albert spun against the wall falling to his knees. Now Bob and The Crip faced each other, the Crip panting and holding his throat where Wencha had hit him. They stood like that for a few seconds, Crip wondering what Bob was going to do, Bob wondering the same thing. The only difference was Bob was smiling.

Then Crip noticed that the front door was open and the girls were gone. He took a step towards it and Bob did the same. There was no

way The Crip would get there before Bob.
"Look, Bobby, those girls are getting away. Don't make me have to hurt you okay?" As he was saying this he spied the gun on the floor where he had dropped it. Bob just laughed. But his eyes went there too, as did Wencha's and Albert's.

Then there was the sound of car doors closing and the small, grey sedan went into gear and the tires screeched against the tarmac and the car tore off down the highway. The Crip swore again. There was another moment and then all four men pounced for the shotgun.

Meanwhile, Nascha, having crawled out of the back door, was now running towards the Mesa. He ran and as he did so, a clear path opened up before him through the storm and he could see the road leading up to the top. It was as though someone had blown wide a path for him. He felt weak and stumbled and fell but as he did so he felt something sharp and powerful grab him beneath the arms. His feet left the ground and within moments he was hovering fifty feet in the air, held skyward in the claws of Crow. Then he was down on the mesa top in front of a fire that had already been set for him. Crow placed him beside it and then took to the sky and disappeared. Nascha looked down and could see only the house below. All else was still obscured by the storm. He had seen the girls drive away and he knew now for sure that Big Jim was dead. He turned, unhappily, his heart racing, towards the fire and muttered, "I am sorry for this, Kai..." Then he reached into his bag and took out an ancient talisman and some herbs. The herbs he threw onto the fire, the talisman he grasped to his chest as he began to chant once more; loudly, ferociously and with tears in his eyes, for he knew that what he was about to do was a sin.

Then from down below came the muffled explosion of the shotgun.

*   *   *

The teachers fanned out amongst the tents, each taking a quadrant of the canvas city, preparing the students for the trek back to the bus. The storm was less fierce now but maneuvering through the maze of ropes and tent pegs was still difficult. Okay and Harry disappeared quickly to their areas. Steven watched Karen head towards her section and then turned and started his task, made that much harder because he had to preface each set of instructions with a quick introduction of himself and why he was there. But the kids seemed to take it in stride. Now that the immediate danger had abated somewhat and nobody had been hurt they were a bit more relaxed as a whole.

When he got to the tent containing Anton Remy's group, Éclair bolted out from the mesh, eager to be free of the confining, airless covering. He tore away down the line of tents as Anton shouted after him in vain. He tried to follow the dog but Steven grabbed him and held him back, reassuring him that the dog wouldn't go far in the storm and would soon get tired and return. Anton reluctantly returned to the tent.

Karen approached the final tent in her line, the one that Steven had first entered upon his arrival at the camp. It was the tent containing CJ, Hattie and Melissa. Karen reached down, unzipped the flap and called in. "Hi girls… It's Karen. We're going to…"

But then she stopped in mid-sentence; froze, in fact. There was only the one girl, Hattie, still in the tent and she was sitting on a sleeping bag in the middle of the floor with her arm around a huge, red dog. Not quite a dog, though…

Karen slowly entered into the tent. The dog was staring at her, its tongue hanging loose as it panted in the heat of the enclosure. The tent reeked of its dirty fur. It wagged its tail. Karen put an arm out towards Hattie and the tail stopped wagging and a growl began to grow in its throat.

"Who's your friend, Hattie?" Karen said slowly and quietly once she had found her voice.

230

"He was scratching at the door when the storm started so we let him in. We couldn't leave him outside in the sand," Hattie replied, stroking the dog's mangy neck. Hattie had a strange tone to her voice; as though she was struggling to get the words out.

"Where are CJ and Melissa, Hattie?" Karen asked.

"I don't know, Miss."

"Did they go to the teacher's tent?"

"I don't know." Hattie paused, unsure of what to say next. "They wanted to put the doggie outside. They thought we'd get into trouble if he stayed inside after the man came. But the doggie didn't want to go. He wouldn't... So they... Now they're gone... and I'm tired, Miss." Hattie lay down beside the big animal that still hadn't taken its eyes off Karen. She seemed to go to sleep the instant she was prone.

Karen looked at the dog but quickly looked away again as their eyes met. Karen knew better than to look an animal in the eyes. It might see the gesture as being aggressive so she just stared at the ground and started to inch her way around the other way towards Hattie. If she could get there and take her away gently she could get her outside perhaps. And there was something else about this animal's eyes... Who knew what it was doing there? It was obviously wild and its bizarre behaviour might be chalked up to the storm's effect. On the other hand it could be rabid. Either way, she had to get Hattie away from it. As she moved she could feel the animal tense and then it yelped at her. Karen jumped back. She knew now what she was facing. She had seen enough wild life shows to know a Coyote bark when she heard it.

The big animal was looking at her with what could only be described as a grin on its face, Karen thought. But that was impossible; just a trick of its facial markings probably. She knelt down as low as possible. The coyote sat back on its haunches and Karen thought she heard the words "aoo' adeezhi" in her ear, as on a wind. "Yes, sister..."

Then there was a sudden scuffling at the tent door and Éclair bounded through, barked once and skidded to a silent stop about two feet from the big coyote. The little dog immediately started to growl and sat back, his ears and tail down to the floor. He bared his aging, yellow teeth at the coyote and tensed his back. Karen looked at the coyote that hadn't moved an inch. Then Karen heard something that made her reel. The

Coyote laughed. Not a yelp, not a growl that could be mistaken for a laugh; an actual laugh.

Éclair looked almost resentful of this laugh in the face of her best attack pose and in a black blur attacked her huge adversary. The Coyote barely moved a muscle as it sank its teeth into the back of Éclair's neck and turning for a moment to look at Karen, trotted out of the tent with the struggling dog in its jaws. Karen, shaking, grabbed Hattie and took her slowly outside making sure the animal was away from the front. She turned once when she heard a bark from off to one side. The coyote had released the dog and they were sitting, facing each other, a short distance apart about twenty feet out into the desert. They sat that way for a moment and then Éclair calmly turned and trotted off into the storm.

Karen hurried back towards the teacher's tent, grateful to have Hattie safe but sick to her stomach with fear for the other two girls. If they weren't in her tent now then where had they gone?

*   *   *

Doug Wencha was beginning to get his breath back. What was left of Mystic Bob's shattered body lay over his lower legs and Wencha could see The Crip's expression as he lowered the shotgun to the level of his face. It was only going to be a couple of seconds before he was dead. He felt like crying actually. Not from fear but regret. Regret that he wouldn't be spending the last few moments of his life in the arms of the woman he loved. Regret that he hadn't been able to make Joey's life easier and regret that his own life had been so hard.

For a little guy with a bad leg, The Crip was fast and even though Wencha had reached the shotgun first he had easily taken it from Wencha's shaky grasp. Then, when Bob lifted up the broken leg of a chair to use as a club, he had unloaded the first chamber into Bob's neck, effectively decapitating him. Then he had put a foot into Doug's chest and sent him reeling to the floor. Now the shotgun barrel was a few inches from his face and The Crip was ready.

"Crip, don't." It was Albert, slowest of the four to go for the gun and the last to find it gone. "We need the keys to the truck."

The Crip's face contorted, sweat dripping from his forehead down to his eyes. "What?" he managed to get out.

"The cop truck is the only one going and the keys aren't on him. So maybe he knows where they are."

The Crip grimaced again but the angle of the gun increased upwards and finally it was resting on his shoulder. "You know where the keys are, friend?" he asked. "You get me the keys and maybe we tie you up and leave you alive, huh?"

"I doubt that," Wencha said, struggling to get Bob's body off of his feet.

"Well, we don't get that truck going, it's not a question of 'if' but 'when', you know?"

"I might have dropped it when you hit me with that board. Or when I was coming around back," Wencha said, trying to find the right angle with which to stay alive.

The Crip looked at Albert. "You finish getting that stuff together. Then see if the old man is still hanging around. I'll take the pig outside and see if we can't find those keys. Hand me that flashlight."

Albert looked to one side and spotted the big, box flashlight on the shelf. He tossed it over to The Crip and then grabbed the food bag off the floor and returned to the kitchen. The Crip hauled Wencha up to his feet and shoved him towards the back door. When they were out on the porch, Crip looked up and saw the fire burning high on the mesa. Wencha saw it too. Maybe someone had heard what was going on. The Crip read Wencha's mind.

"How the fuck do you think they managed to get a fire going in this?" The Crip asked. The storm was just a shadow of itself now but still there was quite a wind and the dust in the air was still clogging.

"That's probably my guys," said Wencha. "They'll be down here any minute."

"Yeah, right... You know what I think? I think if you keep fucking around with me I might just waste you anyway. Now get down there and find those fucking keys." The Crip jammed the butt of the shotgun into the back of Wencha's knees and sent him sprawling to the side of the house where the kitchen window was located. He tossed the flashlight down beside him. Wencha tried to pretend he was looking for something he knew wasn't there. He had already stuffed the truck

233

keys down behind the cushion on the couch. So they definitely weren't out here. He knew that his time was running out. But he did wonder who was burning a fire on the mesa. Maybe someone was signaling for help. Well if so they had come to the wrong place for that.

Up on the mesa Nascha stopped his chant. The air had become still and cold and the flames of the fire burned straight up into the air. Another odd thing about that fire, he thought, there was no smoke. Then he saw the first of two shadows on the other side of the blaze. Then another appeared. Nascha knew what it was that stood before him but his mind raced and his vision blurred. He could feel the indescribable hatred that emanated from them, the two he had called forth, releasing them from their subterranean prisons. He grasped the small statue of Monster Slayer close to his heart and prayed that he had not done the wrong thing. He knew in his heart that he almost certainly had but he was sick with the fear and hatred for these men that had killed his grandson and probably many others and ruined the lives of them all... these white men.

The two across the flames stepped forward and Nascha drew a quick breath as the horror of that which he had brought forth was revealed.

Tse-Nill Chindi had escaped from the bindings first and had found himself manifested on the plane of mortals as a being roughly human in shape but grotesquely flattened into a wider-than-tall creature that had no neck, barrel arms and legs and a face that found the entire spectrum of features condensed into an area not two inches in depth. Wide swaths of skin hung from the head to the shoulders and down the back; its spine was bent like a bow, outwards, and the vertebrae protruded like spikes beneath a tarp of flesh-coloured sausage casing. Its mouth swung open like an angler fish and rows of thin, razor teeth lay within, trying to force themselves from the gaping maw. It had hands of a sort at the end of its arms. But the single digits protruding from each wrist had but one long claw fastened on. And that claw, thick and jagged and wide as a board, hung like machetes from either side.

Naz-Tsaid Chindi, however, could not even begin to pass for humanoid. It was happy to be what it was; a fur-bearing mass of bone and sinew that boasted no facial features other than a dull, glowing, reddish orb that might pass for an eye in the centre of what could be its head. It had, arguably, three appendages, one extruding from each side and one in the centre of its midsection. The two on the sides had several large claws rooted on them that resembled hooked knives. They gleamed like steel in the fire and shuddered as the huge creature moved. The central 'arm' had knuckled fingers of a sort that were covered in the same wiry hair and were constantly moving as they searched for something to grab onto. The thing that likened the two demons was that they could move faster than the eye and they made no sound as they did so.

Then Nascha died.

As the two things passed by him, not touching him, but throwing themselves off of the mesa roof to pass on the wind to the ground below, their reek filled his lungs. They were on their way to do that which they had been summoned to do. Destroy the interlopers; the white ones. Nascha, his mind crumbling, turned slightly and then felt his heart stop. No pain, just a single out-rush of air and then his old body, abused by this world, left it behind.

Crow swooped down and picked up the old man and flew to the place by the river that Nascha had left when he had bravely decided to return to the fourth world and help those he could. He wondered now if he had actually accomplished anything. Or had he just played into the hands of a great malevolent spirit that had used him for its own ends.

Crow set him down by the river near the grassy place that he had found so peaceful and healing before. Nascha grew sad and tears swelled in his eyes but then he heard his name called by a familiar voice. Looking up he saw Big Jim on the other side of the river. Jim waved to him and together they advanced through the cold water. They met in the middle and as the stream coursed around them they embraced each other. Jim held Nascha back and looked into his eyes. They smiled at each other and then they returned to the shore and sat in silence by the fire there.

Wencha, on his knees outside the Ahiga house, stopped his pretense of searching for the keys and began to pray. From where they sat, Nascha and Big Jim stopped talking and looked to the sky. Wencha heard the click of the shotgun hammer and waited for the sound that was to follow. But it didn't. There was another sound however, a gurgling, and when he looked up he saw Crip being dragged by his throat into the house. He was being held tightly in the grasp of something that Wencha couldn't quite understand. There was a loud drumming in his ears. He pushed himself to his feet and stumbled to the stairs of the porch. He paused; not knowing whether he really wanted to see what was inside or not.

Then the screaming began.

Wencha drew a breath and smashed in through the screen door. Up against one wall The Crip was being held about four feet off the ground and the something that held him there was slowly ripping his flesh away in long, silky red strands with razor-sharp talons. Wencha staggered back and tried for the kitchen door again but missed it and fell by the stove. He knelt up and looked at his hands, soaked in something and raised his head but quickly looked down again, away from what was before him. Another thing, shorter and even more grotesque than the other, had Albert Bader pinned backwards over the kitchen table and was using what looked like scaly blades attached to its arms to slowly hack him to bits. With unbelievable precision it was only taking off about a half an inch at a time. Like an industrial meat-slicer, it was rapidly reducing Albert's appendages to stumps in tiny increments. Albert, in shock and unable to scream anymore, watched with fascination as the blood that showered over them all coated his face like a wet, red mask.

When both the men were dead, the two demons stopped their strange noises and came together in the hallway. One carried the head of Albert Bader, ripped from his neck; the other carried that of The Crip, cut away neatly from the shredded body. The two faces of the once-vicious bikers seemed to be looking sadly at each other. The demons looked down at Wencha. Wencha, in shock now himself and thankfully losing consciousness, stopped shaking and rolled to his side. Then the demons moved past, were out the door and away. They paused outside, sniffed at the air and looked to the west; to the other side of Black Mesa. Yes, there was more work to be done yet.

CHAPTER SEVEN

HEADCOUNT

The wind was still stinging and the sky was still a dirty brown but the constant, shrill whine of it had started to lessen. The kids were standing beside the teacher's tent, shielding themselves from the storm with their arms. Most of them had towels or jackets wrapped around their heads and necks and they resembled a group of Arabian tribesmen as they milled about.

Harry Babcock arrived with a long length of rope from the supply tent and he and Steven stretched it out, Harry at one end, Steven at the other. When the rope had been laid straight on the ground the students stepped up and each took their position along it as they had been told. Then they raised it up and stood, waiting for the command to go. Virtual Jones in the Jones device was at the head of the line, just in front of Harry. The front end of the rope was attached to the back of the rover. Virtual took out his goggles that he carried in a pouch on the vehicles side and slipped them on. Then came Cam and Louie, Louie chosen for the front because of his large size and hence greater visibility. Then Tommy Wong and Finn Esterhaus, Finn coughing constantly and wiping at his running eyes with a handkerchief. Micki Valence, who would rather be up front in the protective lee of Louie, was next, with the Remo Twins behind her. Attibi kept an arm solidly around his sister. Then Allison and Kai, Kai impatient and wondering whether this wasn't a crazy thing they were trying to do. Anton Remy came next, now totally despondent as Éclair had not returned and soon would be left to an uncertain fate. Ricky Ray, behind him, tried to joke with him and lift his spirits, but to little avail. Cookie Johanson and Alice Bird stood on either side of the line with little Hattie between them. They were given the task of looking after her as she was still slightly dazed. David Smith and Angela McReary were next with Linwood Desmond taking up the last student position with strict instructions to anchor the line if Steven had to let go to rescue a straggler. He was glad to be given this important job and was determined to do it well.

Steven kept looking over at the teacher's tent and wished the other two adults would hurry up and join the party. He could hear what sounded like raised voices coming from the tent and considered going inside but didn't. In the tent, Okay and Karen were arguing about who would stay behind in case CJ and Melissa returned.

"Look, I was in charge of this project and the girls are my responsibility, okay, so I'm staying. That's the end of it." Okay paced back and forth across the width of the tent, more and more desperate as he realized the chances of finding the two girls in tact grew slimmer by the minute. But what could he do? He couldn't wander around out there in this; he'd be lost in minutes. That's what had stopped them from sending anyone out further than a few yards from the camp up until now. Karen felt sorry for him but also felt that her point was important.

"Herman, it's ridiculous. It makes far more sense for me to stay. You can't do anything here for the girls except wait for them. The kids out there could really use another man in the centre of the line. You're stronger and bigger than I am and it just makes sense for me to wait. It's just wasting you to have you sitting here."

Okay stopped pacing and looked directly at her. "Karen, it's alright. I'm making this decision and it's done, okay? I tell you, if those girls don't come back or I don't find them, then I might not be coming back myself. Understand?"

Karen half-smiled but then realized that he probably meant what he was saying. If he was thinking like that then maybe he should just wait here. The last thing they needed on the trek back was someone who wasn't focused on the job.

"Alright, Herman, alright," she said and stood up and went over to him. As she slung her pack with the extra water in it, she leant over and gave him a peck on the cheek. "We'll be back for you soon with a proper search party. Don't go wandering around out there, the girls will be okay. They're probably hunkered down by some rocks or something. They're both pretty bright girls and fit too. We'll get them back."

She bent over and let herself out of the tent door and was immediately met by the gaze of twenty-one pairs of expectant eyes, all waiting in silence. Okay came out behind her and stood beside Steven.

"Okay, everyone…! Do what Mr. Babcock tells you and everything will be fine. I'm going to wait here until CJ and Melissa come back and by that time you will be out on the highway and everything will be alright!" Okay looked at Steven. "For god's sake get them out of here, okay?"

"Don't worry about it," said Steven, "we'll be fine." Karen took up her place in the centre of the line and picked up her section of the rope.

"Alright, Virtual," Harry called out above the roar of the wind. "Let's move out. Nice and slow now!"

"Okay, Mr. Babcock," Virtual called back and started the motor. Slowly the device ground into the drifting sand and lurched forward. The line sagged a little and then went taut and the entire line of students, teachers and cops moved off.

Okay watched them go and started a bit as Alice stumbled and fell. But Cookie yanked her back up quickly and they marched on. As the last of the students disappeared into the gloom, Steven turned once and waved and then he too was gone. Okay shivered as the wind whining around his head now became the only friend he had. He turned his collar up tighter and called out into the wind. Called out the names of the two girls he had lost.

*   *   *

Father Sky was angry. Spider Woman and Ever-Changing Woman were beside themselves. And the focus of their anger was the Coyote.

It was one thing to trim the operation of the world with healthy cynicism. It was one thing to walk amongst men and offer them their own weaknesses to see and learn from. But it was another to take a child of woman and use them for your own malignant purpose. And he had also released prisoners that Father Sky himself had condemned!

Yes, Coyote had gone too far and the other gods knew this and knew that he must be brought to heel. So Father Sky summoned his child Born-Of-Water and delivered him a message. His son knelt before him and the old god whispered into his ear and then Child-Born-of-water rushed away and, in his own time, summoned Crow who was his messenger and servant. Crow had no love for Coyote and was pleased that it would be he who showed Coyote the error of his ways.

Crow knew of Coyote's time with the young girls in the desert and didn't approve of this at all. To show himself to the people was one thing, to cast about with the whites and the others was beyond the pale. Crow flew to the desert and the mesa and found Coyote fairly jumping with anticipation and excitement. Coyote danced along the mesa rim.

"Oh, Crow! Crow! What a glorious day!" Coyote yelped to the sky as Crow approached from the clouds of sand and settled beside the fire that Coyote was maintaining. From where they stood they could see in all directions; a three hundred and sixty degree panorama from the Black Mesa despite the storm. They could see all that was happening there and about. Crow was sickened by some of what he saw and although he knew that Nascha and Jim were now in the spirit world, he was more concerned with those that were still living; both of the Dine and the other folk. For were they not people and was not the pure of heart still blessed in this world?

"There are many that are angry with you, old friend," sighed Crow and watched as the big Coyote strode about, yelping with glee.

"Angry? Why angry?" Coyote said, and paused for a moment to contemplate the Crow, the big bird's black feathers glistening in the glow of the flames. "You have not told them of my plans have you?"

"Foolish one, I didn't have to tell anything to anyone. Your work is plain for all to see. There has been much pain this day. "

"And more to come," said Coyote. "I am glad you are with me. There is something about sharing such an adventure that is more pleasing than to be by oneself. I am sure, when you see the intricacy of it all that you will be impressed."

"You should not have gone to the young ones. They are the innocents. The great father and mothers are sad for their trouble. You should have let them be. You must stop all this before things happen that cannot be undone!"

"I will not! I will not!" Coyote shouted and bounded up on to a rock. "I am a god! What I will shall come to pass! I am only doing that which I was created to do! It is not for anyone to question that. And today I shall see the outcome of all my plans. The two ancient ones from below are now amongst the living. It was not I which brought them forth. It was not I who committed the crimes for which vengeance is their goal!"

"No, but it was your doing nonetheless," said Crow. "And this time you have gone too far."

"That is nonsense. I have done that which should be done. And now I shall look and see all that is the glory of my deeds. Foolish Crow, there shall be songs sung of this day and this world itself will change. And it is all of my doing! Mine! Oh, I cannot wait to see that which unfolds!"

"Well, you will be sorry for all that will follow," said Crow, sadly. Crow hopped over to the flames and looked down into the shining red coals. He remained still and didn't move an inch for several minutes and finally Coyote noticed this.

"What is it you are looking at?" he said, distracted from his view of the desert floor.

"There are pictures of the future in the flame. You don't really have to wait, you know. You can witness the events to come here; right now."

Coyote bounded down to the fire's edge and stuck his snout close to the flames. "Show me," he cried. "Show me! I cannot wait!"

Crow reached down with his beak and although it caused him great pain he scooped up some of the red-hot and embers and flung them into the face of the Coyote.

"My eyes! I can't see!" screamed the Coyote and he rolled in the dirt trying to fling it into his face. "What have you done?"

Crow took to the air and circled about, keeping well away from the frantic beast below him. "You will not witness that which you have wrought, tragic beast!" he called from above. "All that you have schemed to bring about will be as nothing to you. For you are the cursed one and the songs that they sing about you now will be that of disdain and the words will mock you for a thousand years."

"Damn you! Damn you!" Coyote shouted at the top of his lungs. "This will not stop what will happen!"

"No, I cannot stop that. Nor can the other gods. Only a Dine can change things now. But at least you will not profit by it. And when Father Sky calls you before him you will tremble at his rage."

The blind Coyote screamed in terror and ran into the night. He stumbled about, this way and that, in a frantic effort to find some water with which to cool his wounds. It would be many years before he regained his sight; many years in which his only balm would be to hear the tale of what followed that day.

*   *   *

An hour into the forced march, the wind started to pick up. From where he followed, at the end of the line, Steven could barely make out Karen's back, midway up the line. Every now and then she would turn and look back and smile at him. He knew that she was finding this arduous. They all were. The students were coughing and unsteady on their feet but to a person they were gamely moving on. As far as he could make out they were about two hours from the bus parking lot, maybe a little more. It was hard to tell how much progress they were actually making in this atmosphere.

At the front of the line, Harry Babcock watched with admiration as Virtual's rover picked its way between rocks and gullies. By rights, any machine should have gummed up and stopped with this airborne soup clogging the works. But onwards it went with Virtual veering this way and that, sometimes on his own accord, sometimes at Harry's request. Harry had done this route a hundred times but it all looked different now, covered in small dunes, the paths obscured and only the larger rock faces and barrel cactuses standing out as landmarks.

Karen felt the sand making its way into the various folds of her clothing and was thankful now for the heavier khakis she was wearing. To look at some of the other children, especially the girls, she realized that everything she was feeling in the way of irritation at the intruding dirt was probably doubled in their flimsy shirts and pants. Every now and then she would turn and make sure Hattie was doing okay but the young girl was still somewhat in a daze and gave no hint of being particularly disturbed by their difficult journey.

Ahead of her Kai and Allison were holding hands over the line and she thought of telling them to take back the rope but decided that they were okay. They were joined at the hip, as it were. At that moment, as though he had heard her thoughts, Kai turned and looked back at Karen. He had a strange expression on his face and Allison was looking up at him, confused. Kai opened his mouth to say something but it didn't come out. Then they were in an impossible dream…

The wind stopped, the noise stopped, the sand hung motionless in the air. Nobody in the line made any movement; the rover had come to a halt and Virtual looked back, unable to explain to himself why his machine had suddenly stopped. For some reason, Harry looked at Virtual and smiled. Virtual smiled back.

Karen couldn't understand what was happening. The sand was hanging in the air as if each grain had been pasted there, suspended by invisible strings. She heard a noise and looked slowly to her left and saw, at the extreme periphery of her vision, a large figure outlined against the quivering brown backdrop. The figure raised an arm as if to signal. Karen turned and looked to her right. Another figure, smaller and wider and again on the extreme edge of vision was there. And it, too, lifted an arm. She turned and looked back at Kai. Kai was slowly taking Allison to his side under the rope.

Then there was a slow rush of air and a roar that seemed to come directly from above and when she looked up to the sky Karen was immediately blinded by a column of sand that was descending directly down upon them.

Then there was nothing but chaos. With the sound of an oncoming locomotive, the storm, which had been quieted for a moment, came down upon them full force. It hit like a Tsunami and the shock wave knocked most of them off their feet. Then the rope, like some sort of charmer's snake whipped up and curled into a tight knot and rose and flew into the air. Some, whose hands had still been grasping it, rose into the air four or five feet before letting go with yells and tumbling to the ground.

They ran in all directions as lightning, blue and hot, broke between them and scattered them like seeds to the wind. Steven started to yell something, to try to keep them in a group but a branch of something, carried in the wind like a javelin, struck his shoulder and sent him spinning to the ground. Karen screamed and lunged for Hattie as the little girl was lifted by the squall into the air. She pulled her down and together they started to run. She instinctively headed towards Steven and found him, groggy but conscious, against a rock.

"Get to some shelter," he said, on the verge of passing out. Karen helped him to his feet and, together with Hattie, they found refuge at the base of a large sandstone outcrop. The three of them crouched there as Karen tried to make out what was happening. At one point a pair of feet, followed by another pair, ran past and she tried to grab at one of them but missed. Steven had passed out and Hattie just sat beside him on her haunches, staring at Karen.

Near what, at one point, had been the front of the line, Harry had reached Virtual and had hauled him out of the rover and was carrying him away from what he perceived to be the centre of the electric activity. Then Tommy was at his side struggling to keep a hold of Cookie Johanson who was cut and bleeding from her forehead. The four of them ran until Harry suddenly yelled, "Stop!"

But it was too late; Cookie and Tommy disappeared over the side of an unseen gully and fell with short screams into the sands below. Harry looked down and could barely make them out below. They were still moving.

"Hold on tight, Virtual, I'm going down there!" Harry shouted. Virtual just nodded and Harry felt the boy's strong forearms grab into his jacket.

Together they slipped and slid down the side of the arroyo and came to a stop beside the other two who were just managing to pick themselves up. To one side Harry could make out the opening of a spring cave and he pulled at Tommy.

"Get in there! Get Cookie and get in there!" he shouted. Tommy grabbed Cookie and soon all four were lying on the wet side floors of a cave which was the opening of a small creek that was dribbling down to a place somewhere below.

The others were gasping for breath and Harry's heart was pounding. It was racing and his head was splitting and his left arm felt like it was being squeezed in a vise. Oh god, Harry thought, not now, don't let it happen now. Just a few more hours; please, then I won't care. But a minute later Harry realized that a few hours would be hard to come by for he saw the thing that was coming for them along the creek bed.

*   *   *

Herman Kilagrew lay on his bunk, staring at the ceiling and listening to the wind whipping around the tent ropes. His arm was strung across his forehead and his face was beaded with sweat. He wasn't really the panicky type; he didn't have the imagination for that, but he was about as close to it as he could be. A loose tent fly flapped against the tent next door and added to the symphony of storm that was playing all around him. But he scarcely noticed it now.

He felt very tired and although he was bent on staying awake he began to drift off. The fatigue of all the physical work plus the nervous exhaustion was catching up to him and his mind wanted desperately to shut off. So part of it did and his head rolled to one side and he slept.

He had a dream that was in complete contradiction to where he actually was. Instead of the hot sandstorm and dry air, he was walking in a field and a light rain was falling on his face. He felt easy and happy and unburdened; idyllic in his world of semi-light and peace. He could see a road at the edge of the field and he hopped lightly over the wooden fence there and began to stroll along it humming to himself. Not far along from the field he came to a wood and at the edge of that a short, stone path and a cottage. He knew this place. From somewhere a long time ago. It was familiar and warm and when he entered the door he was immediately taken back to a childhood scene filled with complete serenity. He walked about the house that he recognized now as the one he had lived in when he was ten. It had easily been the best year of his life. There was the picture of the family on the kitchen wall and when he looked closely at it, he saw his father. His father had died in a war the day Herman turned twelve. As he looked at the picture the image of his father faded away. Then he heard his name being called. It sounded like his mother. It was coming from outside and he wanted so much to be with her now but he found the door to the cottage bolted shut and he couldn't open it and he pounded at it as someone called his name louder and more demandingly.

And then he was coming too and for a second he couldn't remember where he was or how long he had been asleep. But he heard his name again; again coming from outside. It was one of the girls!

He leapt to his feet and almost tore the tent zipper getting it open as he tripped and spilt out onto the sand. The storm was still there but lighter now. He heard the call from his right side and from his knees he turned and saw two, small figures standing about thirty feet away, at the extreme limit of his vision.

He called their names and started to run towards them but as he did, they turned and moved off into the gloom. He called again and ran forwards and again saw them, but now further away and walking away from the camp. Why were they walking away from the camp?

"Melissa! Stay there!" he shouted, but the two figures continued to move along the rocks and around a bend in the mesa wall. "God damn it! What are you doing?" he yelled. "Stay still, okay!"

When he rounded the bend he saw the two girls turn and head into a small canyon with high, steep sides. As he got to it he realized that the canyon opening was only about six feet wide but beyond that the passage expanded somewhat as it made its way up the side of the mesa. He moved forward, running again, through the sand and the clustered cacti and finally came to a dead end. Again he heard his name only this time from above.

He looked up and about twenty feet over his head the two girls were standing on a narrow ledge of rock and scrub, faces against the wall of the canyon. Their hands were at their sides and they were perfectly still. Their hair blew and fluttered around the back of their heads and shoulders.

"For god's sake...! What are you doing? Melissa?" They didn't respond, just maintained their still poses beside the rock wall. "Stay there, I'll come and get you," he shouted above the wind that, whistling over the mesa edge, was almost like a siren. He clutched at the bush in front of him but pulled back cursing, his hands covered in small, sharp thorns. He found another hold and started up, hand over bleeding hand. How had they climbed up there so quickly, he wondered?

Finally he was over the edge and standing on the ledge about six feet away from them. "Don't be scared, okay?" he said calmly. "Just keep facing the wall and don't look down. I'll carry you each down on my back."

He reached out to Melissa and slowly turned her around and smiled. But there was nothing to smile back. Above her body and below her hair, there was nothing. No face, no eyes, no chin, no neck; nothing. And the hair that had been flying about them blew away and the body of the young girl, pinned to the jagged rocks, where it had been slammed, slipped off its bloody mooring and slid to the ground leaving the crazed Herman Kilagrew looking down at a handful of hair.

He stuttered something and staggered backwards, his face a stretched mask of terror. He reached behind him, but there was nothing there, of course, and he fell to the canyon floor. His body landed with a dull thud and a sickening crack, his back broken on the spine of a narrow boulder. The wind continued to moan. Something appeared slowly from the gloom behind him and as the last few sparks of his life, one by one, were extinguished, Tse-Nill Chindi reached down and took Herman Kilagrew's head.

*   *   *

"Louie!"

"Right here, Cam!"

Cam Proctor caught up to Louie who was half helping, half dragging Finn Esterhaus. Finn was even more pale than usual and was coughing. And each time he coughed something nasty and green was coming up.

"What the hell's the matter with him?" Cam said as he made his way to Louie. The big centre just muttered something under his breath and kept walking forwards. "What?" said Cam.

"He's sick, okay? Help me. Get his other arm."

Cam took Finn under his other arm and between them Finn was carried. "Where is everyone?" Cam said over the din of the wind.

"I don't know. The rope broke and then I kind of went dizzy. Now I don't know where the fuck we are."

"Mr. Babcock!" Cam yelled, stopping. "Ms. Armitage!"

Nobody answered their calls and the twenty foot radius of their vision also brought them nothing useful.

"Let's put him down," said Cam, tiring now and finding it hard to catch his breath.

"No, don't," Finn gasped. "I can't breathe."

"We have to find some shelter," Louie said over his shoulder. The thin kid, suspended between them could hardly move his legs. "He's asthmatic. We have to get him out of this dirt."

"What's that over there?" Cam said, pointing to the left of where they were standing, "Some kind of shack?"

"C'mon!" Louie said without bothering to answer the question and together he and Cam dragged Finn towards the ramshackle hut. Louie kicked the door open when they reached it and Cam and Finn and he fell forwards onto the dusty floor of the abandoned equipment shed. Louie shut the door behind them and, for the moment anyway, they could get air into their lungs. They lay as they fell for a few minutes and finally Louie got himself up and looked around. Not much; just an old table, a couple of chairs that were sort of falling apart and a cabinet. Loose, ragged curtains hung at the windows and the cloth flapped up and back in the wind where there were broken panes. Strangely, there wasn't much noise and the howling of the storm seemed more than just muted. It almost seemed absent entirely. In one corner there was an old cot with a moth-eaten blanket on it.

"Help me get him over there," Louie said and he pulled Cam to his feet and they dragged Finn over to the cot and laid him down. "Better?" Louie asked after Finn was settled.

"Yeah, I can breathe a bit better now," Finn said in a thin voice and he put his head back.

"What are we gonna do?" Cam said.

"Wait until somebody finds us," Louie answered.

"But that could be hours."

"Yeah, okay, so it's hours. We won't get anywhere out there in that. Besides, he can't walk around," Louie said, pointing a thumb at Finn.

248

"Look, let's just leave him here. He'll be okay out of the storm. We can find the others and then come back for him."

"No way, Cam, he might have a heart attack or something. We can't just leave him."

Cam looked over at Finn who was staring at the ceiling and breathing heavily. Cam was no hero. Cam thought mostly about himself. It was what he had been taught to do. Louie knew that Cam didn't give a shit about Finn, or him for that matter. Not when it became a question of who was going to suffer. He thought back on all the times that he'd looked out for Cam and wondered why the hell he had ever done that. Micki had always wondered the same thing and Louie had just shrugged and said something about the football team. He wished with all his heart that Micki was here now. He was afraid for her.

"Well, to hell with this, Louie. You wait here if you want to, I'm going to find the others and get out of here."

"No you're not," Louie said with a determined edge to his voice.

"The hell I'm not," Cam said angrily and opened the hut door. Louie hurled himself at Cam and dragged him down to the floor.

"You'll get yourself killed out there," Louie yelled and grunted as Cam elbowed him in the gut. "Stupid bastard... don't make me knock you out!"

Cam didn't stand a chance against Louie's size and was quickly pinned against the boards. "Let me up, Louie! I mean it, let me up!" he shouted. He was almost in tears it seemed. Cam got an arm loose and struck up at Louie and connected with his fist to one of Louie's eyes. Louie jerked back and sat up with his hand to his face.

"Stupid bastard!" he shouted. Cam stood up triumphant, framed against the open doorway. "Go if you want to!"

"Yeah, well, you shouldn't..." and that was all Cam was able to get out. He looked down at the red smear that had appeared on his chest. He turned his head and looked at Louie with a questioning stare as Louie jumped to his feet. Cam was now slowly rising up off the floor, something hard and sharp protruding from his ribs and then, with a choked-off yell, he was pulled outside. Louie ran to the door and peered out into the haze. He could just make out two figures now; one large and one small. One, a screaming boy jammed against a small, dead tree. The larger figure raised the smaller one up over its head for a moment and then the smaller figure dropped to the ground, separated into two pieces; one large, one small.

Louie slammed the door shut and turned to see Finn struggling to get up out of his bed. Behind him, silhouetted against the window over the cot, was a face, if you could call it that, of something that Louie couldn't define. He shouted at Finn to get away from the window but before Finn could get up off the bunk a thin arm smashed what was left of the glass, snaked in and dragged Finn by his face to the opening. Louie ran forward and tried to drag the terrified boy back in but all his weight and strength were as nothing and Finn Esterhaus was pulled through a hole only half his width. Large splinters of the shattered frame with pieces of Finn's flesh stuck on them remained behind as Louie fell back onto the bunk.

Then a pounding started on the cabin wall and Louie felt the side of the flimsy building begin to shake. Dust fell from the ceiling and more wood began to splinter. He ran to the door and flung it open and hurled himself out into the storm. He could hear the sound of footsteps in the sand around the cabin now. Something was running after him. Something was behind him. He ran faster than he had ever run but the sound got closer and closer until it was right off his shoulder. He didn't look back. He didn't stop to see what it was. That is what saved him. And then he fell.

As he tumbled to the ground, the big teen-ager thrust his hands into the ground, raising a cloud of the newly disturbed sand that blinded him for a moment. He wiped at his tearing eyes with one big hand and tried to swipe at something that he knew was beside him with the other.

"Hanot-Dzied Chindi" said a voice like a sack of dead leaves. "Know me."

Louie's hand made contact with something that was flesh but not flesh. He collapsed into himself and sank to the sand. He heard himself make something of a whining sound and then he coughed into his chest. There was a laugh close to his ear in the same dead leaf tone. "Know me!" But Louie stayed as he was, cowering with his face in the dirt and then... he was alone. He got to his feet and staggered off into the sand.

Harry turned to the others and shouted "Back, get back into the cave! Keep going!" The others, their faces paled by the sight before them, fled into the darkness. Tommy reached into his bag as they ran, fishing for something.

The spirit thing, splashing and flinging itself down the creek gully, was almost at the cave entrance. Then it stopped. Harry turned and looked at it. Harry had seen many things in his long career as a cop, some pretty horrific things, some strange, inexplicable things; but nothing could have prepared him for his. This was partly why his reaction to the horror that was before him now was to laugh. The thing laughed back at him.

"What the hell…" he muttered and took a step back. As he did so, the thing, this thing that had what could only be described as meat-hooks or small axes for hands also moved back a step. Harry stopped, it stopped. He could hear the splashing of the kid's footsteps as they ran back into the cave. Harry took another step back and stopped; the creature did the same. Harry, always looking for the angle, took a step towards it. It moved two steps closer. "Well, it was an idea," Harry said under his breath. He grinned. The thing grinned.

He could sense by the sound of the others that they must be at least fifty yards away now down the dark passage with the creek running along its floor. Harry knew instinctively that if he turned and ran that this thing, whatever it was, would be on him and it would be over. He turned and looked over his shoulder. About ten feet further down the passage there was a split and the main tunnel veered off from a smaller chute that went straight on. He backed up to this 'y' section, the thing mirroring his movement each step of the way but seemingly in no hurry. Harry turned down the smaller channel knowing that the others would have taken the larger route. He backed slowly along into the darkness. There was still some light from the cave opening but very little. The thing in front of him stopped at the dividing line and sniffed at the air in both directions. It turned its squat, horrible features towards Harry and something long and slimy shot out from its mouth and down the tunnel and landed at Harry's feet.

"Did you just spit at me?" Harry murmured. Then the thing turned and started down the main tunnel. "Oh no, you don't," Harry said and taking the long knife that he had bought from Al McReary, hurled it at the demon. The blade spun and landed in the side of the thing's neck. The thing reached around and pulled the knife from its neck. Then it turned, backed Harry into a corner and with one swipe, sliced him from chin to groin. As Harry died he felt the blade begin its work, cutting through his neck.

Further up the tunnel, and unaware of the big cops sacrifice, Virtual, Tommy and Cookie were making their way forward with the help of Tommy's flashlight. Cookie led the way and Virtual clung to Tommy's back.

"What the hell *was* that?" Virtual said in a half-crying, half-spoken voice. He spoke low so that Cookie wouldn't hear his fear.

"I don't know" Tommy answered, breathing heavily as they splashed along, "A bear or something."

"In the desert..." Virtual said, "With knives for paws?"

"This is the end. We can't go any further," said Cookie, shining the light upon a wall that stopped any further progress.

"Well, where does the water go?" said Virtual.

"Down there," Tommy replied, pointing to a ground-level opening that seemed to disappear on an angle. Looking down they could see a dim light through the water below. "There must be another place further along where the stream meets the open air again," he said.

"Listen…" Cookie whispered. They all fell silent. They could hear the slow splash of something moving down the tunnel towards them.

"Maybe its Harry", Virtual said.

But when they saw the shape of the thing coming slowly toward them, etched against the grey backdrop of the tunnel, they knew it wasn't.

"We're going to have to go down there," Tommy shouted and they looked towards the small opening. There was no way more than one of them could get through it at a time. Then the splashing steps started speeding up and the thing behind them was only forty yards away.

Tommy pushed Cookie to the entrance and shouted "Go!" Cookie bent down and slid on her butt over the first edge of the rise and then disappeared down the smooth, watery slide. "Now you, Virt," said Tommy.

"No, you go," said Virtual.

"Get in there, damn it!" Tommy shouted.

Virtual saw the small rock directly behind Tommy and he smiled at his best friend as he said, "Hey man, this is the only time I'll ever get to really impress her. I really love her, you know?" He looked down the chute and from his sitting position put a hand out and pushed Tommy in the chest. Tommy tripped backwards over the rock and fell, feet first, down the chute and disappeared.

Virtual dragged himself towards the hole as the footsteps behind him grew louder. He tried to jam himself through but his pant leg had come unraveled and had snagged against the same rock he had used to throw Tommy. Frantically, he tore at the jeans with his hands but it was too late. The shadow of the demon was there, over him. He looked up and was eye to eye with Harry Babcock; or rather, with a decapitated piece of Harry Babcock, strung on a leather thong hanging at the demon's waist. The thong had been laced through Harry's eye sockets. Virtual only had time to scream once before there was silence in the cavern once again.

The great Chindi looked down at the hole. There were two more down there. It moved forwards. Down... It hesitated. No, it would not go down. Never again would it allow itself to be trapped in a prison of stone below the world. This tunnel was as far into the earth as it would go. The demon turned and flew back to the entrance. There were others to be found.

*   *   *

He had always found her feet erotic... incredibly erotic, actually. He had never thought of himself as a 'foot man' but the sight of her delicate feet just drove him somewhere unusual. He had, therefore, always started there when they were in need of each other and he would work his way up her calves as he did now, using each inch of her to satisfy his craving of her and also her desire. The backs of her knees were particularly sensitive so he stopped there for a moment and found her taste and let it fill his senses. He kissed her softly, there. Then, slowly, he worked his way up, his saliva and her skin meeting and forming new scents and the delicate and satin skin of her inner thigh, shaking so slightly in anticipation of his...

But there was something aggravating him and now there was pain that wound its way up through his arm to the source of it, at his shoulder. He fought to get up from the bed but couldn't find the strength. The mesmerizing tones of her flesh gave way to sharp, red insistences that were now riveting stabs of pain. And he sat up and yelled and slumped back down again.

"Steven. Lay back. Please, lay back," Karen said gently and pushed him down so that his head rested on her jacket once again.

Steven, now finally awake, groaned and fell back, Karen's hand under his head. The shoulder that he now knew must be separated, throbbed and sung to him and it took all of his strength just to open his eyes and look at her. But she was there, her face dirty and her hair askew, looking down at him. She put pressure on his arm and raised it so that it was straight out. He cried out.

He turned his head and as he extended his arm saw the girl, he thought her name was Hattie, crouching in the corner of the shelter provided by an overhanging rock. She was looking at him with a stunned expression on her face and he could see that she was almost in a state of shock. It was beginning to get dark.

"How long was I out?" he managed to say. Karen put a flask with some water to his lips. He drank it down.

"A couple of hours," Karen replied and took the flask and drank some herself. "The storm seems to have finished." And when he looked out at the landscape he saw that this was true. The desert was actually quite beautiful now. The last twilight was fading and the shadows of the rocks and cactus cast on the desert floor was stark and still and peaceful.

"How do you feel?" she asked.

Steven pondered this. It was an odd sensation, being in so much pain in one area of the body but so glad to be with this woman at the same time and glad that he could be here to help her through whatever this was; although, he wasn't going to be of much help right now.

"Hurts like hell," he answered, eventually. "But it's okay."

Karen, having kept up a brave face for the last hours for Hattie's sake, started to tremble now. "I thought maybe it was your heart…"

"My heart?"

"Well, you never went for those tests like you were supposed to… and the stress…" Tears started to well up in Karen's eyes and Steven reached out and put his hand on hers.

"Karen, I…"

"It's over there…" That came from Hattie. Karen turned her head and looked at her. Hattie was looking out across the flat towards a dune that fell away about forty feet from them.

"What's over there, Hattie?" Karen asked.

"The big monkey thing…" Karen looked at Steven. He was looking towards where Hattie had been looking.

"There is something over there, Karen," Steven said.

Karen stood up. "Maybe it's one of the kids," she said. She started to move towards the large shadow moving slowly across their line of vision. Steven jerked her back down with his good arm.

"It's not a kid, Karen. It's some kind of animal. Keep quiet. Don't draw attention to us."

Karen squatted back down and moved closer to Hattie. There was a copse of bushes close to them that permitted them to see out but obscured them from anyone looking their way. She pulled Hattie closer to her as the shape in the night came closer to them. Then it was all she could do to stop from screaming as the shape materialized into something that she could actually make out. It wasn't an animal; it was an impossible thing that shredded all reason. She started to black out. As she did so, she felt Steven's hand grasp at her arm.

"Don't look at it," Steven whispered, almost choking. He felt her arm relax slightly as she averted her eyes. Why he had said what he did he didn't really know. Partly because he didn't want her outburst to give away their position, he supposed. But there was something else.

He had to fight his every impulse to force himself to watch the thing as it moved slowly across the clearing. It was dragging something and when Steven realized it was part of a body, he started to shake too.

The only one who seemed unfazed by the whole thing was Hattie who, her back to a small tree, was rocking back and forth and murmuring something about Melissa.

Then there was a pounding in his head and he realized that he was about to lose consciousness again. The last things he saw were: Hattie standing up, Karen's arm going up towards her and, as his head hit the ground, the thing moving their way.

*   *   *

Kai, Allison and Ricky Ray had stumbled and run out into the desert with the howling wind at their backs. But after regaining his senses from the blast that had scattered them all, Kai shouted out for them to stop. After explaining that there was nothing ahead but more desert, Kai suggested that they head back the way they had come and try to find the others. Allison and Ricky had agreed but when, against the diminishing winds, they had finally forced themselves back to the approximate position from which they had started, there was no one to be found.

After searching about for a bit Ricky eventually found a pile of bags and the long rope that marked the last place the school party had been together. There was a mishmash of footprints in the dirt going off in all directions giving evidence of the mayhem that taken place. Then Allison stopped and stood looking down at something.

"What is it?" Kai asked, coming up to her. Then he, too, stood staring silently at the massive print in the sand. Ricky joined them and after taking it in for a moment, coughed and then laughed.

"Desert bear," he said with a grin. "This place is crawling with them."

"There aren't any bears here," Kai said, pointlessly.

"I know, I was just kidding," Ricky said. Then he, too, fell quiet.

Allison looked around. The wind had died down now to a soft moan and when it paused occasionally there was an awful silence beneath it.

"Where is everyone?" she asked, of nobody in particular.

Ricky cupped his hands around his mouth and started to shout but Kai pulled his arms down saying, "I don't think that's a good idea right now, Ricky."

"What? Why?" Ricky said. "What, because of those prints? That's stupid. It's probably just Éclair come back and running around or something. You said there are no bears, right?"

"I think Kai's right, Ricky," said Allison. "They aren't dog prints; unless he's grown about eight feet high."

"This is stupid!" Ricky complained. "How else are we going to find everyone?" And he put his hands to his mouth and bellowed out into the encroaching dusk. "Mr. Kilagrew! Hey! Mr. Babcock!"

Then the soft wind stopped. And from an uncomfortably close distance came a reply to Ricky's plea. It started as a gravelly, low-pitched wail and then rose in volume and became a shrill screech. Then it abruptly ended.

Ricky looked at Kai. Allison did, too.

"I think we'd better get out of here," Kai said in a low voice and started walking quickly in a direction away from the sound and towards the cliff face of Black Mesa. The others hurried along behind him, Ricky looking back now and then over his shoulder.

It was almost dark now and a low moon was beginning to peek over the edge of the mesa and brought a sepia glow to their surroundings. When they reached the mesa wall, Kai looked around but could see nothing that resembled a path.

"If we follow the mesa wall to the north we'll find the parking area eventually," he said. "That's probably where the others are."

"Why don't we just go back to the rope and follow the path?" Ricky asked.

Then the screech call was repeated in the night, only somewhat closer than before.

"Oh yeah, right..." Ricky said and started moving forward along the rock face. They hadn't gotten very far when the call came again only now it was not behind them anymore but somewhere to the front. Then a few seconds later it was back behind them again.

"How is it moving around so fast," Ricky said, panic slowly beginning to show in his voice.

"It isn't," Kai answered.

"Then how can…" Ricky started to say.

"There must be two of them," Allison whispered and Kai could tell from her voice the fear that was in her now. He looked around as two more calls echoed out, one after the other, as if the two creatures, whatever they were, were calling to each other.

"They're positioning themselves," Kai said.

"What do you mean, they're positioning themselves!" Ricky said, far more loudly than necessary. "What do you mean? What the fuck are they?"

Kai didn't answer. He was looking up at a series of crevices and ledges that skirted this part of the mesa.

"We should go up there," he said and started to remove his belt.

"Up there? Why?" Ricky asked.

"We can see what these things are and hide if we have to. We might be able to spot the others, too. It's getting pretty bright with the moon."

"Yes, let's get up there," Allison said and their eyes met. Kai smiled. She looked a little calmer now.

"It'll be alright," he said and started to climb up to the first ledge. "I'll hang my belt over the edge there and you can use it to pull yourself up if you have to."

"Okay," Allison said. Ricky didn't say anything but started to climb up another way.

When they were all standing on the first ledge, about fifteen feet off the desert floor, Ricky pointed to a dark, shambling shape approaching from the east. "Look! There it is!" he whispered, hoarsely.

"Come on," Kai said and pulled himself up to a vertical crevice and swung over to another ledge about seven feet higher. Allison got up next with Ricky right behind her. Five minutes later they were on a fourth ledge, now fifty feet above the ground. Then the things in the bush were down directly below them.

"What is that?" Ricky cried. "What are they?"

The two things looked up. Close to the wall, they were hard to make out but one was smaller and the other immense. Both were standing upright and had arms of a sort. Each had a cluster of round objects bouncing from its middle. They were too far up to make out anything more.

Then Kai felt a tingling in his hands and against the moon a large, black shape swooped down into view.

"Look at that!" Allison said, pointing at the shape.

"Oh great, now they're coming by air," Ricky groaned.

"It's a crow," Kai said, the relief palpable in his voice. "Thank god."

"Oh yeah, great! A crow! That'll keep them away."

Kai didn't bother answering him as the big bird landed on another ledge somewhat higher and to one side of them. The two things below were watching the bird and after a moment, one of the things made a coughing sound and moved off into the bush. The bird rose into the sky and circled once, looked at Kai and shook its tail. A large black feather broke away and wafted down towards the teenagers. Kai reached up and grabbed it as it floated by. The bird circled once more, cawed loudly and flew off in the direction of the disappearing Chindi.

Kai took the feather and tied it to the leather necklace he had around his neck; the necklace that his grandfather had given him with a talisman on it. The feather fluttered in the night breeze.

Down below, the remaining Chindi looked up and its eye gleamed as it started to rise into the air. Ricky croaked and fell to his knees as Allison began to cry. The demon rose steadily until it was hovering directly in front of their ledge. Kai stepped forward and positioned himself between the thing and the other two. The reek of the huge thing almost made him vomit and he felt himself grow numb when he saw what it was that was hanging from the things mid-section. He grasped the talisman and held the feather out in front of him. The Chindi hesitated and tried to get closer but could not. It was held away by forces that Kai couldn't understand but was very grateful for. When it was about six inches in front of Kai's face the demon screamed. A deafening, soul-killing scream that Kai thought would split his skull open.

Ricky screeched and jumped to his feet and ran to the other edge of the ledge and started to try to climb up further.

"No!" Kai shouted at him. "Stay behind me!"

The demon stopped its screech and its eye turned lazily up to see the scrambling boy. The eye turned back to Kai and Kai began to cry too, as he heard a rumble in the things chest. Then in a flash it was gone, up to the unfortunate Ricky. Ricky's scream dissipated into the night sky as the Chindi and most of Ricky disappeared over the top of the mesa, its claws firmly planted into the tendons at the base of Ricky's brain.

Kai turned and saw that Allison had fainted. He poured some water from his water bag onto her face and she started to come to. Kai sat back against the rock, shaking and trying to understand.

*   *   *

It was dark but the moon glinting brightly off the shattered windshield of the school bus could be seen from quite a distance. Towards this beacon the small group of kids still shepherded along by Linwood Desmond struggled the last quarter mile. Linwood still held onto the piece of rope that had come free in his hand when it had ripped apart during the first onslaught of the storm. Alice Bird, holding onto the other end of it, stumbled weakly as she was dragged along. The Remo twins, arms linked, supported David Smith whose shoes had been lost somehow and his legs, feet caked with mud and bleeding badly, hardly functioned as the twins helped him along. He groaned every now and then. Out in front of them all, Micki Valence, the diminutive gymnast girlfriend of Louie Ostermann, walked about ten yards ahead, warning them every now and then about rocks and obstacles on the ground. Micki had her eyes trained on the glinting windshield and when they had reached the clearing of the parking lot she went over to the bus. The rest of the group waited silently. She pushed on the damaged door and crept up inside. She looked around and, after seeing the state of it, returned to the others.

"Something has happened to the bus," she said to Linwood.

"What do you mean? From the storm?" he replied.

"Well, I guess so. But it looks like someone broke it up on the inside too. The radio is busted."

"Great. Well, we might as well get everyone inside anyway. There should be a first-aid kit somewhere and we can take care of David's feet."

While the others climbed aboard the bus, Micki went over to Steven's car and checked it out. It was unlocked but Steven had taken the keys with him. There were some apples on the back seat sent along by Tommy Wong's parents so she took them over to the bus and handed them out. And she told Linwood about the missing keys.

"Does anybody here know anything about hot-wiring a car?" he asked of them all. "You take car shop don't you, Attibi?"

"Yeah, but I don't know about that. We just started electronics this year. I guess I could look at it though," he said off his sister's glance.

"Here's the first-aid kit," said Alice, removing it from under the bus dash. She took it over to where David had been stretched out at the back and, putting it down, started to undo the cloth they had tried to tie to his feet. She cleaned the dirt as best she could and tried to squirt some anti-bacterial cream on the wounds but David howled so she stopped.

Linwood and Attibi went over to the car and popped the hood open and looked down into the engine. Attibi pointed out some of the ignition connections and then entered the car and tried to take off the plate protecting the ignition system on the steering column.

"I need a knife or something, to cut through the wires," he called out to Linwood and Linwood went back to the bus to see what he could find. When he was about half way across the lot towards the bus there was a loud wail from off in the distance. A coyote, he thought and kept going.

There was nothing onboard that would do the cutting so Attibi gave up eventually and they all sat, staring out the windows of the motionless bus like cut-outs peering into the night.

"What are we going to do?" Enye said.

Linwood looked over at her and said, "I guess we have to wait. There'll be someone out to collect us soon enough."

"Should we go and look for others?" said Micki.

"I don't think so. We'd probably just get lost again."

Then there was another wail. This time closer and sounding deeper and less like a Coyote yelp.

"Just Coyotes," Linwood said, before anyone could ask.

The moon was becoming eclipsed by cloud now and the darkness spread across the lot and filled the bus with night. One by one the teens fell asleep. Linwood was last and in a daze he stared off across the desert. As he, too, finally succumbed he had one last thought that maybe he had just seen something moving a short distance away.

Linwood jolted awake, his head falling from his arm and grazing the metal bracket of the window. He reached up to his forehead and rubbed at the spot. Then he realized that the back emergency door was open. And David, who had been spread across the rear seat, was gone.

Micki whispered at him from across the aisle. "There's something out there," she said, tensely."

"What do you mean?" he asked.

"Shh!" she waved at him and he lowered himself back down from his half-risen position. He could barely see Micki in her seat but could vaguely make out the shapes of the still sleeping Remo Twins and Alice. Now he could hear something too. Sort of like something metal being dragged across cement.

"What is that?" he asked. "And where's David?"

"I don't know. He was gone when I woke up. He can't be far. Maybe he had to pee or something."

"Yeah, maybe. I'll go to the back and call him."

"No don't, there's definitely something out there. Some animal or something…"

Again the sound of metal, definitely metal, and now it sounded like metal being stressed, creaking or groaning under weight…

"What the hell…"

Just then the cloud cover broke and the moonlight hit, full bore, on to the parking lot. Micki screamed as Steven's car came hurtling across the space, twenty feet off the ground, and smashed with a deafening crunch into the front end of the bus. The car stood up almost vertically on end, balanced on its hood for a second and then slid slowly over to one side and scraped and whinged down the side of the bus. Where it had impacted, a huge hole in the metal appeared. Then the bus started to rock violently.

"What's happening?" Alice screamed as she woke up. The Twins jumped up together but immediately fell back to the floor as the whole bus started to rock again. Linwood turned and looked out the other side and screamed himself when he saw what it was that was rocking the bus.

"Get out! Get out of the bus!" he shouted and they tried to get up but the bus was shaking so crazily that they couldn't get to their feet. Then as suddenly as the rocking had started it stopped. That lasted for a second or two and then something wet hit the bus from the rear and what was left of David Smith came spinning in through the open door.

The bus started to rock again as the terrified children tried to get away from the horror of the body. But now the bus was starting to rock from front to back. And now the front end of the bus was rising from the ground and foot by foot the angle was increasing. Alice lost her grip on the metal of the seat in front of her and slid in the slush provided by David to the back of the bus, trying vainly to hang on to the doorframe. Somehow she fell out of the emergency exit and rolled over and found herself standing upright about ten feet behind and to the right of the bus. She could make out arms of some sort holding onto the undercarriage of the bus front and then something peered at her from around the bus fender. She screamed and lunged to one side and tripped on a parking lot divider and sprawled down into the ditch at the end of the lot. As she fell she struck her head and was unconscious by the time she hit the long grass on the other side.

The bus was now sitting perpendicular to the ground and those still on board found themselves lying or sitting on the backs of the seats. Then the bus was let go and the whole thing fell over backwards onto its roof. Gas from the ruptured tank started to spill through the lines and onto the forward seats. Linwood grabbed Attibi and together they shoved at Enye to get her towards the back of the bus. But as they crawled along the roof of the bus that was now the floor something was starting to crawl in the door. Micki saw what was happening and hurled herself towards the front exit and managed to squeeze herself out of the door and in through the window of the sedan that had slid off the bus and was lying back on its wheels in an upright position.

Somehow the windows had remained in tact and as she looked up over the edge of the back seat she saw what was happening in the bus. She choked as she watched the inside of the bus windows slowly shade red. Then the back door of the car jerked open and something was dragging at her; trying to pull her out. She screamed and pounded at it with her feet.

"Stop it Micki!" someone shouted and she was lifted up into a pair of strong arms and then they were running towards the road leading to the open highway. Micki did pass out now. But not before she had looked up into the sweating, beautiful face of Louie Ostermann.

*   *   *

Kai, Allison, Karen, Steven and Hattie stood evenly spaced along the edge of the Black Mesa and looked down on the Ahiga house below. Kai had spotted Hattie fumbling along the mesa wall on the north side and then, not far behind her, Karen helping Steven hobble along. Together they had all agreed to take the one path up the north face to the mesa top and cross over and down the other side to the village. This, they had hoped, would help them avoid meeting up with the... But there was no mutual consensus between them as to what it was exactly that was hunting them.

Somehow Karen had managed to pull Hattie down into the rill where Steven lay when the big creature had stopped and looked their way some time ago. It had moved towards them but at the last second was distracted by something, a sound possibly, from the direction of the parking lot and had moved off that way. Hattie had started to cry after it had gone and the crying had become more and more hysterical and louder and Steven had to hit her, stun her, before they were discovered. Afterwards, when she had recovered, she had been fine and had actually started to lead the party along the mesa until they met up with Kai and Allison.

They had climbed up the mesa path with some difficulty, Steven being in a great deal of pain, but eventually reached the top and walked the five miles or so to the other edge.

Kai, looking to his right, saw Nascha's fire some distance away. It was still burning brightly, almost supernaturally bright and rising straight as an arrow into the sky. It seemed to be perched directly above the cave over Face-in-the-rock. He considered going over to it for it seemed to hold a possible answer to this nightmare but instead he decided that he should get the others down to the house first.

They managed to get Steven over the gap in the downward path and about an hour later were standing in Kai's back yard looking at the shattered back door.

"What are we waiting for?" Allison asked, her voice still shaking. "Let's go inside and phone someone."

Steven and Kai looked at each other. "One of us should go in and check it out first," Steven said. "Looks like it might have to be you."

"Maybe we should just walk to the village," Karen said, sitting on a stump by the fence.

"Somebody's moving in there," said Hattie and ran to shelter behind Karen and Steven.

It was true. There was a large shadow moving about in the kitchen. They all got down low to the ground and Steven put his arm around Hattie when he saw that she was starting to panic. The broken porch door, smashed in by Albert Bader, hung uselessly on its hinges. But now it was starting to swing away to the inside of the house. A bloodied arm appeared in the porch light and pushed the screen door back out. Doug Wencha stumbled out onto the deck.

Kai leapt up and ran to him, helping him onto one of the porch chairs.

"Kai..." Wencha said and lost his breath.

"Is there anyone else inside?" Kai asked.

"No. They're all... Do you have a car?"

"No, we just came down off the mesa. Have you seen those... things?"

Doug looked up into Kai's face. Even now he felt like denying it. Even now that he had seen the things and knew that Kai had too.

"Yes. I saw them." Then the rest of it sank in. "You mean they attacked the school group?"

Kai sat down on the wooden planks and put his head between his knees. The others got up and walked over to the porch. Doug looked up and saw Steven.

"You were with them out in the park?"

"Yeah," Steven replied. "What the hell..." And then he stopped. There were too many questions; too many things to tell; too many thoughts.

"Listen, Kai, we should get everyone inside but we'll have to clean something up first. You all wait out here, okay?" Doug led Kai into the house and together they covered up the bodies there with curtains and bed sheets. By the time it was done, Kai was numb. Then the others were allowed in and they all sat in the living room.

"We'll have to get into town somehow," Karen said as she distributed some bread and water to the others.

"We don't know where those things are," Steven said.

"Still, she's right Steve," Wencha said. "We're not any safer here, believe me."

They were silent for a moment. Kai, standing by the back window and looking up at the mesa said slowly "There's something about that fire..."

"What do you mean, Kai?" Doug said.

"I think I should go up and see. I remember Granddad used to build a fire there when he was trying to make medicine. Maybe it has something to do with all this.

"Like what, Kai?" Karen asked.

Kai paused and looked down at the floor. "I don't know. Just a feeling I guess."

Doug looked at Steven. "Look, I'll try to get to the town. You okay to stay here with the kids?"

"Yeah, you go. We'll try to see if we can get one of the cars going."

Wencha went to the front door and bent down to re-tie one of his boot laces. His head came even with the small window half way down the wall and he froze. Down the road about fifty feet, one of the creatures was standing, looking up towards the fire. Then it reared back and holding up one of its arms, screamed at the sky. Wencha fell backwards onto his backside and grabbed at the wall, at nothing. The sound of the thing's wail drove through him like a knife. He turned and saw the others, pale and shaken, staring at him. Hattie broke and ran to the rear door before Karen could stop her. But then she stopped dead. Through the screen, Karen and Hattie faced the other Chindi that was moving through the grass towards the fence. Karen slammed what was left of the door shut as Steven approached.

"Help me push the fridge over here!" she screamed.

Together, joined by Kai, they toppled the fridge over in front of the door.

"We have to get down into the cellar!" Kai shouted and moved to show the others the way. Steven scooped Hattie up and Allison and Karen followed down the stairs into the dark basement. Kai stood with Wencha.

"There're no windows down there," Kai said.

"So what?" said Wencha, breathlessly.

"Those things would have to go by us and I don't think they can."

"What do you mean?" Wencha said.

"On the mesa, one of them tried to get at Allison but it couldn't get by me."

"What are you saying? That they won't hurt us because we're Indians? That's insane."

They stood side by side for a moment by the basement door. Then they looked to the rear door as the fridge began to shake and, with a loud crash, it was flung aside like a matchbox. The frantic scream of the Chindi preceded its horrible face as it tried to squeeze its huge shape through the door frame.

"Don't look at it, Doug!" Kai shouted and together they faced each other, eyes down at each others boots. The Chindi stopped its scream and moved to the living room about ten feet away and sat on its haunches, watching them curiously.

"Where's the other one?" Wencha whispered. The Chindi in the room snuffled and moved a couple of feet closer. The smell of it was sickening.

"I don't know," said Kai. "I can't see it."

Then the Chindi rushed at them, screaming, and they both yelled. But the Chindi pulled up three feet away and stood, swaying, looking down at them. Its hot breath flowed down on them.

After a minute, Wencha finally breathed and said, "Looks like you're right, Kai."

"Do you think you can hold on here, if I go up to fire?" Kai asked.

"Maybe. Unless this thing figures out how to move me without hurting me."

Kai edged out from the doorway and moved towards the rear door. "Doug, if you move that thing will kill them all down there."

"I know," Wencha said and turned his back against the door.

Kai grabbed a nylon rope from the rack on the back of the house and ran across the back yard, leaping over the fence. He could hear the demon start to scream again and shuddered as he recalled what it was like to have that blast in your face. He knew he had to be quick. Wencha wouldn't be able to take it for long.

Kai made his way back up along the rock path, slowly beginning to feel the effects of the previous climb and his exhaustion and when he eventually got to the top he wasn't sure he could make it all the way to the fire. But he did and when he stood there, looking down at Nascha's body, he had finally had enough and he collapsed and cried into his fists. He rolled to the edge of the mesa and struck at the dirt with his hand. He stopped when, down below, he saw the other creature making its way to the mouth of the old cave. It had something, several things actually, that looked like balls of something, in its claws and when it got to the mouth of the cavern it stopped and then floated inside. Kai looked back at Nascha and stopped as he caught a glint of something shining by his side. The old man was holding something wrapped up in his fist. He walked over and gently removed the talisman from his grandfather's hand and held it up to the fire to look at it. He began to feel a heat around his neck and remembered the artifact that he had been given to wear. It was hot as if it, too, was being held near the fire. He snapped it off in his hand and held it up. It was similar to the other one yet somehow slightly different. Then he realized what it was he was holding. He had two miniature carvings that were identical to the two things that were trying to kill them. But not him or Doug really; the others. The whites, but why…

He thought about the two eviscerated men in the house and remembered now seeing them in town. And for the first time, he thought about Lucy and Mary. Where were they? Had those men harmed them? Was that what this was all about; revenge? It was hard to imagine that Nascha was responsible for this after all that he had said about tolerance and two societies and such. And how could he do it? Was he that powerful?

He held one of the talismans closer to the fire and it started to glow red hot. He heard a wail come from down below, down where the cave was, and on a rush of air and heat Tse-Nill Chindi swooped from below and descended until it was there, crouching, on the other side of the fire.

The vile thing kept its distance but its single-eyed gaze never left the two clay figures in Kai's hand. Kai brought his hand closer to the fire and the demon moaned slightly and made a motion towards him but hesitated. Around the maw that passed for its mouth a dribble of pale liquid oozed out and dripped to the ground.

In the house, Wencha was now looking at his father. Or what had become his father. Before his eyes, the flesh on the thing had slowly transformed itself into a grotesque image of his old man. But with no mouth and its eyes were shut. Still it spoke…

"Why do you hurt me, son?" came the stiff, coarse whisper. The demon crept closer to Wencha. Doug wept but kept his back to the door. When it was about a foot away from Wencha the thing raised one thin arm. The bracelet that Morton Wencha had been buried with on that rainy Saturday dangled from the wrist. Wencha grabbed at it. He pulled his hand back and a razor thin line of blood appeared across his palm.

"Let me through the door, son," the voice said, the monster's mouth now inches from Doug's ear. "Let me have them. What have they ever done for you but cause you hurt?"

Wencha was growing cold, his mind wandered and he thought of his father, ten years ago, dying in slow stages because the hospital in the city refused to care for him. There had been no money. The pitiless faces of the doctors and nurses (white doctors and nurses) turning the boy and his ailing father away. Wencha's hand found the door latch and began to slowly turn it.

"That's it, my son, that's it. Turn away from them."

As Wencha fought the urge to stand aside for the beast, Kai was raising his arm with a single talisman in it; the fetish that was Naz-Tsaid Chindi; the Chindi that now stood before Wencha in the form of his father. As Kai tossed the icon into the burning fire, Wencha pulled his knife from its sheath and plunged it uselessly into Naz-Tsaid. The knife met only with air though as, with a blood-curdling wail, the great Chindi disappeared from view. A league below the surface of the earth it found itself back where it had started, in its prison of stone. It screamed again, franticly.

Kai, hearing the wail even from this height, realized that he had thrown the wrong figure into the fire and quickly hurled the remaining talisman into the flames. The Chindi in front of him was too fast though and it thrust its hooked paw into the fire, screaming with pain as it did so. It withdrew with the steaming talisman in its grasp and spat at Kai as it ran to the edge and over the mesa wall. Kai ran to the edge as well and saw the Chindi disappear into the old, cliff dwelling. Then he looked down to the house and saw Wencha emerge from the door and wave up at him.

Kai tied off one end of his line to the ancient pitons, still stuck into the rock from the ill-fated university excursion of so long ago. He lowered the rope to the cave floor and looking once more at the body of old Nascha, still sitting upright against a boulder, staring back at him with dark, lifeless eyes, he started to climb down.

Once on the ledge below he found the old kerosene lantern and matches where the boys had left them such a long time ago. The Chindi was nowhere to be seen. Kai lit the lantern and, staying by the wall, entered into the cave. He passed the bag they had deserted in their hurry to leave the cave before. He passed the crushed spiders that had covered Virtual. And then he raised the lantern and let the light cast itself about. The talisman hung from a stone hook below the odd shelf that they had seen before. On the shelf, carved into the rock of the side wall (the shelf that they had wondered about) Kai could make out a dozen or so dark, round shapes stacked up on it. Those hadn't been there before. He grasped the talisman and slowly raised the lantern higher.

Wencha, down below on the mesa path, heard Kai's scream echo from the cave and cannonade down the valley. He started to run faster. Then he looked up and saw Kai jerk out of the cave entrance and stand with his feet on the edge of the cliff, wavering; his hand over his eyes. The lantern lay at his feet and he teetered there, the hundred foot drop to the broken rock before him. Wencha called out Kai's name as loud as he could.

Kai heard the call through the loud buzzing that filled his head and he looked to one side, stunned, alone, terrified and on the verge of blacking out. He couldn't move. He couldn't turn back to that sight; to those eyes. He felt himself losing his balance, tried to fight the darkness crowding in on him. But it was no use. He started to topple...

There was a flash and then he was standing before a tree; a lone tree, barren of leaves and alone on a patch of rocky ground. It was daylight all of a sudden and a light wind whistled through the black branches. He stood with his back to the tree and far away he could see a figure approaching. The figure was moving fast and quickly covered the sandy ground between them. In a brief moment Monster Slayer stood beside him. Kai could not look up at Monster Slayer, for he was a god, but he heard his words.

"Kai... Willow."

In the dream that Kai believed he was having, he took the hand that was offered to him. It was his grandfather's hand. He immediately felt stronger. Then he heard a bird call and looking up saw an eagle.

"Be calm, Kai. I will help you," the soft, strong voice from Monster Slayer floated down to him. A feather, from the wing of the eagle also came down with the words and Kai let go of the hand and grasped the feather to him.

A cold wind blew and his head began to spin once again, and then clear. He opened his eyes and once again he was on the cliff ledge. He held the lantern up one more time and the light hit the rear wall, where the opening to the stone chute that led to the caverns below was located. Something was coming out of it.

Kai dropped the lantern, leapt and grabbed the dangling rope end. He began to haul himself up, hand over hand, as Tse-Nill Chindi moved to the mouth of the cave and began to rise up towards him. He covered the last ten feet of the rope, the thing hovering before him, spitting and swiping at him but making no contact.

Kai ran closer to the fire. The Chindi swept down towards Nascha's body, scooped it up and used it to block Kai's access to the pit. Kai, insane with anger, watched as his grandfather's body, a helpless, horrific marionette, pranced and flopped in front of him. Kai lunged forward and tore the old body from the demon's grasp. He held it with one arm and with the other hurled the talisman into the flames. With a revolting retch, Tse-Nill Chindi vanished into the night.

Kai laid his grandfather down. The flames of the fire grew dimmer and smaller and finally extinguished altogether. Doug Wencha emerged from the darkness and walked slowly over to the smouldering embers and stood looking down at Kai. Kai held Nascha in his arms and rocked slowly and sang the only song that he could remember.

EPILOGUE

Many years later Kai Ahiga lay on his death bed and peered through the mist gathering throughout the room. He looked over at his son, Joshua, asleep in the hospital chair as he had been for the last hour, resting fitfully, waiting for his old man to die. Kai smiled and wished he could reach over and brush the hair from the young man's face as he had done when Josh was just a child.

He turned his head slightly and gazed out the window. It was cloudy again as it had been for the last few days. The slight drizzle smattering against the pane washed down and made the whole landscape, such as it was, melt and become a surreal image of itself.

Kai had been troubled by the weather ever since Allison had died. When it was gray he was depressed. When it was clear and sunny he just missed her. She had died three years ago, her heart finally giving out. It had been weak and problematic since the events of so many years ago and when she had at last succumbed it had not come as much of a shock, really. Still, he missed her a lot.

The years that they had spent together had held few triumphs other than managing to stay out of the asylum. The birth of Joshua, in later years, and the move north had brought them some relief. But there had been terrible struggles as well. The endless battle with the media and the years of therapy for Allison had both taken their toll. But if you considered what they had endured during those few days so long ago, all in all it could be said they had survived well and had managed to make something good from their broken lives. Josh lived with his aunt Lucy and helped to take care of her. The boy knew he could help ease some of her constant sorrow and had gladly taken on the responsibility. Kai loved Josh a lot.

Kai had stayed in touch with Tommy Wong for a long time. Sometimes they even went climbing together but Tommy had moved up to Seattle eventually and they had lost contact after that. When Kai had moved further into the reservation, up by Tuba City, he had tried to make time to visit Karen and Steven back in Newton. Karen had fought the urge to get away from the high school and had managed to stick it out there and did what she could to help others deal with the aftermath of the murders. Steven had left his job in San Francisco and moved to Newton so he could be with her. After Kai had made a few such visits, mostly vain attempts to share their common burden, the three of them had come to realize that seeing each other was more difficult than any of them wanted and so the visits had stopped.

The shock of the tragedy had left all of them weak and walking a fine line as they tried to live day to day with the knowledge of that other, strange world that had now proven to be all around them. The media had been abusive and sensationalistic. They had tried to explain what had happened out in the desert to readers who were doubtful and, in some cases, vindictive.

273

The general consensus was that a group of murdering drug-runners had a run-in with a bunch of kids who were in all likelihood high on desert plants and that the whole story had been concocted by them and the teachers to cover up who-knows-what. Of course, other than some terribly abused bodies there was nothing to substantiate any of what those involved knew to be true. The pain that they had all endured had been doubled by that doubt and suspicion. It had caused Doug Wencha to retire and move his family away to another state.

And so they had lived out their lives, mostly in the shadows. Not so in the case of Alice Bird, however, who hadn't had the strength to persevere through it all and had ended her own life a few years later.

Joshua stirred and Kai watched as the boy adjusted to relieve some cramp in his leg and then fell back to sleep. Kai was getting very tired again himself. He leaned his head back against the cool pillow.

There was a sudden, muffled flurry of feathers at the window and Kai sat up, grinned and laughed softly as Crow alighted and began to hop about gingerly on the ledge outside, dancing with the rain. Then the big bird stopped moving and for a moment their eyes met. A sad requiem of the ever-changing world resonated in that contact. Then the window opened. A breeze caught the curtains as Crow cawed loudly once, flew up into the sky and with that Kai Ahiga was gone.

*   *   *

www.ingramcontent.com/pod-product-compliance
Lightning Source LLC
Chambersburg PA
CBHW071824020726
47502CB00004B/1225